KU-532-947

Fugitive from the Grave

EDWARD MARSTON

Allison & Busby Limited
11 Wardour Mews
London W1F 8AN
allisonandbusby.com

First published in Great Britain by Allison & Busby in 2018.
This paperback edition published by Allison & Busby in 2019.

Copyright © 2018 by EDWARD MARSTON

The moral right of the author is hereby asserted in accordance with
the Copyright, Designs and Patents Act 1988.

All characters and events in this publication,
other than those clearly in the public domain,
are fictitious and any resemblance to actual persons,
living or dead, is purely coincidental.

All rights reserved. No part of this publication may be reproduced,
stored in a retrieval system, or transmitted, in any form or by
any means without the prior written permission of the publisher,
nor be otherwise circulated in any form of binding or cover
other than that in which it is published and without a similar
condition being imposed on the subsequent buyer.

A CIP catalogue record for this book is available from
the British Library.

10 9 8 7 6 5 4 3 2 1

ISBN 978-0-7490-2351-5

Typeset in 10.5/15.5 pt Adobe Garamond Pro by
Allison & Busby Ltd.

The paper used for this Allison & Busby publication
has been produced from trees that have been legally sourced
from well-managed and credibly certified forests.

Printed and bound by
CPI Group (UK) Ltd, Croydon, CR0 4YY

This one is especially for Judith

CHAPTER ONE

1817

London was awash with beggars. Hardly a road, street, lane or alleyway was free of them. They haunted the riverside, lurked in doorways and descended on St Paul's Cathedral like a swarm of locusts. Some worked alone while others were members of criminal gangs. Begging was a profession open to all: males and females, children and old folk, the blind, the diseased, the disabled and those returning from the war with hideous wounds. Everyone had his or her favourite pitch, jealously guarded against intruders.

Striding through the heart of the city, the man peered out from beneath his umbrella. His clothing and demeanour suggested wealth, so he raised a chorus of appeals wherever he went. Most of those he passed earned no more than a glance, their pathetic cries scarcely reaching his ears. Pickpockets hid in the shadows but none dared to single him out as their prey. Tall, robust and moving swiftly, he exuded a sense of strength and determination. When he turned down a side street, he saw that the beggars had largely disappeared and that he could actually walk a dozen yards or more without being subject to a desperate plea from some sodden wretch.

It was when he reached the end of the street that someone finally caught his eye and brought him to a halt. Sitting on a doorstep, an old man was staring into space. There was an air of desperation about him. Though his clothing was threadbare and his hat crumpled, he was clearly no ordinary beggar. Gaunt and unshaven, he nevertheless had a strange dignity about him. It was ironic. Having ignored those who'd called out imploringly to him, the newcomer had stopped beside someone who'd remained silent and who seemed to be locked in a private world. He knelt down beside the man, shielding him from the rain with his umbrella.

'You don't belong here,' he said, solicitously.

'What's that?' The old man came out of his reverie and looked up nervously. 'Am I doing something wrong, sir?'

'On the contrary, my dear fellow, I believe that something wrong has been done to *you*.'

'They keep moving me on. Wherever I stop, someone tells me that I've taken his place. They use harsh words and often add a punch or a kick to send me on my way. Do forgive me, sir,' he went on, struggling to his feet. 'I hadn't realised that this spot was reserved.'

'It should never have been occupied by you in the first place,' said the other, putting a friendly arm around his shoulders. 'What brought you to such a condition?'

'I have no money. I beg or I starve.'

'What of your family and friends?'

'My dear wife died years ago and our only child lives abroad. When I had a thriving business, there were many who sought my company. Now that my fortunes have declined, they look the other way. Poverty is the surest way to exile, sir.'

'You look ill. Why have you not sought a doctor?'

'They require money.'

'When did you last eat?'

'I can't remember.'

'Where do you sleep at nights?'

'Wherever I can.'

'Look at you – you're nothing but skin and bone.'

The man gave a wan smile. 'That's what I'm reduced to, sir.'

'Then the first thing we must do is to get some food inside you.'

'Thank you, kind sir. This is unexpected kindness.'

'And we must get you out of that tattered apparel. It's no longer fit for a man of your breeding.'

'Oh, I had to forfeit my breeding, alas.'

'There are some things a man never loses.' The newcomer glanced over his shoulder. 'I've no time for those wailing beggars with their tales of woe. They were born to this life. You, I can see, were certainly not. Come, sir, lean on me and keep under the umbrella. We'll stop at the first tavern we come to and let you taste wholesome food again. It's no more than you deserve.'

The older man was overwhelmed with gratitude. 'I'm a complete stranger,' he said in disbelief. 'Why are you being so good to me?'

'You need help. It's my duty as a Christian to provide it.'

Slowly and gently, he guided the old man away.

CHAPTER TWO

When he walked slowly past the house, Peter Skillen appeared to show no interest in it at all. Out of the corner of his eye, however, he made a swift assessment of the building. It was a nondescript three-storey house in the middle of a row of dwellings that were all in need of repair. For most people, there'd only be two possible exits, one at the front of the property and another at the rear. But the man he was after that morning would also have a third means of escape. Notorious for his ability to evade arrest, Harry Scattergood had more than once fled over the rooftops of his latest refuge. Small, agile and fearless, the thief was a master at shaking off pursuit. Peter had resolved that Scattergood would be caught and convicted at long last. It was not only because of the large reward on offer. He had a genuine interest in meeting the man face-to-face.

Turning back, he crossed the road and approached the house. As soon as he used the knocker, he heard a bedroom window open above him and caught a glimpse of a man's head popping out before vanishing quickly out of sight. The front door was opened by a middle-aged woman of generous proportions with a powdered face and a startling ginger wig. When she saw the handsome, elegant man on her doorstep, she exposed yellowing teeth in a crooked smile.

'Good day to you, sir. Can we be of service to you?'

'Indeed, you can. I need to speak to Mr Scattergood.'

Her smile became a scowl. 'We've nobody of that name here.'

'My information is usually very reliable,' said Peter. 'I believe that, in all probability, he is at present occupying the front room on the first floor. You may, of course, know him by a different name. He has a whole range of them.'

'There's no gentleman staying here at the moment,' she said, raising her voice so that it could be heard throughout the house. 'I've never even heard of Mr Scatter-thing.'

'His name is Scattergood and he's certainly no gentleman.'

'You've come to the wrong address.'

'I don't think so.' He lifted a warning eyebrow. 'Are you aware of the penalty for aiding and abetting a criminal?'

She folded her arms defiantly. 'I've done nothing wrong.'

'The magistrate will think differently.'

'Good day to you, sir.'

She tried to close the door in his face, but Peter stopped it with a firm hand. The look in his eyes was easy to translate. Whether she liked it or not, he was going to come into the house, even if he had to do so by force. There was no way to stop him. With great reluctance, she stood back out of his way.

'Thank you,' he said, bestowing a benign smile on her.

Harry Scattergood, meanwhile, was listening to the conversation from the top of the stairs. Now in his late forties, he was remarkably lithe for his age and confident in his ability to get out of any awkward situation. One confronted him now. He remained in position until Peter came to the foot of the stairs. Having taken a good look at him, Scattergood then set off like a greyhound, dashing into a room at the rear of the house and barricading it swiftly with every piece of furniture he could lay his hand on. He flung open the window, clambered through it and dropped feet first through the air, landing on the cobbles below with the lightness of a cat. Since discovery had always been a possibility, he'd taken the precaution of leaving his horse saddled in the stable and ready for instant departure. Once again, he congratulated himself that he'd made a miraculous escape. Taking a good run at the hindquarters of the animal, he vaulted effortlessly into the saddle, intending to ride swiftly away from danger.

But there was a problem. The moment he landed on the horse, the saddle gave way completely and he was tipped violently onto the ground. Before he could move, he felt a sword point at his neck.

'We had a feeling you'd leave this way,' said Paul Skillen, stepping into view, 'so I took the trouble of cutting the girth on your mount. You won't be riding a horse for a very long time, Harry.'

Mouth agape, Scattergood stared at him in amazement.

'How the hell did you get out here so fast?' he demanded. 'I left you standing at the bottom of the bleeding stairs.'

'That was my brother. Come and meet him.'

Taking him by the scruff of the neck, Paul dragged him out of the stable, then yanked him to his feet. 'There he is,' he went on, pointing upwards. 'You fled from Peter into the arms of Paul.'

'We always work together,' explained Peter, leaning out of the window through which the thief had leapt. 'Strictly speaking, Paul made the arrest, but we always share reward money equally.'

Scattergood looked first at Peter, then at Paul, then back again at Peter. Realisation slowly dawned on him.

'I've heard about you,' he said. 'You're twins.'

'We've heard about *you*,' said Paul, grinning. 'You're nabbed.'

It was the time of day when Micah Yeomans and Alfred Hale were usually to be found at the Peacock Inn, eating a warm pie and washing it down with a pint or two of its celebrated ale. The pub had long ago become the Runners' unofficial headquarters, the place where they could relax in comfort and from which they could deploy the various patrols they supervised. Yeomans was a big, hulking man in his forties with dark, bushy eyebrows dominating an excessively ugly face. Hale was shorter, slighter and a couple of years younger, enjoying the power his status gave him yet always deferring to his companion. They were on their second pint when a breathless Chevy Ruddock came into the bar and looked around for them. A member of the foot patrol, Ruddock was proud to be involved in law enforcement and to be working with the two most famous and successful Runners in the city. He was a tall, ungainly, ever-willing individual in his twenties. Panting heavily, he sped across to them.

'I was hoping to find you here,' he said, gulping for air.

'Get your breath back first, lad,' advised Hale. 'There's no rush.'

'Yes, there is, Mr Hale.'

'Why is that?'

'I've brought you important news, sir.'

'What is it?' asked Yeomans.

'I've just come from Bow Street.'

'That's not news, you idiot. You go there every day.'

'But today is different, Mr Yeomans. You'll never guess what's happened. A certain person is finally in custody.'

'Don't stand there gibbering, man. What's his name?'

'Spit it out!' urged Hale.

After pausing for effect, Ruddock made his grand announcement.

'Harry Scattergood is finally behind bars.'

'These are wonderful tidings,' said Yeomans, leaping to his feet. 'That slippery little monkey has been caught at last.'

'Congratulations, Chevy!' said Hale, getting up to pat him on the back. 'In arresting him, you've done this city a great service.'

'I wasn't the person who caught him,' admitted Ruddock.

'Well, whoever it was, he deserves our thanks.'

'There may even be a promotion in this for him,' said Yeomans, beaming. 'We've been chasing Harry for years without so much as getting a glimpse of the rogue. I'd love to shake the hand of the man who made the arrest. Who is he?'

'In point of fact,' said Ruddock, taking a precautionary step back, 'it was not one person but two.'

'Then I'll buy a pint of ale for both heroes. Who are they?'

'Peter and Paul Skillen.'

Yeomans blanched. 'What did you say?' he growled.

'It was the Skillen brothers who tracked him down, sir.'

'I thought you'd brought us good news, damn you!'

'These are the worst tidings possible,' said Hale.

'Credit where credit is due,' said Ruddock, reasonably. 'The two of them did something that we couldn't manage, even though we have far better resources, not to mention an army of paid informers.

Those twins have a knack that we somehow don't possess.'

'Shut up!' barked Yeomans.

'We should learn from them, sir. I believe that—'

The rest of the sentence became a gurgle as Yeomans grabbed him by the throat and lifted him bodily from the ground. A former blacksmith, the Runner had immense power. It was usually reserved for malefactors but, on this occasion, the hapless Ruddock felt its full force. When he was dumped back down on the floor, he shuddered.

'*We* are the official guardians of law and order,' said Yeomans.

'Yes, sir.'

'The Skillen brothers are mere interlopers.'

'But they're remarkably clever ones,' said Hale.

Yeomans glowered at him. 'Don't *you* start as well.'

'What Chevy said was good advice, Micah. We ought to wonder why it is that Peter and Paul Skillen are better thief-takers than we are. What's their secret?'

'They have outrageous good fortune, that's all.'

'How did *they* find Scattergood when we didn't get so much as a sniff of that little toad?'

'We'd have caught him in due course.'

'It's too late now,' Ruddock pointed out. 'He's already caught. The Skillen brothers have stolen our thunder.'

'They're trespassing on our territory,' said Yeomans, angrily. 'I've warned them before about that. They need to be stopped.'

'You tried to stop them once before, sir.'

'It's true,' said Hale. 'We arrested one of their friends in the hope that it would teach them a lesson. All we got in return for our efforts was a stern rebuke from the chief magistrate and a demand that we release the prisoner at once. Jem Huckvale walked free and we ended up in disgrace.'

Ruddock was rueful. 'You made me swear I'd seen him stealing a leg of mutton in the market,' he said, 'and I was very uneasy about doing that.'

'I know,' said Yeomans, shooting him a disdainful glance. 'Had you given your evidence with more authority, Huckvale would have been convicted and the Skillen brothers would be devoting all their time to saving him from transportation. Jem Huckvale is vital to them. He's their intelligencer. He *hears* things.'

'So does my wife, sir,' said Ruddock, sighing, 'and it's always in the middle of the night. She's convinced a burglar has got in. Some nights I'm in and out of bed three or four times.'

'There's one sure way to stop her from hearing noises at night.'

'Is there?'

'Stuff something in your wife's ears – if not elsewhere in her anatomy.' He and Hale shared a ribald laugh. 'But I return to my point. The Skillen brothers would be helpless without Huckvale. He always seems to be in the right place to pick up information. It's quite uncanny.'

When he was dispatched with a message to deliver, Jem Huckvale had been offered the use of a horse but he preferred to run to and from Covent Garden, maintaining good speed and threading his way expertly through the crowds. He was a diminutive figure in his twenties, but his stature belied both his strength and his ability to defend himself. Having handed the letter over, he began the journey back to the gallery where he lived and gave instruction in shooting, boxing, fencing and archery. Huckvale reached the edge of the market when he noticed a striking young woman and her male companion. Looking around in dismay, they were clearly lost. Because their attire marked them out as visitors from abroad, Huckvale stopped to offer his help.

'Are you lost?' he asked, politely. 'I was born and brought up in London, so I can give you any directions you need.'

'That's very kind of you,' said the woman, appraising him for a moment before deciding that he could be trusted. 'I, too, was born here but I've lived in Amsterdam for many years. To my shame, I've forgotten my way around. We're looking for Bow Street.' She gave a hopeless shrug. 'At least, I think that we are.'

'Don't you know?'

'I thought I did but, now that we're here, I'm not at all sure that we'd be going to the right place.'

'Wherever you wish to go, I'll be happy to conduct you. My name is Jem Huckvale,' he explained, 'and I'm at your service.'

There was something about his open face, his soft voice and his pleasant manner that appealed to her. For his part, he was delighted to be able to help a beautiful and well-spoken woman so obviously in distress.

'I'm Mrs van Emden,' she said, then indicated her chaperon, 'and this is Jacob, my footman. He speaks very little English.'

Huckvale grinned. 'I don't hold that against him, Mrs van Emden,' he said. 'I can't speak a word of Dutch. It always sounds such a difficult language to learn.'

'It is,' she agreed with a smile. 'It's taken me years to get my tongue around it. Fortunately, I have a very patient husband.' She became serious. 'My dilemma is this: I returned to England because I heard that my father had died. I'm desperate to learn the circumstances of his death. That's why I thought my search might start in Bow Street.'

'Do you suspect that a crime might have taken place?'

'No, no, I've no reason to think that. I just need someone to find the information I want. My immediate thought was a Runner.'

'Why not begin your search at the church where he was buried?'

'I don't know where it is.'

'Someone in your family will surely tell you.'

'It's not as simple as that, Mr Huckvale,' she said, looking around at the jostling crowd. 'If you don't mind, I'd rather not discuss my private affairs out here in the street.'

'Then you have a choice,' he told her. 'You can either turn to the Runners and hope that they have a man who'll take an interest in your plight, or you can engage the best detectives in London.'

'Who are they?'

'Their names are Peter and Paul Skillen, seasoned men who've solved murders, caught endless criminals and tracked down dozens of missing persons. They'll certainly take on your case.'

'How can you be sure?'

'I have the honour of working for them, Mrs van Emden.' He could see her hesitating. 'Why not at least speak to them?' he suggested. 'It will cost you nothing. If you have any doubts about their abilities, you can go to the Runners instead.'

'Well . . .'

'What can you lose?' asked Huckvale, with a reassuring smile. 'This is no chance encounter. I believe that fate guided our footsteps today. We were *meant* to cross each other's paths. Don't you feel that?'

'No,' she replied. 'In truth, I don't feel that at all.'

CHAPTER THREE

Having chased Harry Scattergood without success for so many years, the Runners couldn't resist going to see him in custody. The infamous thief was being held in a dank cell at the Bow Street Magistrates' Court. Mindful of the man's reputation, Eldon Kirkwood, the chief magistrate, had ordered that he should be kept in handcuffs. Yeomans and Hale went to satisfy their curiosity. Expecting to find the prisoner cowed and resentful, they were surprised to see him sitting cross-legged on the floor with a contented smile on his face. It turned into a broad grin when he saw the Runners.

'Good day to you, gentlemen,' he said, breezily.

'I'd have thought it was a bad day for you,' said Yeomans. 'Your miserable career has just come to an end.'

Hale was sarcastic. 'We feel so sorry for you.'

'Save your sympathy for Welsh Mary,' said Scattergood.

'Who's she?'

'Mary Morris from Wales is the sweet little darling who was about to enjoy the moment of a lifetime when I was rudely plucked from between those wondrous thighs of hers.'

'So that's it. You were caught in a brothel.'

'I was tricked by those damnable brothers. When one of them banged on the front door, I had to leave Welsh Mary high and dry so that I could quit the premises. No sooner had I done that and mounted my horse than I was lying on the ground with a sword at my neck. Paul Skillen, the cunning devil, had cut the girth so that the saddle gave way beneath me.'

Hale guffawed. 'I'd have loved to have seen that.'

'Well, I wouldn't,' said Yeomans, malevolently. 'Don't ask me to praise the Skillens' handiwork. This flea-bitten wretch was *ours*.'

'Except that you couldn't catch me,' taunted Scattergood.

'We got close many a time.'

'But I always escaped your clutches.'

'It remains to be seen if you'll escape the hangman. At the very least, you'll be shipped off to Australia with the scum of London. If the voyage doesn't kill you, the hard labour certainly will.'

'We'll see,' said Scattergood, airily.

'How can you be so cheerful?' asked Hale.

'I have Welsh Mary waiting for me.'

'Your days with the trulls of the capital are over.'

'I paid her in advance. I want my money's worth.'

'Forget her, Harry. You'll never see her again.'

Scattergood became pensive. 'What I want to know is this,' he said, 'how did those brothers know where to find me?'

'They've got noses like bloodhounds,' said Hale, enviously.

'But I never leave tracks.'

'Someone must have betrayed you.'

'They wouldn't dare,' said Scattergood, eyes glinting. 'Yet those clever twins picked up my scent somehow.'

'So can we,' complained Yeomans, turning his head away in disgust. 'You stink to high heaven.'

'Who was your stall?' asked Hale. 'Who always got in our way whenever we tried to chase you?'

Scattergood was insistent. 'I work alone.'

'We don't believe you. I'll wager you had a lookout.'

'I didn't need one when I was up against fools like you two. I've been buzzing all my life, you see. I started off as a snakesman, then a mutcher, then a dipper, then a dragsman, stealing from carriages. When I learnt how to break a drum,' he boasted, 'there was no stopping me. I've been burgling houses ever since. Nobody could touch me.'

'The Skillen brothers did.'

'I'll get even with them somehow.'

'How can you do that from Botany Bay?' asked Yeomans.

'Oh, I've no intention of being transported.'

'There's no way to prevent it.'

'You'll see – and so will Welsh Mary.'

'What's she got to do with it?'

'She owes me fifteen minutes of paradise,' said Scattergood, with a smirk. 'That's what I paid for and that's what I intend to get.'

Even when they'd reached the shooting gallery, Clemency van Emden was still undecided. Though she'd been persuaded to go there by Jem Huckvale, she was unimpressed by the shabby exterior of the building and wondered if she should bother to go inside. After thinking it over for a few minutes, she agreed to enter and was shown into the room that was used as both an office and a place for storage. To her amazement, she was welcomed by Charlotte Skillen, a poised, handsome woman of her own age who seemed out of place in such surroundings. After formal introductions, Jem explained how the visitors from abroad came to be there, then left them alone with Charlotte, confident that she would soon remove any doubts they might have.

When she'd taken a seat, her footman stood behind her. Clemency started with a confession.

'I have to tell you that I'm to blame for all the confusion,' she said, penitently. 'The fact is that my father and I have been estranged for a number of years because . . . he disapproved strongly of my marriage.'

'Why was that?' asked Charlotte.

'He disliked my husband and he disliked the idea that I'd be taken off to live in Amsterdam even more. When I defied him, he told me that he no longer had a daughter. That was very hurtful, Mrs Skillen.'

'It sounds to me as if there was pain on both sides.'

'Oh, there was – intense pain.'

'Were no efforts made towards reconciliation?'

'None were made by my father,' replied the other. 'I yearned for his forgiveness but the steady stream of letters I sent to him went unanswered and, I fear, probably unread.'

'That must have been a very sad state of affairs. How did you hear of his death?'

'I received an anonymous letter. It gave no details, merely

stating that my father had died and that the funeral had taken place. Since my husband was unable to come to England, I set off without him. From the moment I arrived in London, I've met with quite an alarming series of discoveries.'

'That must have been disconcerting for you.'

'It's frightening,' said Clemency. 'When I went to the house where my father had lived for most of his life, I was told that he'd left there several months ago when he became bankrupt. Yes – think of that – *bankrupt*. How could that possibly be true? He was a successful engineer and draughtsman. How could he possibly have got into dire financial straits?'

'What about his solicitor? Did you contact him?'

'I went straight to the man who used to act for him, but I learnt that they'd fallen out and parted company. He had no idea who'd replaced him as a legal advisor.'

Clemency explained that she'd visited a number of her father's friends and discovered that nobody had seen him for months. Such as it was, his social life had ceased to exist. All that she heard were rumours that he'd taken to drink and been seen begging in the streets. Charlotte felt profoundly sorry for her. It was clear that she blamed herself for the rift with her father and felt that her disappearance abroad had robbed him of any purpose in life. Having left him in good health and in constant demand for his skills, she'd come back to hear of his rapid decline into penury.

'If only he'd *told* us he needed money,' Clemency wailed. 'We'd have sent it at once. My husband is a wealthy man and as eager as I was for an amicable reunion. It can never take place now.'

She lapsed into silence and Charlotte let her brood quietly on the sorrowful events. Then, without warning, Clemency was

25

suddenly jerked out of her reverie by the sound of a gun being fired in the room directly above them. She jumped to her feet, but Charlotte didn't turn a hair.

'Someone is receiving instruction in the shooting gallery,' she said.

'How can you bear such a noise?'

'One gets used to it, Mrs van Emden.'

'That helpful young man we met earlier, does he really work here?'

'Oh, yes, Jem is an important part of the enterprise. So, for that matter, are my husband, Peter, and his brother, Paul. Between them, they'll quickly solve the mystery of your father's death.'

'Do you really mean that?'

'Yes, of course.'

'I simply must know the truth, Mrs Skillen.'

'That's only natural.'

'I'll understand if you place all the blame on me.'

Charlotte was surprised. 'Why on earth should I do that?'

'You must think I acted wilfully in disobeying my father.'

'I think that you followed your heart, Mrs van Emden, and I'd never criticise any woman for doing that.'

While his wife was talking to their visitor, Peter Skillen was hearing from Jem Huckvale how the woman came to be there in the first place. The two men were in the long room reserved for archery practice. As they chatted, Jem was whitening the target. Peter was perplexed.

'I'd have thought it was very easy to find out where her father is buried,' he said. 'All that Mrs van Emden has to do is go to the church where he attended services on a Sunday.'

'On the walk back here, she told me that she'd done that.'

'And what was the result?'

'The vicar had no idea that her father was dead. It seems that George Parry – that's his name – stopped going to church altogether when his daughter left. Wherever the funeral took place, it wasn't in his parish church.'

'Oh, I hadn't realised that.'

'I promised her that you and Paul would come to her rescue.'

'We'll be happy to do so, Jem. Most of our assignments involve great danger so it will be a welcome change to deal with a case entirely devoid of jeopardy. It's so straightforward.'

'It may not be *that* straightforward,' said Huckvale.

'What do you mean?'

'Mr Parry was so upset at what his daughter did that he cut off all links between them. What if he left instructions in his will that he was to be buried in a place where she was least likely to find him?'

'In other words,' said Peter, thinking it through, 'he may not even be here in London.' Huckvale nodded. 'That could complicate matters. I like that. Our job has suddenly become more interesting.'

'Mrs van Emden hasn't hired us yet.'

'Leave that to Charlotte. She'll persuade the lady to engage us.'

'Her father used to be an engineer. He designed a bridge once.'

'Then he'll have had lots of business associates. One of them is bound to be able to shed light on what actually happened to him.'

'They didn't step forward when he lost all his money.'

'There must be a reason for that, Jem.'

'Mrs van Emden is desperate to know what actually killed him.'

'From what you've told me about her father, there are lots of possibilities. He wouldn't be the first person who drank himself to death. If he was forced to beg on the streets, he'd have been vulnerable to attack from one of those predatory gangs that smell a weakness instantly. Then again, he could simply have withered away from starvation. It's even conceivable,' Peter went on, 'that he actually *wanted* to die.'

'That's Mrs van Emden's greatest fear.'

'Is it?'

'Yes, Peter. She didn't say it in so many words, but I could guess what she was thinking.'

'And what was that?'

'Because of what she did,' said Huckvale, sadly, 'Mrs van Emden believes that her father died of a broken heart.'

Paul Skillen could still not believe his good fortune. Sharing his life with Hannah Granville, the finest actress of her generation, he woke up every morning with the most extraordinary feeling of joy and fulfilment. There were, however, some disadvantages. Superb onstage in any part she played, Hannah could, in private, be volatile, demanding and headstrong, requiring Paul to read her moods and exercise considerable tact. Then there were the hordes of male admirers who competed for her attention, showering her with gifts and offers of a more intimate alliance. When he'd first met her, Paul had enjoyed the thrill of escorting her from the stage door of a theatre through a melee of devotees, but that pleasure had soon evanesced into annoyance at the brutal fact that most of them simply wanted another conquest.

But the major disadvantage of being her chosen partner was that Hannah was always in demand by theatre managers in London and elsewhere. Her latest engagement was at the Theatre Royal, Bath, where she was due to play Rosalind in *As You Like It*. While he was excited by her unwavering success in a highly precarious profession, Paul hated being apart from her. As her luggage was being taken out to the waiting cab, they were about to exchange farewells. Hannah could see the sadness in his eyes.

'You could always come with me,' she said.

'I have work that keeps me here, my love.'

'Then I'll write to you every day.'

'Make sure that you do,' said Paul. 'It was torture when you went to Paris. Your letters took an age to reach me and they contained only the merest hints of the terrible problems you were facing there. Had I known the truth, I'd have set out for France at once.'

'Thankfully, you did come in due course.'

'That episode ended happily, as it was, but it could easily have had appalling consequences. At least Bath is easier to reach than Paris.'

'I hope that you'll come to see my performance.'

'If it were left to me, I'd be there every day.'

'And every night . . .'

Hannah gave him the smile that had first enchanted him, then went into his arms for a final embrace. When he pulled away, he looked at the beautiful opal necklace she was wearing.

'Whenever you're travelling, Hannah, you really shouldn't have any valuables on display.'

'This was a gift from the dearest man in the world,' she said, one hand to the necklace, 'and I can't thank you enough for it. When I'm wearing this, I'm reminded of *you*, Paul.'

'I'd feel happier if you kept it out of sight during the journey.'

She snapped her fingers. 'I'd never dream of it. When you have something wonderful,' she went on with a grand gesture, 'you're entitled to flaunt it, and that's exactly what I intend to do.'

CHAPTER FOUR

After their visit to see the prisoner, Yeomans and Hale returned to the Peacock Inn to drink more ale in a futile bid to dispel the feeling that they'd been thoroughly humiliated. The Skillen brothers had surpassed them yet again and Harry Scattergood had mocked them. It was the thief who unnerved them most. Since the protection of property was one of the cornerstones of British justice, Scattergood was facing the prospect of execution. Anyone else in his position would be showing fear and begging for mercy, yet he did neither. Scattergood was sitting blithely on the floor of his cell as if he were a guest at a hotel. When the Runners went to see him, he'd actually taunted them.

'I don't like it, Micah,' said Hale.

'Neither do I,' agreed the other. 'He was far too sure of himself.'

'He could just be trying to bluff us.'

'I doubt it. Harry knows something that we don't and that worries me. It's almost as if he's certain of escaping.'

'Nobody can escape from the cells in Bow Street.'

'That woman did,' Yeomans reminded him. 'Don't you remember? We had Miss Somerville safely locked away then Captain Hamer came to her rescue by holding a pistol to Chevy Ruddock's skull. We had to let her walk out of there.'

'They didn't get clear. Thanks to Chevy, we stopped them.'

'Ruddock was irrelevant.'

'Be fair, Micah. He was a real hero that day.'

'It was our heroism that foiled the escape, Alfred,' said Yeomans, unwilling to let the younger man enjoy any of his deserved praise. 'But the case is different here. Harry Scattergood is no beautiful young damsel about to be carried off by a dashing soldier. He's a hideous little runt without a true friend in the world.'

'What about Welsh Mary?'

'*She's* not likely to rescue him, is she?' He quaffed his pint and brooded for a while. 'All the same,' he admitted at length, 'he disturbs me. It's one thing to fail to catch him. To let him slip through our fingers when we actually have him in custody would be unforgivable.'

'So what do we do?'

'What I'd like to do is strangle him with my bare hands. It's no more than he deserves. Since I can't do that, unfortunately, we need to take extra precautions.'

'Do you want him in leg irons?'

'I want him watched day and night, Alfred.'

Hale was alarmed. 'Do you mean that we have to stand guard over Harry for twenty-four hours?'

'No, you fool. This is work for an underling – someone who is ideal for slow, simple, boring, undemanding work.' He sipped more ale. 'I know just the man for the job.'

Hale chuckled. 'So do I,' he said. 'Chevy Ruddock.'

After tapping gently on the door, Peter let himself into the room where his wife had just finished her conversation with Clemency van Emden. Charlotte introduced her husband to the two visitors then summarised the situation so concisely and accurately that she took the other woman's breath away.

'What a memory you have, Mrs Skillen!' said Clemency.

'It's only one of my wife's many attributes,' said Peter, fondly. 'Charlotte has a vital role in the service we offer.'

'I'm beginning to see that, Mr Skillen.'

'In essence, then, the situation is this: in your search for details of your father's death and burial, you've come up against what appears to be a conspiracy of silence. Old friends deny any knowledge of what actually happened and, since he was forced to sell the house, there are no servants you can question. The one person on whom you think you can rely,' said Peter, 'is this gentleman from Norwich.'

'Mr Darwood was my father's best friend.'

'Then why didn't he send you his condolences on your loss?'

'I don't know,' said Clemency, 'but the obvious explanation is that he was unaware that Father had died. I wrote to him from Amsterdam, asking if he could possibly meet me here in London. I gave him the name of the hotel where I intended to stay.'

'And did Mr Darwood reply to your letter?'

'I'm afraid that he didn't, Mr Skillen.'

'There was no message waiting for you at your hotel?'

'No. It was very disappointing.'

'It's more than that,' said Charlotte. 'You told me that you'd always been on good terms with Mr Darwood. If he and your father were so close, you'd have thought he'd be anxious to help you.'

'Since he clearly is not,' said Peter, 'I may have to go to Norwich to ask him why.'

Clemency gaped at him. 'You'd do that for me?' she asked in disbelief. 'You'd go all that way?'

'Oh, I'd go much further than that, Mrs van Emden. The truth is that your situation intrigues me. While he was alive, your father was a man of means and prodigious talent. Now that he's dead, it's as if he never even existed. Why is everyone so keen to bury and forget all about him?'

'That question has been troubling.'

'Who could have sent that anonymous letter, telling you that Mr Parry had passed away?'

'I wish I knew, Mr Skillen.'

'Do you still have it, by any chance?'

'As a matter of fact, I do,' she said, opening her reticule to take out the missive. 'It caused me a lot of pain when I first read it, but I felt that I should bring it with me, nevertheless.'

'I'm glad that you did,' said Peter, taking it from her. 'This is the only piece of evidence we have that your father is deceased.'

Unfolding the paper, he read the terse message written in capitals.

YOUR FATHER IS DEAD AND BURIED

'There's no sign of grief or sympathy,' said Charlotte, looking at it over his shoulder. 'It's so blunt as to be . . . cruel.'

'When I first read it,' admitted Clemency, 'I almost fainted. Not a word comes from England for years then – out of the blue – I get this thunderbolt. It was a dreadful shock.'

'I can well imagine it, Mrs van Emden.'

'My husband thought at first that it might be a hoax, but I knew in my heart that it wasn't. What I saw in the message was a definite sense of reproach. It's as if someone is telling me that this was the result of me defying my father.' She turned to Peter, who'd been studying the six words carefully. 'What do you think, Mr Skillen?'

'I think this person had a reason to conceal his or her identity.'

'It doesn't look like a woman's hand, Peter,' said his wife.

'It does and it doesn't. The gender is indeterminate. That was the intention. What it tells me is that this letter was sent by someone well known to Mrs van Emden, someone whose calligraphy would have been recognised by her.' He turned to Clemency. 'May I keep this, please?'

'Yes, by all means,' she replied.

'But I'm getting ahead of myself. You haven't even had time to decide if you wish us to act for you. We're more than willing to do so, but you may have reservations about us. Don't worry about the financial commitment,' he went on, smiling, 'because we ask for no money in advance. Until we provide you with everything you seek, you won't have to pay a single penny.'

'You surely need some kind of deposit?'

'We prefer to be paid by results, Mrs van Emden.'

'That's always been our policy,' said Charlotte. 'And it isn't only a question of money. We have the additional satisfaction of seeing one or more criminals paying for their crime.'

Clemency blanched. 'Is that what we have here – a crime?'

'It's too soon to say.'

'But it's a possibility that's getting to feel more and more likely,' said Peter, thoughtfully. 'Someone wanted you to suffer,' he added, holding up the letter. 'This was designed to hurt. By withholding any details, the person who sent this knew that it would cause real distress. That's wicked, in my view.'

'What's your decision, Mrs van Emden?' asked Charlotte. 'Do you wish to hire our services or go elsewhere?'

'Oh,' said Clemency with passion, 'I'm *begging* you to help me. You've been so kind and understanding that I couldn't conceive of finding anyone better able to solve the mystery. It's strange, isn't it? Jem Huckvale told me that, in meeting him, my steps had been guided by fate.' She smiled wearily. 'All of a sudden, I'm starting to believe him.'

It took them some time to run Chevy Ruddock to earth. The younger man was on patrol with William Filbert, a stout, red-cheeked man in his fifties with a drooping moustache that always looked as if it was about to fall off his face altogether. When they'd first worked together, Filbert was the senior man in years and experience, but Ruddock had learnt quickly. He'd become a resourceful member of the foot patrol and, more often than not, Filbert now deferred to his judgement. The two of them had paused on a corner so that the older man could light his pipe, a difficult operation because of his trembling hands and rheumy eyes. When the tobacco was finally ignited, they moved off again, only to find two sturdy figures blocking their way.

'We've found you at last,' declared Yeomans.

'Good day to you both,' said Filbert, touching his hat.

'Be quiet, Bill. We're not interested in you. We're here for Ruddock.'

'You might as well be on your way,' advised Hale. 'You'll be on your own for the rest of the day.'

'Yes, sir,' said Filbert, shifting his pipe to the other side of his mouth. 'Is Chevy in trouble?'

'No, we've got a special assignment for him. He'll tell you all about it next time you're on duty together.'

'Goodbye, Bill,' said Yeomans, firmly. 'Keep your eyes peeled.'

After releasing a loud cackle, Filbert ambled off on his way.

'What's he laughing about?' asked Hale.

'He can't keep his eyes peeled,' explained Ruddock. 'As soon as the light starts to fade, Bill is as blind as a bat. Luckily, his other senses more than make up for his poor eyesight.'

'Forget about Bill Filbert,' said Yeomans, dismissively. 'We've come to talk about Harry Scattergood.'

'Has he been up before Mr Kirkwood yet?'

'No, he's being kept as the last case of the day so that the chief magistrate has time to go through the full catalogue of his crimes.'

'There must be dozens of them.'

'And the rest,' said Hale. 'I'd be amazed if there are not more than a hundred. Harry was a real master of his craft.'

'You have to admire the man's skill in dodging us.'

'I don't admire *any* criminal,' said Yeomans. 'In my view, they should all be strung up as a warning to others. Thieves like Harry have contaminated this city for too long. They're like a plague of rats. Our job is to trap and kill the vermin.'

'In Harry's case, the Skillen brothers did the trapping.' Ruddock gasped as he was punched in the stomach by Yeomans. 'I'm sorry, sir. I promise not to mention them again.' He rubbed his stomach. 'What's this assignment you have for me?'

'I want you to keep an eye on Scattergood.'

'But they already have a gaoler in Bow Street.'

'He's simply there to lock and unlock the cells,' said Hale. 'He's more of an usher than anything else, taking prisoners into court.'

'What we want,' said Yeomans, 'is someone sitting on a chair outside Harry's cell and watching him like a hawk. You'll be responsible for taking him into court and, when he's convicted, for seeing him safely locked up again.'

'Am I allowed to talk to him?' asked Ruddock.

'No, and you mustn't listen to him either. He'll try every trick in the book to bamboozle you. Take no chances. Keep your mouth shut and your ears blocked.'

'Yes, sir.'

'If you need to communicate with him,' said Hale, 'just fart.'

'We've chosen you,' Yeomans stressed, 'because we wanted someone alert and reliable. Your task is not as simple as it may look. Whatever happens, Harry Scattergood must not escape.'

As the day wore on, there was a lot of coming and going at Bow Street Magistrates' Court. Secure in his cell, Scattergood rarely had more than a few minutes alone. New prisoners were arriving, while those already there were being hauled out in turn to appear in court. The little thief had to wait a long time before there was a definite lull in activity. On his arrival there, he'd been thoroughly searched and all the tools of his trade had been removed from his pockets. What nobody had done, however, was to search his shoes properly. They'd made him remove them in case he had anything hidden inside but, when nothing was found, he was allowed to put them on again. Salvation was still possible.

He moved swiftly. Pulling off one shoe, he twisted the heel sharply so that it swung outwards to reveal a hollow into which a number of skeleton keys had been jammed. He selected one that unfolded to four times its original length, inserting it in the handcuffs one at a time. In less than a few seconds, he heard a satisfying click and the first wrist was free. The second quickly followed. He now turned his attention to the lock on the cell door, probing gently for over a minute until he got it in the right position. Once again there was a positive click. Putting the key back in its hiding place, he twisted the heel into the position, put the shoe on again, then opened the cell door with a flourish.

As he thought of the joy that awaited him, he grinned broadly.

'Get ready for me, Welsh Mary,' he whispered. 'I'm coming.'

CHAPTER FIVE

When Hannah Granville was driven to the Flying Horse, Paul rode alongside her so that he could savour her company for a short while before she quit London. Though he still had concerns about her decision to wear the opal necklace – albeit it was covered by a pelisse – he didn't challenge her again. The last thing either of them needed before they parted was an argument. He therefore elected to humour her. On reaching the inn, Paul dismounted, then helped Hannah out of the cab. A groom came to take care of her luggage, allowing the couple to go into the hostelry. The first person they saw was Jenny Pye, the short, roly-poly, middle-aged woman who'd been Hannah's dresser for many years and, in that time, had become a trusted friend. Getting up from her seat, she waddled across to the newcomers and was embraced warmly by Hannah. About to set off on what was a new adventure for them, the two women began to converse excitedly.

Paul, meanwhile, was looking around the room. While he was delighted that Hannah had female company for her journey, he was more interested in the security of her travel. The actress had only agreed to join the company in Bath if the theatre manager could provide a bodyguard to get her there safely. Paul soon picked out the man. He was in his thirties, tall, craggy, roughly attired and reassuringly muscular. Realising that he was being assessed, the bodyguard got up to walk across to him.

'Are you looking for me, sir?'

'You've been sent from Bath, haven't you?'

'Yes, sir, I'm Roderick Cosgrove. My orders are to protect Miss Granville on the journey there.'

'Have you done this kind of work before?'

'Yes, sir. I'm very experienced.'

'That's good to know.'

'I don't foresee any trouble,' said Cosgrove. 'We travelled from Bath to London without incident. I trust that the return journey will be exactly the same.'

'Take good care of Miss Granville.'

'I will, sir. My years in the army prepared me well for this kind of employment. Nothing that could happen will in any way compare to some of the battles in which I fought. Besides,' he said with quiet confidence, 'I carry a pistol, and I'll not be the only man aboard with a weapon. We can repel any attack, though one is highly unlikely to happen.'

'I'm glad to hear that.'

Paul took him across the room and introduced him to the two women. They were pleased to meet Cosgrove and struck by his polite manner. When it was time to go, they followed the other passengers out to the stagecoach. The four horses were restive and their harness was jingling as they moved about, hooves clacking on the cobbles. After checking everyone's name against a list, the driver allowed them to get inside the vehicle or, in Cosgrove's case, to a seat on the top. Hannah was the first to enter the coach and chose a window seat facing the direction of travel. Paul spoke to her through the window.

'Write to me the moment you arrive,' he told her.

'I'll be far too jangled to hold a pen,' she said, laughing. 'By the time we get there, we'll have explored every pothole on the way.'

'I'll need to know that you reached your destination safely.'

'You will, I promise.'

'I'm going to miss you sorely.'

'You don't have a monopoly on feelings of loneliness, Paul.'

He grinned. 'How can you feel lonely when hundreds of people will see you onstage every night?'

'They mean nothing to me,' she said, earnestly. 'You are the only audience I want. When you're with me, I'm happy. When you're not, I suffer a terrible sense of loss.'

'It is the same for me, my love.'

After taking a last kiss, he bade her farewell. Bath was a popular destination, so the stagecoach was full. Hannah was already collecting admiring looks from the male passengers and envious glances from their wives. When everything was ready, the driver cracked his whip and the horses set off. Cosgrove waved to him and Paul lifted a hand in response. He watched the vehicle bouncing and rattling along the street until it was eventually out of sight. Knowing that he wouldn't be seeing Hannah for some time, he turned away with a sigh.

From now on, his bed would feel painfully empty at night.

Gully Ackford was a big, rugged man of middle years. As the owner of the shooting gallery, he provided work as instructors for his friends and, more importantly, a base from which they could operate when their detective skills were in demand. When the gallery closed at the end of the afternoon, he was alone with Peter Skillen, listening to his account of their latest client. With her footman in tow, Clemency van Emden had gone to her hotel, Grillion's in Albemarle Street. Moved by her plight, Peter was eager to assist her.

'When I first heard her plea,' he recalled, 'I thought that it would be easy to find out where, when and how her father had died, but it's proving to be a more complex case than I imagined.'

'So it seems,' said Ackford.

'What I am certain of is that he's buried somewhere in London.'

'Why do you think that, Peter?'

'George Parry was born here, married here, employed here and – if rumour is to be believed – ended up as a beggar here. According to his daughter, his only surviving relatives are up in the wilds of Yorkshire somewhere.'

'How could he get there if he had no money?'

'There was another reason he'd stay here. Mrs van Emden said that he was a very proud man. He'd be far too ashamed to admit that he was in such straitened circumstances. Mr Parry was the sort of person who'd suffer in silence, rather than throw himself on the mercy of relatives he hardly ever saw.'

'What a sad way to end his days,' said Ackford, running a hand through his hair. 'He must have felt marooned, completely cut off from his family, friends and the people he'd once worked with. There seems to have been nobody to whom he could turn.'

'It's true.'

'What state is his daughter in?'

'She's consumed with guilt, poor woman.'

'How will you find out what happened to him, Peter?'

'There are two possible ways,' replied the other. 'First, we must locate the church where he was buried. To that end, I've loaned Jem my horse and sent him off to make enquiries.'

'But there are scores of churches in London,' warned Ackford. 'It will take him days.'

'I tried to save him the trouble by going to Lambeth House, hoping that they might have a register of all deaths in the capital, but I got short shrift there. They don't allow random strangers to inspect their records.'

Ackford laughed. 'Is that what you are – a random stranger?'

'I've been called worse, Gully.'

'You said that there were two possible ways.'

'The second one is to turn to the medical profession. Someone must have signed the death certificate. Mr Parry couldn't afford the services of a physician but, even as a pauper, he'd have been examined by someone qualified to pronounce on the cause of his death.'

'Knocking on the doors of every physician or doctor in this city would take an age, and there are many of them who simply never divulge confidential details about their patients.'

'I know. The churches remain our best option.'

'Jem will be exhausted when he gets back.'

'Not if he brings good news, Gully. It will lift his spirits.'

'What if he doesn't find the right churchyard?'

'It's a result that I won't even entertain,' said Peter, 'because I have complete faith in Jem. He's always been lucky. Somehow or other, he'll find it.'

Facing the chief magistrate was an ordeal at the best of times. Though he was a short, slight, insignificant man in appearance, Eldon Kirkwood took on size, power and dignity whenever he sat in court. Summoned to his office, Yeomans and Hale got the impression that he was twice his actual weight. He had bad news to impart.

'Harry Scattergood has gone,' he announced.

'Has he been remanded to Newgate?' asked Yeomans.

'No – he's escaped.'

Hale goggled. 'But that's impossible, sir.'

'The empty cell would seem to contradict that claim.'

'He can't have got away,' said Yeomans, still reeling from the news. 'I ordered Ruddock to sit outside his cell to watch every move that the prisoner made.'

'Well, he didn't watch him escaping,' said Kirkwood. 'He arrived far too late. Scattergood was long gone.'

'*How* did he get out?'

'I'm counting on you to tell *me* that.'

'Did he overpower someone?'

'He didn't need to, Yeomans. One minute, he was here; the next, he was gone. Nobody saw a thing. Now, unless he sprouted wings and simply flew out of here, there has to be a logical explanation. I want the two of you to examine his cell and come up with the answer.'

'He must have had a means of opening doors,' said Hale.

'I disagree,' said Yeomans. 'He was thoroughly searched before he was locked up. They'd have done everything but strip him naked.'

'Harry was a cunning devil. He always dodged us.'

'There's no need to bring that up,' said the other, glaring at him. 'The main thing is that we weren't to blame for his escape. In fact, I took steps to prevent it by sending Chevy Ruddock here. If anyone is culpable, it has to be him. Yes, Ruddock has to bear responsibility.'

Kirkwood silenced him with a raised palm. 'I'm not apportioning blame to any of the three of you,' he said. 'I sent for you so that you can tell me how a man in handcuffs can discard them, unlock the cell door and stroll out of here without anyone catching sight of him.'

'We'll soon establish what actually happened, sir.'

'Once you've done that, I have another task for you.'

'What is it?'

'I want you to find Scattergood again. Bring him back here, bound hand and foot, and laden with the heaviest chains you can find. He's mocking us,' he went on, sourly. 'Wherever he might be, that incorrigible rogue is enjoying a laugh at our expense.'

At that moment in time, Harry Scattergood was, in fact, pumping away vigorously between the blue-veined thighs of Welsh Mary. At the height of his pleasure, he let out a long, loud yell of triumph then rocked with mirth before flopping down on the obliging young woman beneath him.

'I told you that I'd be back,' he said, breathlessly.

'You always did keep your promises, Harry.'

'And I always ask for you, my darling.'

She giggled. 'I'm glad about that.'

'You're my favourite, Mary.'

'When will I see you again?'

'It won't be for a while,' he told her. 'I escaped from custody. Every Runner in London will be hot on my trail. I'll have to disappear.'

'You won't forget me, will you?'

'I could never do that.' Leaping off the bed, he dressed with remarkable speed, then pulled on his shoes. 'A word of warning,' he said. 'Two gentlemen, who look so alike you can't tell them apart, might come here searching for me. Say nothing at all to them. Understand?' She nodded obediently. 'Good girl.' He took a last, guzzling kiss. 'Or – if you *do* open that delicious little mouth of yours – speak to them in Welsh. That will get rid of them.'

Jem Huckvale had forgotten just how many churches there were in the city. Over thirty had been destroyed in the Great Fire of 1666, but most had been swiftly rebuilt and new ones had also sprung up. Within the first hour, he'd visited four St Michaels and six dedicated to other saints. Thinking of the twins, Ackford had told him of the parish church of St Peter and St Paul but, since it was in Dagenham, Huckvale hoped that he didn't have to go that far afield. At each place he'd stopped, he'd spoken to vergers or to curates. In every case, they denied having heard of George Parry or having held his funeral at their respective churches. When he reached his thirteenth church, he learnt something that made him think he might never find Parry's last resting place.

The vicar was a white-haired old man who listened patiently to the enquiry, then raised a possibility that had never occurred to Huckvale.

'How do you know Mr Parry is buried in consecrated ground?'

'Where else would he be?'

'There are all sorts of places. If they can't afford even a cheap funeral, some families may be forced to bury their loved ones in any isolated patch of land they can find.'

'But that's against the law,' protested Huckvale.

'It's also in violation of the Church's prerogative. Are you certain that this gentleman had a legitimate funeral?'

'Yes, sir.' Doubts crept in. 'At least, I think so.'

'Then it would certainly have been at his parish church.'

'They have no record of that happening.'

Huckvale thought about the letter he'd been shown by Peter Skillen. Sent to Parry's daughter, it had simply declared that her father was dead and buried. There was no mention of a funeral. If it had been an unnatural death, he reflected, then the person or persons responsible might have dug a grave in a place where people were unlikely ever to venture. In short, his peregrinations were a complete waste of time. Huckvale's first impulse was to return to the gallery to say that they'd never find where the man was buried, but his innate stubbornness made him decide to go on.

'You could be on a fool's errand, young man,' said the vicar.

'It will be for a worthy cause, sir.'

'I admire your tenacity.'

'Thank you for your help.'

'Did you know Mr Parry well?'

'I didn't know him at all,' said Huckvale, sadly, 'but I've met his daughter. She's a charming lady and I'll do everything in my power to help her. We're convinced that he's buried somewhere in London. However long it takes, I'm determined to find him.'

In the wake of Hannah's departure, Paul Skillen was already feeling bereft, but he couldn't simply abandon his duties at the gallery and go after her. When he joined his brother and Gully Ackford there, they had no difficulty in diagnosing his condition.

'Don't worry,' said Ackford. 'Hannah will return before long.'

'Yes,' added Peter, 'and it's not as if Bath is on the other side of the world.'

'If it was a mere five miles away,' confessed Paul, 'I'd still pine.'

'And so you should.'

'We've news for you,' said Ackford. 'A gentleman I instructed this afternoon in the noble art of self-defence had just come back from Bow Street Magistrates' Court where he'd been giving evidence against someone who'd unwisely tried to steal his purse. He told me that the place was all abuzz.'

'Why was that, Gully?' asked Paul.

'Someone had just escaped.'

'It was not—'

'Oh, yes it was – Harry Scattergood has vanished into thin air.'

'If he's not convicted, we won't get our reward.'

'We'll have to catch him all over again,' said Peter, resignedly.

'It's easier to catch moonbeams in a jam jar,' moaned Paul. 'He led us a merry dance last time.'

'The search will help to keep your mind off Hannah. I'm involved in a case of a missing body, so you'll have to manage on your own for the time being. It won't be long before the Runners are hammering on the door, demanding to know where we found Harry in the first place.'

'I'm not giving any help to *them*,' said Paul, fiercely. 'They had their chance to catch him and they failed. I'll track him down somehow.'

'Before you do that, tell us about Hannah.'

'Yes,' said Ackford, 'I know that you were concerned for her safety during the journey. Have your fears been allayed?'

'They have, indeed,' said Paul, relaxing a little. 'I met the bodyguard assigned to look after her. Cosgrove was in the army, so he clearly knows how to handle a pistol. Not that he'll need to draw it from its holster, mind you. There have been no reports of highway robbery on that particular route for months,' he went on. 'I have no worries about Hannah on that score. She's in good hands.'

It was always going to be a testing journey. While efforts had been made to increase the comfort of the passengers by padding their seats, nothing could be done about the roads over which the stagecoach was destined to travel. Rutted, uneven and treacherous, they made the vehicle lurch and shudder at regular intervals. Time and again, Hannah was thrown against Jenny Pye, causing both women to apologise repeatedly to each other and making their male companions regret that they were not seated beside the actress. Cosgrove, meanwhile, was also enduring discomfort on the top of the vehicle. It was swaying to and fro and, when one of its wheels hit a large stone or a deep pothole, it sent tremors through his whole body. Since he was seated at the back of the stagecoach, Cosgrove was facing in the opposite direction to the way they were travelling. He could see nothing of what was ahead, only the road snaking away behind them.

They were making good time until they came to a hill that rose steeply towards a wooded summit. Though the driver used his whip to get extra effort out of his horses, the stagecoach nevertheless slowed. It was when they got within reach of the top that the attack came. It was so swift, sudden and unexpected that they were all taken unawares. Three masked men cantered out of the trees. One of them stopped his mount in the path of the

51

oncoming stagecoach with a pistol drawn. The driver immediately hauled on the reins with all his strength and produced a barrage of protest from the horses. Before the man beside the driver could reach for the weapon beneath his seat, he found himself staring at the pistol held by the second highwayman.

As the stagecoach skidded to a halt and sent up a cloud of dust, the third member of the trio went to the back of the vehicle to stifle any resistance there. Cosgrove had been the first to recover. Pulling out his pistol, he discharged it at the third man with a loud bang, narrowly missing his target. In response, the highwayman fired from close range, forcing the bodyguard to drop his pistol with a cry of pain. It was the second of the highwaymen who was their leader. Tall, bolt upright and clad entirely in black, he barked out his orders, motioning with one of the two pistols he held. Everyone was to get out of the vehicle at once. Those who refused would live – or not live – to regret it.

Terrified by the attack, the passengers got out of, or down from, the vehicle in a panic. Though he alone remained cool in the crisis, Cosgrove moved gingerly, nursing the wounded hand around which he now had a bloodstained handkerchief. The last person to alight was Hannah, who was shaking. Using his other hand to help her out of the coach, Cosgrove gave her a look of profound apology for his inability to protect her. He was then shoved roughly aside by the leader of the highwaymen who'd dismounted to take a closer look at their prisoners. His eyes went straight to Hannah.

'Well, now,' he said, with a disarming smile, 'this *is* a pleasant surprise, Miss Granville.' He reached forward to flick the scarf back from her neck to reveal the opal necklace. Laughing with delight, he swept off his hat and held it out to her. 'I'll relieve you of those baubles, if you don't mind.'

Hannah was outraged. 'They are not baubles,' she retorted.

'Whatever they are, they belong to us now.'

'Don't you dare touch me!'

Putting a hand to the necklace, she stared at him in token defiance. It was a futile response. Clicking his tongue and raising a meaningful eyebrow, he pointed a pistol straight at her.

CHAPTER SIX

Perseverance finally brought its reward. After hours in the saddle, Jem Huckvale finally had something to show for his efforts. Having been to what seemed like an unending series of churches, he went further afield, riding north and leaving the stench and pandemonium of the city for the fresh air of rural villages. When he reached Islington, he thought it pretty, unspoilt and blissfully tranquil. He drew another blank at St Paul's Church, then pressed on into the village until he came to St Mary's, an imposing structure built half a century or more earlier to replace the ancient church that had fallen into ruin. It looked too large, stately and symmetrical to be the burial place of a man who'd reportedly died in abject poverty.

Huckvale nevertheless tethered his horse and went across to it.

Light was fading fast now, and he realised that this might well be the last church he was able to visit before heading back to the gallery to admit that his search had been fruitless. He let himself into the gloomy nave and looked around. Nobody was there. Since every church was obliged to keep a record of births, marriages and deaths in the parish, he hoped that he might be able to look at the appropriate ledger. To his disappointment, the door to the vestry was locked, so his visit had apparently been in vain. Huckvale trudged back down the aisle, footsteps echoing eerily, and went out, intending to ride straight back to the gallery. A banging noise from behind the church then alerted him.

When he walked to the rear of the building, he found a stocky figure bent double over an upturned wheelbarrow. The man looked up to reveal a face that was almost hidden by a bushy beard and by the long, straggly hair poking down from his filthy cap.

'Evenin' to you, sir,' he said. 'I were just mendin' this afore it gets too dark. Can I 'elp you?'

'I doubt it,' said Huckvale. 'I wanted to ask about recent burials here, but there's nobody about.'

'I'm 'ere, sir, and there's no better man than me.'

'Why is that?'

'I'm the gravedigger,' said the other, wheezily. 'Any grave dug in this churchyard in the last thirty years or more was dug by these two 'ands.' He held out large, dirty, calloused palms. 'I always dig well and dig deep.'

'Have there been any funerals lately?'

'Why do you ask, sir?'

'I'm desperate to find where a certain man is buried.'

'Name?'

'George Parry.'

'Look no further, sir,' said the other, pointing a gnarled finger. 'Mr Parry's over there, near the wall.'

'Really?' asked Huckvale, hopes rising. 'Will you show me?'

'There's not much to see, sir, just a mound of fresh earth.'

He led the way between the headstones and the occasional piece of statuary to a plot close to the far wall. It was in the shade of a yew tree. All that Huckvale was interested in was the mound that covered the last remains of Mrs van Emden's father.

'It were a strange business,' recalled the gravedigger.

'Why was that?'

'Only one person were 'ere for the funeral.'

After several hours, they were still shaken by what had happened. The robbery had reminded them just how perilous the open road could be. Three highwaymen had got away with all their valuables and, in the case of Hannah Granville, some of her luggage as well. The one consolation was that the women had escaped any kind of physical abuse. In the eyes of two of the highwaymen, Hannah had seen the burning desire to take full advantage of their plight, but they'd been overruled by their leader, a man who blended courtesy with criminality. At his command, they'd taken their booty and galloped off.

Along with the other passengers, Hannah was now at a coaching inn where they'd decided to spend the night to recover. There was one bonus. Coaches going in the opposite direction stopped at the inn, enabling her to get a message about their predicament to Paul. Having lost all her money, she was unable to pay the driver to see her letter safely delivered but assured him that he – or any messenger he engaged – would be rewarded by the recipient of the letter.

Hannah was having a light supper with Jenny Pye in the quietest corner of the taproom. It had been provided free of charge by a sympathetic landlord, shocked to hear of their predicament. Still deeply upset by the robbery, neither had much appetite. The older woman was curious about what was in the letter.

'Did you mention the pendant?'

'No,' said Hannah.

'Mr Skillen is bound to wonder.'

'I'd rather tell him face-to-face, Jenny. It was my own stupid fault. Because it was such a treasured gift from Paul, I hated taking it off. The chances of having it stolen seemed so slim as to be negligible.' Hannah grimaced. 'I know better now.'

'What puzzled me was why they took that valise of yours. All that it contained was clothing.'

'Perhaps they wish to give them to their wives.'

'Men like that don't get married,' said Jenny, darkly.

Before she could continue, she was interrupted by the arrival of Roderick Cosgrove. He cut a sorry figure. His hand was now covered with heavy bandaging and his earlier confidence had disappeared.

'I just came to apologise once more, Miss Granville,' he said. 'I let you down badly.'

'You were not to blame, Mr Cosgrove. You were outnumbered. In trying to take them on, you were too brave for your own good.'

'There've been no highwaymen on this road for ages.'

'We were spared our lives,' said Hannah, 'and we should be grateful for that.'

'We were spared ill treatment as well,' observed Jenny. 'Villains of that kind usually have no respect for women.' She looked at the bandaging. 'How is your hand?'

'It was only a flesh wound,' replied Cosgrove, 'but it does smart. When we reach Bath tomorrow, I'll visit a doctor to have the wound dressed properly. However,' he went on, 'I'm interrupting your meal. I'll disturb you no longer.'

After a polite bow, he withdrew to the other side of the room.

'Poor fellow!' said Hannah. 'He was hired to escort me to Bath yet failed to prevent my being robbed. That means he'll probably be denied any payment.'

'That would be monstrously unfair.'

'I'll put in a word for him, Jenny.'

But her mind was not really on the bodyguard, nor was it on her performance in a Shakespearean comedy at the Theatre Royal in Bath. She was brooding obsessively about Paul Skillen. When he heard about the robbery, he'd rush to her side to offer love and sympathy. How would he react at the news that the expensive gift he'd bought for her to show his love had been stolen? It was an uncomfortable question. Trying to answer it would give Hannah a sleepless night.

When she'd left the gallery earlier, Clemency van Emden had told them that she would stay awake at the hotel in case they made any progress in the search for her father. Peter therefore had no qualms at calling on her so late. She was summoned from her room and adjourned with him to the parlour. Her face brightened.

'You have news for me, Mr Skillen?'

'I believe so,' he said, 'but any thanks must go to Jem Huckvale. He's been riding from church to church until his head was going round in circles, but his efforts were eventually repaid.'

'He found out where my father is buried?'

'We believe so – he's at St Mary's Church in Islington.'

Clemency frowned. 'Islington?' she repeated. 'How did he end up there? He's never had any connection with the place.'

'He may have developed one during the time you were estranged.'

'That's possible, I suppose. Is Jem *certain* that it was my father's grave he saw?'

'He was shown it by the gravedigger himself,' said Peter. 'George Parry is not an uncommon name, but it was a recent funeral held not long before you received news of his death.'

'Who organised it?'

'The gravedigger didn't know. What he did say was that only one person turned up to pay his respects. When I take you there tomorrow, we'll speak to the vicar and get more details.'

'Why can't we go right now?' she asked, eagerly.

'It's too late and too dark, Mrs van Emden. I promise you that I'll pick you up early tomorrow morning.'

'I'll be waiting for you.'

'The news should at least bring you a measure of comfort.'

'It does and it doesn't, Mr Skillen. At least I finally know where my father is and that brings some relief. At the same time, however, I feel rather disturbed without quite knowing why.'

'When we go to Islington, the vicar may be able to put your mind at rest.'

'I still have the urge to go this instant.'

'Then you'll have to master your impatience,' he said, softly. 'Try to get a good night's sleep. I'll be back tomorrow.'

There were two of them and they were dressed in black to blend with the darkness. One of them led the horse by the bridle until they reached the wall of the churchyard. The other man climbed off the cart with a spade.

'Is this it?' he asked.

'Yes,' said the other, reaching for the lantern on the driving seat. 'Come and see for yourself.'

Walking across to the wall, he lifted the lantern to illumine the grave on the other side of it. Conditions were ideal. It was a dark night and the mound of earth was obscured by the branches of the yew tree. Recent rain had kept the ground damp and easy to dig. Since it was now almost midnight, the whole of Islington was fast asleep and wouldn't hear a thing. They worked swiftly and with minimal noise, showing no respect for the fact that they were on consecrated ground. To them it was merely a task they'd been given. The man with the lantern held it up so that they had a good view of the grave.

'That'll give the vicar something to think about,' he said.

Paul Skillen had found it very difficult to maintain his concentration. His mind kept drifting to Hannah Granville. Though he tried hard to school himself to address the task in hand, he failed. It meant that the person he was after might have come and gone without being seen. The news of Harry Scattergood's escape had been at once amusing and annoying. While it would give him the chance to tease Yeomans and Hale about the incompetence at Bow Street, it had also caused him profound irritation. He and Peter now had to recapture a man they'd been trailing for months. It would be a severe test of their skills.

Reasoning that the thief might return to the place where he'd been caught, Paul had put it under surveillance. Scattergood was too cautious to return there in broad daylight, but it was possible that he might try to sneak in there after dark. When the brothers arrested him, he railed at them for coming between him and his pleasure, saying that they'd deprived him of the delights for which he'd paid. In fact, he'd seemed less angry about being apprehended than he was about having to abandon a Welsh prostitute at a critical moment. Scattergood had paid for something he didn't get. He was the kind of man who'd go back.

Paul took it in turns to watch the front of the house, then the back. Clients went to and from the brothel, but none of them had the thief's distinctive profile and gait. At one point, he started wondering once again how Hannah had fared and wished that he could have travelled with her. It took the chimes of midnight to bring him back to reality. He was still scolding himself for letting his attention wander when someone plucked at his sleeve. It was a slim, young woman with a Welsh lilt in her voice.

'I'm to tell you that he's not here, sir,' she said.

'Who?'

'We haven't seen Harry since he was took away.'

'He escaped.'

'Did he?' she exclaimed, feigning surprise.

'Yes, he did,' said Paul, wishing that she was not wearing such unpleasantly pungent perfume. 'You must be Welsh Mary.'

She was thrilled. 'You've heard of me, sir?'

'Harry talked of nobody else.'

'*Diu!* What a sweet old thing he is.'

'Have you any idea where he might be?'

'No, sir, but he'll be miles away from London.'

'Did he never talk to you about moving on somewhere?'

She tittered. 'We didn't do much talking, sir.'

'How long have you known I was out here?'

'Mrs Ginniver, who owns the house, saw you arrive in daylight,' said the woman. 'She hoped it would rain hard so you'd get soaked to the skin for your pains, but it didn't. So she decided to keep you out here till midnight.'

Paul was livid with himself. He'd not only failed in his mission, he'd given himself away. It was an unpardonable lapse. He was tempted to storm into the brothel to make absolutely sure that Scattergood wasn't there, but he knew he'd only face derision. After thanking her for coming out to him, he watched Welsh Mary run back to the house on tiptoe, then he collected his horse from the place where he'd left it. The ride home was accompanied by remorse and recrimination. He was not looking forward to delivering his report to his brother and to Gully Ackford. They would be justifiably critical of him.

All that he wanted to do was get back to the privacy of his home and go straight to bed. When the silhouette of his house finally came into view, he felt a surge of relief. He could put his mistakes behind him. Paul was unsaddling his horse in the stable when he heard footsteps. One of the servants came out to him with a lantern.

'I'm so glad you're back, sir.'

'Why is that, John?'

'This came for you,' said the man, handing him the letter. 'The messenger wouldn't part with it until he was paid. Since it was sent by Miss Granville, I gave him the money at once.'

'Who brought it?' asked Paul, snatching it from him.

'He was an ostler from the Flying Horse.'

It was the coaching inn from which Hannah had departed. Telling the servant to hold the lantern closer, Paul opened the letter and read the contents, noting that it had been written in a shaky hand. After thrusting it into his pocket, he grabbed the saddle and hoisted it back into position.

'Are you going out again, sir?'

'Yes,' said Paul, hastily. 'Send word to my brother in the morning that Miss Granville's coach was waylaid on the road to Bath. Warn him that I may be away from London for a considerable time.'

It was impossible even to doze, let alone sleep properly. Hannah lay in the darkness and relived the horror of the attack. When she heard the bed beside her creak, she realised that Jenny was also wide awake.

'Can't you sleep either?' she asked.

'I'm too scared.'

'We're safe enough here, Jenny.'

'I thought we were safe in the coach, especially with Mr Cosgrove to look after us. We could've been *killed*.'

'But weren't,' emphasised Hannah. 'Be thankful for that.'

'I've been sending prayers up to heaven for the last hour.'

There was a lengthy pause before Hannah spoke again.

'I keep thinking about that highwayman.'

'Which one do you mean, Miss Granville?'

'The one who was in charge – he wasn't like the others. They were just nasty, uncouth and frightening. Their leader had an educated voice and he dressed more smartly than them. Did you notice his boots? They were gleaming.'

'I didn't have time to see what he was wearing,' admitted Jenny. 'To be honest, I kept my eyes closed for most of the time.'

'The people with him were unlettered ruffians. One of them kept spitting on the ground in that disgusting way. And when everyone got out of the coach, he pushed them around for the fun of it.'

'Then their leader ordered him to stop.'

'He actually had some manners, Jenny. His companions obviously wanted sport with us. He seemed to understand just how deeply upsetting the robbery must have been for us. That's why he showed mercy.'

'Taking our valuables like that was not exactly merciful,' said Jenny, sharply. 'He deserves to hang with the others.'

'Oh, I'm not excusing him. He was a vile criminal, but one with a measure of decency in him and a concern for his appearance. In the circumstances, those boots of his were rather incongruous.'

With a full day at the gallery ahead of them, Ackford and Huckvale were up shortly after dawn for an early breakfast. They were surprised when they heard the front door being unlocked. Moments later, Peter Skillen came striding into the room.

'We weren't expecting you for hours,' said Ackford.

'There's been an emergency,' Peter told them. 'A message from Paul arrived to say that he's ridden off to be with Hannah. Highwaymen stopped her coach and robbed everyone in it.'

'Heavens!' cried Huckvale. 'Was anyone hurt?'

'I don't know the details, Jem. All I was told is that Hannah somehow managed to have a letter delivered to Paul, explaining where she was and why. Needless to say, he went racing off into the night.'

'Was there any news about Harry Scattergood?'

'There was no mention of him, so we can assume that he's still at liberty. In any case, Paul has somebody more important to worry about at the moment. Harry will have to wait in the queue.'

'As we predicted,' said Ackford, 'the Runners called here after you left yesterday. They demanded to be given the address where you and Paul had caught him.'

'We didn't give it to them,' added Huckvale, grinning. 'We gave them *an* address, but it was a long way from the place where he was hiding. They'll have spent last night sitting outside a pub in Southwark in the hope that Harry will turn up.'

'And he certainly didn't.'

'That will have served Yeomans right,' said Peter. 'He's always trying to bully information out of us. The Runners need to rely on their own intelligence. However,' he went on, 'I must go and have breakfast with Charlotte, then I'll be off to Mrs van Emden's hotel to take her to Islington.'

'I wish I could come with you,' said Huckvale, then he caught Ackford's eye, 'but I have work to do here. Please let me know what you find out.'

'I'll make a point of it, Jem. But for you, we'd never have found out where Mr Parry was buried. Mrs van Emden will want to thank you in person. Learning the truth about her father will make it an important day for her.' Peter moved towards the door.

'But spare a thought for Hannah as well. She's been through a terrible experience.'

'My sympathies are with Paul,' said Ackford. 'He must be worried to death. If I know him, he'll have been in the saddle for hours, riding like mad through the night.'

CHAPTER SEVEN

It was yet another of the many occasions when Hannah Granville realised just how much she owed to her dresser. Jenny Pye offered far more than female companionship. As well as supervising the actress's costumes during a performance, she provided practical advice, unconditional loyalty and wise comments about any role that her employer was due to perform. The two of them sat alone at a table in the corner. Like them, the other passengers were still very upset by their confrontation with the three highwaymen. Cosgrove, they noticed, was eating with one hand.

'I was hoping that Paul might be here by now,' said Hannah.

'It's a long way for him to come.'

'I'm afraid that he didn't get my letter.'

'Oh, he must have done, I'm sure,' said Jenny, trying to inject some optimism into the conversation. 'When you spoke to that driver, you impressed upon him how vital it was for the letter to be delivered.'

'What if Paul set out and was ambushed on the way?'

'Then I'd feel sorry for the people who tried to ambush him.'

Hannah laughed. 'You're right. The one thing he does best is defend himself. He's been in any number of perilous situations and he always comes out alive in the end.'

'He might even enlist the aid of his brother.'

'Paul won't need to do that.'

'How can you tell him apart from Peter? I still confuse them.'

'I always know the difference, believe me,' said Hannah, smiling. 'Peter is charming, but I like that element of danger in Paul.'

'Are you going to tell him about the pendant when he arrives?'

'No, Jenny.'

'Why not?'

'I need comfort not criticism. If and when he gets here, all that he'll want to know is that I'm alive, well and capable of fulfilling my contract with the theatre in Bath. Talking of which,' she continued, 'I'll look to the manager for unstinting sympathy.'

'Mr Teale will be shocked to hear what happened to the famous Hannah Granville on her journey.'

'He should have sent more men to guard me. I deserve it.'

'And he'll realise that now. You're his prize asset. Your name alone is enough to fill the theatre for a month.'

'The engagement is not for that long, Jenny.'

'That's a real pity!'

'Why do you say that?'

'As soon as our work is done there,' said Jenny, 'we'll have to travel back to London along that same road. I'm afraid that the man in the shiny boots might be waiting for us again with his two cut-throats. They might not be so lenient with us the next time.'

In the privacy of a room in the tavern where they'd spent the night, they put all their takings on the table and gloated over them. The stagecoach had yielded up a minor treasure chest. Apart from an abundance of banknotes and gold coins, there was a selection of fine jewellery, tugged uncaringly from its previous owners, and the two guns they'd confiscated from Cosgrove and the driver. All in all, it was their most profitable raid in years. The tall, urbane gentleman who was their leader divided the spoils up carefully.

There was the usual protest from one of his henchmen.

'You've got more than us,' he said, accusingly.

'It's no more than is my due,' replied the other. 'I was the one who found out when the coach was coming and decided where best to launch our attack. Left to yourselves, you'd have bungled the whole enterprise.'

'Why are you keeping that opal necklace? It's worth more than anything we have. I say we should play cards for it.'

'If anyone has designs on that piece of jewellery, he's more than welcome to fight a duel with me. Mark my words, it's the only way he'll get it. Well,' he challenged, looking at the others in turn, 'is either of you man enough to try?'

The surly one who'd spoken up cursed under his breath and turned away. Though he felt cheated, he valued his life too much to take on their acknowledged leader. With sword or pistol, he was invincible.

'Right,' said the tall man, admiring himself in the mirror and flicking some dust off the shoulder of his frock coat, 'that's all for the time being. Spend your money sensibly. Don't draw attention to yourselves by being too free with your booty. We don't want people asking questions about how you acquired it.'

'When do we meet again?'

'It will be when I send for you. Let the hullabaloo from today's little venture die down. When word of our ambush gets around, coaches will start to travel with more guards aboard. We'll wait until they become more lax again.'

'How do we find you?'

'You don't,' said their leader, turning to face them. 'I find *you*. Now, get out.'

After looking covetously at the opal necklace, the surly man nodded to his companion, and they gathered up their haul before leaving the room. The leader picked up the one item that he'd kept for himself. It was the valise belonging to Hannah Granville. Made of the finest leather, it was a handsome piece of luggage. He noted that her initials had been delicately sewn into the valise. After rubbing his hands together in anticipation, he opened it up and peered inside.

'Now, Miss Granville,' he said, with quiet excitement, 'it looks as if I have something you wear very close to that delectable body of yours.' Taking out a long, thin, fur-edged petticoat, he stroked it gently. 'What more can any man ask than the pleasure of running it slowly through his fingers?'

Peter Skillen didn't have to go into the hotel on Albemarle Street because she and her footman were waiting for him outside. He got out of the curricle he'd been driving and held the door open for her to get in. Her footman took the rear rumble seat. Peter climbed back on to the vehicle and flicked his whip to set the two horses in motion. Clemency had to raise her voice to hold a conversation with him.

'I've been on tenterhooks all night,' she confided. 'I've been tormenting myself with what we're about to discover.'

'Let me counsel you against expecting too much.'

'What do you mean?'

'All that Jem was able to find was where your father was laid to rest. There may be little that the vicar can tell us in addition to that. The person we really need to speak to is the one who turned up at the funeral.'

'It must be someone who knew my father,' she said. 'It's vital that we find this man.'

Peter turned his head briefly towards her. 'How do we know that it's a man?'

'It has to be, surely?'

'It could equally well be a woman, Mrs van Emden.'

Clemency's face puckered with anxiety.

On receipt of Hannah's fraught letter, all that Paul had wanted to do was gallop through the night to the inn where she was staying. But he had more concern for his horse than that. They'd be travelling a long distance to their destination, so he had to pace the animal and allow it periods of rest when it could quench the thirst it was bound to build up. In spite of this, they made good time and, thankfully, encountered no danger on the road. It was daylight when the coaching inn finally came into sight. Paul used his crop to get a final spurt out of his mount.

When he reached the cobbled yard of the inn, however, he met with a setback. The ostler who ran out to hold the bridle of his horse told him that the coach he was after had departed well over twenty minutes earlier. If he wanted to catch up to Hannah, therefore, he realised that he had to chase after her. Since she'd already be miles ahead of him, it was too much to ask of his tired horse to gallop in pursuit. Paul decided to hire a horse from the stable and leave his own there to have a well-earned rest. He could return to collect it at a later date. The ostler was glad to do as he was bidden, removing the saddle and harness from one animal to another with remarkable speed. After pressing some coins into the man's hand, Paul used his heels to spur his new mount into action.

During the journey to Islington, she was unable to sit still. Clemency kept shifting her position and looking out of the curricle impatiently to see where they were. Peter felt sorry for her. She was clearly still blaming herself for her father's untimely death.

'There must be a vicarage nearby,' he told her.

'I have to see the grave first,' she insisted. 'I want to pay my respects.'

'Jem described the location to me. We must look for a yew tree growing near the wall of the churchyard.'

'I can't wait to see it.'

'It won't be long now, Mrs van Emden.'

She put a hand to her breast. 'My search will be over at last.'

Peter was not as sanguine. Finding where her father was buried, he believed, might only be the start of a search rather than its conclusion. There would be so much more still left to find out. He didn't want to upset his companion by reminding her of that. It would be cruel to introduce reality at such a delicate moment.

When the curricle eventually rolled to a halt, they were beside the churchyard. After alighting himself, Peter helped her to get out. His gaze soon picked out the yew tree.

'It's over there,' he said, indicating the tree.

Lifting the hem of her dress, she entered the churchyard and tripped along on her toes. Clemency was impelled by a mingled curiosity and sense of foreboding. As they got close to the spot, she broke into a run and went around the yew tree. Coming to a halt, she let out a scream of horror. Peter ran to her side and saw with dismay what had frightened her into crying out. The grave had been opened and the earth scattered wildly in every direction. While the coffin was still there, its former occupant most certainly was not. The lid had been levered off and cast aside. George Parry had gone. The empty coffin was a grim epitaph. Clemency's father was the victim of grave robbers. Unable to cope with the enormity of the shock, she wobbled slightly and emitted a low moan before swooning. Reacting quickly, Peter was only just able to catch her before she tumbled into the open grave.

Although he was weary from his marathon ride, Paul Skillen didn't give himself a moment's rest. He galloped on along the road with a blind determination to overhaul the stagecoach on which Hannah Granville was travelling. He could well imagine the fear and anguish she must have suffered and chided himself yet again for not accompanying her to Bath. The sun came out, brightening the countryside all around him, but he hardly noticed the sudden intensity in the various colours. His eyes were fixed on the road ahead, his mind driving him on, his aching body rising to the challenge. When he crested a hill, he finally had a glimpse of the coach, rumbling on with a cloud of dust in its wake.

Paul used his crop on the horse's rump to increase his already fast pace. Convinced that he'd certainly catch them up now, he came up against an unforeseen hazard. Some of those seated on the roof of the stagecoach were looking directly at him. When they saw the desperation with which he was riding, they mistakenly took him for a highwayman and yelled a warning to the driver. The coach picked up even more speed. Paul nevertheless closed on it and was able to pick out the figure of Roderick Cosgrove on the roof. Worried that the bodyguard might try to shoot him, he snatched off his hat and waved it in the air. To Paul's relief, Cosgrove recognised him and told the driver they were not in danger. The stagecoach slowly lost its forward impetus and, when they came to a flat piece of land, it veered off the road and slowed to a halt. Heads came out of the vehicle to see what had caused the unscheduled stop.

One of them belonged to Hannah. When she saw Paul approaching, she heaved a sigh of relief and flung open the door. He reached the coach, reined in his horse, then leapt from the saddle to help her out.

'You got my letter, after all,' she said.

'I came as soon as I read it.'

'You're running with perspiration and covered in dust.'

'That's immaterial, my love. How are you? That's what I want to know. Were you hurt? Threatened? Mistreated in any way?'

'All is well now that you're here,' she said.

'Well, I want to know *everything*.'

'And so you shall.'

'Do you have any idea who the highwaymen were?'

'We can't hold up the coach like this, Paul. I'm not the only passenger and we've lost enough time, as it is.'

'Then I'll delay you no longer.'

'Ride on with us to Bath and I promise you'll hear the full story.'

After kissing her hand, he helped her back into the vehicle.

* * *

The Reverend Hubert Corke, vicar of the parish church of St Mary's, was a tall, slender, hollow-cheeked man in his sixties with a natural dignity. Peter, Clemency and the footman were invited in. She was offered a glass of wine to revive her. They were in the drawing room of the vicarage, a large, comfortable, well-proportioned room with a crucifix over the mantelpiece and devotional paintings on the walls. Only when his female visitor seemed to have calmed down did the vicar speak.

'We meet in unfortunate circumstances, Mrs van Emden,' he said. 'While I'm pleased to meet the daughter of George Parry, I regret the shock you must have had when you saw the grave.'

She was aghast. 'Who could have *done* such a thing? It's inhuman.'

'Unhappily,' said Peter, 'it's all too common. There's such a demand in the medical profession for cadavers for dissection that an army of grave robbers has sprung up.'

'The worst of it is,' added Corke, 'that they are sometimes called resurrectionists, a word that lends their work an undeserved spiritual significance. It's a grotesque appellation. In stealing bodies from their last resting place, they are committing acts that are simultaneously evil and blasphemous.'

'Has this ever happened here before?' asked Peter.

'No – thank God.'

'Perhaps you could tell us how Mr Parry came to be there in the first place – if, that is,' he said, with a glance at Clemency, 'Mrs van Emden feels able to hear the full details.'

'Indeed, I do,' she said, nodding.

'It's a strange tale,' said the vicar, apologetically. 'I must warn you about that in advance. In all my years in the church, I've never seen the like. What happened was this: almost a fortnight ago, a gentleman was riding through Islington when he caught sight of someone underneath a hedge. Thinking it was some desperate soul who'd slept in the field all night, he went to investigate. What he found,' continued Corke, 'was a man so close to death that he was unable to speak or move of his own accord. The gentleman came to the vicarage for help.'

'Who was this kind person?' asked Peter.

'The name he gave was Alderson – Mr Sebastian Alderson. I sent for the doctor and we repaired to the place where the man still lay. He was, alas, beyond help. By the time we'd brought him back here, he was fading fast. He died in the night.'

'What was the cause of death?' asked Clemency.

'The doctor said it was a mixture of malnutrition and a bad chest infection. He never stopped coughing. From the condition of his clothing, it was evident that he'd been sleeping rough for a long time. You couldn't help but pity him.'

'How did you know it was my father?'

'We didn't, Mrs van Emden. We had no idea what his family situation was. All that we had was his name.'

'And how did you discover that?'

'It was on a piece of paper in his pocket. In fact,' said Corke, 'it was virtually the only thing he had in his possession.'

'Let me go back for a moment to Mr Alderson,' said Peter. 'What manner of man was he?'

'He was a true Christian. Most people seeing someone cowering under a hedge would be too cautious even to approach him, still less to summon help. Mr Alderson was different. Having made the discovery, he took an interest in the deceased and – when we were unable to find out anything at all about him – he insisted on paying for the funeral.'

'That was very generous. How old was Mr Alderson?'

'He'd be in his forties, I suppose, Mr Skillen. He seems to be a man of independent wealth and the freedom to go where he wishes, yet he found time to take an interest in a poor, lonely, dying man.'

'I must thank him,' said Clemency, impressed by what she'd heard. 'Where does Mr Alderson live?'

'He has a house in High Barnet and was visiting friends in the city.'

'Could you furnish me with his address?'

'You can have it gladly.'

'You told us,' resumed Peter, 'that you were unable to learn anything at all about Mr Parry.'

'I sent out letters here, there and everywhere, Mr Skillen, but nobody was able to help. And we were up against time, you must remember. A once-healthy body can be kept for some time after death but one in such a sad condition is more difficult to preserve. When the doctor recommended burial,' he went on, 'I discussed the matter with my bishop and he agreed that we should follow the advice.'

'How did you get in touch with Mr Alderson?'

'I wrote to the address he'd given me and told him of our decision. As you can imagine, the funeral was a rather dispiriting affair. George Parry was consigned to his grave with only a complete stranger to mourn him.'

It was too much for Clemency. Overcome with grief, she pulled out a handkerchief and began to sob into it. While Peter put a consoling arm around her, the vicar left the room and returned with his wife, a practical old woman who took charge of Clemency, talking softly to her, then shepherding her slowly out of the room.

'My wife has a gift for offering comfort,' said the vicar.

'The wonder of it is that Mrs van Emden has managed to hold in her emotions for so long. Though she did faint at the graveside, she somehow managed to rally.'

'That was admirable. However, now that we're alone, I can give you certain details that I thought it best to keep back.'

He went on to tell Peter about the doctor's examination of the dying man. His body was badly bruised and his face was covered in dried blood. He didn't have a single penny to his name.

'We felt that he'd been set on by blackguards of some kind,' said the vicar. 'It's by the grace of God that he fell into the tender hands of Mr Alderson. I saw the corpse when it was being prepared for burial. I tell you, Mr Skillen, the fiends who dug him up will not get much for their pains. Professors of anatomy prefer to dissect bodies that were once in a far healthier state.' He looked hopefully at his visitor. 'Is there any chance of discovering to whom the cadaver was sold?'

'If there is,' affirmed Peter, 'we'll find it. Meanwhile, I must ask a favour of you. In addition to Mr Alderson's address, there are two things I'd like. The first is the name of the undertaker hired for the funeral.'

'What's the second request?'

'When you found Mr Parry's name, did you keep the piece of paper on which it was written?'

'Of course, I did,' replied the vicar. 'It's in a drawer in my study. If you'll excuse me for a moment, I'll fetch it instantly.'

Peter was left to mull over what he'd been told. Crossing to the window, he looked out at the churchyard and wondered how Clemency's father had come to end up there. Had he not been rescued from under a hedge, he would certainly have rotted away and been vulnerable to predators. His injuries showed that he'd

80

been badly beaten by someone, distressing information that Peter resolved to keep from the man's daughter. One thing brought solace: at the very end of his life, Peter reflected, George Parry had been shown some sympathy and kindness.

The vicar came back into the room with a sheet of paper.

'This is what we found in his pocket,' he said, handing it over.

'Thank you.'

'When I first saw it, I wondered if he was one of those unfortunates born deaf and dumb. We've had people like that calling here from time to time. They speak with their hands or hold up a card to explain what their deficiencies are. The deaf live in private worlds.'

Peter was in a private world of his own at the moment. Five words were written on a piece of paper and they jumped out at him.

MY NAME IS GEORGE PARRY

He recognised the lettering at once. He'd seen it on an identical sheet of stationery. The hand that had written the terse message had also sent word of the man's death and burial to his daughter.

CHAPTER EIGHT

'Who told them where to find him?' asked Hale.

'They always guard their sources carefully.'

'Someone must have seen him in that tavern we visited yesterday.'

'I'm not convinced he was ever there in the first place,' said Yeomans, ruefully. 'I fancy that Huckvale sent us off to Southwark out of mischief. I'd like to wring his neck.'

'So what do we do next, Micah?'

'We squeeze our informers until the blood seeps out. One of them must have some idea where Harry Scattergood goes to ground.'

They were seated in the Peacock Inn, drinking a restorative pint after their latest failure and wondering how they could get the upper hand over the Skillen brothers.

'We must eclipse them somehow,' said Yeomans.

'There's one simple way to do that, Micah.'

'I can't see it.'

'Why battle against them when we can fight side by side? All we have to do is recruit them. Those brothers would make excellent Runners.'

Yeomans snorted. 'You have a habit of coming up with truly nonsensical ideas, Alfred,' he said, scornfully, 'but that one is far and away the most ridiculous. They'd never take orders from us.'

'They might if they knew how much they could earn.'

'They already make a small fortune in reward money.'

'Yes,' agreed Hale, 'but they could still be tempted by all the extra cash we make over and above our wages. Private commissions have lined our pockets for years.'

'I'm not letting that pair have a sniff of those,' said Yeomans, possessively. 'They're rewards for our status. Besides, there's something you haven't considered, and that's Mr Kirkwood. If those twins were allowed to become Runners and were seen by the chief magistrate as being more effective than us, we'd be demoted and they'd hold the whip hand over us. Is that what you want?'

Hale sagged. 'No, Micah,' he said. 'I never thought of that.' When he saw someone entering the room, he rallied. 'Here's Chevy Ruddock with a smile on his face. I think he has good news for us.'

Ruddock marched across to them as if expecting applause.

'Well,' said Yeomans. 'Have there been any sightings of Harry?'

'No,' admitted Ruddock, 'but I've learnt something that will please you. Three highwaymen robbed a coach on the road to Bristol yesterday.'

'Why should we take the slightest interest in that? It's well outside our territory.'

'I have a friend who works at the Flying Horse.'

'Spare us details of your private life.'

'But this is relevant, I promise you. Davey, my friend, told me that one of the passengers in that coach was Miss Hannah Granville, the famous actress. He saw her arriving at the inn yesterday with a certain person. Do you catch my drift, sir?'

'I do,' said Hale, grinning. 'That certain person was Paul Skillen. If Miss Granville is in any kind of trouble, he'd fly to her side at once. This is good news, Micah. He could be away from London for days.'

'His brother is still here,' complained Yeomans.

'Perhaps,' said Ruddock, 'but he wasn't at the gallery yesterday when we called for details of where Harry Scattergood was caught. Don't you remember what Gully Ackford told us? He said that Peter Skillen had his hands full, looking for a missing person. In other words, neither of the twins will be able to get in our way.'

'This *is* good news,' conceded Yeomans. 'You deserve a tankard of ale for bringing it.' Ruddock beamed. 'Buy one for Alfred and me while you're at it.' The younger man grimaced. 'In the search for Harry Scattergood,' Yeomans went on, 'we have a clear field. So let's drink up, then go and find that devious little bastard.'

Deciding that it was wise to quit London for a while, Harry Scattergood was in St Albans, riding slowly around the town and looking for likely targets. When he found the district where the more prosperous citizens lived, his face lit up. The houses would present no obstacle to him. All that he had to do was familiarise himself with the town so that he could move about it easily after dark. He'd come to the right place. It was positively brimming with rich pickings. The only thing it lacked was the stimulating presence of Welsh Mary in his bed.

On the way to the undertaker, Peter suggested that, since she'd been so shaken by what they'd found, it might be better if Clemency remained in the carriage.

'It's no place for a woman,' he argued.

'I'm the daughter of a man I loved very deeply,' she said, 'and I want to know everything we can find out about what happened to him.'

'You might hear some rather unsavoury details.'

'I'm not as fragile as I may appear, Mr Skillen.'

'Then I withdraw my suggestion,' said Peter, courteously. 'We'll visit this fellow together.'

Islington was known for the quality of its milk and the purity of its water. Much of the land was given over to dairy farming, but what attracted visitors most to the village – apart from its tea gardens and its glorious parks – was its spa. It was ironic that George Parry had perished near a place whose water had medicinal properties that might even have revived him.

Mokey Hiscox, the undertaker, lived in a house almost a mile from the village. When they arrived there, they could hear the sound of hammering in the large, rickety shed set apart from the dwelling. Peter hoped that the mere sight of the place might deter Clemency from entering it but she was adamant. If there was anything new to hear about the funeral, she wanted to be present. As they walked closer to the shed, they heard another noise. It was the rhythmical clink of a chisel on stone. Peter banged on the door with his fist and waited. There was no response. He therefore grasped the knob and found that the door opened. After ushering Clemency inside, he went after her.

Three people looked across at them. Hiscox, a stooping man with a fringe beard, had been working on a new coffin and put down his hammer. His wife, an emaciated creature, was the monumental mason in the family, chiselling a block of marble into the shape of an angel. She stopped to stare at the newcomers. But it was the third person who caught their attention. Seated cross-legged on a table was a moon-faced girl with a board across her knees on which was a piece of paper. Two things struck them at once. She seemed far too young to be the child of such elderly parents and she was suffering from some kind of disability. Her head seemed too large for the little body that was permanently twisted out of shape. She gave them a half-witted grin of welcome, then returned to her drawing.

Hiscox came across to them and spoke with practised solemnity.

'You 'ave my profound sympathy on your loss,' he said. 'I'm Mokey 'Iscox and this is my wife, Matilda, and that's our daughter, Sally.' He wiped the back of his hand under his nose. 'When is the funeral due, may I ask?'

'It's already taken place,' said Peter, indicating Clemency. 'Mrs van Emden's father, George Parry, was buried recently in St Mary's Church, Islington.'

'I remembers it well, sir.'

'Unhappily, the grave has been opened and the body removed.'

'Dear God!' exclaimed the wife.

'We've spoken to the vicar and heard all that he could tell us. Since you took charge of the body and attended the funeral, we'd like to know if you have anything to add.'

'It was a sad business,' recalled Hiscox. 'I've never seen a corpse in so bad a state. We did what we could – Matilda sees to that kind of thing – but we couldn't make him look anything but wasted away.'

'What happened to his effects?' asked Clemency.

'Mr Parry didn't 'ave none, Miss. When I picked him up from the vicarage, 'e was wearing an old nightgown as the vicar'd given 'im for the sake of decency. Your father's clothes stank so much, they burnt 'em.'

Peter could sense how upset Clemency was getting and wished he could get her out of there so that he could press Hiscox for more detail. It was, however, impossible. Letting her take over the questioning, Peter glanced across at the girl. She was looking at them intently before gazing down at the paper. Sally Hiscox lifted her head after a few moments, then looked away once more.

'What my 'usband tells you is right,' said Matilda, intervening. 'Forgive me for saying so, but your father was no more than a bag of bones. We can prove it if you like.'

'How can you possibly do that?' asked Peter.

'Sally can show you.'

'She's not like other children,' said Hiscox, quietly, 'but we love 'er no less for that. The one thing that Sal *can* do is draw. It's 'er passion. Show 'em, Sal.'

The girl gave them another toothy grin and held up the piece of paper on which she'd been drawing. Before they'd arrived, she'd been working on portraits of her parents. Two new faces had now been added. Peter and Clemency were startled to recognise each other. Their portraits were crude and inexact but, with relatively few lines, the girl had somehow caught their essence. They were looking at real talent, an unexpected counterpoint to the handicaps that fate had visited on her.

While Peter was alarmed at the thought of the girl being allowed to view the dead bodies routinely brought in, he saw that

88

it might just be of advantage to them. He glanced at Clemency and she nodded, ratifying the question she knew he was about to ask.

'Does your daughter keep the drawings she makes?'

'She'd never part with them, sir,' replied Hiscox.

'I'll get them,' added his wife. 'Come with me, Sal. The lady and gentleman want to see some more of your work.'

Lifting the girl off the table, she took her by the hand and led her slowly out. Peter and Clemency winced when they saw that she had a pronounced limp. How such a child could produce work of that quality was baffling. They thought it such a tragedy that her gift was limited to the production of portraits of her parents and drawings of corpses. And yet Sally was immensely proud of her achievements. When she returned with her mother, she had a large sheaf of drawings under her arm. Placing them on the table, she began to sort them out.

'It was that man with the broken nose, Sal,' said her father. 'That's what they want to see. Find 'im for us.'

'My father had no broken nose,' said Clemency.

'Oh, yes, 'e did – and a missing ear as well.'

Peter saw her shudder slightly and put out a steadying hand.

'Perhaps we should go,' he suggested. 'Do you really want to see the macabre doodles of a young child?'

She gritted her teeth. 'Yes, I do.'

'Then this is Mr Parry,' said Matilda, finding the appropriate portrait. 'Show it to the lady, Sal.'

Holding both sides of the paper, the girl held it aloft. Much more time had gone into the drawing than into the sketchy likenesses of Peter and Clemency. There was considerable detail. The body lay on its back in the coffin, eyes closed and arms crossed over its chest. The broken nose and missing ear were apparent, and there were other salient features.

Clemency let out a cry that blended shock with disgust.

'What's wrong?' asked Peter.

'That's not my father!'

'Are you sure?'

'It's nothing at all like him, Mr Skillen,' she said, firmly. 'He was a handsome man when he was younger, whereas this fellow is ugly to the point of being repulsive.' She put both hands up to her face. 'I've had the most dreadful thought.'

'What is it?'

'If this drawing is anywhere close to a true likeness, then the man they buried was an impostor.'

'That raises an interesting possibility, Mrs van Emden.'

'Does it?'

'Yes,' said Peter. 'Your father may still be alive.'

While the city was no longer quite as fashionable as it had been forty years earlier, Bath still exerted an attraction for the rich, titled and leisured. At heart, it remained what it had always been – a place of frivolity, fashion, social nuances and posturing dandies. When they reached the White Hart, the city's well-known coaching inn, Hannah was the first to alight, aided by Paul Skillen, who'd dismounted to run across to the vehicle. Neither Hannah nor Jenny Pye had the slightest interest in viewing the delights of Bath. Both of them simply wanted to go to the hotel in order to rest after the long and troublesome journey from London.

Rooms had been reserved for them at an establishment within easy walking distance of the theatre. Hannah's suite was the larger and more luxurious, Jenny's being small and functional by comparison. The first thing that greeted the actress in her room was a basket of fresh flowers and an effusive note from the theatre manager, commiserating with her over the robbery and assuring her that concern for her safety would now be his priority. Paul had been restrained yet attentive while they had company. The moment they were alone together, however, he swept her up in his arms and kissed away some of her distress. They adjourned to the elegant two-seater sofa and sat entwined.

'Tell me *everything*, my darling,' he said.

'It's a long story.'

'I insist on hearing every syllable of it.'

Paul was not simply hoping that, in going over the details of her ordeal, she might somehow draw some of the poison out of it. He knew that he'd also be treated to a private performance from a sublime actress. Hannah held nothing back, embellishing her narrative with gestures, vocal tricks and a whole battery of facial expressions. While she'd been desperately worried about her own fate at the time, she spared a thought for the other passengers, including Cosgrove.

'He was fortunate they didn't shoot him on the spot,' she said. 'Had their leader not forbidden it, the others would have punished him for trying to fight back. As for what might have happened to us . . .'

Her eyes rolled and she wrapped her arms around her body in a display of defence. Paul needed no elaboration. There were rumours of female travellers being subjected to rape, humiliation, even torture at the hands of highwaymen. Thanks to the leader of this particular gang, the women had been spared violation. In Paul's eyes, that didn't lessen the severity of their crime.

'All three are destined for the noose,' he said.

'But we have no idea who they are, Paul.'

'That's not true, Hannah. From what you've told me, it's clear that the man in charge poses as a gentleman when he's not robbing coaches. Where better to do that than here in Bath? There's another telling feature about him. He's a cultured man who is fond of the theatre. He identified you at a glance.'

'That's true.'

'It wouldn't surprise me in the least if he turned up at one of your performances.'

She started. 'What a frightening thought!'

'Be grateful that he is patently an admirer of yours. It may bring him within reach of me. As for those other rogues,' said Paul, throbbing with anger, 'I'll get their names out of him if I have to tear the loathsome devil apart limb by limb with my bare hands.'

It was late morning before Gully Ackford and Jem Huckvale could stop work for some rest and refreshment. When they joined Charlotte, they found that she had food and drink prepared for them.

'There may be long days ahead for both of you,' she warned. 'Paul is probably in Bath by now and unlikely to stir from Hannah's side until he's certain that she's in no danger.'

'That's not enough for him,' said Ackford. 'Your brother-in-law will not be happy until he's tracked down the highwaymen who robbed her coach.'

'How can he possibly do that?' asked Huckvale.

'He'll find a way somehow, Jem.'

'I'd love to be there to help him.'

'You're needed here,' said Charlotte. 'That's what I meant when I talked about extra work falling upon you and Gully. There'll be no help from Paul in the foreseeable future and Peter is preoccupied with the search for Mrs van Emden's father.'

'I found him in Islington – what was left of him, that is.'

'She'll want to know how he came to be there.'

'I keep thinking about Mr van Emden,' said Ackford. 'Why isn't he here with his wife?'

'She explained that,' said Charlotte. 'He's very busy.'

'Rich men can always make time for things of importance and I'd have thought that his wife's search was very important.'

'Perhaps he didn't like Mr Parry,' suggested Huckvale.

'That wasn't the impression Mrs van Emden gave us,' recalled Charlotte. 'She told us that her husband was as anxious as she was to be reconciled with her father.'

'Then he should offer her proper support.'

'What do you mean, Jem?'

'Well,' he said, 'when I first met her, she was completely lost and the only person with her was Jacob, that young Dutchman who speaks very little English. I think her husband should have sent her off with a maidservant and at least two able men who spoke our language fluently. I'm not married myself,' he continued, 'but if I was, I'd take more care of my wife than Mr van Emden has.'

'That's a good point,' said Charlotte.

Ackford grinned. 'You're going to be an excellent husband, Jem.'

He winked at Charlotte and she suppressed a smile. They both knew how fond Huckvale was of Meg Rooke, the pretty young servant who lived with her and Peter. Some sort of understanding had grown up between Huckvale and the girl. Whether or not it would blossom into marriage, it was too soon to tell.

'Put it this way,' said Huckvale, reinforcing his argument, 'if Peter sent *you* off to Amsterdam, would your only companion be a man who didn't speak a word of Dutch?'

'Peter would come with me and, if we were likely to be there some time, I'd take Meg Rooke.' She saw Huckvale blush slightly.

'No, the more I think about it, the more convinced I am that Jem is right. Mr van Emden is definitely letting his wife down.'

Clemency was stunned. She sat in the curricle and stared unseeingly ahead of her. Hopes of finding her father's grave had been cruelly dashed. Instead of getting the answer she sought, she'd been left with even more questions. Peter Skillen made no attempt to speak to her, prepared to wait as long as was necessary for her to come out of her daze. Understanding how she must feel, he felt profoundly sorry.

Eventually, her face turned to him.

'What is going on, Mr Skillen?' she asked, despairingly.

'I wish I knew.'

'Do you really think my father could still be alive?'

'It's one explanation, but there are probably others.'

'Such as?'

'Well,' said Peter, 'it could be that the man in that grave really *was* named George Parry. It's not an unusual name. What's happened is that we were brought here by an unfortunate coincidence.'

'Do we have to start searching all over again?'

'That's a decision only you can make.'

'I simply must know the truth,' she said, clenching her fists. 'I can't go back home until I know what happened to my father. So please give me your honest opinion. I'm far too shaken up by what we learnt from the undertaker. You're much calmer and more reasonable.'

'Then my opinion is this,' he told her. 'You were not meant to find out the truth. Whoever sent that message to you in Amsterdam did so on purpose to cause distress. But for our help, you'd never have discovered that a Mr George Parry was buried in Islington.'

'But he's not my father.'

'I believe he was intended to pass as Mr Parry.'

She frowned. 'What evidence do you have for that, Mr Skillen?'

'When you were taken out of the room by the vicar's wife,' he explained, 'I asked how the dead man had been identified. I was shown a piece of paper found in his pocket. All it said was that his name was George Parry, but the lettering matched that on the letter sent to you and the stationery was identical.'

'Why didn't you tell me this earlier?'

'I thought it would only intensify your grief, Mrs van Emden. I wanted to protect you from further pain. Someone is playing games with you,' he said, 'and I'll go to any lengths to find out why. When you feel ready, we'll take the first step towards finding out who's behind it.'

'And how do we do that?'

'We visit the gentleman who actually found the bogus George Parry. I can do so on my own, if you wish.'

'Oh, no,' she said, sitting up and asserting herself. 'I want to be there as well. Just because we've been deceived, I'm not giving up. We'll go to High Barnet together, Mr Skillen.'

CHAPTER NINE

Having him at her side made all the difference. Even though she'd been troubled at first by the suggestion that the leader of the highwaymen might actually live in the city, Hannah Granville was no longer afraid because Paul Skillen had vowed to remain in Bath and would be staying with her in the hotel. When she felt sufficiently recovered from the jolting ride in the coach, she decided to acquaint herself with the manager of the Theatre Royal. Vernon Teale had only taken over from his predecessor six months earlier and was keen to stamp his character on the theatre. By engaging Hannah Granville, he was announcing to his audiences that he'd bring the finest members of the acting profession to the city.

'What do you know of Mr Teale?' asked Paul.

'He's obviously a kind and considerate man,' she replied. 'These lovely flowers are evidence of that.'

'Have you had any reports of him?'

'Yes, I've spoken to actors who've performed here since he took over. They were uniformly favourable in their comments. Mr Teale is a true man of the theatre.'

'I hope that you get on with him, Hannah.'

'I *always* get on well with theatre managers.'

Though Paul disagreed, he thought it best to hold his tongue. The previous year, she'd brought the manager of one London theatre to his knees by making impossible demands, pursuing a vendetta with the playwright and causing endless turbulence. Of her talent there was no doubt, but it came – as Paul knew only too well – with changeable moods and a tempestuous nature. He hoped that Vernon Teale would be able to cope with her caprices.

After changing her dress, she left the hotel on Paul's arm and collected approving glances on all sides. When they entered the foyer of the theatre itself, Hannah was given a little round of applause by the employees standing there. It was a good start. She and Paul went up the carpeted stairs to the manager's office. In response to a knock on the door, Vernon Teale flung it open, let out a cry of delight, then bent double to kiss her hand.

'You're here at last, dear lady,' he said, effusively. 'The theatre is honoured to have you within its walls.'

'Thank you,' she said, turning to Paul. 'Let me introduce Mr Paul Skillen, who will safeguard me throughout my time here.'

'You'll be perfectly safe now.'

'Miss Granville is always plagued by her admirers,' said Paul.

'That's unavoidable, sir.'

Standing aside, he motioned them into the room, then closed the door. Vernon Teale was a tall, slim, middle-aged man with a benign smile and a skilful tailor. He looked quite immaculate. Paul veered towards ostentation, but he couldn't compare with Teale. Every item of the latter's attire was striking and in the height of fashion. Even in a procession of peacocks, he would stand out.

'First,' he said, 'let me say how shocked I was when I heard that your coach had been attacked by highwaymen. It must have been a terrible experience.'

'I'm trying to put it out of my mind and to concentrate on my performance.'

'You'll be the perfect Rosalind,' he said, spreading his arms. 'The rest of the cast are thrilled that you've joined the company.'

'I'm thrilled to be here, Mr Teale.'

'But it's no thanks to you that Miss Granville got here in one piece,' said Paul, sounding a note of criticism. 'In the best sense of the word, she is precious cargo. More care should have been taken to ensure her safety.'

'I provided the bodyguard that was requested,' said Teale.

'Two or three were needed.'

'Cosgrove is a reliable man. I've used him before.'

'He was unable to protect Miss Granville.'

'It was not for the sake of trying,' she said. 'Mr Cosgrove is not to bear any blame. He showed courage. However,' she said, 'let's try to put all that behind us, shall we? I'm well, I'm happy and I'm here.'

'Nobody could be more welcome,' said the manager, beaming.

'I feel at home already, Mr Teale.'

'That's wonderful to hear. Ah,' he said, remembering something, 'I have a gift for you. It was left in the foyer with a letter that bears your name. I'll get it for you instantly.'

Crossing to a large cupboard, he took something out and held it up for her. Expecting to see her smile in gratitude, he was given a very different response. Hannah drew back with fright because what he was holding was the stolen valise. The sight of it sent a bolt of lightning through her. After making an effort to master her fear, she stepped forward to snatch the letter attached to the handle by a pink ribbon. Hannah opened it quickly and read the message. Unsigned, it consisted of one short sentence, written in a neat hand.

I tender my profoundest apologies.

High Barnet was a flourishing medieval town whose growth had been stimulated by the fact that it stood on the main route north from London. It was situated on a hill ridge and commanded a fine view of the Brent valley. Peter was impressed by its size, quality and number of inns. Countless buildings had survived from earlier centuries. Sebastian Alderson lived in a more recently built house that conformed to all the dictates of Georgian taste and would not have looked out of place in one of the capital's squares. Peter and Clemency took a few minutes to rehearse what they were going to say so that they obtained all the information they wanted. They then approached the house with a curiosity tempered by misgivings.

A manservant opened the door and heard their request. Inviting them into the hall, he went off to speak to his master. Sebastian Alderson soon appeared, appraising them as he walked along the corridor. He was a tall, well-built, well-dressed man in his forties.

'You wish to see me?' he asked.

'Yes,' replied Peter. 'It's in connection with a recent funeral that took place in Islington.'

'Ah, I see. Let's talk in comfort, shall we?'

Alderson took them along the corridor until they came to the library. Taking a seat, he waved them to the chairs facing him. Peter made the introductions and apologised for disturbing him.

'Not at all, not at all,' said Alderson, pleasantly. 'I'm interested to meet you. The only thing that could have brought you here is that you have some link to the deceased. Is that the case? If it is, I'd be delighted to hear more about the fellow.'

'We thought that he might have been Mrs van Emden's father,' said Peter, 'but we were mistaken.'

'It certainly was not him,' she added.

'How can you be so sure?' asked Alderson.

'We saw the drawing that the undertaker's daughter had made.'

He was appalled. 'The child was allowed to look at corpses?' he said, grimacing. 'That's unforgivable.'

'She should never have been allowed near them.'

'Dear me!' he said. 'I wish I'd known about this when I had dealings with Hiscox. I'd have protested in the strongest manner. That poor malformed creature shouldn't have seen the body of George Parry. It was in a gruesome state.'

'How exactly did you find it?' asked Peter.

Alderson told them what they'd already heard from the vicar of St Mary's. There were a few new facts to digest. Alderson's attention had been attracted to the hedge by the barking of a dog. When he'd ridden into the field, he saw that the animal had been bothering someone crouched so far into the hedge that he was almost invisible. The dog had fled, Alderson had examined the man, seen how ill he was and gone for help. When they got him to the vicarage, Alderson stayed until the man was offered some food. He'd grabbed it eagerly but, the moment he put it in his mouth, he spat it out again.

'It was not his fault,' said Alderson. 'My guess is that he hadn't eaten for so long that he was no longer able to swallow any sustenance. I could see that he was fading, so we did the one thing we could do.'

'And what was that?' asked Clemency.

'The vicar and I prayed for him. Though he was in a parlous state at the end, he was a human being and must have known better times. I wondered what sort of family he'd had and how he'd become separated from them.'

Out of the corner of his eye, Peter saw Clemency twitch guiltily.

'The vicar will have told you the rest,' said Alderson. 'Having failed to discover where he'd come from, we took on the responsibility of giving him a proper funeral. I was happy to pay the cost and be there at the service. Someone had to mourn his passing.' Inhaling deeply through his nose, he let the breath out in a long sigh. 'That's how he came to be buried under the yew tree in the churchyard.'

'He's not there any longer,' Peter told him.

'Why not?'

'The grave has been opened and the body taken away.'

'Whenever did this happen?' asked Alderson in alarm.

'Last night, it seems.'

'Hasn't the wretch suffered enough indignity in life? Even in death, he has no rest.'

'That's why I was so upset,' said Clemency. 'Convinced that it might be my father, I was horrified that he'd be dissected in front of a crowd of medical students.'

'Yet you say that he was *not* your father, Mrs van Emden.'

'No,' said Peter, stepping in. 'We were misled. Thank you, Mr Alderson. You've been most helpful.' He rose to his feet. 'We'll trouble you no more.'

102

'Can't I offer you some refreshment?'

'Thank you, but we must head back to London.'

Clemency rose. 'It was kind of you to talk to us.'

'The theft of the body must be reported,' said Alderson. 'Grave robbers are a detestable species. Nothing is sacred to them.' He stood up. 'I'll see you both out.'

As he led them towards the hall, he probed for details about the other George Parry, wondering why he'd gone missing. Taking her cue from Peter, Clemency said very little. She didn't want to discuss such a delicate matter in front of a stranger. They took their leave and returned to the curricle.

'Why did you wish to get out of there?' asked Clemency.

'We'd learnt all that we were going to learn, Mrs van Emden.'

'I had the feeling that you didn't like the man.'

'That's not true at all,' he said. 'I thought him sincere and admired him for what was, after all, an act of Christian compassion. Something puzzled me, however.'

'What was that, Mr Skillen?'

'Well, you saw all the coffins stacked up against the wall in the undertaker's. What did you notice about them?'

'Apart from variations in size, they were much the same.'

'But they weren't, you see. Different timbers were used. The better ones were made of elm or oak and crafted with care. The cheaper ones were made of unseasoned wood and hacked roughly into shape. That was the case with the coffin that contained the other George Parry.'

'I'm not sure that I follow your reasoning.'

'You heard the vicar. He told us that Mr Alderson is a wealthy man. He'd have to be to afford that lovely house of his. Now then,' said Peter, pensively, 'if his conscience inspired him to rescue the person he found under that hedge, why did he send him off to his Maker in the meanest coffin he could find?'

Jem Huckvale had just finished two strenuous hours instructing clients in the art of fencing, so he was grateful for a rest. When he came into the office, he was surprised to see Chevy Ruddock talking to Charlotte.

'Mr Ruddock has been sent with a complaint,' she explained. 'The Runners believe that you and Gully gave them the wrong information about Harry Scattergood's arrest.'

'Mr Yeomans is very unhappy,' said Ruddock. 'You sent us south of the river, whereas Harry was caught north of it.' He pulled himself up to his full height. 'I'm to give you a stern warning.'

'What is it?'

'If you or Mr Ackford dares to mislead us again, you'll be hauled off to Bow Street.'

'Thanks to you, that happened to me before.'

Ruddock was embarrassed. 'Yes, I'm sorry about that.'

'You were put up to it, weren't you?' said Charlotte.

'I *did* see someone stealing that leg of mutton . . .'

'But it wasn't Jem.'

'It looked a little bit like him.'

'That's nonsense,' said Huckvale. 'It was a nasty experience at the time, but I bear no ill will against you. It's Mr Yeomans who's to blame. As for sending you off to the wrong part of London, we only gave you the information we received.'

'That's not true.'

'What makes you say that?' asked Charlotte.

'We found your informer,' said Ruddock. 'That's to say, *I* did. He denied it at first, but I got the truth out of him in the end.

Harry Scattergood was hiding in a brothel on Old Street. Mr Yeomans and Mr Hale are on their way there right now.'

'I didn't know they used such places,' said Huckvale, pretending to be shocked. 'They're both married, aren't they?'

'You lied to us on purpose, Huckvale.'

'We were simply trying to protect our informer.'

'What we can't understand is why he came to you and not to us.'

'I can answer that,' said Charlotte. 'He knew that we'd have a far better chance of catching him than the Runners.'

'We think it was because you paid him more than us.'

'We didn't need to pay him a penny,' said Huckvale. 'It's only the Runners who have to buy their intelligence or beat it out of people with their fists. Some people prefer to work with us. Harry Scattergood is the king of the thieves and that's made him a lot of enemies among his rivals. They want him dethroned so they're not in competition with someone who's so much better at his trade.'

'As you discovered,' said Charlotte, 'our informer was a thief.'

'He'd fallen out with Harry,' said Huckvale, 'and wanted revenge.'

'*We're* the ones wanting revenge now,' Ruddock told them. 'Step out of line again and you'll be punished.'

'What are you going to do – arrest me for stealing another leg of mutton?'

'I wish you wouldn't keep on about that.'

'It's no fun being carried off by force.'

'Can't we just forget it?' asked Ruddock, earnestly.

When he'd arrested Huckvale, it hadn't been the first time he was obeying orders of which he'd disapproved. Yeomans and Hale seemed to delight in giving him the most unpleasant duties to perform. Wanting to cause havoc at the gallery, they singled out Huckvale. It had been on the Runner's conscience ever since. He'd been roundly criticised by the chief magistrate for being about to bear false witness. The case was dismissed. Charlotte and Huckvale felt some sympathy for him. They knew how ruthlessly he was exploited by Yeomans and Hale.

'You're too honest to be a Runner,' said Huckvale.

'I'm proud of my station in life,' said Ruddock, straightening his spine. 'I've got the most important job in London.'

'Then why can't you do it better?'

'We have our triumphs.'

'Letting Harry Scattergood escape wasn't a triumph.'

'We'll capture him again, don't you worry. Mr Yeomans and Mr Hale will track him to his lair. The Skillen brothers may have had the luck to catch him last time,' said Ruddock, 'but it's *our* turn now.'

Before they even reached the front door, it was opened wide. Hands on her hips, Binnie Ginniver stared at them with undisguised distaste.

'I can smell a Runner from miles away.'

'Hello, Binnie,' said Yeomans, familiarly. 'So you've moved to Old Street, have you? We've been wondering where you were.'

'Why? Did you and Mr Hale want to do business with me?'

'We prefer wholesome women,' said Hale.

'Mine are as a ripe and succulent as can be.'

'Yes, and they'd give us ripe and succulent diseases.'

'We've come for Harry Scattergood,' said Yeomans.

'I've never heard of him.'

'This is where he was arrested.'

'I know nothing of that,' she said. 'As for the man you just mentioned, we don't get many here as give their real names. In any case, why are you bothering to come here if he's already behind bars?'

'He escaped.'

'We need to search the house,' said Hale.

'You can't come in here,' she said, indignantly. 'How would you like to be interrupted when you were taking your pleasure? It can cause terrible things to a man's bodily functions if he's stopped at the wrong moment. I'm not letting a pair of Runners rampage around my house. Think of my reputation.'

'You don't *have* a reputation, you ugly old bawd.'

'And you'll no longer have this house if we arrest you,' added Hale. 'We've done it before, remember.'

'Yes, I remember,' she said, grimly.

'Last time our paths crossed, you had the sense to pay us to look the other way.'

She was adamant. 'Harry Scattergood is not here.'

'A moment ago, you said you'd never heard of him.'

'You jogged my memory.'

'We'll come in, all the same,' said Yeomans.

'You're too late,' she insisted. 'One of those twins who actually caught him came back last night looking for him. Harry disappeared like a scalded cat. God knows where he is. That's the gospel truth.' They looked at each other in disappointment. 'Since you're here, you're welcome to sample my wares. There's no charge.'

Clemency van Emden swung like a pendulum between hope and despair, clinging to the remote possibility that her father might actually be alive, then plunging into utter dejection. Nothing that Peter could say brought any comfort. He was not even sure that she heard what he told her. As he drove them back towards London, he held his peace. Suddenly, she seemed to remember that he was there and raised her voice.

'Would you *really* do that for me, Mr Skillen?'

'I don't follow.'

'When I first met you and told you that my father's best friend lived in Norwich, you volunteered to go there, if need be.'

'That promise still stands.'

'Mr Darwood might be able to help me.'

'Then why hasn't he come to London in answer to your appeal?'

'I don't know,' she admitted, 'and the only explanation I can think of is that my letter to him went astray.'

'What age would Mr Darwood be?'

'Oh, he was older than my father.'

'Then that might be the answer,' suggested Peter. 'If he's declined in years . . .'

'He'd still have replied to my entreaty.'

'He could only have done that if he were still alive to do so, Mrs van Emden.' Her face clouded. 'Let's not fear the worst. I'll ride to Norwich tomorrow.'

'You're so kind, Mr Skillen.'

'When someone hires us, they get value for money.'

'I'm sorry that Islington proved to be such a waste of time.'

'But it wasn't,' said Peter. 'We learnt a great deal that you weren't expected to learn. You were not meant to find that grave, let alone discover who'd been in that coffin.'

'Is there any way of finding that other George Parry?'

'The crime has already been reported to the authorities. Sadly, it's a growing problem. Grave robbers can earn good money from corrupt physicians who are so desperate for a fresh supply of corpses that they don't ask questions about their origin. I've known some churchyards in the city where they keep vigil over graves that have been recently filled. I don't need to tell you how distraught family members feel when they realise that their loved ones have been stolen from their coffins.'

'It comes as a shattering blow, Mr Skillen.'

'In your case, you suffered unnecessarily. The deceased was not actually your father.'

'Yet he had my father's name in his pocket.'

'I'm determined to find out how it got there.'

'You are truly a remarkable man,' she said. 'When Jem Huckvale told me that you and your brother were the finest detectives in London, I thought he'd simply been paid to say that. Now I know that it's true.'

'Thank you.'

'You're so dedicated to the task in hand.'

'It's the only way to solve a mystery, Mrs van Emden.' He pulled on the reins to turn the horses into Albemarle Street. 'Here we are at last. I daresay you'd be glad to rest at your hotel.'

'Please keep in touch.'

'There's no need to ask me that.'

When he brought the curricle to a halt outside her hotel, someone came out to hold the bridle. Peter helped her out of the vehicle before escorting her into the foyer. The moment she appeared, an old man used his walking stick to hobble towards her.

'Clemency!' he called out. 'Here you are, at last.'

Mungo Darwood had answered her summons, after all.

CHAPTER TEN

Hannah Granville had seen the Theatre Royal before, but she had not been there since the change of management. Vernon Teale had made visible improvements to the place. Money had been spent on making the foyer more welcoming and new furniture had been bought for the bars. Proud of his changes, he took Hannah and Paul on a short tour of the building so that he could point them out. Though most of the attention had been lavished on the public areas, work had also been done on the main dressing rooms. The one that Hannah was destined to occupy was the largest and most comfortable, with mirrors giving the impression of a much bigger room.

Paul was impressed, but Hannah seemed a little distrait. Teale talked about his future plans for the theatre and assured her that she would be invited back there on a regular basis. Pleading fatigue, she eventually said that she wished to retire to her hotel. After bidding farewell, she and Paul departed.

'It's a wonderful theatre,' he acknowledged. 'I'm sorry that you were in no mood to appreciate it.'

'My mind was on something else.'

He held up the valise. 'It was this, wasn't it?'

'Yes,' she replied. 'Seeing it again gave me such a shock.'

'You should be glad, Hannah. You not only had your property returned, you had cast-iron evidence that the man who stole it from you is here. In other words, he's within reach of *me*.'

'I thought I'd accepted the idea that he might come to Bath, but now that it's happened, I feel unsettled.'

'There's no need, my love.'

'I won't feel safe until that devil is caught.'

'I'll snare him somehow.'

'He has dangerous friends, Paul. Beware of them.'

'I'll go armed,' he said. 'With sword, pistol or bare fists, I'd take on all three of them without a tremor. Not that I'm likely to be in that position,' he continued. 'The man in the shiny boots might be a theatregoer but his confederates sound as if they prefer baser pleasures. I doubt that I'll ever meet the trio in its entirety.'

'Promise me that you'll act with great caution,' she said.

'That's something I can never promise, Hannah. If I have a chance to catch any of them, I'll throw caution to the wind.'

They reached the hotel and went in together. The first thing that Hannah did was tap on the door of Jenny Pye's room. When the dresser opened it, she saw the valise in Paul's hand and let out a gasp of amazement.

'Where did you get that?' she asked.

'It was waiting for me at the theatre,' said Hannah.

'Are you saying that the highwayman *returned* it?'

'He wrote a short note to convey his apology.'

'There's not an ounce of sincerity in it,' said Paul, harshly.

'Has he sent everything back?' said Jenny.

Hannah shrugged. 'Who knows? I haven't dared to look. In fact, that's the reason I knocked, Jenny. I need your help.'

She glanced at Paul, who realised that she wished to be alone with her dresser. After arranging to meet Hannah later, he handed over the valise and went off. The two women, meanwhile, went into Hannah's room. She gave the valise to Jenny.

'Open it, please.'

'Why are you so afraid to do so yourself?'

'Just open it, Jenny.'

The other woman obeyed, taking out the items one at a time and placing them on the table. Hannah watched nervously. When everything was laid out, she gulped.

'There's one thing missing,' she said.

'I know.'

'Where is it?'

Jenny looked up at her. 'He's kept it as a souvenir.'

After pulling on his gleaming boots, the highwayman turned to let his servant help him into the immaculate tailcoat with its high-rolled collar and its tight sleeves. He examined himself in the full-length mirror for several minutes until he was satisfied that everything was in order. He took the hat from his servant and put it on his head, angling it slightly for effect. When he was completely ready, he left his house and strolled in the direction of the theatre.

* * *

'By Jove!' exclaimed Mungo Darwood, eyes bulging in astonishment. 'It's such an extraordinary business. When I had my last letter from your father several months ago, he said that he was in good health.'

'A lot has happened since then,' said Clemency.

'So it appears. I had no idea that he'd died.'

'We're not entirely certain that he did,' Peter told him. 'We haven't as yet established the truth.'

'I'm grateful that Mrs van Emden has had the good fortune to engage you, Mr Skillen. From everything you've told me, I can see that you have amazing diligence and tenacity.'

They were seated in the hotel parlour. Clemency had always known Darwood as a jovial businessman who came to stay with them from time to time. Not having met him for years, she was upset to see that he'd put on considerable weight and was a martyr to arthritis. Without his walking stick, he could hardly move. Between them, she and Peter had told him about their search for George Parry and their frustration at the latest turn of events.

'I curse myself for living so far away,' said Darwood, 'but my dear wife had made me promise that we'd return to Norfolk one day. As a result, I rather lost touch with all my London friends.'

'My father missed you,' said Clemency.

'He missed *you* even more. His letters may have been few and far between but every one of them was full of regret about the way that you and he had drifted apart.'

She was astounded. 'It was his decision to disown me.'

'When he made that decision, he was acting on impulse. It was not long before he was chiding himself for not accepting that you had the right to choose the man you wished to marry. Well,' said Darwood, 'you must have realised from his letters how eager he was to see you again.'

'I never received any letters from him,' she complained. 'I wrote several to him but never had an answer.'

'You must have done.'

'I didn't have a single word.'

'That's bizarre!' he said.

'I think I see what may have happened here,' said Peter, weighing up the evidence. 'Mrs van Emden never even saw her father's letters because someone prevented them from reaching her. By the same token, her pleas for reconciliation were never allowed to get into Mr Parry's hands.'

'That's outrageous!' cried Darwood. 'They were deliberately kept apart.'

'That's how it seems to me, sir.'

'What fiend was behind this skulduggery?'

'It was someone whose best interests were served by keeping the two of them estranged. In doing so, he or she was causing intense pain to both father and daughter.'

'It's monstrous!' cried Clemency.

'I'd call it downright criminal,' said Darwood.

'It's only supposition on my part,' Peter warned them, 'but, now that we know the truth, Mrs van Emden can at least take some comfort from the fact that her father loved her and was keen to see her again.'

'Comfort?' she said. 'I feel nothing but anger at the person who kept the two of us apart on purpose.'

'Think back to the time when you lived in London,' said Peter. 'Your father lived well and employed a number of servants. Can you remember any of them?'

'I think so.'

'Then I'd like their names, please. I'm not accusing any of

them,' he was careful to add, 'but I would suggest that a servant was in the best place to intercept any correspondence.'

'That's true,' said Darwood. 'Start with the servants.'

'I may be maligning Mr Parry's servants unfairly,' said Peter. 'I hope that I am. One of them may well have posted a stream of letters to his daughter in Amsterdam.'

'Then why didn't they reach her?' asked Darwood.

'We have servants of our own,' said Clemency, providing the answer with obvious discomfort. 'I'd swear that they were all loyal but . . . one can never be entirely sure.' She looked at Peter. 'What are you going to do, Mr Skillen?'

'First of all,' he replied, 'I'll try to track down anyone who was in your father's house here in London. If that turns out to be a fruitless exercise, I may have to sail to Amsterdam.'

While Hannah was resting at the hotel, Paul decided to take a closer look at what had been, for many years, one of the most fashionable resorts in England. People still flocked to its famous mineral spas to take the waters. Bath was a beautiful city. Set in the Avon valley, it was effectively divided into two halves, the lower one being the older part and the upper, distinguished by its classical magnificence, being the newer. Paul headed for The Circus, a stunning example of architecture modelled on the Coliseum in Rome. It consisted of thirty-three terraced houses arranged in a circle around a wide road. He stood and marvelled at it for some time.

To the west of The Circus, he came upon the equally startling Royal Crescent, a row of terraced houses arranged in a semicircle to produce yet another striking example of style and symmetry. Only the rich could afford to buy such delectable places in which to live. Some of the occupants would doubtless come to the theatre to see Hannah Granville in one of Shakespeare's most popular comedies. Among them would be a number of aristocrats, dandies, rakes and men about town who would come to gloat at her for reasons other than her ability to bring the character of Rosalind vividly alive. Paul would be kept on his toes, defending her from being propositioned and pursued. And somewhere in the ranks of her ardent admirers would be the man with the shiny boots who made a living by robbing stagecoaches on the public highway before passing himself off as a gentleman in Bath.

Paul could not wait to introduce himself to the man.

Peter returned to the gallery to find Charlotte and Ackford together in the office. Eager for news, they listened intently while Peter told them about the visit to Islington and the meeting with Sebastian Alderson. What really interested them was the information that Mungo Darwood had finally emerged to make an unexpected claim.

'Is that true?' asked Charlotte, dubiously. 'Mr Parry really wanted to be part of his daughter's life again?' Her husband nodded. 'Keeping the two of them apart like that was tantamount to cruelty.'

'Who stood to gain from it?' said Ackford.

'Perhaps Mr van Emden did. If he's possessive by nature, he might want to exclude Mr Parry from their lives.'

'The husband is an unknown quantity,' said Peter. 'His wife talks very fondly of him. When she expressed a desire to come to London in search of the truth about her father, her husband didn't try to stop her. In fact, he urged her to go.'

'Yet he couldn't bother to come with her,' said Ackford.

'He's a businessman, Gully. He has commitments.'

'Mr Parry clearly took against him.'

'He didn't want his daughter taken out of the country.'

'How did she and Mr van Emden meet in the first place?'

'That's something I'd like to know,' said Peter. 'To that end, I've invited his wife to move in with us for a while. I hope you don't mind, Charlotte.'

'Of course not,' she said. 'We've plenty of room and I'd feel more involved in the search if I spent time with her.'

'She's more likely to confide in you. Mrs van Emden hasn't been dishonest with me, but I sense that she's holding something back. With luck, you might be able to draw it out of her.'

'What about her father's will?' asked Ackford.

'We don't know that he left one.'

'He must've done, Peter. If he was so keen to patch up any differences with his daughter, he must have left everything to her. She was his only child, wasn't she?'

'Yes, she was, but there's a slight problem.'

'What is it?'

'Mr Parry might not have had anything worth bequeathing to her. Wherever she enquired, Mrs van Emden was told that her father had lost his house, his position as an engineer and his place in society. There was talk of excessive drinking and the claim – by various people – that he'd ended up begging in the streets.'

'Something perplexes me,' said Charlotte. 'If he wanted to be reconciled, why didn't he take a ship to Amsterdam to find his daughter?'

'Perhaps he didn't wish to be rebuffed,' argued Peter. 'From his point of view, she'd cut all ties with him when she refused – as he believed – to reply to his letters. For the same reason, his daughter didn't come to England. She feared being rejected again. It's a tragedy,' he went on. 'Two people, still loving each other and fervently hoping to be reunited, are kept apart by some malign person who wishes them to suffer.'

'Why?'

'I don't know, Charlotte. To get at the truth, we must learn more about her courtship with Mr van Emden. He's an important factor in the situation. We must discover how he persuaded her to defy her father's wishes and marry him. It's one of many questions that, as a man, I feel unable to ask her. That's why I'd like to bring the two of you together,' he explained. 'She'll feel at ease with you and talk more freely.'

Since he'd made the effort of coming to London to see her, Clemency was very grateful. She readily accepted Mungo Darwood's invitation to dine with him. When they met again at a restaurant, she was sad to see, once again, how slowly and painfully he moved. Already afflicted by agonising conditions, his problems had been accentuated by the long, bumpy ride from Norwich. As he lowered himself into his seat, she saw once again how decrepit he now was.

'Forgive me,' he said, with a weary smile. 'You must show me some clemency, Clemency.'

'I'm just so pleased that we were able to meet again.'

'As, indeed, am I.'

'You're the only one of Father's friends who agreed to talk to me.'

'That's shameful on their part.'

'It was almost as if my father had contracted leprosy.'

'He caught something just as bad,' said Darwood, wryly. 'It's a disease called poverty and it can be contagious. Once caught, it may even be fatal. But I have problems of my own to worry about. My memory is like a sieve.'

'I'm sure that you exaggerate, Mr Darwood.'

'Talk to my wife. She taxes me about it day after day.'

'You remembered who I was,' she said, 'and that's all that matters to me.'

'But it doesn't, you see. As soon as I left you and Mr Skillen, I recalled things that I should have told you.'

'What sort of things do you mean?'

'Let me try to gather in my scattered thoughts and I'll tell you.' He needed time to collect himself. 'You were never really aware of what your father did, were you?'

'I knew that he was an engineer. That's all I needed to know.'

'Had you been a boy, I'll wager that you'd have been groomed in what is a very honourable profession. George Parry thrived in it. I could show you examples of his genius all over London.'

'He did take me to see that bridge he designed in Oxford.'

'It was a miniature work of art. Because of his inventive skills, he stood out from the crowd.'

'That wouldn't have made him popular.'

'He was respected, Clemency. That meant more to him.'

'What happened to that respect when he really needed it?'

'One moment,' he said, reaching in his pocket for a piece of paper. 'Knowing that you'd ask me that, I wrote down the answer lest I forget it.' Taking out a pair of spectacles, he put them on. After studying the piece of paper, he looked up at her. 'I had letters about him from his former friends. They said that he'd taken to drink out of sorrow.'

'I was responsible for that sorrow,' she admitted.

'That's untrue. You offered him an olive branch, but he never even got to see it. What I'd forgotten – and it saddens me to relate this – is that your father's drunkenness cost him dearly. Unable to work, he had no regular income. As a last resort, he decided that the only way to restore his fortunes was to do so at a card table.'

'But he had no experience of gambling,' she protested.

'Exactly – he was a lamb to the slaughter.'

'He must have been so desperate.'

'I reckon that George was both desperate and misguided. When his money ran out, he seems to have gambled his house.'

She was heartbroken. 'He gambled it and lost it?'

'He did just that, alas.'

After putting the piece of paper away, he removed the spectacles and slipped them into the case before setting it down on the table.

'If I'd known of his debts, I'd willingly have given him money.'

'We'd have done the same, Mr Darwood.'

'That fine, intelligent mind of his must have crumbled. I admired his achievements so much, Clemency. My work was simple compared to his. All that I did was to import goods from abroad. If you keep well informed, there's no real skill involved in that. What your father created, however, was highly individual. George Parry had a touch of magic.'

'He spoke so well of you.'

'I treasured his friendship.'

'You *remembered* it, Mr Darwood. Others didn't.'

'We'll see about that, Clemency,' he said, banging the table with a fist. 'While I'm here, I'll make a point of calling on one or two of those "friends". I may be able to dig some information out of them.'

'Anything you can find out will be useful.'

'I'll pass it on to Mr Skillen. He seems a thoroughly decent fellow and an effective one to boot.'

'Oh, he is.'

'How did you come to choose him?'

'I was acting on the recommendation of someone who works for him. It was the best decision I've made since I arrived in London.'

Jenny Pye had worked with her long enough to know by instinct when Hannah wished to be alone or with someone else. Having helped the actress into a change of clothing in preparation for going out, Jenny sensed that it was time to go. Minutes later, Paul arrived. Hannah ran into his arms.

'Thank goodness you're here,' she said. 'If you hadn't come, I'd be in a state of terror.'

'There's no need to fret. You're among friends.'

'They can't reassure me the way that you do.'

'It's nice to know that I can do something of value,' he teased. 'My advice is that you must stop worrying.'

'How can I?' asked Hannah. 'That man is in Bath.'

'He can't touch you when I'm here and, besides, he won't know where you're staying.'

'He kept something back, Paul.'

'I don't understand.'

'When he stole that valise of mine, he took something out before he returned everything else.'

'What was it?'

'A petticoat. As for the other garments, I'm afraid to put any of them on, knowing that he's probably examined each one in detail. They've been soiled.'

'Then we need to buy you replacements. Bath has a good reputation for its dressmakers and its sense of fashion. Now, let me take you out and make you forget all about your highwayman with the gleaming boots.' He kissed her on the cheek. 'Put on your hat and we can go.'

'I'll be ready in a moment,' she said, buoyed up by his confidence.

Collecting her hat, she walked across to the mirror and put it on with care, adjusting it until it had the desired effect. Hannah crossed to the window to look out at the balmy evening, but she saw instead something that made her shudder. Standing on the opposite side of the road was a man staring up at her room. He seemed eerily familiar. When he saw her appear, he raised his hat in greeting. Hannah backed away, as if reeling from a blow.

'It's *him*,' she gasped. 'I'm certain of it.'

'Where?' asked Paul, running to the window.

But he was too late. The man had already fled around the corner.

CHAPTER ELEVEN

In spite of the number of trials over which he had to preside in the course of a normal day, the chief magistrate always found time to deal with his voluminous correspondence and to read any reports he'd commissioned. One of them was causing him particular anxiety that morning, so he sent for Yeomans and Hale. Thinking they'd been summoned in order to be chastised for failing to recapture Harry Scattergood, the Runners entered the office with trepidation. Yeomans had his excuse ready.

'We've looked high and low for him, sir,' he said, nervously, 'but we've not seen so much as a whisker of Scattergood. Our sources tell us that he's left London altogether until the search for him eases off.'

'It must never ease off,' insisted Kirkwood.

'Oh, I agree, sir. We'll remain vigilant.'

'As soon as he dares to come back here,' said Hale, 'we'll be waiting for him.'

'Then he'll be locked in a cell with two armed officers watching him day and night. He won't get away again.'

'I should hope not,' said Kirkwood. 'While you're waiting for Harry Scattergood to sneak back into the capital, I have other work for you to do. It concerns this,' he went on, waving a sheaf of papers at them. 'It makes grim reading.'

'What is it?' asked Yeomans.

'It's a report into one of the most heinous and disgusting of crimes that's now reached intolerable proportions. It *must* be checked before it gets completely beyond control.'

'Are you talking about prostitution, sir?'

'That's heinous, in my view,' said Hale.

'And it's certainly disgusting.'

'What I'm talking about is even worse than that,' said Kirkwood, slapping the papers down on his desk. 'I refer to the vile practice of bodysnatching, of trespassing on consecrated ground to dig up the recently deceased in order to sell their corpses. As you know only too well, the law allows the medical profession to have access to the cadavers of executed criminals, but there aren't enough to satisfy the demand so they look elsewhere.'

'It's despicable,' said Yeomans. 'Anyone who robs a grave should be buried alive in it.'

'We have to catch the villains first and that, I fear, has not been happening to any degree. It's a problem that every city faces. Because they have colleges of surgeons, London and Edinburgh have the highest demand. This report tells me that, in Scotland, there are fiends who, rather than put themselves to the trouble of using a spade, prefer to commit a murder, selecting young, healthy victims because their bodies bring the highest price. It's happening here as well.' He hit his desk hard with a fist. 'It has got to be stopped.'

Hale was confused. 'You're not going to send us to Scotland, are you, sir? We have no jurisdiction there.'

'I want you and your men to concentrate on the problem in London. Funerals happen almost every day. Ghouls lie in wait. Last weekend alone, as many as five bodies were hauled unceremoniously out of their coffins. Imagine the pain and misery that must have caused the families and friends of the deceased.'

'We've met some of them,' said Yeomans. 'In one case, a family kept vigil in a churchyard for a full month. The day after they stopped guarding the grave of their dead child, it was opened and plundered.'

'Undertakers are seeking the legal right to inter in iron,' observed Hale. 'I agree with them. The coffins will be much heavier but at least they'll keep intruders out.'

'My orders are simple,' said Kirkwood, looking from one to the other. 'Stop these raids on the city's graves. Bring the chief malefactors to me and I'll make an example of them.' He offered the report to Yeomans. 'Read this first. It will tell you how and where these rogues operate.'

'Leave it to us, sir,' said the Runner, taking the document from him. 'We'll interrupt this foul trade somehow. And when we've done that,' he added, triumphantly, 'we can have the supreme pleasure of arresting Harry Scattergood.'

Having found his way around St Albans, he soon began to mark out his first potential targets. The town was much smaller than

127

London, so it lacked the teeming crowds into which to disappear and the rookeries into which officers of the law rarely ventured. It was nevertheless irresistible. Having taken a room at a seedy pub down a dark alley, he studied the rough street map he'd drawn and looked at the crosses he'd placed on it. Each one represented a property that had excited his interest. He selected the most tempting of them, then folded his map before slipping it into his pocket. The decision had been made. He'd leave his signature on the town at midnight.

Charlotte Skillen was glad that Clemency van Emden was now staying under their roof, along with her Dutch chaperon. From the moment they first met, she'd liked the woman and was very sympathetic to her plight. The latest twist had exacerbated her pain and bewilderment because Clemency was no longer even certain that her father was actually dead. Charlotte could see the effect of it all etched in the woman's face. Stress had put years on her.

It was not until after breakfast that the two of them were alone at last. Some gentle probing was now possible.

'I hope that you slept well,' said Charlotte.

'I didn't sleep at all. I may have dozed off now and then but I spent most of the night simply wondering what was going on. It's . . . baffling.'

'The truth will come out in the end.'

'I sincerely hope so,' said Clemency, 'but I have doubts.' She forced a smile. 'It's so kind of you and Mr Skillen to invite me into your home. Instead of being surrounded by strangers in that hotel, I feel as if I'm among friends.'

'You're welcome to stay as long as you wish, Mrs van Emden.'

'Thank you so much.'

'Since we *have* become friends,' suggested Charlotte, 'we might even waive the formalities and call each other by our Christian names.'

'Yes, please,' said Clemency. 'I'd like that.'

They were seated opposite each other in the drawing room. While Charlotte was relaxed, however, her companion was tense and drawn.

'I can see that you're eager to ask me more questions, Charlotte. Don't hold back. Please speak out.'

'Thank you, Clemency. I'll do just that.' Charlotte paused to choose the right words. 'Your marriage interests me. It's so . . . unusual.'

'I married the man I adored. There's nothing unusual in that.'

'No, there isn't,' agreed Charlotte. 'I did the same. In your case, however, you acted against the express wishes of your father. There must have been a bitter confrontation at some point.'

'There was.'

'Did he refuse you permission to marry?'

'He did at first. When he saw how resolved I was, he relented, much against his will. But he wouldn't take part in the service itself.'

'Who took you to church on his arm to give you away?'

'My uncle performed that office.'

'That must have made for more dissension in the family.'

'I'm afraid that it did. It drove my father and his brother apart. The worst of it was that my uncle died not long after the wedding, so the two of them were never reconciled.'

'How did you meet your husband?'

Clemency smiled. 'It was a chance encounter,' she recalled. 'Jan was here on business, hoping to buy various items for import. He was invited to dinner at the home of a friend who sold equipment

129

for marine engineering. I happened to be there as well because my father had worked for the host at one point in his career. Everything went well at first, especially for me and Jan. It never occurred to me at the time,' she said, 'but the very first glance we exchanged was a form of contract. I was his choice and he was mine. Since my father was bound to disapprove, it had to be a very clandestine romance.'

'Why do you say that?'

'To begin with, Jan was much older than me and he'd been married before. His first wife was drowned in a terrible accident. They had no children.'

'That's a reason to feel sympathy for the man.'

'Not in my father's eyes,' said Clemency. 'He has this hatred of foreigners. It's quite irrational. When he realised that I not only wanted to marry a Dutchman but that I was ready to live with him in Amsterdam, he went almost berserk. I was locked in my room for days.'

'It must have been a trying time.'

'It was unbearable, Charlotte. I was forced to choose between two men I loved and respected. Whichever path I took, it would have involved great sacrifices. Sadly, I had to lose a dear father.'

'But you *didn't* lose him, Clemency. Remember what Mr Darwood told you. In time, your father came to see that he'd behaved badly and wanted to heal the rift.'

'I never realised that.'

'It was only because somebody concealed the truth from you.'

'My father was kept in the dark as well. He was never allowed to read any of my letters.'

'My husband will root out the culprit.'

'He won't know where to begin.'

'Peter will find a way somehow,' said Charlotte, confidently. 'He always does.'

Peter Skillen's search began at the former home of George Parry and his family. It was a moderately large house in the middle of a terrace on the edge of a fashionable area of the city. Peter appraised it from the opposite side of the road, wondering what dark secrets it held. Clemency had told him everything she'd learnt from Mungo Darwood, including the way that the house had been recklessly lost at the card table. Peter knew all about the lure of gambling because his own brother had fallen victim to it. During a turbulent period in his life, Paul had often lost more than he could afford to lose, but he'd never been foolish enough to bet his house on the turn of a card. George Parry had done just that, revealing, in doing so, his utter desperation.

When he'd finished studying the house, Peter rang the bell and was soon looking into the face of a short, dapper old man. Peter's hope that he might have been retained from the original staff was soon dashed. The old man had only been there for a matter of months.

'We were brought here from our former house,' he explained.

'And where was that?'

'We lived in the country, sir. Do you wish to speak to the master?'

'I'd rather talk to you. I'm trying to track someone down and you may be able to help me.'

'That's very unlikely, sir. I'm a stranger here.'

'Before your master moved in, you must have been sent ahead to prepare the house.' The old man nodded. 'I daresay that some of the original servants were here.'

'There were two of them, sir.'

'Can you remember their names?'

'I'm not sure that I can,' admitted the other.

'Then let me offer a few suggestions.' Peter took out a piece of paper on which he'd written the names given to him by Clemency. 'Tell me if any of these sound familiar – Mary Culshaw, Joseph Rafter, Edmund Haines, Verity Bartlett . . .'

'Those names are all new to me, sir.'

'What about Abigail Saunders?'

'Ah,' said the other, eyebrows shooting up, 'now that's different. The man kept calling her "Abby", so I suppose that it could have been the woman you just mentioned.'

'Describe her to me.'

'To be honest, sir, I didn't pay much attention to her.'

'What age would she be?'

'A little older than you, I'd say, but at least twenty years younger than me. I felt sorry for her. Every now and then, she burst into tears because of what happened to Mr Parry.'

'And she was with a man, you say?'

'I never heard his name mentioned.'

'And where was Abigail Saunders going? Did she give you any idea where her next employment would be?'

'She'd searched for a new position in vain.'

Peter was unable to hide his disappointment. He'd learnt nothing of use. He was about to thank the servant and depart empty-handed when the old man remembered something.

'One moment, sir,' said the other. 'I did overhear something she told the man.'

'What was that?'

'She was going to live with her sister and brother-in-law at their tavern.'

'Can you remember what it was called?'

'Yes, sir, it was the Red Cow.'

'Where is it?'

The old man shrugged an apology. 'I've no idea.'

'Not to worry,' said Peter, quietly elated. 'I'll find it.'

It took Paul Skillen the whole evening to convince Hannah Granville that she was not in any immediate danger. The unexpected appearance of the highwayman had shaken her to the core. The idea that he knew where she was staying and which room she occupied had terrified her. She finally fell asleep out of fatigue. By morning, her apprehension had returned with a new intensity. So upset was she that she only ate the most frugal breakfast. Later that morning, she was still pacing the room, afraid even to glance out of the window. Paul tried to reason with her.

'You don't even know that it *was* the highwayman,' he said.

'It was him – without question.'

'Then where was he when I looked out of the window?'

'He must have fled.'

'I think there may be another explanation, Hannah.'

'What is it?'

'He was never there in the first place.'

'Of course he was there,' she cried. 'I saw him with my own eyes.'

'You only *believed* that you saw him. He was a phantom.'

'That's absurd!'

'Just hear me out, please. Ever since I got to Bath, you've talked about nothing but the robbery. It's bound to loom large in your mind. Because of that, you're likely to mistake every shadow for the man who dared to rob you. That's all you saw yesterday, my love – a meaningless shadow. Nobody was there.'

'But he *was*, I tell you.'

'It only took me a second to reach the window and he was gone. Human beings can't move that fast. You imagined it.'

Hannah was suffused with anger. Biting back the angry words she was about to hurl at him, she took a series of deep breaths to calm herself down. When she felt ready, she spoke with slow deliberation.

'Let us look at the facts,' she said. 'The coach in which I was travelling was set upon by highwaymen. They took all our valuables. I not only lost some jewellery that was very precious to me, their leader also took a valise containing items of apparel. Agreed?'

'It was taken and then returned.'

'But we both know that he kept something back for . . . reasons of his own. And the fact remains that he's definitely in Bath.'

'He's not the only admirer of yours who knows that you are here,' said Paul. 'Your army of avid would-be suitors has been waiting for you to arrive. The clever ones will have realised you'd stay in the hotel nearest the theatre, and they'd have bribed members of the staff for confirmation.'

'They don't worry me in the least – the highwayman does.'

'You only had a brief glimpse.'

'It was enough.'

'I still think that—'

'No,' she said, interrupting him, 'don't you dare suggest that he's a figment of my imagination. I stood within feet of that man, Paul. Yes, he was in disguise at the time, but there are some things you can't hide.' She swallowed hard. 'He's here in Bath and he has designs on me.'

'He won't be allowed anywhere near you,' he said, taking her in his arms. 'When you step onstage, you're in front of huge numbers of people. The law of averages means that the audience will always contain a smattering of criminals, adulterers, drunkards and other unsavoury individuals – even a highwayman or two, perhaps. You handle that situation with complete aplomb. Why get unnerved by a single individual?'

'It's because he intends me harm.'

'You're still shocked by what happened to you.'

'I'll probably have nightmares about it for the rest of my life.'

'There's no need, Hannah.'

'You don't know how menacing that man was.'

'I think that you may have misjudged him.'

'How on earth can you say that?' she demanded.

'Those three men had you at their mercy. They could have subjected you to untold horrors. Thanks to their leader, that didn't happen. He's a man of taste, Hannah. He reveres you as an actress.' Paul tightened his hold on her. 'All I have to do is wait until he comes close enough.'

The Runners had caught bodysnatchers before and knew how difficult an exercise it was. Men who robbed graves tended to work in gangs and use lookouts to warn them if anyone was coming. They chose their targets with care and worked at speed.

'It all comes down to intelligence,' said Yeomans. 'They find out where the burials are taking place and make a first visit to the churchyard or cemetery to get the lie of the land.'

'How do we stop them, Micah?' asked Hale. 'We've tried to do it before and our record is not a good one. There are far too many of them and far too few of us.'

'There has to be a way, Alfred.'

'What is it?'

'The answer is slowly evolving in my mind. Another tankard of ale would help it to pop out like a newborn baby.'

Hale responded to the hint. They were back in the Peacock Inn, discussing the latest directive from the chief magistrate. Seated at a table in the corner, Yeomans was not alone for long. Chevy Ruddock came into the inn and went over to him.

'You sent for me, sir?' he asked.

'We have an assignment for you.'

'I hope that it doesn't involve standing outside a brothel all night in the rain. You made me do that once before and I felt sick at the thought of what was going on inside those four walls.'

Yeomans sniggered. 'I'd have thought you'd be consumed with envy.'

'Heaven forbid!'

Yeomans told him that they would be giving preference to the pursuit of bodysnatchers from now on. It was an assignment that Ruddock relished. Religious by nature, he had a strong aversion to men involved in such a repulsive activity and was quick to offer his opinion on how the problem should be tackled.

'There's one easy way to stop them,' he said, helpfully. 'You must cut off the demand. If nobody is prepared to pay for a supply of corpses, there's no point in digging them up. Look to the hospitals, sir,' he urged. 'That's where the bodies end up.'

'But they're almost impossible to identify. When a corpse has been sliced into fifty or sixty different pieces, how can you tell who they once were? Besides,' said Yeomans, 'professors of anatomy always have a convincing explanation for where their bodies come from. Some even have documentation to prove it.'

'It must be forged, sir.'

'Yes, Ruddock, it probably is. The medical profession, like any other, has its share of villains. To get what they want, they'll break the law without a twinge of conscience.'

Carrying two tankards, Hale returned to join in the debate. He resumed his seat at the table and left Ruddock standing there. Neither of the senior Runners offered to buy a drink for the newcomer, but he made no complaint; he was preoccupied by the problem they faced.

'Perhaps we could set a trap,' he said.

Yeomans belched. 'What are you talking about?'

'We could out-think the bodysnatchers for once.'

'And how are we supposed to do that?'

'We arrange a funeral that's only a sham,' suggested Ruddock. 'It must be in a church that's fairly isolated and has a small congregation.'

'That's ridiculous,' sneered Hale. 'No vicar would dare to take part in a mock funeral. The Church of England would never condone it. What is someone supposed to do – deliver a eulogy over an empty coffin?'

'No eulogy will be needed,' said Ruddock, 'because there's no actual service. All that I'm talking about is a burial. We can invent a name for the deceased and go through the motions of committing him to the earth. The more isolated the church, the better. It will tempt bodysnatchers because they're unlikely to be disturbed and – since there's no funeral service – local people won't be involved in any way.'

'We'd never persuade a vicar to agree to the idea.'

'I think a number of them would be glad to join forces with us, sir. They revile bodysnatchers as much as we do. All over London, there are clergymen who've seen their churchyards robbed.'

'Well, I think it's a stupid idea,' said Hale.

'Not so fast, Alfred,' warned Yeomans. 'As it happens, I was thinking along the same lines as Ruddock. Why go after these rogues when we can make them come to us? We're only borrowing a churchyard so that we can bury a coffin full of stones in it. Then we simply watch and wait.'

'I'd volunteer to do that, sir,' said Ruddock.

'You'd be one of the team I'd station nearby. The important thing would be to let them actually dig up the coffin so that we could have the pleasure of seeing their faces when they open it.'

'Yes,' said Hale, quickly persuaded. 'It's not such a stupid idea, after all. Well done, Chevy.'

'Thank you, sir,' said Ruddock.

'I thought of it first,' announced Yeomans, deftly stealing the notion. 'It was taking shape in my mind before Ruddock even got here. Since we won't be using a *real* body to entice someone to commit a crime, I can't see that we'd be causing any offence.'

'It's a stroke of genius on your part, Micah,' said Hale, raising his tankard in tribute. 'Your plan might well work.'

'It *will* work, Alfred.'

Both of them turned to Ruddock for approval.

'Yes,' said the other, dutifully. 'It's an excellent plan.'

CHAPTER TWELVE

Animals proliferated on the inn signs of London. Within easy walking distance of his house, Peter Skillen knew of a Black Horse, a White Horse, a Waggon and Horses, an Eagle and Child, a Black Dog, a White Hart, a Brown Bear, a Red Bull, a Greyhound and a Golden Lion. Most famous of all was the Elephant and Castle, a former smithy that had been turned into an inn and given its name to one of the city's most important junctions. Many more creatures belonged in the London menagerie. To speed up the search, Peter had enlisted Jem Huckvale, who cantered around the city and came back to the gallery with his findings.

'I found two Dun Cows,' he declared.

'That's the wrong colour, Jem. I'm after a Red Cow.'

'There are three of them, at least.'

'They'll do for a start,' said Peter. 'Thank you very much for your help. Since you were responsible for bringing Mrs van Emden to us in the first place, I thought you'd like to be involved in the hunt.'

'Yes, please. Feel free to call on me any time.'

'I will. Now, where exactly are these three Red Cows?'

After Huckvale had given him precise instructions, Peter set out for the closest address. When there was no sign of Abigail Saunders there, he went on to the second inn and found to his dismay that the landlord had never heard of the woman. That left him with one last hope and the worrying possibility that she was not there either. All that Peter had to go on was a name. It could conceivably refer to a pub that was outside the city or even in some distant county. His earlier optimism began to wane.

The last Red Cow on his list was in Wapping, a dockland area to the east where sailors abounded and where there were dozens of lively taverns in its high street. It had a reputation for the boisterous behaviour of its inhabitants. Peter found his destination in Anchor and Hope Alley. The Red Cow was a long, low building whose original profile had been distorted over time by subsidence. Tethering his horse outside, he went into the inn and was met with a barrage of sound. Rowdy sailors were enjoying a drink and indulging in crude banter.

The sudden appearance of a well-dressed gentleman caused some of the patrons to jeer at him, but Peter ignored them. He headed for the bar, behind which a stocky, beetle-browed, middle-aged man was standing with arms folded. The landlord looked at him with an amalgam of surprise and suspicion.

'What can I do for you, sir?' he grunted.

'I'm looking for Abigail Saunders.'

'Why?'

'I'm hoping that she might be able to help me.'

'What business have you got with Abby?'

Peter was thrilled. 'She's here, then, is she?'

'Abby is my sister-in-law.'

'Thank goodness I've found her!'

The landlord remained surly. 'Who are you?'

'My name is Peter Skillen and I'm acting on behalf of the daughter of George Parry. Abigail Saunders worked for him.'

'I know. He was good to her.'

'May I speak to her, please?'

'I'll see if she's agreeable.'

'Tell her that it's very important.'

Curling a lip, the landlord looked him up and down.

'Wait here,' he said.

The walk to the theatre was an ordeal for Hannah Granville. Though it was only a short distance, it seemed like a mile or more, each step an individual effort. Not daring to look either side of her, she clung to Paul's arm and drew strength from his support. His gaze roved everywhere as he searched for the man whose appearance the previous day had disturbed her so much. Nobody they passed remotely fitted the description she'd given him of the highwayman. They reached the theatre and went in. Hannah was able to breathe a sigh of relief.

'You see?' he said. 'There was no sign of him.'

'He could have been watching from a window somewhere.'

'Nobody was there, Hannah. I promise you.'

'Then why did I feel so uneasy?'

'You're always a little on edge when you meet the rest of the cast for the first time. That's only natural.'

'There's more to it than that.'

Before she could enlarge on her comment, they saw the manager swooping down on them with a broad grin. Vernon Teale wanted to introduce her to the rest of the company but, since she was still a trifle nervous, she asked if Paul could come as well.

'Mr Skillen is welcome to be at your side at all times,' said Teale, flashing a smile at him, 'as long as he doesn't follow you onstage during a performance, that is.' They laughed. 'On the other hand,' the manager went on, studying him carefully, 'he'd make a fine Orlando in this play.'

'Hannah's place is onstage,' said Paul, 'and mine is well off it.'

'So be it.' He waved an arm. 'Shall we join the others?'

'I'd like a moment alone in my dressing room first,' said Hannah.

'Yes, of course. There's no hurry. Take as long as you wish.'

While the manager headed for the auditorium, Paul took Hannah to the dressing rooms at the rear of the building. He opened the door of the one assigned to her. She sat in front of a mirror and inspected her appearance.

'You look wonderful,' he said.

'I just need time to compose myself.'

'Would you like to be alone?'

'No,' she replied. 'I want you at my side.'

'You're perfectly safe inside the theatre, Hannah. No strangers will be allowed in here. Once the play starts, of course, you'll have Jenny to stand guard over you. Nobody will get past her.'

'That highwayman did.'

'Try to put him out of your mind.'

'I simply can't.'

Paul said nothing. There were times – and this was clearly one of them – when silence was the best option. It suited Hannah's mood. It took her the best part of ten minutes to recover her composure, then she got up. She took Paul's arm and squeezed it gratefully.

Her decision to visit the dressing room was dictated partly by vanity. Hannah knew that the remainder of the cast was seated in the front stalls awaiting her arrival. She would have had to walk down the aisle in order to meet them. By approaching from the back of the theatre, she was able to make a dramatic entrance on to the stage itself. That appealed to her. Paul was less enthusiastic about the idea because he wasn't actually a member of the company, but he was ready to be at her beck and call whenever needed.

The first reading of the play would take place in the auditorium, but the cast would move on the following day to the rehearsal room because the stage still had the scenery of the current production standing on it. Instead of entering the Forest of Arden, therefore, Hannah made her first appearance on the set of Goldsmith's *She Stoops to Conquer*. The effect was powerful. The moment she glided gracefully into sight, the whole cast leapt to its feet and applauded her as if acknowledging the end of a performance. Shakespeare's Rosalind had arrived.

Hannah shook off all her misgivings and beamed at the faces before her. All that Paul could do was to stand there self-consciously and wish that the ovation would soon cease. Nobody looked at him. The applause was for a remarkable actress whose presence in any play lent it quality and definition. Thanks largely to her, they knew, no seat would ever be empty during the run of

As You Like It. Teale clapped as hard as anyone, knowing that the production would be an unqualified success. Hannah, meanwhile, looked from person to person, spotting friends with whom she'd worked before and giving each one of them a separate smile of recognition. Among such a cast, she knew that her stay in Bath would be one of continuous pleasure.

Then her smile vanished abruptly and her body tensed. Paul became instantly aware of the radical change in her manner. Her eye had just alighted on someone below her. Trouble lay ahead.

Peter Skillen was astounded. He'd never met twins who looked so dissimilar. Because he and Paul were identical, it was almost impossible for most people to tell them apart. The one difference between them was that, while Peter was right-handed, his brother was left-handed. Abigail Saunders and her twin sister, however, had almost no matching features. While Abigail was skinny and decidedly plain, Betty Kingzett, wife of the landlord, was plump yet still attractive. Abigail might be subdued and fearful, but Betty had the bubbling personality needed in the Red Cow. Peter was glad that the effervescent Betty stayed to help her sister answer the questions fired at her.

'Abby was fond of Mr Parry, weren't you, Abby?'

'Yes,' said the other.

'He treated her well. After his wife passed away, he became very sad and Abby thought he was going to dwindle away – didn't you?'

'I did, Betty.'

'What kept him going was his love for his daughter.'

'Miss Parry meant everything to him,' explained Abigail. 'He lived for her, really. Then she met a Dutchman and things changed.'

'Her father didn't like him,' said Betty, taking over. 'I don't know why. We get a lot of Dutch sailors in here and they're no trouble at all. Wapping was built on land reclaimed by a Dutchman named Cornelius Vanderdelft. I think it's strange, really. I mean, Mr Parry was an engineer, wasn't he? You'd have thought he'd appreciate an engineer who could drain marshes.'

'What I really wish to ask your sister is this,' said Peter, finally seeing a gap in the conversation into which he could jump. 'Were all the servants as loyal as her?'

'Were they, Abby?' prompted Betty.

'I think so,' said her sister.

'Who was the one Mr Parry trusted the most?'

'That was Edmund Haines.'

'Yes,' said Peter. 'Mrs van Emden gave me his name. She spoke quite well of him. In fact, she spoke well of all the servants, especially you.'

'That's so kind of her,' said Abigail, smiling for the first time. 'How is Miss Parry – Mrs van Emden, that is?'

'As you'll appreciate, she's very upset at the moment.'

'From what you've told us, Mr Skillen,' said Betty, intervening yet again, 'she has every right to be upset. She doesn't know if her father is alive or dead, and did someone really stop her letters reaching Mr Parry?'

'It wasn't me,' Abigail blurted out.

'Do you have any idea who it *might* have been?' asked Peter.

'No, I don't.'

She lapsed back into a watchful silence. Losing her position in a comfortable house had been a blow to Abigail Saunders. Even more distressing had been the decline of George Parry that had preceded it. When she spoke again, she talked about him as if he was no longer alive, telling Peter that the sight of her former employer begging in the street had made her feel ill for days.

'Did you blame his daughter for what happened?' asked Peter. 'Mrs van Emden feels very guilty.'

'And so she should,' said Betty, bluntly. 'If my daughter ever tried to defy me and my husband like that, we'd never forgive her.'

'My question was for your sister, Mrs Kingzett.'

'Answer it, Abby.'

'It wasn't my place to blame anyone,' said Abigail.

'That's typical of you. You're always so timid.'

'I liked Miss Parry. I still do.'

'Then perhaps I should arrange for you to meet her,' said Peter. 'Would you be happy to do that?'

There was the flicker of another smile. 'Yes, I would.'

'Leave it to me. I'll speak to her.'

'Thank you, sir.'

She was clearly in awe of her visitor. Head bowed and shoulders hunched, she sat on the edge of her chair. Betty, by contrast, stood there with her hands on her hips. Feeling that he'd got as much out of the servant as he was likely to at a first meeting, Peter rose to his feet.

'Thank you, Miss Saunders. What you've told me has been very interesting. I have one last question.'

'What is it?' asked Betty.

'Two servants were left behind at the house to welcome the staff of the new master. One of them was you. Who was the other one?'

'That was Joseph Rafter, sir.'

'Why was he selected?'

'Even though he'd actually left Mr Parry's employ, he'd been in service there far longer than any of us.'

'Where might I find this man?'

'He's still in London, sir, but that's all I can tell you.'

'Then we'll leave it at that for the time being.' He turned to Betty. 'Thank you for your assistance, Mrs Kingzett.'

'I'm always here to help, Mr Skillen. And now that you've found the Red Cow, don't forget us. We serve good food and the finest ale you could ask for. This is no ordinary inn, you see. If you come back, I'll show you the exact spot where that black-hearted villain, Judge Jeffreys, was arrested, him that hanged all them people when King James was on the throne. He was hiding here in the guise of a sailor. They hauled him off to the Tower.'

'I never realised that,' said Peter. 'The Red Cow clearly has its place in history.'

Having devised a plan, the Runners hired a gig and went in search of a suitable church. Yeomans was firmly of the opinion that the idea was really his, but Hale felt that Chevy Ruddock ought to get some share of the credit. His companion dismissed the suggestion out of hand.

'He's got to be kept in his place, Alfred.'

'Chevy needs to be encouraged. He's learnt fast since he joined us.'

'His reward is that he hides all night in a churchyard.'

'A word of praise from you wouldn't come amiss.'

'Well, he's not going to get it. I rose to the position I hold because I had an iron hand. It gains us universal respect. If we start befriending people like Ruddock from the foot patrol, everyone will think we've gone soft. Discipline is vital in our job.'

'So is having good ideas,' said Hale.

'I have a steady stream of them.'

'This one was not entirely yours.'

Yeomans silenced him with a glare. All that concerned him was winning back the esteem of the chief magistrate and that could best be done by making a significant arrest among the bodysnatchers of London. The timing was propitious because they would have complete freedom of movement.

'At least, we won't be tripping over the Skillen brothers,' he said. 'Paul is still in Bath with that fetching actress of his, while Peter is busy looking for a missing person. Let's hope the pair of them stay out of our way.'

'Our task is so much easier when they're busy elsewhere.'

'Paul Skillen will certainly have a lot on his plate, Micah,' said the other. 'We know what he's like when he's roused. Miss Granville was robbed by highwaymen. That means he'll want to wreak his revenge.'

'It could keep him out of London for weeks.'

'What about Peter Skillen?'

'I don't think that he'll bother us, Alfred. Of that we may be certain. Hunting a missing person in London is like trying to find a particular grain of sand in the Sahara Desert. No,' Yeomans went on, flicking the reins to get more speed out of their horse, 'someone is doing us a favour by hiring him. The one thing he won't be doing is hunting bodysnatchers.'

When Peter returned home, Charlotte and Clemency were waiting for him, eager to hear his news. His account was clear and concise, wisely editing out the role played by Abigail's effusive sister. While she was pleased to hear what the servant had told him, Clemency was saddened that she couldn't explain how letters from Amsterdam had been prevented from reaching

148

her father. She was, however, very willing to meet the woman.

'I liked her,' she said. 'Abigail was as quiet as a mouse, but she did her job well. Joseph Rafter was also efficient, though he always let the other servants know that he was in charge.'

'Would he be capable of hiding correspondence from your father?'

'I wouldn't have thought so.'

'What about the others?' asked Charlotte.

'Abigail didn't say much about them,' said Peter. 'I'm hoping that Clemency can get more out of her. The poor woman was afraid of me for some reason.'

'Did you get the feeling that she was hiding something?'

'No, Charlotte, I didn't. If someone in that house betrayed Mr Parry, it wasn't Abigail Saunders. It's not too much to say that she loved him as a master. When she saw him begging in the street, she was appalled at how low he'd fallen.'

It was agreed that Peter would bring the servant to the house so that Clemency could have a long conversation alone with her, hearing about her father's life during the years when they were apart. Peter was loath to take Clemency to the Red Cow in Wapping. The raucous atmosphere would be a problem. The two women needed peace and privacy.

'What will you do next?' asked Clemency.

'I'll begin the search for Joseph Rafter,' replied Peter. 'The chances are that he's gone into service somewhere in London. Did he ever mention a family to you?'

'Yes – he had a brother who worked as a shipwright.'

'Then I'm already one step closer to locating him. There are countless servants, but shipwrights are much smaller in number. Thank you, Clemency. You've just saved me a lot of time.'

149

'I feel so guilty for monopolising you like this. I know how much in demand you and your brother are.'

'Paul is the one who's being monopolised at the moment,' he said with a light laugh. 'Knowing how Hannah must be feeling, I doubt if he ever leaves her side.'

My way is to conjure you; and I'll begin with the women. I charge you, O women, for the love you bear to men, to like as much of this play as please you. And I charge you, O men, for the love you bear to women – as I perceive by your simpering that none of you hates them – that between you and the women the play may please. If I were a woman I would kiss as many of you as had beards that pleased me, complexions that liked me and breaths that I defied not. And I am sure, as many as have good beards, or good faces, or sweet breaths will for my kind offer, when I make curtsy, bid me farewell.

The applause was spontaneous. Hannah had not only delivered the final speech of the play with perfect timing, she did so without a copy of *As You Like It* in her hands. She had learnt the entirety of her part beforehand, amazing some of the company and shaming others because of their lack of preparation. As a character, Rosalind had stiff competition in the play, notably from the actors playing Jaques and Touchstone. Each of them was capable of stealing scenes and remaining most prominent in the minds of the audience as it left the theatre. Hannah had just served notice that, in this case, she would dominate the play completely.

Paul watched everyone gather around her to congratulate her on her performance. While he was pleased that she'd been outstanding during the reading, he knew that something had upset her deeply, and it was not just the memory of being robbed. He'd studied

150

her carefully when she remained silent during scenes in which Rosalind didn't appear. Though she seemed poised, involuntary glances and tiny gestures gave her away.

After rhapsodising over what he'd just heard, Vernon Teale showered praise on the whole company and told them when they'd be needed for rehearsal on the morrow. He then took Hannah aside to thank her for the way she'd set such a high standard for the others, predicting that her curtain speech would be a sensation. She lapped up his comments and sailed out of the theatre with a contented smile on her face. Once out of the building, however, she started to seethe with anger. Paul decided to wait until she was ready to speak to him. He concentrated on scanning the street on both sides for signs of the highwayman. None were seen. It was a source of great relief to him.

He escorted Hannah up to their room. Once inside, she closed the door behind her and vented her spleen.

'I'll not endure it!' she yelled, stamping a foot.

'What do you mean?'

'I should have been warned beforehand.'

'I don't know what you're talking about, Hannah.'

'Didn't you *see* her? Didn't you notice that smirk on her face?'

Paul was mystified. 'No, I didn't—'

'The manager betrayed me. He'll pay for that.'

'Why? I can't understand what's upset you so much.'

'Elinor Ingram.'

'Who?'

'Elinor Ingram,' she repeated, raising her voice, 'that ugly, malicious, two-faced harridan who is to play Celia to my Rosalind.'

'I thought she was rather impressive,' said Paul, 'and, to be fair, the woman is far from ugly.'

151

'How can you possibly say that? She has a face like a diseased pig. She's entirely devoid of talent and shouldn't be allowed anywhere near a public stage.'

'Then why did Mr Teale engage her?'

'He didn't – that's the point. When he first approached me to join the company, he told me that he'd already persuaded Henrietta Doyle to accept the role of Celia. She is an actress for whom I have the highest respect. I looked forward to renewing my acquaintance with Henrietta, but she is not there. In her place,' said Hannah, quivering with fury, 'was Elinor Ingram. It was an unforgivable insult.'

'I can't believe that Mr Teale would dare to insult you, my love.'

'That woman is anathema to me.'

'The manager didn't know that and nor did I. Miss Ingram showed you no animosity. Why do you rail against her?'

'There are lots of reasons, Paul. The main one is that she once tried to ruin my career onstage. She's nothing but a venomous snake.'

'Calm down,' he advised. 'There's no need to get so vexed.'

'*Vexed?*' she echoed. 'That's far too puny a word to explain the emotions that I feel. I'm enraged, frustrated, infuriated, exasperated, maddened, incensed and provoked beyond all measure. My immediate impulse is to summon Jenny to pack all my things so that we may shake the dust of Bath off our feet for ever.'

'But you still haven't told me why you are in such a state.'

'I did so in pronouncing her foul name – Elinor Ingram.'

'Would you really quit the company because of her?'

'Mr Teale faces a choice between us,' warned Hannah. 'He either replaces that vixen or he'll need to look for another

Rosalind. I'll not soil my reputation by playing scenes with that unprincipled back-stabber.'

'Is that what you're going to tell the manager?'

Grabbing him by the shoulders, she looked deep into his eyes.

'No, Paul – it's what *you* will say to him.'

CHAPTER THIRTEEN

Though he was inclined to be lazy, Micah Yeomans could move with speed and purpose when required to do so. He and Hale visited several churches that might serve their purpose but, in each case, the parish priest objected strongly to the plan they put to him. The Runners widened their search, looking for a more remote location with a more amenable vicar. After meeting another series of disappointments, they eventually found themselves in Islington and decided that St Mary's might suit their needs. Unknown to them, the grave robbed earlier had now been filled in and was no more than a mound of earth. All that they saw was a churchyard likely to attract criminals because of its isolated location.

The Rev. Hubert Corke gave them a cordial welcome and invited them into the vicarage. He was delighted to hear that the Runners were taking a special interest in the problem of bodysnatching and were determined to arrest those behind it.

'We issued a report,' said Yeomans, giving the impression that he'd done so of his own volition, 'and were shocked at the increase in attacks on churchyards. None of them is safe.'

'I know,' said Corke, gloomily.

'We don't view our task solely as a case of catching depraved criminals. It has a religious purpose as well,' said Yeomans, striking a pose. 'I was brought up as a true Christian and believe my work has a missionary side to it. I drive out the evil from society in order to protect the good.'

'Micah is true to his name,' Hale pointed out.

Corke smiled benignly. 'Then I'm glad that his parents chose to name him after a Hebrew prophet who lived in the kingdom of Judea,' he said. 'There are other Micahs in the Old Testament, you know. One of them lived in the country of Ephraim and stole eleven hundred pieces of silver from his mother. When she cursed the thief, he gave the money back, but she used some of it to pay a silversmith to make a graven image. Micah set up an altar to the idol.' He turned to Yeomans. 'I'm sure that you'd never approve of that.'

'Mine is the way of the Lord,' said the Runner, borrowing the phrase from a half-remembered sermon. 'To that end, we wish to safeguard the dead from the sinfulness of the living. I have a plan that will help us to snare the malefactors.'

'Let me hear it.'

'We're going to meet cunning with cunning.'

He went on to describe the scheme that had been devised,

making it sound as if it was entirely his idea. Hale had a vestigial pity for Chevy Ruddock, the true author of the plan, but he didn't dare to voice it. Yeomans could be vindictive. Having heard him out with a mixture of patience and head-bobbing approval, Corke pronounced his judgement.

'It's a wonderful plan, Mr Yeomans.'

'Thank you.'

'It has the virtues of simplicity and effectiveness.'

'Does that mean you'd allow us to use your churchyard?'

'In theory,' said Corke, 'I'd be happy for you to do so but your idea is rather redundant here. If you'll forgive a rather crude comparison, it's a case of closing the stable door after the horse has bolted.'

'I don't understand,' said Hale.

'One of our graves has already been robbed. We'll be more vigilant in future. We don't wish to lose anyone else entrusted to our care.'

'You've been a victim yourself?' said Yeomans, with interest. 'Tell us the details and we'll do our best to catch the villains responsible.'

'As it happens, someone has already taken on that task.'

'It's a crime that only we are best placed to solve.'

'The gentleman swore that he'd find the culprits,' said Corke, 'and I believed him. He spoke with such resolve.'

'And who was this gentleman you mention?'

'A Mr Skillen.'

Yeomans was stunned. '*Peter* Skillen?'

'That's right.'

'You were wrong,' said Hale. 'It looks as if Peter Skillen *has* started chasing grave robbers, after all.'

* * *

When he returned to the Red Cow that afternoon, Peter travelled by Hackney cab so that he could bring Abigail Saunders back to his home in comfort. The inn was noisier than ever and she was glad to escape its pandemonium. Seeing how apprehensive she was, he spent the journey trying to calm her nerves and prepare her for what was to come.

'You'll find Mrs van Emden much changed.'

'I'll still be pleased to see her again, Mr Skillen.'

'She remembers all of the servants' names and told me that it was a very happy house.'

'Oh, it was – if only it could have stayed like that.'

'Things change as time passes. That's inevitable.'

'I know.'

'When I met you earlier,' he recalled, 'I asked you to rack your brains to see if there's anything you can remember about the other members of staff that might make it easy to track them down.'

'I tried very hard,' she said, 'but there's nothing.'

'Can't you remember if they talked about their families?'

'Two of them didn't *have* families, sir. They were orphans. We all thought that we were part of a family at Mr Parry's house.'

'You talk of him as a kind man, yet he tried to lock his daughter away when he learnt about her romance. That doesn't sound like an act of kindness.'

'He thought he was doing the best for her.'

'And what did you think?'

'It doesn't matter what I thought, sir.'

'You must have taken sides, surely?'

'Most of us wouldn't have dared to do that.'

'What about Joseph Rafter?'

'He was different.'

'In what way?'

There was a pause. 'You'll have to speak to him.'

Because of his relationship with Hannah Granville, Paul was on the fringes of the theatrical world, but he still didn't understand its strange rules or speak its overblown language. Actors and actresses seemed to thrive on hyperbole, exchanging extravagant greetings whenever they met, yet falling out with each other at will and indulging in bitter feuds. Competition between them was fierce. Much as he loved Hannah, he'd come to accept that she was prone to rash judgements, dividing people into lifelong friends or hated enemies. No middle ground existed. In every production in which she took part, there'd been someone she identified as her bête noir. Most recently, it had been the author of *The Piccadilly Opera* who'd aroused her ire so much that she'd had a tantrum at almost every rehearsal. In the end, she reached a point where she refused to continue unless he stayed well away from the theatre. The war of attrition between actress and playwright had reduced the manager of the theatre to tears.

Paul suspected that Vernon Teale would be made of sterner stuff. Behind the flamboyant manner and the beaming amiability, he sensed that there was a shrewd businessman well versed in dealing with the demands of egotistical actors and distraught actresses. In one way, he was glad that Hannah had asked him to speak on her behalf. It showed how much she trusted him and gave him the opportunity to find a compromise that would enable them to remain in Bath, where she'd play Rosalind and he'd have the opportunity to catch the highwayman who'd robbed her. In another way, however, he wished that she'd fought this particular battle on her own because he simply didn't

159

understand the subtleties of negotiating with a theatre manager.

When he stepped into Teale's office, therefore, he did so with some misgivings. Hannah had told him exactly what she expected, but Paul felt that she was asking far too much. He vowed to take a more cautious approach.

'Come on in, Mr Skillen,' said Teale, motioning him to a seat.

'Thank you, Mr Teale.'

'Do you come on your own account, or are you here as an emissary of Miss Granville?'

'Hannah asked me to speak to you.'

'Then you do so as a much-envied man, sir. Miss Granville's fabled beauty has dazzled every actor in the cast. They look at you with a mixture of wonder and resentment because of your privileged position in her affections. I congratulate you on your good fortune.'

'I'm not here to talk about myself, Mr Teale. What happens between Hannah and me is a private matter. What happens between *you* and her, however, affects the future prospects of your theatre.'

Teale's smile faded. 'The dear lady is unhappy in some way?'

'I fear that she's distressed.'

'Tell me the problem and I'll deal with it immediately.'

'I sincerely hope that that will be possible.'

'I can deny her nothing,' said the other, with a sweeping gesture.

'You may change your mind when you hear what she wants.'

'I'm not sure that I like the sound of that,' said Teale, eyelids narrowing. 'I'm a very reasonable man, but I must warn you not to go beyond the bounds of reason.'

'Warnings are unnecessary,' said Paul, firmly. 'Please remember that I am only the messenger here.'

'Then be so kind as to deliver Miss Granville's message.'

'It concerns Miss Ingram.'

'What about her?'

'Hannah feels that you deliberately misled her in one respect. When you submitted your cast list to her, the part of Celia had been given to someone else.'

'It's true,' said Teale. 'Miss Doyle was my first choice for the role. Until two days ago, I fully expected her to join the company. Then word came that she was seriously ill and had lost her voice into the bargain. Compelled to find someone else at short notice, I chose Miss Ingram.'

'Hannah strongly objects to your choice.'

'For what reason, may I ask?'

'There's a history of dissension between the two ladies.'

'That's not what Miss Ingram told me,' said Teale. 'She adores Miss Granville and feels honoured to play opposite her. Well, you were at the reading. Didn't you think that she was a perfect Celia?'

'As a matter of fact, I did,' said Paul.

'Miss Granville can't possibly object to her abilities.'

'There are personal issues at stake here,' said Paul, uncomfortably. 'What they are in detail, I don't rightly know. I'm simply telling you that the future of *As You Like It* will only be secure if Miss Ingram leaves the cast and is replaced by someone else.'

Teale received the news with apparent equanimity but, beneath the calm exterior, he was extremely annoyed. He was grateful that Paul had been sent with the demand. A confrontation with his leading lady would have been considerably more fraught. Paul's manner made the discussion far less hostile.

'The message you may take back to Miss Granville,' said the manager, quietly, 'is that she should be grateful to Miss Ingram. To get the services of someone of her quality in what was an unlooked-for emergency was a gift from God. Had she not been prepared to step in, we'd have been left stranded. As a last resort, we'd have had to fall back on some unseasoned beginner who could never hold her own onstage against Hannah Granville.' He sat back in his chair. 'That is my message, Mr Skillen.'

'Then I am to give you a reply,' said Paul.

'But you haven't delivered it to Miss Granville.'

'I know what she will say, Mr Teale, and I regret having to tell you what it is. Unless Miss Ingram departs, you will lose your Rosalind.'

Teale took a few moments to absorb the news. Then he opened a drawer in his desk and took out a document, glancing at it before passing it across to Paul.

'What is it?' asked the latter.

'It's the contract that Miss Granville signed. Can you confirm that that is her signature?'

Paul looked at the bold calligraphy. 'Yes, it is.'

'Then I ask you to do two things for me, please,' said Teale, taking the contract back and putting it away. 'The first thing is to apologise to Miss Granville for inadvertently employing someone whose presence in the cast is not to her liking.'

'And what's the second?'

'Tell her this contract is legally enforceable.'

Paul stiffened. 'Don't try to scare Hannah.'

'I am merely drawing her attention to our agreement.'

'If you threaten her, she'll leave Bath within the hour.'

'Is she aware of what the consequences will be, Mr Skillen?'

'They don't worry her in the least.'

'Well, they should,' said Teale, his tone hardening. 'Miss Granville will not only be sued by me, her reputation will be damaged so much that she'll have difficulty finding anyone else to employ her. To put it bluntly, she must play Rosalind with the cast we have or risk being ousted from the profession.' He became almost avuncular. 'You've been put in an awkward position, Mr Skillen, and I sympathise with you. I've had more experience of dealing with people like Miss Granville, creatures of such abundant talent that they rise effortlessly above everyone else whenever they take on a new role. Almost to a woman, however, they tend to be both passionate and capricious. I've yet to deal with a leading lady who didn't make intemperate demands simply to flex her muscles. I fear that that is what Miss Granville is doing.'

Paul sat there motionless for some time as he weighed up the manager's comments. Then he extended a hand.

'I'd like to read the terms of that contract,' he said.

After delivering Abigail Saunders to his house, Peter went off in search of another of the former servants. He'd expected Clemency to speak to Abigail alone but she wanted Charlotte to remain, even though her presence might inhibit the servant. All three of them settled down in the drawing room, Abigail perching nervously on the edge of the chair. After an exchange of pleasantries, Clemency asked for an account her father's life after she had left for Amsterdam. Slow of speech and meek of manner, Abigail was nevertheless able to give a clear picture of how George Parry had fared in the wake of his daughter's marriage. It was a tale of loneliness and decline. Parry had suffered. It was clear to all of the servants that he was having second thoughts. Full of regret at the way he'd treated his only child, he'd written letters of apology and implored her to forgive him.

'It was Joseph's job to send the letters off,' she said.

'And he'd also have been the first to see any correspondence that came to the house,' observed Clemency. 'Isn't that so, Abigail?'

'Yes, it is.'

'He'd be far too honest to tamper with it.'

'Yes,' said Abigail, less readily. 'He would.'

'I thought that he was dismissed,' recalled Charlotte. 'Why was that, Abigail? Did he upset Mr Parry in some way?'

'I think it was the other way around, Mrs Skillen.'

'What did Mr Parry do?'

'He lowered Joseph's wages. It was the same for all of us, mind you, and we had to accept it. Joseph didn't. He refused to do the same work for less money so Mr Parry sent him on his way.'

'Was he replaced?'

'Oh, no, the master couldn't afford to do that. He'd stopped working and was starting to drink a lot. It made him short-tempered with us and that wasn't like him at all.'

'It certainly wasn't,' agreed Clemency. 'He loved his work. I can't believe that he gave it up. What did he do all day?'

'He just moped around the house, Mrs van Emden.'

'It must have been very unpleasant for all of you.'

'Mr Parry was in pain. We could see that. All we could do was carry on with our duties.'

As she listened to the servant's sad tale, Charlotte was very sorry for George Parry, but it was Clemency who was deeply moved. The contrast was stark. While she had gone on to forge a new life with a caring husband, her father had reached a point where he'd felt his existence was worthless. His descent had been swift. When Abigail finally came to the end of her recitation, Clemency's eyes were full of tears. The poignancy of the situation was too much to bear. Guilt was overwhelming her once more. In deserting her father, she'd taken away his reason for living.

It was the horse that bore the brunt of his anger. As he drove the gig, Yeomans was so enraged at the news that Peter Skillen was in competition with him yet again that he used the whip hard on the animal's rump. In the end, Hale had to plead on the horse's behalf.

'There's no need to flay the creature, Micah.'

'Peter Skillen is the one I'd like to flay.'

'You always say that Paul Skillen is worse.'

'The pair of them are damnable nuisances, Alfred. We can't seem to do anything without one or the other getting in our way.'

'It's just a coincidence that Peter Skillen went to that church in Islington. He may think he's more intelligent than any of us, yet I'll wager he doesn't have a plan like the one Chevy Ruddock suggested.' He gasped in pain as he was elbowed sharply. 'I know that it was *your* idea as well, Micah.'

'Ruddock stole it from me.'

'Yes, yes . . . of course he did.'

'It was my inspiration and mine alone.'

'You have much keener instincts than him.'

'And I have a better knowledge of the criminal mind.'

'You put Chevy in the shade.'

'Don't let me hear his ridiculous name on your lips again.'

'No, no, it's a promise.' They came to a fork in the road and swung off to the right. 'We came here on the other road, Micah.'

'That's why we're going back by another route. There's no point in travelling any further away from the city. This road will get us back there in due course. Meanwhile, we must hope we find another country church with a vicar as willing to help us as the Reverend Corke.'

'I'm sure we will,' said Hale, with confidence. 'Bodysnatchers are vermin. Any parish priest with an ounce of sense ought to rush to put your brilliant plan into action.'

'It's not as if there's anything that's offensive to the church. We don't need a mock funeral service inside the building – that would be blasphemous. I know how these gangs work,' said Yeomans. 'They're constantly on the lookout for signs of a forthcoming burial. They keep a constant watch on churchyards near and far.'

'All we need to tempt them is a hole in the ground.'

'Peter and Paul Skillen would never think of a trick like that.'

'No, Micah, they don't have your brain.'

They rolled on over the bumpy surface until a distant steeple came in sight. Yeomans had an upsurge of optimism.

'We've found the right church at last,' he said, sitting up. 'I feel it in my bones.'

Hannah Granville couldn't understand why Paul had been gone for such a long time. In her mind, all that he had to do was deliver her ultimatum, wait for a reply, then bring it back to her. She was not only eager to hear that her command had been obeyed by the manager, she wanted Paul beside her. Alone in her hotel room, she felt uneasy. She was too afraid to look out of the window in case the highwayman was keeping her under surveillance, and so nervous that – whenever the floorboard creaked outside her room – she drew back from it as if an interloper was about to batter his way in. While she regretted sending Paul on an errand she could have done herself, she believed that her decision had been a sound one. It was unwise to have a confrontation with the manager so early in the proceedings. She was far better off staying in the shadows and using an intermediary. Vernon Teale worshipped her, she told herself. He'd be glad to comply with her demand.

Yet there was still no word from Paul. A new fear arose. Had he been intercepted and stopped from reaching her? Did his position as her bodyguard make him a target? She remembered how Roderick Cosgrove, another man appointed to look after her, had been shot when trying to defend her. Would Paul meet a similar fate? Hannah was working herself up into a state of hysteria when she suddenly heard footsteps ascending the stairs outside. The floorboard on the landing creaked, but this time the footsteps didn't continue. Someone had stopped outside the door. Knuckles rapped on the wood. There was something assertive about the knocking and it made her scurry to the far side of the room. After a few moments, the door was rapped even harder.

'Miss Granville?' asked a voice. 'It's the manager.'

'What do you want?' she croaked.

'I've come to deliver a parcel for you.'

'Who sent it?'

'I've no idea.'

'One moment . . .'

Gathering up her strength, Hannah ran to the door and opened it. The manager – a short, angular man with a lopsided wig – was standing there with a small parcel in his hand. When he passed it to her, she saw that her name was written on it.

'Did a tall, lean man deliver this?' she asked.

'No, Miss Granville – it was a young girl.'

The information helped to still her beating heart. After thanking the manager, she closed the door and bolted it again. Curiosity got the better of her anxiety. Tearing the parcel open, she took out a small box with a velvet interior. Lodged inside was a beautiful diamond brooch. Hannah was jolted. She'd seen and admired the brooch before. It had been worn by one of the passengers who'd sat opposite her on the coach. Like anything else of value, it had been stolen by the highwaymen.

She flung the brooch onto the bed as if it was red hot.

Peter was finding the search far more difficult than he'd either hoped or anticipated. He'd forgotten that he lived on an island with a rich maritime heritage. Shipbuilding was a major industry that employed a vast number of men. Most of them – it seemed to Peter – earned their living somewhere along the River Thames. Depending on the size of the vessels being constructed, the boatyards varied, but they all had one thing in common: they were deafening establishments. A symphony of mallets, hammers and other tools was being played at full volume. Peter could hardly hear himself speak, let along catch what others were saying to him. Wherever he went, the result was the same. Nobody had even heard of a shipwright by the name of Rafter. It was time to move on to the next place.

As his horse trotted along the riverbank, Peter was alarmed by the thought that the man he was after might not even be in London. Most ports tended to have shipwrights. Joseph Rafter's brother might be working in Harwich or Portsmouth or Dover or one of the countless other ports or river towns. If that were the case, finding him would take a whole lifetime. Peter pressed on hopefully and his luck eventually changed. He came upon a small boatyard where some men were at work on a barge. Reining in his horse, he asked one of them if the name Rafter meant anything to him. The man pointed to a brawny figure using a plane with methodical precision on a length of timber. When Peter dismounted and went across to him, the shipwright drew himself up and gave him a hostile glare.

'Mr Rafter?' asked Peter.

'That's me – I'm Nick Rafter.'

'I wanted to ask about your brother, Joseph.'

'Then you're wasting your time.'

'Why is that?'

'It's because I hate the bastard,' said the other, vehemently. 'I haven't seen him for the best part of fifteen years. I'd be more than happy if I never see him again. What's your business with him?'

'I'm hoping that he might help me.'

'There's no chance of that.'

'Isn't there?'

'If he can't help his own brother,' said the shipwright, sourly, 'he certainly won't help *you*. Don't mention his foul name to me again. If you want the plain truth, I'm ashamed to belong to the same family as him.'

CHAPTER FOURTEEN

There was no escape from him. Cowering in her hotel room, Hannah Granville felt more vulnerable than ever. The man who'd robbed her might not be keeping vigil outside the building but he'd unsettled her in another way. By sending her an unwanted gift, he'd terrified her. There was no message with the diamond brooch, but its purpose was explicit. A man she feared and hated was actually trying to woo her. Worst of all, she'd received his gift when Paul wasn't there to protect and advise her. Unable even to touch it, Hannah stood by the bed and stared down at the brooch. She was still mesmerised by it when she heard a tap on the door. Her first thought was that the highwayman was coming to get her, and she fled to the other side of the room.

'Hannah!' said Paul. 'Let me in.'

'Is it really you?' she asked.

'Who else are you expecting?' She ran across the room and unlocked the door. He stepped in. 'What on earth are you playing at, Hannah?'

She grabbed him impulsively. 'You're here at last!'

'I was held up. I'm sorry about that.' She began to sob. 'You're in a dreadful state. Has someone been here while I was away?' His eye fell on the bed and he saw the brooch. 'What's that?'

'It arrived not long before you did.'

'Who sent it?'

'*He* did, Paul.'

'After what he did to you,' said Paul, 'he has no right to make any contact with you at all. Did he actually deliver it to the hotel?'

'He got someone else to do that,' she explained. 'I was horrified when I saw it. That brooch was stolen from a woman in the coach with me. He's trying to court me with stolen property.'

'It will have to be returned to its rightful owner.'

'I'd already decided that.'

'And we must move to a hotel where he can't find us.'

'I wish that we could!' she said, with a sigh.

'What's to stop us?'

'*He* is, Paul. He knows my every move.'

'We'll leave at night when it's too dark for us to be seen.'

'He'd find us somehow,' she moaned. 'He has eyes everywhere. Those other highwaymen probably live in Bath as well. They might even take it in turns to keep watch on me.'

'Now, don't panic,' he warned, easing her across to the little sofa and sinking down beside her. 'We have to make decisions. We need to be calm and collected when we do so.'

'Imagine how I felt when I saw that brooch. I threw it on the bed as if it had been infected.'

'What if it had been the opal pendant he stole from you? I don't think you'd have thrown that away, Hannah.'

Though he spoke softly, there was an implied reproach. Against his advice, she'd deliberately worn the treasured gift on the journey to Bath. Had it been left back at Paul's house, it would never have been stolen. She was penitent.

'I was too headstrong.'

'You weren't to know that it would be stolen.'

'I was being held at gunpoint,' she wailed. 'I couldn't stop him. You've no idea how sickened I felt. It was only because I loved your gift so much that I had to wear it.'

'I'll get it back,' vowed Paul.

She started sobbing again and he wrapped his arms around her, rocking her gently to and fro. Minutes went by before she gradually began to recover. When she pulled away to look up at him, she had a question to ask.

'What happened when you met Mr Teale?'

Paul sighed.

At first, Abigail Saunders had felt out of place talking to Clemency and Charlotte, two women she could never meet on equal terms, but the longer the discussion went on, the more relaxed she became. Choosing her moment, Charlotte excused herself, convinced that Clemency would get far more out of her visitor when left alone with her. Having repaired to the kitchen, Charlotte asked Meg Rooke to make some tea and to serve it with light refreshments. She was about to talk further with the servant when she heard the doorbell ring. Meg instantly moved towards the passageway, but she was stopped by an outstretched arm.

'You make the tea,' said Charlotte. 'I'll see who it is.'

She went to the door to open it with a flourish and saw the sad figure of Mungo Darwood standing there. Struck by her appearance, he lifted his hat courteously.

'Good day to you,' he said. 'I believe that you are Mrs Skillen?'

'I am, indeed,' she replied, 'and you, I fancy, are Mr Darwood.'

'At your service, dear lady.' He gave a token bow. 'I called to see Mrs van Emden at her hotel and was told she was now staying with you and Mr Skillen. This address had been left for me.'

'Do come in, Mr Darwood. Clemency will be glad to see you.'

'I have some news for her.'

'I do hope that it's good news,' said Charlotte. 'She's sorely in need of it. There's been a succession of bad news so far.'

'I make no promises, Mrs Skillen. My tidings are mixed. There's good in them, I think, but there's also disappointment.'

Peter arrived at the gallery in time to see Gully Ackford pouring himself a reviving glass of beer. He offered one to his friend.

'It's not alcohol I need, Gully,' said Peter, sinking into a chair. 'It's someone who'll listen sympathetically to my woes and tell me what my next step should be.'

'As a rule, you don't need telling.'

'I seem to have come up against a brick wall this time.'

'Then you must either climb over it or knock it down.'

'There you are – good, practical advice already.'

'Tell me what's happened so far,' he said, settling back in his chair and sipping his beer. 'I'm all ears.'

Peter described his visit to Wapping and how he felt he'd made significant progress when he tracked down Abigail

Saunders. Bolstered by what he'd been told by the woman, Peter had set off in the certainty that he'd find Joseph Rafter's brother among the shipwrights of London and discover where the former servant now lived. His overconfidence had been sapped to the point where it ceased to exist.

'What would you do in my place, Gully?' he asked.

Ackford grinned. 'I'd pour a second glass of beer.'

'I don't deserve it.'

'You mentioned the name of another of Mr Parry's servants at one point – Edmund Haines. Isn't it possible to find him?'

'I'm afraid not. Abigail Saunders had no idea where the others went when the house was sold. It looks as if she's my only source.'

'Yes, but finding her was no mean achievement.'

'That was Jem's doing. He located the Red Cow for me.'

'You're the one who got the woman to talk.'

'It's a pity she wasn't as loquacious as her sister or I'd have had more detail. The truth is,' admitted Peter, 'that I'm not only looking in the wrong place, I may be searching in the wrong country.'

'Quash that thought immediately.'

'Perhaps I should go to the Netherlands.'

'No,' said Ackford, decisively, 'the answers don't lie there. I made the mistake of thinking that Mr van Emden had sent his wife back to London ill-prepared. My guess was he'd been deliberately keeping father and daughter apart out of spite by making sure that her letters never reached him and *his* letters – we now know Parry wrote some – were intercepted before his wife was even aware of them.'

'My thinking was starting to veer in that direction.'

'Then consider this, Peter. Did he stop his wife coming here?'

175

'No, he didn't.'

'Did he encourage her?'

'According to Clemency, he did just that.'

'Then he's absolved of any blame. Had he gone to lengths to deny her any contact with her father, Mr van Emden would never have sent her here because she'd find out somehow that her correspondence never reached her father. She's an intelligent woman, Peter. She'd have realised that her husband was to blame.' He took several more sips of his drink. 'Do you follow my reasoning?'

'I follow it and agree with it,' said Peter. 'You've just saved me from an expensive, uncomfortable voyage. It would have been followed by an embarrassing meeting with Jan van Emden.'

Ackford chuckled. 'How well do you speak Dutch?'

'Thanks to you, I won't have to speak it at all.'

They laughed companionably. The talk with Ackford was a tonic for him, lifting his spirits and making him review events from a slightly different perspective. As they discussed what steps should be taken in the future, Peter issued a plea.

'I need help, Gully. I can't do this on my own.'

'Then you must have Jem at your side.'

'Don't you need him at the gallery?'

'Of course I do,' said Ackford, 'but your need is greater than mine. I'll manage somehow. I have friends on whom I can call in a situation like this. You take Jem Huckvale. It won't be for very long.'

'I don't know about that.'

'I do. You'll either solve this mystery in a day or two or have someone else to work alongside you.'

'Who would that be?'

'Your own brother, of course,' said Ackford. 'Paul isn't going to stay in Bath, is he? He'll come back fairly soon.'

Paul Skillen had returned from his meeting with the manager, knowing that Hannah wouldn't like what he had to tell her. On his way back from the theatre, he'd been searching for phrases that might be palliative but, in this case, the English language seemed strangely bereft of them. In the end, he decided to break the news without any embellishment at all, then weather the raging tempest that was bound to follow. As it was, Hannah's strictures about Elinor Ingram had been submerged beneath her fears of the amorous highwayman. She had now remembered the rival actress and wondered why her question had provoked such a response from him.

'Why did you pull such a face?' she asked.

'It was . . . a difficult discussion, Hannah.'

'I would have thought it to be a remarkably easy one. You simply had to pass on my complaint to Mr Teale, hear his apology and return here with his guarantee that Elinor Ingram would disappear from the cast at once.' He gave a mirthless laugh.

'What did the manager say?'

'We had a frank and meaningful talk.'

'And what was the outcome?'

'He said that he'd have preferred to speak to you directly.'

She was dismissive. 'That's neither here nor there, Paul.'

'It's an important point, my love,' he said. 'I'm no silver-tongued advocate. You know the inner workings of theatrical life. I don't. To be honest, I felt that I was a little out of my depth.'

'You still haven't told me what Mr Teale said.'

'Promise me that you'll listen in a tranquil mood.'

177

'Tell me,' she demanded, standing up.

'Hannah . . .'

'*Tell me!*'

Paul plunged straight in. 'Mr Teale was bewildered,' he said. 'He simply couldn't understand the reason for your dislike of Miss Ingram.'

'It's not dislike – it's pure, unvarnished detestation!'

'He sets a high value on her talents.'

'Then his judgement is woefully awry.'

'Beware of what you say, Hannah,' he told her, rising from the sofa. 'You didn't question his judgement when he chose you to perform in this play. The manager has an eye for quality.'

'What he lacks is an insight into character. Miss Ingram has been selected on the grounds of her supposed talent. If Mr Teale knew what a sly, cunning, deceitful, disruptive reptile she was, he would never dream of employing her. Didn't you tell him how I described her?'

'He laughed off your comments as the kind of rivalry that always exists between actresses.'

'Laughed them off?' she said, almost apoplectic. 'I must speak to him myself at once.' She headed for the door, but Paul barred her way. 'Stand aside, please.'

'No, Hannah.'

'Do as I say. I must have this out with Mr Teale.'

'It's not in your best interests to do so.'

'What the devil do you mean?'

'I've read the contract that you signed.' It was enough to silence her and let him continue. 'I went through every line of it, Hannah. If you are in breach of any of its terms, there will be legal penalties. You would be sued.'

'I'm the one who should be taking legal action,' she said. 'Mr Teale should be prosecuted for engaging an actress like Elinor Ingram without first consulting me. I'd have stopped the malevolent harpy from getting anywhere near this theatre.'

'You can bluster all you wish, my love. A contract is a contract.'

'And you say that you read it?'

'I perused every word.'

'Then you'll have noticed the special provisions relating to me. I refused to sign the document until they were included.'

'All your demands were accepted, Hannah. It was a point that the manager emphasised. He felt that he'd gone out of his way to give you certain privileges. Unfortunately,' he went on, 'they do not include the right to have anyone else dismissed from the company.'

'They *will* do.'

'Don't put Mr Teale in an impossible position.'

She was outraged. 'Are you taking his side against me?'

'Of course I'm not,' he said. 'I'm here to do whatever you ask. I just beg you – before you confront the manager – to look to the future.'

'I will do, Paul. I'll make sure that any contracts I sign from this day forth will give me the right of approval over the cast.'

'You're assuming that there'll *be* future contracts.'

Hannah gaped. She'd been struck dumb this time.

Paul told her flatly that, if she chose to leave the company forthwith because of the presence of another actress, word of her precipitate action would soon spread. After her endless rows with the playwright of *The Piccadilly Opera*, she'd already acquired a reputation as a combative personality. If she defied Teale and stormed away from Bath, other managers would hesitate to employ her. Paul added that the only way that he would ever find the highwayman who'd stolen her opal pendant was by remaining in the city. His final argument was the one he felt would be most telling.

'There's something you haven't considered, Hannah.'

'What is it?' she asked.

'If you desert the company – Mr Teale assured me of this – he would have to assign the part of Rosalind to Miss Ingram. She would garner all the praise in your stead. Do you really want *that* to happen?'

The church of St Saviour's in the parish of Tottenham satisfied all their requirements. Set in a village, it was outside the bustle of London yet easily reached from the city. More to the point, it had a vicar who was eager to put their plan into action. The Runners wished that they had found the church earlier on instead of having to visit so many beforehand. Yeomans and Hale surveyed the churchyard. The fact that a corpse had been stolen from there less than six months earlier showed that it had been watched by bodysnatchers. The crime had made the vicar resolve to thwart any future attacks on his churchyard. The plan put to him seemed to be the ideal answer.

'It's good to find a clergyman prepared to see sense,' observed Yeomans. 'Most of them were terrified they'd be reported to someone.'

'They'd be doing nothing illegal, Micah.'

'They're far too timid. Parish priests are all the same. They're afraid to break wind without written permission from their bishop.'

'This one isn't,' said Hale, 'and nor was the Reverend Corke.'

'I wish he'd told us why Peter Skillen had gone to his church.'

'He was there with a woman for some reason.'

'Yes, but what *was* that reason?'

'You could always ask him.'

'I just want to catch some bodysnatchers before he does,' said Yeomans. 'We need to prove to Mr Kirkwood that we can do what the Skillen brothers can never do.'

'One of them is not even in London.'

'That suits me, Alfred.'

'There's something else that will suit you,' said Hale, as he saw two figures coming around the angle of the church. 'The vicar is as good as his word. He not only approved of the plan – *your* plan – he's doing exactly what you asked him to do.'

Yeomans caught sight of the vicar with a thickset man carrying a spade. They walked to a corner of the churchyard where there was plenty of space. As soon as the vicar pointed to a spot, the gravedigger started work. Yeomans was delighted.

'We'll need to find an empty coffin and bury it after dark,' he said. 'Sooner or later, somebody will come sniffing in this direction.'

'How soon do we need to keep the churchyard under surveillance?'

'They can start tomorrow night.'

'It may be some time before any gang is aware of the burial.'

'They'll come here eventually. Meanwhile, we need a person who is strong, patient, fearless and unlikely to fall asleep while on duty.'

'There's only one man who meets those demands.'

'Chevy Ruddock!' they said in unison.

When he'd called at the house, Mungo Darwood had assumed that he'd be left alone with Clemency to pass on the information he'd gathered about her father. Instead – and he made no complaint – he was given tea and refreshments in a room shared with three women. One of them, Abigail Saunders, was too abashed by his presence to say anything, but the others were full of questions. In spite of his physical disabilities, he'd been busy and had spoken to some of George Parry's old friends. One of whom had been especially helpful.

'What was his name?' asked Clemency.

'Taylor – Mr Geoffrey Taylor.'

'I remember him. He employed my father years ago.'

'Given the choice, he'd have employed him much more. He said that, as an engineer, George Parry was a true pioneer. When he came in search of him recently, he heard your father was no longer in a fit state to do any kind of work.'

'What about the other people you contacted?' asked Charlotte.

'They were all fellow engineers, Mrs Skillen, and they happily admitted that they'd never achieved the same level of excellence as my old friend, George. He was even more gifted than I'd imagined.'

'Why didn't they help him in his hour of need?'

'I asked that very question of all three of them.'

'How did they answer it?'

'With one voice,' replied Darwood. 'None of them knew about the predicament he was in until it was too late. They hadn't spurned him – as George had feared – they were keen to come to his aid. When Mr Taylor set up a fund to pay off George's debts, the three of them contributed readily. The problem was that they couldn't find him. He'd vanished into the masses of poverty-stricken wretches that blight this fine city.'

'Did any of them search for him?' asked Clemency.

'Mr Taylor took on that responsibility. He hired someone to

find your father but the search bore no fruit. Apart from anything else, I suspect, George's appearance had changed so markedly that he might not have been easy to recognise. Since his three friends had last seen him, he'd have aged and lost a lot of weight. The description given to the man sent looking for George might well have been worthless.'

'It's a comfort to know that he still had friends, after all.'

'They were friends and admirers of his work.'

'Did any of them say why he stopped working?'

'They all had theories about that . . .'

Charlotte was happy to let Clemency take over the questioning completely. Curiously, she was less interested in what her father's friends had said than in her memories of visits made to the family house by Darwood. They reminisced happily. Charlotte was pleased to see a smile on Clemency's face at last. Darwood brought the man alive again for his daughter. It was a joy to hear her laugh at one point. While half-listening to the conversation, Charlotte was remembering what their visitor had told them earlier. She singled out Geoffrey Taylor. If Peter had made no headway, she believed it might benefit him to speak to the man at the earliest opportunity.

Hannah Granville was such an ebullient person that her lapse into a morose silence was wholly out of character. At least she was no longer berating Paul and accusing him of siding with the manager. She'd come to realise that her career had reached a turning point. Instinct told her to flounce out of the cast of *As You Like It* and return to London, but that course of action was not as appealing as it had first seemed. It might be as expensive as it was damaging to her professional standing. The fact that she would, in effect, be handing the role of Rosalind to a despised rival was the decisive factor. Though she'd have to endure the woman's proximity during daily rehearsals of the play, it would be preferable to giving Elinor Ingram the chance to shine in her place.

Paul was not used to a prolonged silence in her company. When Hannah was not talking to him, she was usually rehearsing her latest role. He eventually interrupted her reverie by pointing out that neither of them had eaten for several hours and that the restaurant recommended to them was only five minutes' walk away. The anticipated protest never materialised. Hannah was ready to accept his suggestion. Earlier on, she'd been afraid to stir from the room, but she left it without a murmur this time. On the walk there, she did say that it was good to have a breath of fresh air again. Paul sensed that, as soon as they were in the restaurant, she'd become animated, treating the other people there as an audience.

'I was hoping you'd grace our establishment, Miss Granville,' said the head waiter, fawning over her before conducting the two of them to a table in the corner. 'If there's anything you need – anything at all – just beckon me over.'

'Thank you,' she said, taking the seat he held out for her.

'I'm sure you'll find the menu to your liking.'

'We've heard glowing reports of your chef,' said Paul.

When they were both seated, the waiter stared at Hannah as if in the presence of royalty. It required a nudge from Paul to send him on his way. Studying their menus, they were able to have a conversation at last, choosing certain items, changing their minds, then reverting to their original choices. Food and wine were safe subjects. The one thing he was determined not to mention was the theatre. Their discussion brought Hannah back to life again and she actually seemed to be enjoying the visit to the restaurant. When she glanced around, a number of people were staring at her. Those who realised who she was were smiling at her, while those who didn't recognise Hannah simply found her beauty arresting. Between them, the other patrons helped her to blossom.

The meal was excellent and the wine superb. Paul felt that he'd at last regained the woman he loved. Hannah was as vibrant as ever. It was as if she'd forgotten all about the manager's rebuff. She was starting to make the most of her time in Bath. Then a man and woman, who'd been sitting on the opposite side of the room, rose to leave and made a point of going past Hannah's table. The woman simply gazed at her in admiration, but the man brushed against her so gently that she hardly felt his touch. For the best part of a minute, she kept on talking. Then she stopped abruptly and looked towards the exit.

'What's wrong?' asked Paul.

'That man touched me on purpose.'

'I hardly noticed him.'

'Neither did I, but I've just realised who he must be.' Putting a hand to her mouth, she whispered behind it. 'It was *him*, Paul. I swear it.'

CHAPTER FIFTEEN

It was the second time that Paul had been alerted about the man, but there was a longer delay on this occasion. It turned out to be fatal. Leaping out of his seat, Paul charged across the room and almost collided with a waiter who'd just entered with bowls of soup on a tray. Paul mumbled an apology, then ran on. When he got into the street, light was fading badly, and he could only see people in fuzzy outline. He picked out a man and a woman just turning a distant corner. Haring after them, he caught them up and accosted them, realising at once that he'd stopped the wrong people. The man was far too old to be the highwayman. Both he and his wife were justifiably indignant at being challenged. Paul sent the couple on their way with a gesture of apology, then he dashed back to the restaurant, going past it until he came to the first turning. He rushed down it but all he could see was a cab fading away into the gloom. It was too far ahead of him to be caught. Paul was on fire with frustration.

He hurried back to the restaurant and found the head waiter.

'Is anything wrong, sir?' asked the man.

'Two people left the restaurant a minute ago,' said Paul. 'Do you happen to know who they were?'

'I'm afraid that I don't, sir.'

'Have you ever seen either of them before?'

'As far as I know,' said the other, 'the young lady has never been here before, but the gentleman was vaguely familiar. I thought that Miss Granville might have recognised him.'

'Why is that?'

'He was very handsome. He looked like an actor.'

Paul thanked him then went back into the dining area, collecting a lot of inquisitive glances as he did so. Hannah was crushed.

'Did he get away again?'

'Yes,' he said, sinking into his seat. 'They both disappeared.'

'So he's still at liberty.'

'I'm afraid so.'

'He's never going to leave me alone, is he?'

He studied her. 'Are you quite *sure* that it was him, Hannah?'

'Yes, I am.'

'But you never even looked at him properly.'

'He *touched* me, Paul. And he went out of his way to go past our table. They were seated over there,' she went on, pointing. 'The easiest way to leave was to go between those other tables. He must have seen me and bided his time. When he left, he made sure that he brushed past me.'

'There's another explanation for that.'

'I can't see one.'

'The head waiter believes that the man may be an actor. If that's true, he'd certainly have noticed you. He couldn't resist coming across to you and brushing against greatness.'

Hannah's conviction was momentarily shaken. She wondered if she'd been mistaken, after all. Certainty soon reasserted itself.

'It was definitely him, Paul.'

'I'm not so sure.'

'The thought that he's been sitting there and watching me all this time has made my blood run cold.'

'He was with a young woman, Hannah. She might even have been his wife. I don't recall his staring in this direction.'

'I can see how it happened,' she said, face puckered in thought. 'This is the finest restaurant in Bath. It's also the closest to our hotel. He must have realised we'd come here sooner or later.' Hannah grabbed his wrist. 'He was lying in wait for me.'

'That's mere supposition.'

'It's what highwaymen do – they arrange an ambush.'

'But he didn't ambush you, my love. He touched you accidentally. I think that your reaction was far too hasty. If he *was* the man you believe him to be,' said Paul, 'why would he risk breaking cover like that?'

Hannah paused to weigh up his argument before dismissing it.

'I want to leave,' she declared.

'But we haven't finished our meal.'

'I've lost my appetite.'

'Can't I at least drink my wine?'

She rose to her feet. 'Take me back to the hotel, please.'

'Hannah . . .'

'I want to leave *now*!'

On his return home, the first thing that Peter had to do was escort Abigail Saunders back to the Red Cow in a cab. The reunion with the former Clemency Parry had unlocked the woman's memory and she was able to confide much more information about the household in which she'd worked happily for so many years. Peter began to get a clearer picture of domestic life with George Parry.

'His daughter is a very beautiful woman,' he said. 'She must have attracted a number of suitors.'

'That's true, Mr Skillen.'

'Was there anybody in particular?'

'There was a gentleman who'd once worked with her father. He came to the house from time to time. Miss Parry, as I knew her, was fond of him, but it . . . never went any further.'

'So this gentleman was her father's choice of a husband?'

'Yes, he was.'

'That must have been another reason why he was so angry when his daughter chose someone else. She not only rejected the man he preferred, she fell in love with a foreigner. That must have hurt him.'

'It did, sir.'

Peter could see that she was dying to ask him a question but lacked the confidence to do so. He told her what she obviously wished to know.

'My search was futile,' he confessed. 'I'm afraid that I didn't manage to find Joseph Rafter.'

'What about his brother?'

'Oh, I finally located him, but I might have saved myself the effort. Nicholas Rafter told me that he and Joseph lost touch with each other many years ago. They hate each other, apparently.'

'Why?'

'He didn't say.'

'Is there any other way to find Joseph?'

'I hope so.'

Arriving in Wapping, Peter helped her out of the cab and asked the driver to wait while he took her into the tavern. He handed her over to her sister, who was in her element in the riotous atmosphere. Abigail cringed at the sight and noise of inebriated, leering men. Peter left the Red Cow and spent the journey home reviewing what the servant had told him. When he got back to his house, he discovered that Mungo Darwood had left and that Charlotte was waiting with Clemency and her chaperon for her husband to join them for dinner. During the meal, they tried to keep off the subject of the search and were instead diverted by a demonstration of Clemency's fluency in Dutch. Since his command of English was poor, she spoke to Jacob in his native language. When Peter and Charlotte tried to learn a few words in Dutch, they failed miserably to master the correct pronunciation. The others were highly amused.

It was only when he and Charlotte retired to bed that they could talk in private at last.

'Clemency seemed happier,' she said.

'That was because she was able to hear about her father from people she regarded as friends. Abigail always liked her and, I suspect, found the notion of a secret romance rather exciting.'

'I don't think you could say that of Mr Darwood.'

'Perhaps not, but he knew her father well and talked about him with such affection. That bolstered Clemency, I believe,' said

Peter. 'As for real happiness, she'll never achieve that until she finds out the truth about her father.'

'And what *is* that truth, Peter?'

'I honestly don't know.'

'Clemency has suffered a great deal since she came to London,' said Charlotte. 'One setback has followed another. I'm just glad that we've been able to relieve that suffering a little.'

'You've been largely responsible for that,' he said, planting a grateful kiss on her cheek. 'Because she trusts you so much, she's been able to open her heart.'

'She can't believe that I don't condemn her for what she did. Clemency is afraid that everyone else does.'

'Abigail Saunders doesn't condemn her – and neither does Mr Darwood. He accepts the situation for what it is. Hopefully, that will stop her from wallowing in recriminations. The fact that she left Amsterdam the moment she heard of her father's death shows how much she still loved him,' said Peter. 'She came here fearing hostility and criticism, yet she's met neither so far.'

'What surprised me is that – when she first arrived in London – she didn't try to get in touch with Mr Taylor.'

'I can do that on her behalf.'

'From what we were told, I got the impression that he'd been very close to Mr Parry at one time. Why didn't Clemency seek him out?'

'As a close friend of her father, it may be that he disapproved of what she did. Inevitably, many people must have done that. Talking of her husband,' he continued, 'how did they manage to conduct a clandestine romance when he was so far away?'

'They wrote to each other.'

'Mr Parry would never have condoned that.'

192

'That's why the letters never came to the house. Her cousin, Millicent, was her confidante. She posted all of Clemency's letters to Amsterdam and any replies went to her house.'

'Was the uncle aware of the subterfuge?'

'He more or less instigated it, Peter.'

'I can see why he and his brother fell out.'

'Mr Parry was incensed. Tempers did cool somewhat in time, but his brother died before they could settle their differences. Clemency's aunt hailed from Scotland. After her husband's death, she and her family returned there. That's why Clemency could get no help from them when she arrived here. They were hundreds of miles away.'

'No wonder she felt lost in London.'

'Clemency said she'd forgotten more than she remembered.'

'She owed a lot to her cousin and even more to her uncle, perhaps. He made her marriage possible. At least we didn't have that problem with *your* father,' he went on. 'He raised no objections to me.'

'How do you know that?'

'You said that he liked me from the start.'

'Not entirely,' she teased. 'When he first met you, my father thought you were too set in your ways and too opinionated.'

'I'm neither of those things.'

'His other concern was that you were unreliable.'

Peter laughed. 'He must have been thinking of Paul,' he said. 'We're often mistaken for each other.'

Though they'd been back in their room for a couple of hours, they were nowhere near retiring to their beds. Hannah was still worrying about the incident in the restaurant and Paul was unable to soothe her. When he tried to shift the conversation to the theatre, all that he did was set off a second source of anguish.

'How can I possibly face that devious woman tomorrow?' she moaned. 'Mr Teale will doubtless have told her about my attempt at getting her removed, and she'll be smirking in triumph.'

'That is simply not true,' he said. 'To begin with, the manager is far more discreet. He's handled situations like this before. Mr Teale would never dream of telling Miss Ingram about your demand.'

'She'll find out somehow.'

'Show more faith in the manager. As for Miss Ingram, the best way to deal with her is to kill her with kindness. Throughout the rehearsals, be excessively pleasant to her – then act her off the stage once you get in front of an audience.'

Hannah smiled. 'That's the best advice you've given me, Paul.'

'She's here to stay. You must accept that.'

'I do so with the utmost reluctance.'

'I'm sure that Miss Ingram will pose no problem. Like everyone else in the cast, she's aware of the ordeal you faced on the journey here. She admires you for carrying on so bravely. Lots of actresses in your position would have been quite unable to fulfil their commitments.'

'At this moment in time, I feel that *I* am.'

'That doesn't sound like the Hannah Granville that I know,' he said, putting an arm around her shoulder.

They were seated on the sofa and he believed that it was a hopeful sign. For the first hour or so, she'd marched relentlessly up and down the room and gesticulated wildly. Simply getting her to sit down had been an achievement, but it was only an interim stage.

'It's late,' he said, softly. 'We're both very tired.'

'How can I possibly sleep?'

'You could at least try.'

'My mind is in turmoil.' She turned guiltily towards him. 'Oh, it's so unfair on you, Paul. Instead of being home in London, you've had to stay here, putting up with my bad temper and my endless complaints. It must be unbearable.'

'I'd rather be with you than without you, my love.'

'But you were right in what you said a few moments ago.'

'I said lots of things.'

'You told me that I didn't sound like the person you know.'

'That's true. As a rule, whenever you encounter unfavourable circumstances, you always fight back – not in this case, however. Something has happened to your resilience, Hannah, and it's worrying. You were so indomitable in the past.'

'Being robbed by highwaymen made me feel powerless,' she explained. 'You keep telling me to put the experience behind me, but I simply can't when that man is still hounding me.'

'Let's not get into that argument again,' he pleaded. 'We've spent far too long on it already. You know my view. The person who touched you in the restaurant was not the highwayman.'

'But it was, Paul. Look at the sequence of events. Firstly, he stands out there and stares up at our window. Secondly, he sends me that brooch. Thirdly, this evening, he ogles me in a restaurant.'

'He was with someone else, Hannah, and he certainly wasn't ogling you.'

'You must trust my instinct, Paul.'

'I prefer to rely on my own,' he said, stoutly. 'The highwayman who robbed you chose his moment carefully and had all the advantages. He took the coachman by surprise and had armed confederates with him. There was no such help available in the

195

restaurant. If anything, the lady would have hampered his escape. And you were not defenceless this time because I was sitting beside you.'

'That's true,' she admitted, reluctantly.

'If you'd recognised him earlier, I'd have had no trouble catching him.' He pulled her close. 'Are you listening to me this time?'

'Yes, Paul.'

'It would have been folly on his part to give himself away.'

'But I felt so certain . . .'

'It was not him, Hannah,' he said, firmly. 'You have my word.'

'What about the man I saw through the window?'

'You were mistaken, my love.'

'I suppose that I must have been.'

'I've made progress at last,' he said, giving her a gentle kiss.

'I'm sorry I kept you up so late.'

'All I want is for you to feel better.'

She cupped his face in her hands. 'Thank you, Paul.'

As they stood up, she began to drift across to the window. She was just about to tug back the curtain when Paul clicked his tongue. Hannah went back to him. When Paul was there, she felt, she had nothing whatsoever to fear.

Staying out of sight, the man in the street below watched the upstairs window until light finally disappeared from it. He then turned on his heel and walked slowly away from the hotel.

Harry Scattergood's night had been productive. He'd broken into two houses with comparative ease and entered a third by climbing up to an open attic window. Back in his room, he laid out everything on the bed and counted his takings. It was a sizeable haul. St Albans would be a rich source of booty. The only thing it lacked was a wonderful woman like Welsh Mary to take the edge off his exhilaration.

The Runners were back at St Saviour's Church early next morning and they brought Chevy Ruddock with them this time. The three of them scoured the churchyard for the best hiding place. In the far corner was the shed where the gravedigger kept his tools. It had no window but, if the door was left ajar, it would allow anyone inside to see every part of the churchyard. The three of them strode across to the shed. It was unlocked so they were able to open the door. Ruddock ducked his head to go inside but retreated quickly.

'It stinks in there!' he exclaimed. 'It's as if some animal has died and rotted.'

'You'll get used to it,' said Yeomans.

'Do I have to spend all night alone in that shed?'

'No, it's too dangerous to be on your own. You need help to tackle the bodysnatchers.'

'We've got the ideal man for you,' said Hale. 'Bill Filbert.'

'He's far too old, sir. Bill will fall asleep.'

'That's why you have to stay awake, Chevy.'

'Yes,' added Yeomans, 'we've gone for a blend of youth and experience. You and Bill Filbert have well worked together before. As long as we keep him sober, Bill won't let us down.'

'How long must I stay here, Mr Yeomans?'

'It could be one night or a matter of weeks.'

Ruddock gasped. 'Weeks in that pigsty?'

'Put a peg on your nose.'

'What is Agnes going to say?'

'You're not having your wife in there as well. That's forbidden.'

'I'm talking about the stench. If I go home smelling of that, she won't let me anywhere near her.' They laughed coarsely. 'It's no joke.'

'Denial is good for the soul,' said Hale.

'In any case,' suggested Yeomans, 'there's an easy solution. You can either take a bath in the river before you go home, or you buy yourself a supply of perfume. That will hide any unpleasant odours. And there's another advantage – when she inhales the perfume, your wife will think that the Angel Gabriel has come to pleasure her.'

Jem Huckvale proved his worth immediately. Thrilled to be working with Peter once again, he was told what progress had so far been made, then was sent off in search of Geoffrey Taylor. All that he had to guide him were some rather incoherent directions from Mungo Darwood. Peter expected that it might take him all morning to find the place but Huckvale came galloping back in less than an hour. Both of them then rode off towards the docks. The engineering works consisted of a couple of converted warehouses not far from the water's edge. As the visitors entered, there was a grating hullabaloo from the men at their workbenches.

When he heard why they'd come, Taylor invited both men into his office where there was marginally less noise. He was a short, fidgety, intense man who seemed far too old to be still in work.

'I know what you're thinking,' he said. 'Why is a man of my age still coming here six days a week when I could be at home leading a life of leisure?'

'What's the answer, Mr Taylor?' asked Peter.

'I love engineering. It's the reason that George Parry and I got on so well together. We were two of a kind. We lived for our work.' He pulled a face. 'In his case, alas, the magic eventually wore off.'

'We've discovered that.'

'I could kick myself for not realising that George was in such trouble. If he needed money, he only had to ask, but there was a stubborn streak in the man that stopped him doing so. By the time I learnt what had become of him,' he said, 'it was too late.'

'Could you tell us something about his work, please?'

'I should have thought that his daughter would have done that, Mr Skillen. She must have been aware of his achievements.'

'According to her,' said Peter, 'she took very little interest in his career. The one thing she did remember was being taken to Oxford on one occasion to see a bridge that her father had designed.'

'He was very proud of that,' said Taylor, 'and rightly so. After hundreds of years, the old stone bridge was unsafe and close to collapse. I was commissioned to replace it and asked George to submit a design. He came up with the notion of an iron bridge that would be much stronger and far more durable yet still have a certain beauty about it. That bridge encapsulated the journey he'd made in his career, starting as a mason and moving on to leave stone behind and embrace new materials. It's exactly what Thomas Telford did before him.'

'I've heard of him,' Huckvale piped up. 'He built canals.'

'He built everything that a civil engineer could build, young man, and he's still doing it. As we speak, talks are being held to create an Institution of Civil Engineers and Mr Telford will be the obvious choice as its first president.'

'Tell us more about Mr Parry,' urged Peter.

'He was a master of his craft, Mr Skillen. When he put his mind to it, there was nothing he couldn't do, always finding a way to give a structure an individual touch that made it stand out. He was as much an artist as an engineer.'

'I was told he had a gift for invention.'

'He had everything,' said Taylor, 'which is why it was always a delight to employ him.'

He went on to list some of his friend's countless achievements, astounding Peter and Jem with the range and quantity of his work. Taylor was ashamed that he'd not heard about Parry's downfall before it was too late to help him. He wished that he'd been able to speak at his funeral so that people knew what a huge loss Parry's death represented to the world of civil engineering. In spite of the temptation, Peter decided against passing on his belief that Parry might still be alive in case he was raising false hopes.

'You've told us about his virtues,' remarked Peter. 'What about his vices? Did he have any of those?'

'We all have vices, I fear.'

'What were they in his case, Mr Taylor?'

'He was too single-minded.'

'That can be a good thing in some instances, surely?'

'I agree, Mr Skillen. It enabled him to concentrate on the job in hand and that was sometimes to the detriment of his family. His wife loved him, but she also resented his obsession with his work.' Taylor gave a wry smile. 'My own wife makes the same complaint about me.'

'What other defects did Mr Parry have?'

'He could be blinkered and hated compromise. But he was an essentially good fellow at heart.'

'Was he a cruel man by nature?'

'I suppose there's cruelty involved if you treat other people's ideas with disdain and he was sometimes guilty of that. There were complaints about his manner.'

'I was thinking about his treatment of his daughter.'

Taylor's jaw tightened. 'That was an unfortunate business.'

'You think he was right to oppose her choice of husband?'

'I *know* that he was, Mr Skillen.'

Peter was surprised. 'Really?'

'You obviously don't know the full story.'

'What is it?'

'Clemency had as good as given her word to another suitor,' said Taylor, solemnly. 'She discarded him as if he'd never existed. That was unpardonable in my view. The suitor in question happened to be my son.'

Peter was shocked. 'I see.'

'I don't know what tales she's been telling you, but she's not the innocent party she pretends to be. Indeed, one could argue that she was partly responsible for what happened to her father. She drove him to an early grave. If, as you say, his daughter is staying with you,' he warned, 'then you are harbouring an evil woman in your house. Clemency van Emden has blood on her hands.'

CHAPTER SIXTEEN

Given the problems she'd faced in the last few days, Hannah Granville was not looking forward to a second rehearsal. She believed that the manager would be very angry with her for demanding the removal of another member of the cast and that Elinor Ingram would take the opportunity to crow over her. In fact, the opposite happened. When she sailed into the rehearsal room that morning, there was a collective swell of affection towards her. Vernon Teale was even more attentive and obliging, while Elinor Ingram was subdued and respectful. Hannah began to feel at home. All thought of the highwayman had flitted away from her mind. She felt so confident that she relieved Paul of the task of staying there to safeguard her.

He took advantage of the unexpected freedom to learn more about the ambush on the highway. Teale had already given him an address where he'd find Roderick Cosgrove, so he went straight to the man's house. Small, ugly and neglected, it was a far cry from the dwellings owned by the elite of Bath society. The bodyguard only ever ventured into the more prosperous areas of the city when he was employed there. In response to the knock on his door, Cosgrove opened it himself and was taken aback to see Paul standing there.

'Oh, good morning, sir,' he said, recognising his visitor.

'I was hoping to have a word with you, Cosgrove.'

'I've no objection to that, sir.'

'Might I step inside?'

'That's not really . . . convenient,' said the other, glancing over his shoulder. 'I have company.'

'I've never been one to come between a man and his pleasures,' said Paul, with an understanding smile.

'Thank you, Mr Skillen. Now, what can I do for you?'

'I'd like more detail of the robbery.'

'Miss Granville will have told you everything.'

'Yes, but it was the account of a terrified woman still shaking in her shoes at what happened. As a former soldier, you're far more accustomed to coping with a crisis. You know how to hold your nerve.'

'It nearly cost me a serious injury,' said Cosgrove, holding up his bandaged hand. 'Luckily, it was only a flesh wound. I might well have lost a finger or two.'

'When did you first realise there was danger?'

'It was not until the three of them suddenly appeared.'

'Have you ever been in that situation before?'

'Yes, Mr Skillen. A coach I was in was attacked several months ago.'

'Was it at the same spot?'

'No, sir, it was much closer to Bristol.'

'What happened?'

'Luckily, we fought them off.'

'Tell me – in your own words – about the latest incident.'

Frowning in concentration, Cosgrove ran a meditative hand across his face. When he spoke, he gave a straightforward report of the ambush. It tallied in every way with what Paul had heard from Hannah, though it was delivered in a much more measured tone. There were some new details and Paul was grateful for them.

'Could you describe the three men?' he asked.

'I didn't have the time to look at them properly, sir. To be honest, I was too busy trying to stem the blood from my hand.'

'Could you hazard a guess as to their ages?'

'Their leader would be around your age, Mr Skillen, but the other two were older.'

'Miss Granville told me that they were both uncouth whereas their leader was clearly educated. Do you agree?'

'Yes, I do.'

'Would you recognise any of them again?'

'I don't think so, sir. They wore hats and masks.'

'What about their horses?'

'They weren't so easy to disguise. I might be able to pick one of them out because it was ridden by their leader. It was a black stallion with a white blaze.'

'Then you can start looking for it right here in the city,' advised Paul, 'because their leader lives in Bath. The chances are that his two accomplices do as well.'

Cosgrove was startled. 'How do you know that?'

'We have evidence of the leader's presence.'

'Then you'd best keep clear of him, sir.'

'On the contrary,' said Paul, 'I'm looking forward to meeting him one day. I've a score to settle with him.'

'He's a hard man, sir. For all his educated voice and manners, he's as ruthless as the others.'

'Yet he spared you, didn't he?'

'I was lucky. People who try to fight back often get punished for doing so. Last year a guard was shot dead.'

'You have a dangerous profession.'

Cosgrove smiled. 'I'm not complaining.'

'Mr Teale said that he often employs you.'

'That's right, sir. I work at the theatre from time to time, looking out for pickpockets and making sure everyone behaves themselves. I get to see all the plays free. That's a bonus.'

'I'm sure you'll enjoy *As You Like It*.'

'How is Miss Granville? Has she recovered from the shock yet?'

'Oh, yes. She's rehearsing at this very moment.'

'That's good to hear, Mr Skillen.'

'Nobody is more relieved than me,' said Paul. 'Since I won't be needed as a bodyguard every hour of the day, I can start looking for the highwaymen who robbed your coach.'

Cosgrove was eager. 'Count on me, if you need help, Mr Skillen.'

'I'll bear that offer in mind.'

The visit to the engineering works had been a revelation. They'd not only learnt a great deal about George Parry's career, they'd been forced to look at his daughter in a slightly different way. As soon as they'd met her, both of them had warmed to Clemency, but

Geoffrey Taylor had been highly critical of her. It now transpired that her father had not been the only person who felt betrayed by her choice of husband.

They returned to the gallery to discuss the latest development with Gully Ackford. The latter was not surprised.

'I had a feeling there was another side to the story,' he said.

'Mr Taylor was very bitter,' recalled Huckvale.

'Yes,' said Peter, 'it would have suited him to have her as his daughter-in-law. He and Mr Parry would have been drawn closer. Mr Taylor clearly idolised the man.'

'I'd like to see that bridge he talked about.'

'It's a long way to go, Jem.'

'And what was that place Mr Taylor mentioned?'

'Ironbridge – it's in Shropshire. Mr Parry drew a lot of inspiration from Abraham Darby, the man who built it. He visited Ironbridge and Coalbrookdale, where the castings were made.'

'Give me wood and stone any day,' grumbled Ackford. 'They've served us well for centuries. Coming back to what you learnt this morning,' he went on, 'what are you going to do about it?'

'What would *you* do, Gully?' asked Peter.

'Nothing.'

'Nothing at all?'

'I don't see the point. It all happened years ago and is none of our business. If you challenge Mrs van Emden about it, you'll simply upset her. Your only interest should be her father, not some discarded suitor.'

'One thing is explained,' said Peter. 'When Mr Taylor's name was mentioned yesterday by Mr Darwood, she was not keen to talk about him.'

'Now we know why,' said Huckvale.

'We have contradictory opinions here. Mr Darwood, who was a close friend of Mr Parry, obviously likes his daughter and has no qualms about the decision she made with regard to a husband. Mr Taylor, on the other hand, paints her as a scheming woman with no concern for the feelings of other people.'

'That's not how I see her.'

'Nor me, Jem.'

'But she's obviously been avoiding Mr Taylor,' said Ackford. 'He had close ties with her father. When she first came to London, she ought to have gone straight to him for help.'

'It would have been too embarrassing for her,' said Peter.

'So what are you going to do?'

'I'll do what any sensible husband should do, Gully.'

'And what's that?'

'I'll confide in my wife. Charlotte needs to know what we discovered this morning.'

'I've just thought of something,' said Huckvale, blurting out the words before he could stop himself. The others looked at him. 'We've all wondered who sent that message to Mrs van Emden, telling her about her father's death.'

'Go on,' encouraged Peter.

'It must have been someone who hated her.'

'I don't think it was Mr Taylor, if that's what you're about to suggest, Jem. It's just not in his character.'

'What about his son? He's the one with the real grudge.'

Chevy Ruddock was a dedicated, public-spirited officer, but William Filbert had lost the sense of duty that had impelled him to join the foot patrol. When he took Filbert to the churchyard, all that Ruddock heard from the old man were grunts of discontent.

'I hate places like this,' he said. 'They give me the shakes.'

'It may not be for long, Bill.'

'Two minutes is long enough for me. The sight of all these gravestones reminds me that I'll need one myself very soon.'

'You've years left in you yet,' said Ruddock, 'and you won't have to stare at the gravestones. They'll be invisible in the dead of night.'

'Then how are we supposed to see the bodysnatchers?'

'We'll hear them, Bill. Spades make a lot of noise.'

'Where will we be hiding?'

'Over there in that shed.'

Filbert squinted at the rickety shed and let out a snort of contempt. It was the reaction that Ruddock had expected. His companion was known for his habit of moaning at every assignment he was given. There would be a loud protest when he actually put his head inside the shed and inhaled its stench. Notwithstanding the man's defects, however, Ruddock was happy to be working alongside him again. He'd always learnt from the experienced Filbert and knew that the older man would not shirk a fight.

'It was my suggestion, you know,' he said.

'Mr Yeomans told me it was his.'

'I thought of it first.'

'You're an honest man, Chevy. I'd rather believe you.'

'Thank you, Bill.'

'You have to watch them – him and Mr Hale. They always steal ideas and pretend they were theirs in the first place. I'm not saying your plan will work, mind you, but – if it does – Mr Kirkwood ought to be told that you thought of it first.'

'The chief magistrate won't pay attention to me.'

'Then you'll have to make him,' said the other. 'Let's go across to that shed and see what it's like inside.'

'I have to warn you about a nasty smell.'

Filbert bridled. 'Are you telling me that I stink a bit?'

'No, I'm warning you about the shed. It reeks in there.'

'Then I'll have to bring my pipe and baccy with me. The best way to get rid of a nasty smell is to make a nice one. You see?' said Filbert with a throaty chuckle. 'You're not the only one who has good ideas.'

It was during a break for refreshment that Hannah had her first proper conversation with Elinor Ingram. When they'd spoken earlier, they had, for the most part, been using words set down for them by William Shakespeare. This time they could rely on their own.

'I thought you should know that I was reluctant to accept a role in this production,' said Elinor, with an air of deference. 'We've had misunderstandings in the past that I deeply regret, and I didn't wish to discountenance you by turning up unannounced in the cast.'

'That was very considerate of you,' said Hannah, guardedly.

'What changed my mind was the fact that I had the opportunity to play opposite someone whose talent I revere. I always gain so much from you, Miss Granville. It's an education as well as a pleasure.'

'That's very kind of you to say so.'

'I can speak for the whole cast.'

'I'd rather you just spoke for yourself,' said Hannah, with a slight edge. 'And flattery is quite unnecessary. I know my qualities.'

'Then let me just say this: because I'm aware of your attitude towards me, I promise that I will keep well out of your way throughout our time together. If I can make a small contribution to the success of this production, I'll be thrilled to do so, but that is all I ask.'

There was a quiet sincerity in her voice that impressed Hannah. She'd always regarded the woman as designing and highly competitive. Had she changed since they'd last met? It did seem possible.

'One last thing,' said Elinor, looking her in the eye, 'and you don't have to make an instant decision. In view of what's happened between us, you might still wish that you'd prefer me to disappear. If that is the case, I'll withdraw at once, but I'd hate to let Mr Teale down. He has faith in me and may find it difficult to hire an adequate replacement. But your feelings are paramount here, Miss Granville. If my presence offends you in any way, then it is better that I surrender Celia to someone else.' She glanced towards the manager. 'It will mean that I can never work for Mr Teale again, I daresay, but . . . I'll survive somehow.'

Pursing her lips, she gave a little shrug, then walked away.

Hannah was utterly bewildered.

Charlotte Skillen had spent so much time firing questions at her guest that she began to feel she was violating the laws of hospitality, and that it would be better for Clemency to volunteer information instead of having it extracted from her. Since it was a fine, warm day, Charlotte took her into the garden and showed her around.

'I love the artful way that it's been arranged,' said Clemency. 'It's a feast for the eye and that secret bower is delightful.'

'It's where I sit and read – if ever I get the chance, that is.'

'Did your husband design the garden?'

'Oh, no,' said Charlotte, with a laugh, 'Peter never has time to do anything like that. What you see is what I somehow dreamt up.'

'I'm very impressed.'

'I did borrow ideas from friends, Clemency, especially when it came to the choice of flowers and shrubs. My aim was to make the garden seem much bigger than it actually is.'

'You've succeeded.'

'Thank you.'

They strolled around the flower beds once more and discussed the merits of various trees. Clemency seemed well informed on the subject. She stopped abruptly and turned to more personal matters.

'How did you first meet your husband?' she asked.

'It was at a ball,' replied Charlotte. 'I noticed what an excellent dancer Peter was, and he was kind enough to admire my skills as well. He was charming. I longed for an opportunity to meet him again. When it came, however, I was in for a disappointment.'

'Why was that?'

'He no longer danced as well. In fact, he was hopeless.'

'What had happened to him?'

'Nothing at all,' said Charlotte, laughing. 'What I hadn't realised was that the man I saw on the second occasion was not Peter at all. It was his twin brother, Paul. It's almost impossible to tell them apart.'

'Can you do so now?'

'Oh, yes, I'd never confuse them. At the time, it was different. Both Peter and Paul took an interest in me and I was never quite sure which of them was actually wooing me. In the end, I chose Peter.'

'I think you made the right choice, Charlotte. You and he seem to be ideally suited. I like to think the same may be said of Jan and me.'

'You always sound so happy when you talk of your husband.'

'Oh, I am.'

'In order to marry him, you must have spurned a lot of suitors here in London. Had you turned down any other proposals?'

'I'd rather not say,' replied the other, turning away. 'I think I'd like to go back indoors now, if you don't mind.'

Charlotte was shocked by her sudden anger.

The summons from Bow Street made the Runners respond promptly. When they got to Kirkwood's office, they learnt that he was still in court, giving them time to speculate on why they'd been called on. Yeomans had brought the report given to him earlier. The door opened and Kirkwood strutted in, sitting at his desk as if lowering himself onto a throne.

'Do you know what happened last night?' he asked.

Hale smiled ingratiatingly. 'We hope that you slept well, sir.'

'The wonder is that I slept at all. I see that you've returned my report,' he said, gazing at the document. 'I can now add a postscript.'

'What is it, sir?'

'Last night, no less than three graves were robbed in London. That means three families have had their grief intensified and three circles of friends are in despair. You failed them again.'

'We were not on duty last night, sir,' said Yeomans.

'The bodysnatchers knew that. We failed those three families.'

'It's not our fault, sir. We don't have enough men at our disposal. There are just too many churches in London and too many people dying. However,' he went on, deciding to reveal their plan as a means of defence, 'we've set a trap for these night-time monsters.'

'It was Micah's brainwave,' said Hale.

Yeomans beamed. 'I have them from time to time.'

'I hadn't noticed,' said Kirkwood, sourly. 'What is this trap?'

'We've chosen St Saviour's church in Tottenham as our first location. If the venture is crowned with success, there'll be lots of others.'

He went on to describe what they'd done. Kirkwood was at first horrified by the notion, fearing that they'd bring the Archbishop of Canterbury down upon their heads. When he heard that they would not take part in any form of a funeral service, his doubts slowly fell away. Yeomans pointed out an additional benefit.

'We may only catch two of them the first time,' he conceded, 'but they'll know others in the same trade, so I'll be able to beat a list of names out of them – names of villains who dig up dead bodies and names of anatomists who pay them to do it.'

'It does sound promising,' admitted Kirkwood.

'Two of our best men will be on duty tonight, sir,' said Hale. 'Ruddock and Filbert are ideal for this kind of work.'

'Would that be *Chevy* Ruddock?'

'Yes, sir.'

'I remember him helping to foil an escape bid here in Bow Street. He's a young man to watch. I applaud your choice of him.'

'I had thought to lie concealed in that churchyard myself,' said Yeomans, annoyed at the praise showered on Ruddock, 'but my old bones don't like the cold night air. I'll come into my own when I interrogate the captives.'

'Well, you seem to have taken positive steps for once.'

'Thank you, sir,' said the other.

'The moment you catch anybody, I wish to be informed. And I'll also be interested to hear how Ruddock conducted himself in that churchyard. Young men of such promise deserve to be rewarded for their good deeds. Don't you agree?'

Yeomans could only manage a low gurgle.

* * *

Paul had been scouring the city. When he'd spoken to Cosgrove, he'd gone in search of the woman whose diamond brooch had been stolen during the ambush. In the course of the first stage of their journey, she'd told Hannah where she'd be staying in Bath, so Paul was able to find her, hand over her brooch and receive her gushing thanks. He refused to say how the jewellery had come into his possession, merely that he had recovered it. She was delighted and offered him a reward that he declined to take.

He spent the rest of the morning perambulating around the more fashionable part of the city, believing that the highwayman was a Regency buck whose expensive tastes were supported by his criminal activities. He also looked for a black stallion with a white blaze, but saw none being ridden by the kind of person he was after. Acting on Hannah's description of the man, he came across several possible contenders, but none who gave him that tingle of recognition. Eventually, he walked back to the hotel where he found Hannah in a state of indecision.

'Something extraordinary has happened,' she said.

'Yes,' he said, gallantly. 'I met you.'

'Listen to me, Paul. This is serious.'

'Are you saying my adoration of Hannah Granville is not serious?'

She squeezed him hard. '*Listen*, will you?'

Hannah sat him down on the sofa and stood over him. She told him about her strange encounter with Elinor Ingram. He was at once amazed and amused.

'I can't believe it, my love,' he said. 'When you try to have that woman flung out of the cast, your demand is refused. After you've agreed to accept the manager's judgement, Miss Ingram comes to you and offers to go of her own accord. In other words, I needn't have bothered to have that awkward conversation with Mr Teale.'

His brow corrugated. 'Do you think that he put her up to it?'

'I'm certain that he didn't, Paul. He's determined to keep her, as you found out. No manager wishes to be left in the lurch. If she walks out, he has to begin a search all over again.'

'He won't be very pleased with Miss Ingram.'

'He'll never forgive her.'

'Then it's an astonishing act of self-sacrifice on her part.'

'I'm not convinced of that.'

'In that case, accept her offer and bid her farewell.'

'Don't be so hasty.'

'I've remembered everything you told me about that woman,' he said. 'She stirred up trouble whenever you worked together. She deceived you, lied to you, reviled you behind your back and – you once hinted to me – she stole away a man who'd taken an interest in you.'

She flicked a hand. 'That was years ago,' she said, scornfully, 'and I never really cared for him. I was glad to see him go.'

'Elinor Ingram is your enemy. Get rid of her.'

'I'm very tempted to do that, Paul.'

'Why do you hesitate?'

Breaking away, Hannah walked around the room and was deep in thought for a while. When she finally came back to him, she introduced some new information.

'I spoke to one of the other actresses,' she said.

'What did she tell you?'

'Elinor has been very ill. She was unable to work for over six months. That's an eternity for anyone in this profession, Paul. Our careers onstage are short enough as it is. Every minute counts. To be forced to watch others thrive while you suffer is a form of purgatory. Part of me,' she confessed, 'was glad to hear the bad tidings, but another part scolded me for my lack of feeling. That woman is lucky to be alive.'

'I still believe that you should let her go.'

'I'm thinking of the trouble it would cause Mr Teale.'

'You didn't care about that when you demanded he got rid of her.'

'My attitude has softened.'

'You've got what you want, Hannah. Seize it with both hands.'

'It feels so . . . cruel.'

'What's got into you?' he asked. 'I've never seen you dithering like this before. Why can't you make a simple decision?'

She looked helpless. 'I don't know . . .'

CHAPTER SEVENTEEN

Peter Skillen returned home to learn that Clemency van Emden had withdrawn to her room with a show of temper, leaving Charlotte alone for once. While puzzled by the behaviour of their guest, he was pleased to be able to talk freely to his wife. She explained what had happened in the garden and feared that she'd lost Clemency's friendship.

'It wasn't your fault,' said Peter. 'How were you to know that you'd touched on a sensitive subject?'

'Clemency asked me how I met you and I told her. It seemed only natural that I'd ask about her courtship.'

'I can tell you something about that. Before she met her future husband, she'd been very close to a young man named Neville

Taylor.' Charlotte's eyes widened. 'Yes, it was Mr Taylor's son.'

'How close were they?'

'According to his father, Clemency had more or less accepted a proposal from him. He's still embittered at the way his son was cast uncaringly aside.'

'I can't believe that Clemency behaved like that.'

'I'm only quoting Mr Taylor.'

'She's such a caring person.'

'He believes that she should have obeyed her father. In refusing to do so, she contributed towards his death.'

'But, in spite of everything, she loved him.'

'Taylor told us that she had blood on her hands.'

'Clemency can't be held entirely responsible for what happened to her father. He was no angel, Peter. In a bid to prevent her marrying someone to whom he objected, he put her under immense pressure.'

'If she already had a suitor, his attitude is understandable. Marriage into the Taylor family would have been of advantage to Mr Parry. He must have felt embarrassed when she rejected Neville Taylor in favour of a complete stranger from a foreign country.'

'My sympathies are still with her.'

'It would have soured his relationship with Geoffrey Taylor.'

'Yet, according to Mr Darwood, it was Mr Taylor who wanted to set up a fund to help Clemency's father.'

'That's true. He still had the highest opinion of Mr Parry's skill as an engineer.'

'What sort of man was Mr Taylor?'

'He struck me as a decent, honest, hard-working person who'd built a successful business over the years. He was perfectly pleasant until Clemency's name came into the conversation.'

'What are you going to do – question her about Mr Taylor's son?'

'No, Charlotte,' he said. 'In view of the way she reacted to you earlier on, I'm going to keep well clear of her. I need more detail of what actually happened.'

'How can you possibly get that?'

'I'm hoping that Jem can do it for me. I've ask him to find Neville Taylor.'

'Does he have an address?'

'No, but he was very clever. The first thing we noticed when we found the engineering works was that the company trades as Geoffrey Taylor and Son. Neville is also an engineer. As we left the premises,' said Peter, 'Jem took the trouble to ask one of the employees where the son might be found. It transpires that he's supervising a project somewhere in Southwark. Jem will find him.'

Herein I see that thou lovest me not with the full weight that I lovest thee.

In the role of Celia, Elinor Ingram delivered the line with true feeling as if sending a personal message to Hannah Granville's Rosalind. The second scene of *As You Like It* brought the two of them together to discuss the banishment of Duke Senior, Rosalind's father. Many of the lines had a double meaning for the two actresses that nobody else would even notice. After brooding on her decision, Hannah had eventually given her sworn rival the benefit of the doubt and allowed her to remain part of the company. Elinor was profoundly grateful, rewarding Hannah by keeping out of her way when they were not actually playing a scene together and giving her best when they did. As time went on, Hannah felt more and more at ease. She was reassured that her decision had been the right one for the company. While she would never call the other woman a friend of hers, she no longer treated Elinor as an arch-enemy.

The rehearsal was followed by a discussion of costumes and Hannah was delighted with the designs she was shown. Before she was ready to leave, Vernon Teale took her aside.

'I do apologise for not speaking earlier,' he said, 'but, as you saw, my hands have been full. My wife and I would like to invite you and Mr Skillen to join us for dinner.'

'Thank you. We'll be delighted to accept.'

'Excellent.'

'We look forward to meeting Mrs Teale.'

'She's been begging for the opportunity to meet you. My wife is one of your most ardent admirers and will talk endlessly about the plays in which she's seen you in London.'

They arranged a time when she and Paul should arrive. Since the manager's house was within walking distance of the theatre, it would only take a matter of minutes to get there. Her pleasure was mingled with relief at the fact that Teale had made no reference at all to her demand to evict a member of the cast. She'd been forced to accept his ruling on the matter and he'd responded by pretending that the argument had never taken place. That suited her. Harmony had been restored and she was confident that her stay in Bath would now be a pleasurable one.

Paul was less optimistic. He had lingering doubts about Hannah's decision to allow Elinor Ingram to stay in the company, but had not dared to criticise it. His advice had been ignored and he had to accept that with good grace. In any case, a potentially troublesome actress like Elinor was not their major problem; the highwayman occupied that position. Of his presence in Bath, there could be no question. He'd returned Hannah's valise with a note of apology and sent her a gift stolen from one of the other passengers in the coach. What his next step would be was a matter for speculation, but there would definitely be one. Paul was certain of that. He was still not persuaded, however, that the man was bold enough to turn up at the restaurant where Hannah was most likely to dine, and contrive to brush past her. On reflection, he was glad that he'd been unable to catch up with the couple who'd left the restaurant on the previous day.

Having walked around the city that morning, he chose to ride that afternoon, covering more ground and therefore seeing more people from his elevated position. Everyone seemed to be on display in Bath, strolling through the parks and gardens or being driven in a range of vehicles that allowed them to preen in public. When he first set out, he was more interested in horses than in their riders. A man could easily disguise himself, but a black stallion with a white blaze did not have that option. The first animal that had the necessary colouring was ridden by an elderly man with a paunch hanging over the front of the saddle. No sooner had Paul dismissed him as a suspect than another black horse came into view, its head marked with a vivid white blaze. A tall, lean man with a dark complexion was in the saddle. Close to Paul's age, he had the same bearing. He demanded more scrutiny.

After letting him ride past, he pulled on the reins to turn his own mount in a circle, then followed the man from a discreet distance. His pursuit was short-lived. Coming towards him within minutes was an almost identical horse with a rider even taller, leaner and darker of hue. Which one was he to follow? And how many others would he meet who might possibly be the man he sought? Bath seemed to be chock-full of such individuals. Unable to trail them all, Paul eventually abandoned the notion of tracking any of them.

It was time to give up and return to Hannah.

Because he was so short, slight and youthful, people tended to disregard Jem Huckvale, not realising how strong he was or how assertive he could be when occasion demanded. Equipped only with the information that Neville Taylor was working beside the river in Southwark, he began an intensive search of the area. After an hour in the saddle, he found the man at the rear of a large house, watching his men drain the bottom of the garden before creating a barrier to keep out the water in future. They'd erected some iron scaffolding and were using a steam-driven pump. Had he not been there for a purpose, Huckvale would have enjoyed watching the men at work. Instead, he approached their employer. Neville Taylor looked like a younger version of his father, with the same distinctive profile and the same air of self-possession.

When Huckvale introduced himself, he could see from the way Taylor looked at him that the man didn't take him seriously. He'd been schooled in what to say by Peter Skillen, so he pressed on, raising his voice for effect.

'I've brought news that may be of interest to you, sir,' he said.

'What news is that?'

'It seems that George Parry has died.'

'I'm sad to hear that,' said Taylor, 'but not, alas, surprised. My father and Mr Parry were close at one time. When is the funeral?'

'It may already have taken place, sir, but there is a problem. We don't know where and when the service took place. I work for private detectives hired to find out the truth of the matter.'

'I can't understand why there's any confusion.'

'It's too complicated to explain, sir,' said Huckvale. 'The simple fact is that his daughter has come all the way from Amsterdam to pay her respects at his grave and is unable to find where it is.'

Taylor was interested. 'Clemency is back in London?'

'She'll be here until we know what happened to her father.'

'Do you have access to her, Mr Huckvale?'

'Yes, sir, she's staying at the home of one of the people for whom I work. Mrs van Emden is being well looked after.'

'Is her husband with her?'

'He was unable to come.'

'I see,' said Taylor, thoughtfully. 'Is she in good health?'

'She's in very good health, sir, but her mind is troubled. You can imagine the shock she had when she was unable to find Mr Parry's last resting place. Mrs van Emden was even more upset by something she learnt from Mr Darwood, an old friend of her father's.'

'And what was that?'

'I don't need to tell you how she and Mr Parry fell out. She longed to be reconciled with him and wrote many letters. They never reached him, according to Mr Darwood.'

'Were they lost at sea, then?'

'No, sir,' said Huckvale. 'Somebody prevented Mr Parry from seeing them. As it was, he'd been writing to his daughter to say that he'd forgiven her, but she never received his letters either.'

Taylor was outraged. 'Some villain intercepted them?'

'So it appears.'

'Who was the rogue?'

'We don't yet know, Mr Taylor. It was someone bent on keeping father and daughter apart. We'll keep searching until we find him.'

'Thank you for telling me all this,' said Taylor. 'I had no idea that Clemency – Mrs van Emden – was here in London. It is years since we met and she may have forgotten me completely, but please give her my regards in any case. I hope that she soon finds out the truth of what actually happened to Mr Parry. As an engineer, he had few equals,' he went on, pointing a finger. 'That pump over there was his invention. It makes our job so much easier.'

'Do you have any message for Mrs van Emden, sir?'

Taylor was about to say something, then thought better of it.

'My warmest regards will suffice,' he said, quietly.

They stared into the open grave at the church of St Anne's and felt a twinge of guilt. In spite of the way they'd ordered their foot patrols to keep a special eye on the city's churchyards, three had been robbed during the night. This one – at the very heart of Westminster – was the scene of the most daring crime because St Anne's was no isolated church where bodysnatchers could work with relative safety. It was in a populous district where some people would always be abroad at night.

'How did they get away with it, Micah?' asked Hale.

'They worked quickly and quietly.'

'Somebody should still have seen or heard what was going on.'

'It rained heavily last night,' said Yeomans. 'Anyone out and about would have been more interested in hurrying home than in looking into a churchyard. There's another consideration, Alfred. Make allowance for people's fears. Many of them are scared to go anywhere near a place like this at night. They think that ghosts will rise up out of the earth.'

'One of them did rise up, so to speak. They sold the body for a profit. Surgeons pay well.'

'We must stamp the trade out somehow.'

'I agree,' said Hale. 'Whenever I think of my own funeral, I'm terrified that someone will dig me up and take me off to be cut into little pieces.'

'You wouldn't know a thing about it.'

'My wife and children would. I'd hate them to suffer that way.'

'Then make sure you stay alive until the law is changed to allow the use of cast iron coffins. That will deter the ghouls who make their living by ripping corpses out of the ground.'

'Mr Kirkwood told us that this was one of three graves plundered last night. The bodysnatchers go on and on unchecked. How many coffins will be unearthed tonight, I wonder?'

'We know of one that will escape – St Saviour's.'

'But we don't know that it will attract any interest, Micah.'

'Sooner or later, they will come,' said Yeomans. 'Once they get the smell of death in their nostrils, they can't stay away.'

'But there's no corpse being buried in St Saviour's. It's just a coffin with stones in.'

'That will be enough to bait the trap. Let's go and see the other two churchyards that were robbed last night. It's the work of the ungodly,' he went on, lapsing into homiletic mode, 'and they must be struck down by the righteous.'

Charlotte Skillen was still worried. Clemency was a guest in the house and therefore entitled to the utmost consideration. Charlotte blamed herself for speaking out of turn and causing the upset. At the same time, she was bound to wonder why her innocent question had provoked such a reaction. It had certainly revealed an unexpected aspect of Clemency's character. Evidently, there were things in her past that she wished to keep hidden.

When Clemency finally came down from her room, Charlotte

took care to keep the conversation on neutral subjects. For her part, Clemency didn't refer to what had occurred earlier in the garden. Chatting happily, she acted as if nothing untoward had happened. They adjourned to the drawing room and sat down.

'You lead such an adventurous life,' said Clemency. 'I envy you.'

'There's nothing to envy.'

'Yes, there is. You must be the only woman in London engaged in solving crimes or hunting for missing persons.'

'Some of our friends think that I'm mad. They believe that what I do is both dangerous and unladylike.'

'It's also very important.'

'We are there for anyone to hire,' said Charlotte. 'It means that we face new challenges all the time. We're never sure who will knock on the door of the gallery in search of help.'

'I'm so glad I found my way there.'

'So are we. Peter thinks that your father might still be alive.'

'Yes, I know.'

'Doesn't that possibility excite you?'

'It does and it doesn't, Charlotte. I'd hate to meet him in the wretched state that's been described to me. He was such a proud man. Now that he's lost everything, I'm sure that he wouldn't wish me to see him again.'

'But he hasn't lost everything, Clemency.'

'Yes, he has.'

'He's regained a daughter he loves,' said Charlotte. 'No matter what his condition, any father would be glad to do that.'

She saw the tears forming in the other woman's eyes.

Paul Skillen was delighted to hear that the afternoon's rehearsal had gone well. Though he still nursed doubts about the wisdom of allowing Elinor Ingram to continue as a member of the company, he saw virtue in the result.

'Mr Teale is grateful for your acceptance of his decision,' he said. 'This is his way of thanking you, Hannah,' he said.

'I don't follow.'

'Because you didn't try to get Miss Ingram ousted again, he's rewarding you by inviting us to dinner.'

'That's not true at all,' she argued. 'He issued the invitation for two reasons. The first is that I'm his leading lady and deserve the honour. The second is that his wife happens to be a great admirer of my work.'

'Then she's an unusual woman.'

'Why do you say that? Mrs Teale clearly appreciates the finer points of theatrical talent.'

'Most wives think that you should be feared rather than applauded, my love. You beguile their husbands so much. The manager is a perfect instance. Teale is clearly in thrall to you.'

'Then why didn't he agree to my demand?'

'Ah,' said Paul, 'that's a fair point.'

'And if he is really entranced by me,' she added, 'he'd hardly be so eager for me to meet his wife. Married men who take a real interest in me suddenly become lusty bachelors.'

'That's what sets me apart from the herd, Hannah. I'm a lusty bachelor who'd prefer to be a married man.'

She laughed. 'This is no time to make another proposal,' she said, kissing him lightly. 'I've told you before that I'm not ready to become Mrs Skillen just yet. I will do so in time, I promise you, but my career must come first. You accepted that.'

'I did so readily because I'm happy with our arrangement.'

'Is that true?'

'You know full well it is.'

'Your behaviour will be censored accordingly. You risk the disapproval of the public and the condemnation of the Church.'

Paul grinned. 'That's what makes it so infinitely appealing.'

Peter went back to the gallery to find that Huckvale had just returned and was talking with Ackford. They gave Peter a warm welcome. Huckvale gave an account of his visit to Southwark and told them that Neville Taylor was far more personable than his father. They waited for him to finish his report before offering any comments.

'I think that you should go to Mrs van Emden to pass on Taylor's regards,' said Ackford. 'Her reaction will be interesting.'

'I don't believe that she should be provoked,' said Peter.

'Why not?'

'Jem will get the same adverse response as Charlotte. All that she did was ask a harmless question about the past and Mrs van Emden flounced off. It was something she refused even to discuss.'

'Perhaps she should be forced to discuss it.'

'I agree,' said Huckvale. 'If there's something in her past that we ought to know about, we must try to wheedle it out of her.'

'There's something you're both forgetting,' said Peter, reasonably. 'She is a client of ours. Our task is to protect her from anything that might cause distress.'

'What am I to do, then?'

'Bide your time, Jem. There may be a moment when it's safe to mention Neville Taylor to her, but this is definitely not it. Let me pick on something else you told us,' he went on. 'You mentioned a pump.'

'Yes, it was an amazing contraption. It was getting water out of the garden faster than I could have done with a bucket.'

'And you say it was designed by Mr Parry?' asked Ackford.

'Yes, Gully. Like his father, young Mr Taylor has the greatest respect for him.'

'That was my point,' said Peter. 'If he was such a prolific inventor, what happened to all the patents? I can imagine him losing his money and, in a moment of despair, sacrificing his home in an ill-judged venture into gambling. That experience would have sobered anyone.'

'He must have reached the point where he could no longer *afford* to drink,' said Ackford.

'Yet he'd still have his pride. Those patents were proof of his rare abilities as an engineer. I don't think he'd ever have parted with them.'

'Then where are they?'

'And who has them now? That's my question.'

The dinner party was an unqualified success. It was held at the home of Vernon Teale, whose wife turned out to be a delightful hostess. A plump woman with radiant features, she'd abandoned a career in the theatre to look after her husband and raise their three children. Her passion for her old profession was without limit. She kept returning to her recitation of Hannah's achievements onstage. Paul was delighted that she was held in high esteem by both husband and wife, not least because their praise obliterated all memory of the highway robbery and the man who was stalking her.

'You truly are a second Sarah Siddons,' said Amanda Teale.

Hannah glowed. 'Thank you, Mrs Teale.'

'You've played all the Shakespearean heroines for which she became so renowned – Desdemona, Ophelia, Volumnia and

Lady Macbeth. And you're about to add Rosalind, another triumphant role for Mrs Siddons.'

'Whatever Miss Granville touches,' said Teale, 'she turns to gold.'

'Is that how you intend to pay her?' teased Paul. 'In solid gold?'

'Would it were possible, I'd gladly do so.'

'I'm not complaining,' said Hannah. 'Money is always a secondary consideration. Being allowed to serve my art is recompense in itself.'

The conversation flowed freely all evening along with the wine. Time seemed to ripple past. By the time that they had to leave, both Paul and Hannah knew that they had just spent their most enjoyable hours in the city. If it was an example of what they could expect, it would make *As You Like It* a memorable experience. Hannah was transported. As they strolled back arm in arm towards their hotel, Paul felt that she was floating along beside him.

It was when the hotel loomed up in front of them that the mood was rudely shattered. A woman screamed off to their left, causing them both to swing round in that direction. At the same moment, a man dashed out of the shadows on the other side of them, pressed something into Hannah's palm, then fled. It was her turn to scream now. Paul swung round, saw the figure sprinting away and made to go after him, but Hannah clung hard to him.

'Don't leave me, Paul!'

'But he'll get away.'

'Take me back to our room, I beg you.'

Putting an arm around her shoulders, he hustled her along the street, then opened the door of the hotel so that she could go in. He followed her. Once inside, she opened her hand to see what she'd been given. It was an opal pendant. Hannah was at once pleased and disturbed; thrilled that she'd got back her favourite gift

232

from Paul yet so unsettled by its touch that she wanted to toss it away. The opals sparkled under the light of the candles.

'It's your pendant,' she said, holding it up for his inspection.

'Look more closely,' he advised. 'It's very much like it, I agree, but that is not the gift that I bought you.'

CHAPTER EIGHTEEN

It was dark when they entered the churchyard and they needed a lantern to guide them to the shed that was to be their accommodation for the night. Chevy Ruddock stepped into it first, then emerged immediately to gulp in some fresh air.

'It's worse than ever in there, Bill.'

'I don't mind,' said Filbert. 'Before I joined the foot patrol, I worked for a butcher. If you think that stench is bad, you should smell rancid meat or game that's been hung far too long with the innards still inside the animal. The stink is enough to kill you. Go back in.'

'I'll let you do that.'

'You need to get used to it, Chevy.'

'If I stay in there too long, I'll keel over.'

'Not if you take a swig of this,' said Filbert, holding up a large stone bottle. 'This will take away the smell.'

'We're not supposed to drink on duty.'

'Who's going to stop us?'

'Mr Yeomans might take it into his mind to call in here.'

'I know Micah Yeomans better than you,' said Filbert, 'and he won't come here when he can sit in the Peacock Inn with Alfred Hale and drink himself into a stupor.' He patted the bottle. 'That's what I'm going to do. Let's step inside and have a first swig.'

'After you . . .'

Filbert cackled. 'Coward!'

When the older man had disappeared into the shed, Ruddock filled his lungs before he followed. He then sat on an upturned wooden bucket with both hands over his face. Minutes later, he found that the unpleasant odour had abated slightly, and realised that Filbert had lit his pipe and was puffing happily away. Before Ruddock knew it, the shed almost became inhabitable. Thanks to the tobacco, they were able to have a conversation without retching. Ruddock became so relaxed that he even had a swig from the stone bottle.

'Listen,' said Filbert, grabbing his arm.

'I can't hear anything, Bill.'

'Open your lugholes.'

Ruddock pricked up both ears and heard the faint sound of digging.

Filbert was agitated. 'They've come for the body already.'

'Then they're in for a surprise,' said Ruddock, with a laugh. 'What you hear isn't the sound of a body being dug up – it's the sound of one being lowered into the grave and covered up. If anyone did ride past today and saw the open grave, he'll know that there'll soon be a funeral. That means he'll make a point of riding past the churchyard until he sees that the burial has taken place.'

'Nobody told me that, Chevy.'

'Yes, they did – this is the second time. I told you earlier.'

Filbert was upset. 'You *did*? That means my memory's going.'

'The earliest that anyone will come here on the prowl is tomorrow night. All we're doing tonight is getting used to keeping vigil.'

'Did I really forget what you told me?' asked Filbert, with alarm. After a while, he let out his distinctive cackle. 'Mind you, I remembered to bring the drink and the baccy, didn't I? So my memory is still good for important things.'

Arriving back in their room, they found the curtains drawn and candles burning. Hannah held the opal pendant close to a flame so that she could examine it carefully.

'You're right, Paul,' she said. 'It's not your pendant at all.'

'I could see that straight away.'

'So why did he send it?'

'I think he's trying to trick you into believing that he's restoring something of great value to you. This pendant must have come from a previous haul and he just plucked it out.'

'I don't want stolen goods from other robberies.'

'But you *do* want the pendant that I gave you, surely?'

'Yes, of course,' said Hannah, 'but I'd hate to have it thrust into my hand the way that this one was. He flashed past me before I even knew that he was there. It's frightening that he can get so close to me.'

'It won't happen again.'

'You said that before.'

'I'll guard you around the clock, Hannah.'

'You were guarding me this evening, but he still managed to reach me. We were both distracted by that woman's scream.'

'That taught us something new about the man. He has a female accomplice. She screamed at just the right time.'

'If she's his mistress,' said Hannah, in distress, 'he might have given *her* my pendant.'

'We don't know what his relationship is with her,' said Paul, 'but I very much doubt that she's his mistress or his wife. Had she been either, she'd be far too jealous to help him ensnare another woman – if that's what he's trying to do.'

'What he's trying to do is to terrify me.'

'He probably doesn't see it that way, Hannah.'

'That's because he has a twisted mind.'

'He *spared* you, my love – always remember that. But for his intervention, those other highwaymen would have molested you. Their leader knew who and what you were. Unfortunately, your talent attracts men of all kinds, bad as well as good. It's the price of fame.'

'How much longer must I go on paying for it?' she asked, woefully.

'He'll keep on pestering you until I catch him.'

'And when will that be?'

'It will be as soon as is possible.'

She sighed. 'So, until then, I must go on suffering.'

'I suffer as well, Hannah,' he pointed out. 'When you're upset in any way, I share that suffering because I love you. I can't bear to see you under such strain.' He took her into his arms and held her tight. 'What tortures me is that it's partly my fault. I should have insisted on travelling with you in that coach to protect you.'

'I had Mr Cosgrove to do that.'

'He was too slow and only carried one pistol. I teach people how to shoot, remember. After all the time I've spent at the gallery, I can hit any target every time without fail. Had I been in that coach, I'd have shot two of those men from the saddle and the third would have bolted.'

'I don't blame you, Paul,' she said, 'but I would appreciate it if you rode with the coach when we have to return to London.'

'There's no need to ask, my love. It was already my intention.' He held her away from him and gave an encouraging smile. 'Now, let's get ready for bed, shall we, and banish these troublesome thoughts.'

'There's one that won't be so easily banished.'

'And what's that?'

'He set a clever little trap for us,' she said. 'They were waiting for us. How did he know that we'd be returning to the hotel this evening?'

Harry Scattergood's greatest asset was his ability to escape from any danger. On the rare occasions when he couldn't evade arrest, he always managed to escape from custody. Indeed, there had been times in his younger days when he'd deliberately allowed someone to apprehend him for the pleasure of slipping out of their hands and laughing derisively as he ran away. Having had one productive night in St Albans, he planned to enjoy another. He'd singled out one of the largest houses in town. Getting inside it was simplicity itself because he'd long since mastered the art of picking a lock. His other strength was his ability to move around in absolute silence. Creaking boards never creaked under the tender tread of his feet and sleeping dogs somehow remained resolutely asleep. He floated from room to room like a phantom.

When he was ready to strike, he tethered his horse in a copse fairly close to the house and approached on foot. No light showed in any window, so he reasoned that the whole household was abed. After walking slowly around the property, he chose to enter by means of a rear door, picking the lock deftly and easing the door open enough for him to glide in. He then left it ajar in case he had to make a quick exit. He waited until his eyes eventually became accustomed to the dark, then he quickly identified the dining room and felt his way into it. A house of that size and splendour, he'd already decided, would have ample silver plate and tableware. The sack which he'd brought with him was swiftly and soundlessly filled. Back in London, he knew where he could get a good price for his haul and for the items garnered on the previous evening. Scattergood smiled at his good fortune. St Albans was ridiculously easy to rob.

It was an opinion that was hastily revised. Before he could quit the premises, he heard heavy footsteps coming down the staircase. A spill of light came into view under the door. Scattergood immediately ducked out of sight beneath the table. The footsteps went past the dining room, then stopped at the rear door. He heard it being slammed shut and locked, cutting off his escape by that means. A systematic search of the downstairs rooms followed. When the light finally burst into the dining room, he could see the sturdy legs of a manservant and assumed that he was holding a candelabrum. What he couldn't see was that there was a stout walking stick in the man's other hand.

Scattergood stayed where he was, hardly breathing. When the legs walked around the table, he was convinced that his hiding place was safe. The walking stick was then suddenly wielded with great force, catching him on the thigh and making him yelp in pain. He crawled out of his refuge, stood up and saw a stocky man in a dressing gown, ready to take a second swing at him. Scattergood parried the blow with the sack of stolen silver, but it was knocked clean out of his hand. As it crashed to the ground, it made such a frightful clatter that it woke up the entire house. Voices began to shout angrily upstairs. The servant responded.

'There's an intruder in the dining room!' he yelled.

Scattergood tried to dart for the door, but was hampered by the pain in his thigh. Reduced to an agonising limp, he came into the hall only to see another figure lurching towards him with a stick in his hand. The little thief took to his heels and was chased around the entire ground floor. Scattergood was handicapped by the fact that his two pursuers knew the geography of the place far better than he did. When they thought they'd finally cornered him, he dodged past them and fled upstairs, only to find other weapons ready to belabour him. Having been buffeted on all sides, he was dazed by a woman who hit him across the back of his head with an empty warming pan. Scattergood just had sufficient strength to dive into a bedroom and turn the key in the lock.

Mercifully, the room was unoccupied, but he couldn't possibly stay there. Servants were already hammering on the door. He flung open the window and jumped straight through it. Though he made a soft landing on grass, his leg was on fire, the bruises on his body were smarting and his head still pounding. It was all he could do to drag himself to the copse without being seen. There was a final indignity. When he reached the clearing where he'd left his horse, he saw that the animal was no longer there. It had been stolen.

St Albans had had its revenge on him.

* * *

Peter Skillen arrived at the gallery with news. He'd received a letter from his brother that morning describing some of the difficulties that he and Hannah were having in Bath. Patently, their early return to London was out of the question.

'We'll have to manage without Paul's help,' said Peter.

'It seems to me as if he could do with *your* help,' said Ackford. 'He could be marooned in Bath until the run of the play is over.'

'Paul wouldn't leave anyway until the highwaymen are caught.'

'The odds are against him, Peter.'

'That's never troubled my brother.'

'No,' said Huckvale, 'I was with him once when we got caught up in a tavern brawl. Four ruffians set upon him and he fought them all off without any real effort.'

'These highwaymen – their leader, in particular – are not drunken oafs in a tavern. They ply a hazardous trade. It's hardened them. They've obviously learnt not to make mistakes.'

'But they *have* made a mistake.'

'Have they, Jem?'

'Yes, they upset Paul. That's a very bad mistake.'

They laughed knowingly. The three of them were in the room where Ackford was due to spend an hour teaching someone the finer points of swordplay. Until they had evidence to take them on to the next stage of the investigation, Huckvale was going to give lessons in archery. All three of them were frustrated at their inability to find out the full truth about George Parry's disappearance. Ackford had come to accept that he was dead, Huckvale was in two minds as to what actually happened, and Peter believed that Clemency's father might still be alive.

'Has Mrs van Emden said anything about Neville Taylor?' asked Ackford. 'Did she really discard him?'

'She hasn't mentioned him, Gully,' said Peter, 'and Charlotte has the feeling that she never will. Neville Taylor belongs to a difficult period in her past.'

'It can't have been that difficult,' contended Huckvale, 'or Mr Taylor wouldn't have talked about her the way he did. Once he knew that her husband was not with her, he asked me to pass on his warmest regards. Had you not counselled against it, I'd have done just that.'

'It's not Neville Taylor we should be thinking about,' said Peter. 'It's his father, Geoffrey. Of all the people we've met, he's the one who worked most closely with Mr Parry. I've been thinking about what he told us about his old friend.'

'He said that Mr Parry was a genius,' recalled Huckvale. 'And having seen that pumping machine he built, I'd agree with him. It was chugging away with steam coming out of it, sending gallons of water back into the Thames.'

'Geoffrey Taylor boasted about a dredging machine that Parry devised and about his scheme for a tunnel under the Thames.'

'If he was such a clever engineer,' wondered Ackford, 'why did he give it all up? People who love their work – I'm one of them – wouldn't dream of turning their backs on it.'

'It's a good question,' said Peter. 'Why does a man of exceptional talent desert his profession? We know he was rocked by the loss of his daughter, but that would surely make him want to lose himself in his work rather than abandon it. Jem will remember what Geoffrey Taylor said to us as we left,' he went on. 'Without divulging any details, he told us that Parry was on the verge of his greatest achievement yet. Then he stopped working on it. Why suddenly lose faith in the world of engineering?'

* * *

Clemency had breakfast alone with Charlotte. When they adjourned to the drawing room, they were in a relaxed mood. Having finally got her tongue around the few Dutch words she'd managed to learn, Charlotte actually pronounced them correctly. Clemency clapped her hands in appreciation.

'Well done, Charlotte! I'm impressed.'

'The sounds are so alien to me.'

'Before you know it, you'll be speaking Dutch like a native.'

'What use is that? I'm never likely to visit the Netherlands, am I?'

'Yes, you are – we'll invite you to stay with us.'

Charlotte was delighted. 'Thank you very much.'

The offer was spontaneous and sincere. It signalled to Charlotte that their friendship had suddenly moved on to a more intimate level. Clemency confirmed it by returning to the incident in the garden.

'I owe you an apology,' she began.

'Not at all,' said Charlotte. 'The fault was entirely mine.'

'You deserve an explanation so that you can understand why I behaved so badly.'

'I was wrong to probe into your private life, Clemency.'

'And I was wrong to conceal facts that I daresay your husband has revealed to you.' Charlotte nodded. 'When Mr Darwood mentioned the name of Geoffrey Taylor, I did my best to remain calm on the surface, but my mind was in turmoil. Mr Darwood – God bless him – had acted in my best interests, yet ended up by wounding me. He brought back memories I'd sought to suppress for far too long.'

'If they're unpleasant memories, they are perhaps best suppressed.'

'The truth must out.' She paused for a moment. 'When you heard how close my father was to Geoffrey Taylor, you must have wondered why I didn't seek him out the moment I arrived in London.'

'That thought did cross my mind.'

'Having met Mr Taylor, Mr Darwood now understands why I avoided him. Apart from anything else, Geoffrey Taylor would have refused to even see me. I didn't wish to court humiliation, however deserved it might be. I'm sure that Peter told you what he must have learnt.'

'You and Mr Taylor's son were . . . friends at one time.'

'We were more than that,' admitted Clemency, 'and there was a moment when I felt that a proposal was in the offing. As it happened, it never actually came and I was grateful. I liked Neville very much, but didn't have the urge to spend the rest of my life with him.' She took a deep breath. 'This is the moment when you may begin to view me in a less flattering light, Charlotte.'

'Why ever should I do that?'

'There was another man in my life at the time.'

'Yes, you've told me – your future husband.'

'No, this was before I'd even met Jan. I had another suitor, you see, a young man who doted on me. Neither my father nor Neville had any idea of his existence, let alone the strength of my feelings for him. There,' said Clemency, as if expecting disapproval, 'you know the worst of it. I was encouraging the interest of two suitors.'

'Well, don't ask me to be shocked,' said Charlotte, laughing. 'You know full well that I did exactly the same. For differing reasons, Peter and Paul were both attracted to me.'

'Yes, but you actually married one of them.'

'It sounds to me as if you were about to do the same.'

'But I wasn't, you see. In my heart, I didn't feel able to commit myself to either of them. I was being silly and flirtatious. I was simply pretending to be in love for the fun of it.'

'Was this other suitor aware of Neville Taylor's interest in you?'

'Oh, no, I kept the two of them well apart from each other.'

'How did they react when you told them you'd met someone else?'

'They were both hurt, naturally,' said Clemency, 'but they reacted in different ways. Neville was a perfect gentleman and wished me well, but his rival was much more resentful. He accused me of deceit and cruelty in appearing to welcome his advances, and he called me names that brought a blush to my cheek. When he later discovered that I was to marry a Dutchman, he sent me the most hateful letters. And yet,' she continued, sighing, 'I couldn't blame him. I'd raised his hopes, then dashed them. Any man would have been infuriated by that.'

'Neville Taylor wasn't.'

'Geoffrey Taylor was furious on his son's behalf. It made things very awkward for my father and it was entirely my fault.' She lowered her head. 'You must be disgusted with me.'

'I'm not, Clemency.'

'Anybody else would be.'

'You were young and inexperienced, that's all.'

'Don't make excuses. I was wilful.'

'Your mother had died. There was nobody to guide you.'

'I was ignorant and uncaring. I hurt the feelings of others.'

'How much of this did you tell your future husband?'

'I told him everything,' said Clemency. 'He deserved to know the worst about me. Jan was displeased, as you can imagine, but not appalled. Like you, he made allowances for my youth. I'm sure it's one of the reasons I was drawn to an older man. He made me feel grown-up at last. I learnt how to take responsibility for my actions. That's what brought me back to England. I was responsible for my father's misery. I had to face up to that.'

Having reached the end of her confession, she looked relieved to have told the full truth at last. While she could never completely excuse the way that Clemency had treated her suitors, Charlotte nevertheless had some sympathy for her. The other woman had behaved selfishly, but she'd now matured into a person with a more serious view of her obligations and a consideration for the feelings of others.

'You may tell Peter the truth,' said Clemency, willing to face more censure. 'I've nothing to hide now.'

Charlotte smiled. 'My husband will be delighted to hear it.'

They were rehearsing scenes from the play in which Rosalind didn't appear, so Hannah was able to have a free morning. She spent it with Paul, finding it both restful and reassuring. He accompanied her to the rehearsal room that afternoon and stayed there, taking a seat near a window so that he could look out of it rather than at the actors. If the highwayman was lurking outside, Paul wanted to see him. Lost in her role, Hannah was able to forget her fears and worries. It was not the first time in her life that Shakespeare had provided a convenient escape hatch from reality, and she was duly grateful. When she was not rehearsing, she was very pleased that Elinor Ingram was keeping her promise, treating her with the utmost respect and staying out of her way. Except for the scenes in which she appeared as Celia, the actress was virtually invisible.

During a break for refreshment, Hannah had the opportunity to thank the manager for his hospitality the previous evening, praising his cook and saying what a pleasure it had been to meet his wife.

'Amanda was thrilled to meet you, Miss Granville,' he said. 'She'll treasure the way you recited that sonnet of Shakespeare's to us for the rest of her life. Your memory is phenomenal.'

'It's just well-trained, that's all. Tell me,' she went on, 'how many people knew that you'd invited us to dinner yesterday?'

'Someone probably overheard me talking to you. That means that the whole cast knew about it in due course.' He smiled philosophically. 'Our secret was out. Actors are actors. They adore gossip.' He looked at her shrewdly. 'Why do you ask?'

'I'd hate to think that we aroused envy.'

'Your talent does that for you, Miss Granville.'

'Only a happy company can produce an outstanding performance.'

'I'm very aware of that.' He glanced around the room. 'Do you detect any hint of unhappiness here?'

'None at all,' she replied, looking at Elinor Ingram. 'We all get on extremely well together.'

'That's a great relief.'

When he excused himself to go off, Hannah drifted across to Paul. She was pleased to hear that there'd been no sighting of her stalker. One of the reasons the incident on the previous evening had disturbed her so much was that it had taken place in relative darkness. In the full light of day, she could cope with it more easily.

'I've been wondering,' said Paul. 'The lady to whom I returned that stolen brooch told me that she'd had her jewellery box taken as well. Could it be that it used to contain that opal pendant you were given last night?'

'It's more than possible,' replied Hannah. 'When she admired my pendant, she told me how fond she was of opals.'

'Then I'll pay her a second visit.'

'Please do that, Paul.'

'She was overjoyed when I returned that diamond brooch.'

'I'll be overjoyed if I ever get my opal pendant back.'

'You will, my love,' he promised. 'And that's no idle boast. I wouldn't dream of leaving this city until I retrieve it and put those highwaymen where they belong.'

After the pleasure of making a couple of important arrests, the Runners adjourned to the Peacock Inn for a celebratory tankard of ale. As he quaffed his first pint, Yeomans voiced his regret.

'It's a pity we only caught thieves,' he said. 'We do that every day of the week and get no thanks for it from Mr Kirkwood.'

'He's saving up his praise for the day when we catch some bodysnatchers. That's what he really wants.'

'Then that's what he'll get, Alfred.'

'Chevy Ruddock and Bill Filbert ought to get some of the credit.'

'They're just obeying my orders.'

'Yes,' said Hale, 'but they'll also have spent night after night in a shed that stinks to high heaven. That takes courage. It's worse than a privy in there, Micah.'

'They were chosen because they're both reliable.'

'We should have found them somewhere safer to hide.'

'The shed was the best place.'

'I wouldn't have spent five minutes in there.'

'Nor would I,' confided Yeomans. 'Our rank means that we

don't have to take on such unsavoury tasks any more. We have lesser mortals to do them for us.'

'Chevy is not a lesser mortal. He's an intelligent young man.'

'Then he'll have the sense to learn from his experience in that shed. That's what clever people do.'

'I think he deserves promotion.'

'Ruddock has to take his turn in the queue.'

'The chief magistrate has faith in him.'

'Let's just worry about his faith in *us*, Alfred. We need to vindicate our reputations. There are two obvious ways to do that.'

'You've mentioned one of them – arresting some bodysnatchers.'

'The other task may be more difficult.'

'What is it, Micah?'

'We must catch that slippery bastard Harry Scattergood.'

Expecting to return to London after a triumphant stay in St Albans, he was instead going back earlier than intended with both body and pride wounded. As the coach bounced along the uneven road, he was in torment. But it was his injured pride that caused the most intense suffering. Harry Scattergood had not only failed to steal anything the previous night, he'd taken a beating and lost his horse. The fact that he'd stolen the animal in the first place was no consolation to him. The horse had been his property, and someone had taken it. It was an insult with a lasting sting.

Unable to ride, he'd had to resort to coach travel. He still had the proceeds from his first night in St Albans and they would bring enough money to keep him in comfort until he was fully recovered. The real advantage of his early return should have been the reunion with Welsh Mary, but that delight was fraught with danger. In his condition, a night in her seductive arms would be like being driven over a series of jagged boulders in a coach. He'd never survive it. Scattergood thus had another reason to detest the name of St Albans. It had robbed him temporarily of his greatest source of pleasure.

CHAPTER NINETEEN

Peter Skillen was still at the gallery that afternoon when his wife called in. Pleased to see her, he was surprised that she didn't have their guest with her. Ever since she'd moved in with them, Clemency had sought Charlotte's company, relying on her more and more for support and solace.

'Where is she?' asked Peter.

'Clemency has gone to church. Since everything else has failed, she's turning to prayer.'

He was saddened. 'I'm sorry that she thinks we've let her down.'

'She still has faith in us, Peter, and accepts that the investigation will take longer than she'd hoped. And she certainly hasn't fallen out with us. Clemency is even talking about an invitation for both of us to visit Amsterdam.'

'That would be wonderful.'

'Yes, it would. I've never been out of this country.'

'I went rather too often when the war was on,' he said, thinking of his time in France as a British agent. 'It's a very tempting invitation. But we have to earn it first.'

'Yes – she is, after all, employing us.'

'Quite so, Charlotte.' He looked at her. 'I must say that it's lovely to see you back here again. You light up the whole gallery.'

'Thank you.'

After a kiss and warm embrace, they both sat down.

'What I really came to tell you,' she said, 'is what happened with regard to Neville Taylor.'

'Did you coax the truth out of her?'

'She volunteered it.'

Peter sat back. 'I'm all ears.'

Charlotte gave him an attenuated account of the conversation she'd had with Clemency, talking principally about Neville Taylor. In view of the way that Huckvale had described the man, Peter could well believe that he'd behaved with gentlemanly forbearance in the face of rejection. The young engineer had forged another life for himself and – Huckvale had noticed his wedding ring – had obviously married someone else.

'He's not entirely forgotten her, however,' said Peter. 'When he heard that Clemency was here in London, he sent his regards and there was, according to Jem, real fondness in his voice.'

'There's still affection on Clemency's side as well. She liked him. Yet she told me later on that part of her appeal for Neville Taylor was that her father was such a brilliant engineer. Clemency was worried that she'd spend most of her marriage listening to the two of them talking earnestly about their latest projects.'

'That would've been very boring for her.'

'She wanted to be at the centre of her husband's life and not just at the periphery.'

'You're certainly the centre of *my* life,' he said, reaching out to squeeze her hand. 'I dread to think what would have happened to me if you'd chosen Paul instead.'

Charlotte laughed. 'It would have been an act of sheer madness,' she said, 'and Paul would be the first to admit it now. But let's go back to Clemency. She confessed that she had another suitor at the same time, an ardent young man who was outraged when she dared to reject his advances. Unlike Neville Taylor, he became abusive. Could he be nursing a grudge against her? Should he be a suspect?'

'I very much doubt it,' said Peter. 'After all these years, he'll probably have forgotten her. If he's that amorous, it wouldn't have taken him long to transfer his affections to another beautiful young woman.'

'Let's put this second suitor aside for the moment. Now, is there anything I can say to offer comfort to Clemency?'

'You can assure her that I'm dedicated to the task in hand.'

'She knows that, Peter. You've been toiling selflessly on her behalf and so – in my own way – have I.'

'Yet we've nothing to show her in the way of progress.'

'That's not true. You found the supposed grave of her father.'

'But we still haven't discovered what happened to Mr Parry.'

'How do you propose to do that?'

'I was discussing that with Gully and Jem earlier on,' he said. 'The conclusion I reached was not one that you should mention to Clemency.'

'Why not?'

'I'm going to pay a second visit to Geoffrey Taylor. If she knew that, it might upset her again, but I'm certain that he's the man who may help me to solve the conundrum.'

'What about Mr Darwood? He's dying to help.'

'Mungo Darwood was a good friend, but he knew little about George Parry's work life except that it absorbed him. Taylor, by contrast, knew Clemency's father well and employed him regularly. I'm hoping that I can persuade him to forget the way that she treated his son,' said Peter, 'and come to her aid. Neville Taylor seems to have forgiven her. Let's see how much forgiveness there is in his father.'

Reassured that Hannah felt safe with her fellow actors in the rehearsal room, Paul went off to pay a second visit to Mrs Vellacott, the woman to whom he'd returned the stolen diamond brooch. She was staying with friends on the edge of the city. When he showed her the opal pendant, she let out a cry of joy. Minerva Vellacott was a middle-aged woman with a sense of wealth about her. She took the opal from him.

'I never thought I'd see it again, Mr Skillen.'

'May I take it that it *is* your property?' he said, smiling.

'I'm very attached to it,' she replied. 'It doesn't compare with the similar one that Miss Granville wore, but it has immense sentimental value. How ever did it come into your hands?'

'It was given to Miss Granville by the man who stole it.'

'How extraordinary!' she exclaimed. 'First, you bring the diamond brooch and next, the opal pendant. Dare I hope for other miracles?'

'I anticipate the return of the jewellery box itself.'

'But that would entail the arrest of the highwaymen.'

'It's a task I've set myself, Mrs Vellacott,' he said, solemnly. 'You and Miss Granville were only two of the passengers on that coach. All of the others were also robbed of something. I look forward to being able to restore the stolen items to each one of them.'

'Are you a magician, then?'

'I'm a person who believes in the concept of justice.'

She studied the pendant with a beatific smile on her face, then became conscious that she was ignoring him. After profuse apologies, she walked towards the door.

'Do excuse me, Mr Skillen,' she said. 'It was very rude to ignore you like that. I'll just summon my host. Since all my money was taken by those villains, he's promised to lend me whatever I need. I insist on rewarding you this time.'

'I wouldn't hear of it,' said Paul, gently closing the door after she'd opened it. 'The best reward you can give me is to tell me exactly what happened when the highwaymen struck.'

'Miss Granville will have done that.'

'A second version may contain details that she omitted.'

'She behaved with commendable aplomb, I know that. My legs had turned to jelly, but Miss Granville got out of the coach and faced those blackguards without a tremor.'

'I can well believe it.'

Paul knew that, in reality, Hannah had been as frightened as Mrs Vellacott but was able to call on her acting skills to hide her trepidation. The older woman had no such iron self-control. When she'd been ordered out of the coach, she was weeping copiously.

'What do you wish to know?' she asked.

'Tell me everything that you can remember.'

'In truth, it's an episode that I'd prefer to forget.'

'Don't you want these men caught and punished?'

'Oh, yes,' she said. 'I want them to feel the full severity of the law. They deserve to be transported, if not hanged.'

'Then you may help me to achieve that result,' said Paul. 'Sit down again, please, and take your time. Assemble your thoughts.'

She lowered herself into a chair. 'I'll do my best.'

'I've heard Miss Granville's version and I've spoken to Mr Cosgrove, who acted as a guard on the coach. They could only speak from their respective points of view. I'd like you to do the same.'

It was not only the urge to pray that had drawn Clemency to the church. In the dark silence of the nave, there was also the opportunity for reflection. Nobody else came or went. Time ceased to exist. She lapsed into a private world filled with doubt, remorse and accusation. When she looked at the decisions she'd made, Clemency could understand that most people would consider her to be headstrong and ungrateful. The father who had fed, sheltered and brought her up after the death of his wife had pinned his hopes on a marriage that would unite two families in a way that would be to their mutual benefit. All the time Clemency pretended to follow her father's wishes, she was allowing a second suitor to nurse ambitions with regard to her. A third man, differing from the others in age, character and nationality, then wandered into her life and, because she wanted it, slowly took possession of her life.

Clemency might have what she wanted, but those around her were badly hurt in the process. All the sympathy went to George Parry. People felt that she'd betrayed him in the most unforgivable way. Back in England, she found it a rather hostile and judgemental place that opened old wounds and threatened to inflict new ones. In the people she'd hired to launch an investigation, she'd gained some true friends, but London had far more enemies who cursed her name. As she sent up her plea to heaven, she acknowledged that she was unworthy of the help she sought.

Only when she finally left the church did she realise that she'd kept Jacob, her chaperon, standing outside. A devout Huguenot, he would not have felt comfortable in an Anglican church, so had waited patiently in the porch. After apologising for keeping him so long, Clemency set off with him, chastened by the time spent on her knees. On the walk back to the house, there was much soul-searching on her part. When they reached the front door, it was opened before they could even ring the bell. Meg Rooke, the maidservant, came out to greet them.

'You have a visitor, Mrs van Emden,' she said.

Standing out of the way, she revealed the man behind her.

'Jan!' cried Clemency.

Tears streaming, she ran headlong into her husband's arms.

Arriving at the engineering works for the second time, Peter Skillen had to wait until Geoffrey Taylor had finished talking to a potential client. When the man had departed, Peter stepped forward to ask for a little of the engineer's time. Taylor was not welcoming.

'I'm a busy man, Mr Skillen.'

'What I'm doing could have benefits for you,' said Peter.

'I doubt that. You are aiding and abetting a young woman who treated my son disgracefully and disobeyed her father. Two people I love very much were badly hurt by her rash behaviour.'

'I don't deny that, Mr Taylor.'

'Then why should I help a deceitful creature like her?'

'Let's look at the consequences of her deceit,' suggested Peter. 'She admits that she misled your son and has felt guilty about it ever since, but it does not seem to have damaged Neville.'

'You know nothing about my son.'

'It's true, sir, and it's the reason I chose to repair my ignorance. Jem Huckvale, whom you met on my earlier visit, managed to locate Neville at a site in Southwark. When he mentioned that the former Miss Parry was in London once more, your son showed no resentment towards her. In fact, he sent her his warmest regards.'

'That's because he found happiness elsewhere,' said Taylor. 'He's married to a loyal, loving woman and it has bred tolerance in him. I don't share it, Mr Skillen. As far as I'm concerned, Clemency is wicked.'

'Let's turn to Mr Parry.'

'She was responsible for his death. The character she presents to the world is just an illusion. In truth, she's a ruthless, calculating young woman.'

'I'd contest that portrayal of her and I'd also challenge your assumption that Mr Parry is dead.'

'Isn't that what brought her back here?'

'Indeed, it is, but the report she received is starting to look increasingly unreliable. As it happens,' Peter went on, 'we did find the grave into which George Parry was purportedly laid but, unfortunately, the corpse had been stolen by bodysnatchers. After a discussion with the undertaker, however, we established that the person who'd been buried in that churchyard could not possibly have been Mrs van Emden's father.'

Taylor gaped. 'Are you *sure* of this?'

'I'm fairly certain, sir.'

'What proof do you have?'

'I have the evidence of Mrs van Emden's eyes. She knew her father too well to be deceived by a childish sketch of him made by the undertaker's daughter. My firm belief is that someone wanted his daughter to *believe* that George Parry was dead. Had that grave not been plundered, she would have accepted that her father had been laid to rest in it.'

'Who first told her that George had died?'

'An anonymous letter was sent to her in Amsterdam.'

'I'm confused, Mr Skillen,' said the other. 'If he's still alive, why should anyone wish to tell her such a grotesque lie?'

'He wanted her to *suffer*.'

'She could never suffer enough, in my opinion.'

'Would *you* have informed her of his death if it was untrue?'

'No,' said Taylor, indignantly. 'What sort of man do you take me for? I wouldn't stoop to such cruelty. What perverted mind could do so?'

'It's obviously someone close to her family circle. Nobody else would have been aware of her address or of her estrangement from her father.'

'That sounds logical.'

'It has to be someone who hated her.'

'Do you have any suspects?'

'The only one I've identified so far is a man called Joseph Rafter. He was Mr Parry's butler, but left after a disagreement about money.'

'I've met him.'

'What manner of man was he?'

'He was perfectly polite and, as far as I could judge, very

261

efficient.' He hunched his shoulders. 'That's all I can tell you, really. Who looks at servants when you visit a friend's house?'

'So far,' admitted Peter, 'we've been unable to find Rafter. And there's always the chance, of course, that he's not involved in any way. That won't stop me looking for him.'

'You've shown remarkable tenacity, Mr Skillen.'

'I mean to get at the truth, sir.'

'If I can help you in any way,' said Taylor, 'please tell me how. The idea that George Parry is still alive fills me with joy. Where can he possibly be?'

'I believe that he may be being held somewhere against his will.'

'Why?'

'It's because he's of great value to someone,' replied Peter. 'This is where I need your guidance, sir. You told us of Mr Parry's inventions. Jem Huckvale actually saw one in action when he met your son. It was a steam-driven pump.'

'George also invented a dredging machine, twenty times larger.'

'And, presumably, he holds patents for both.'

'It's the only way to stop rivals from stealing your ideas.'

'Is engineering so keenly competitive?'

'It's a dog-eat-dog profession, Mr Skillen. It's full of predators in search of prey. Fortunately, there are laws to protect us against them.'

'When we first met, you told us that Mr Parry was on the verge of developing an idea that would surpass anything else he'd ever done.'

'That's true.'

'What was the idea?'

'I can't divulge that to you, I'm afraid. It was something told to me in the strictest confidence.'

'If George Parry is dead, there's no virtue in preserving his secret. If, as I believe, he may still be alive,' said Peter, 'you may be holding information that will help me to find him. Are you really going to keep it to yourself?'

Taylor blinked. Normally such a decisive man, he was suddenly afflicted by doubt.

The first person to leave at the end of the rehearsal was Elinor Ingram. She gave Hannah a smile of farewell and slipped out of the room. Other members of the cast stayed in the hope of getting a kind word from the leading lady or even some advice about their respective performances. Vernon Teale made a point of thanking her once again. The morning rehearsal had been satisfactory but, when Hannah joined the company in the afternoon, the standard had immediately been raised.

'Everyone followed where you led, Miss Granville,' he said.

'I don't believe that my presence made such a difference.'

'It most certainly did.'

'You've assembled a good company, Mr Teale. That's why there's been visible improvement so early on. The room was full of fine actors.'

'Your modesty becomes you, Miss Granville.'

Before she could reply, she saw Paul entering the room and excused herself to go across to him. He escorted her towards the exit. Inside the building, Hannah had been brimming with confidence. The moment they left it, however, she was assailed by the fear that she was being watched. When they got back to the hotel, she was relieved that no gift or message had been left for her. Paul took her up to their room and listened to her long account of how the rehearsal had gone and how Elinor

Ingram had behaved. It was only when she'd finished that she remembered where he'd been.

'Did that pendant belong to Mrs Vellacott?'

'Yes, it did. Having thought it was lost for ever, she was thrilled to get it back again and asked me to pass on her thanks.'

'I just wanted to get rid of it,' said Hannah. 'If I'm given anything else belonging to Mrs Vellacott, she'll have that back as well.'

'Forget about the jewellery, my love. I need you to help me.' He indicated the sofa. 'Let's sit down.'

'You're very serious all of a sudden, Paul.'

'There's a reason for that,' he said. 'Now, I'd like you to tell me something about the robbery.'

'But I've done that a number of times.'

'There were certain details missing.'

'What sort of details?'

'Mrs Vellacott admits that she was terrified at the time, but she did notice the horses ridden by the highwaymen. She claims that their leader was riding a bay mare.'

'Was he? I hardly noticed.'

'Try hard to remember, please. It's very important.'

Hannah frowned. 'Mrs Vellacott may well be right,' she said, cudgelling her brain. 'One of the others rode a black horse, but their leader had a bay mare. When I was standing in the road, it towered over me.'

'Are you absolutely *certain* about that, Hannah?'

'Why are you being so intense?'

'Because I may have made an alarming discovery,' he said. 'You've never mentioned the horses before and I never asked about them. Mrs Vellacott did remember them and you've just verified what she told me. The leader of those highwaymen was on a bay mare.'

'He was,' she confirmed. 'I remember it clearly now.'

'Then why did Cosgrove tell me that the man was on a black stallion with a white blaze?'

'That belonged to one of the others, though it didn't have a white blaze. Mr Cosgrove made a mistake.'

'No, he didn't,' said Paul. 'He deliberately lied to me. I've been searching for the man you described to me and I've been expecting him to be astride a black stallion with a white blaze. Can't you see what this means, Hannah? Cosgrove is in league with the highwaymen.'

'He can't have been,' she said, incredulously. 'He tried to shoot one of them and was wounded in the hand.'

'That's what it may have looked like at the time.'

'I saw the blood on his handkerchief.'

'That could have been put there before he took it out of his pocket. No, wait a minute,' he went on, stifling her interruption by putting a finger to her lips, 'let me finish. Why did the leader take a special interest in you?'

'He recognised me.'

'But how did he know you'd be in that coach?' About to reply, Hannah had second thoughts. Paul saw realisation dawning. 'Yes, that's right,' he continued. 'He *knew* you'd be travelling in that particular coach because Cosgrove had told him. Otherwise, the highwaymen might well have robbed another vehicle altogether. The leader of that gang is more than simply an admirer, Hannah. He's desperate to endear himself to you. That's why you were spared when at their mercy and why he's been sending you these unwanted gifts.'

'This is shocking, Paul. Mr Cosgrove seemed such a decent man.'

'He's no mean actor himself. It turns out that he works regularly at the theatre and is always hanging about. In other words, he's in a position to inform his friend about your movements. More worryingly, he's been able to divert me on to the wrong track altogether.'

'What are you going to do, Paul?'

'I propose to do nothing at all.'

'But you've evidence that he was party to the robbery.'

'*We* know that, Hannah, but he doesn't. If I apprehend him, I'll throw away my chances of catching the others. I need Cosgrove at liberty so that he can lead me to them.'

'That means he'll still be spying on me.'

'We must never give him the slightest hint that we've unmasked him. If you encounter him at the theatre, give him a polite smile.'

'It will take a great effort to do that.'

'Nonsense!' he said, putting an arm around her. 'You're an incomparable actress, Hannah. Here's your opportunity to prove it.'

On her return home, Charlotte was met with a surprise: Jan van Emden was there. Having gone to the hotel where he'd expected to find his wife, he'd been given the address to which she'd moved. Introduced to Charlotte, he was filled with gratitude.

'I can't thank you and your husband enough, Mrs Skillen,' he said. 'Clemency has been telling me what you've done for her. You've gone beyond the limits of . . . what is the word . . . ?'

'Hospitality,' said his wife.

'We owe you and Mr Skillen a great debt.'

'There are other people involved as well, Mr van Emden,' said Charlotte. 'Clemency may have mentioned Jem Huckvale and Gully Ackford. Mr Darwood, an old friend of Mr Parry's, has also been very helpful. All of us are anxious to learn the truth about Clemency's father.'

'You will be well rewarded for your generosity.'

As soon as she saw him, Charlotte could see what had attracted Clemency to the Dutchman. He was a tall, upright man, with a face that was far from handsome yet full of character. His hair was peppered with grey and he exuded a mixture of kindness and unforced authority. One glance at his rich apparel confirmed that he was a man of some wealth. His command of English was good, though his accent remained throaty. Charlotte had rarely met anyone with so much natural charm. Jan van Emden was a person in whom she felt she could place instant trust.

'You must think me a terrible husband,' he said, apologetically, 'sending my wife off alone like that. The truth is that when Clemency heard of her father's death, she boarded the next ship to England. I was in The Hague at the time, involved in work for the government that kept me there for days. As soon as I got home again, I sailed after my wife.'

'You're here now,' said Clemency, 'and that's all that matters.'

'I'm here and I'll stay until we know the truth about your father.'

'You're most welcome,' said Charlotte.

She felt a degree of relief at van Emden's arrival. His unheralded appearance had not only cheered his wife, it would relieve Charlotte of the burden of being with her most of the time. As she looked at them now, they seemed an incongruous pair, the gap in age making them look more like father and daughter than husband and wife. Yet somehow they appeared to be ideally suited.

'We can't possibly impose on you,' he said. 'Clemency and I will move back to that hotel where she first stayed.'

'I won't hear of it,' said Charlotte, emphatically. 'You belong here and this is where you are going to stay. If I let the pair of you leave our house for a hotel, my husband would never forgive me.'

Because he'd spent the night on duty, Chevy Ruddock had been given most of the day off to recover. By late afternoon, he was ready to call at the Peacock Inn with his report. Yeomans and Hale were in their usual seats. When he got close to them, they drew back in horror.

'Move away,' said Yeomans, flapping an arm.

'You stink as if you've been dead two weeks,' added Hale.

'Don't start on me as well,' pleaded Ruddock. 'I've had enough complaints from my wife. I can't help it if the stench got into my clothes and hair.'

'Open that door and stay near it,' advised Yeomans. 'The fresh air will do us all a favour. Now, what happened last night?'

Hale chuckled. 'We can *smell* what happened.'

'Everything was fine,' said Ruddock, 'while Bill was smoking his pipe. The odour of tobacco filled my nostrils. It was very pleasant. Then he fell asleep and his pipe stopped glowing. The stench came back. If you want us there tonight, I'm hiding in the church porch. Bill Filbert can stay in that shed on his own.'

'You should be with him to keep him awake,' said Yeomans.

'Take pity on him, Micah,' said Hale. 'If Chevy stays in the porch and curls up in a corner, he won't be seen. Bill can stay in the shed on his own and puff away through the night.'

'If anyone does turn up,' said Ruddock, 'I'll be aware of them. I can rouse Bill within seconds.' He yawned extravagantly. 'Though I don't expect anyone will come tonight. It's far too soon.'

When he rode casually past the churchyard, the man glanced at the grave that had now been filled in. The burial must have taken place earlier in the day, he decided. Someone had left a few flowers on the mound of earth. The man sniggered. Another body was ready for collection.

CHAPTER TWENTY

Peter Skillen was glad that he'd decided to speak to Geoffrey Taylor a second time because he'd been given an insight into the world of engineering. On the ride home, he was musing on Taylor's comments about the importance of patents and the advantages of monopoly. Peter was grateful that he didn't work in a profession that had such cut-throat elements in it. To have thrived as an engineer, he realised, George Parry had needed more than a knack for inventing things.

When he reached the house, he discovered that the prevailing mood had changed for the better. Clemency had been transformed by the arrival of her husband. She was buoyant, even sparkling. Jan van Emden's presence had given her confidence. No longer depressed or feeling the need of prayer, she was instead laughing gaily. Peter was introduced to her husband and, like Charlotte, was very impressed by his bearing and obvious intelligence. Jan van Emden was equally struck by Peter and an immediate bond was established between them.

'I'm not simply here to look after my wife,' the Dutchman explained. 'I'm ready to help in any way I can. I can still fire a pistol and give a good account of myself with a sword. Call on me at any time.'

'No, Jan,' said Clemency, 'you're not to put yourself in jeopardy. Peter is an expert with all weapons and so is Jem Huckvale, his friend. Beside them, you are just a raw beginner.'

He laughed. 'Do you hear that?' he said. 'My wife thinks that I know nothing of how to defend myself. My offer stands, Mr Skillen.'

'I'll not be taking advantage of it,' said Peter, smiling. 'With luck, weapons of any kind won't be needed. If they are, Jem will be at my back all the time.'

'You sound optimistic,' said Charlotte.

'It's not out of place.'

'You know what actually happened to Mr Parry?'

'I'm certain of one thing,' he replied. 'He is still above ground.'

'What makes you say that?' asked Clemency, excitedly.

'There are good reasons for keeping him alive.'

'Then why was I told that he was dead?'

'I'm still not sure about that,' said Peter, 'but my feeling is that you're the victim of a conspiracy. You and your father were kept apart on purpose. What I need to know is where your father kept his records.'

'He had a study at the house.'

'Was it kept locked?'

'Oh, yes, I was never allowed in there and neither was my mother.'

'What about the servants?'

'It was the one part of the house from which they were barred. My father told me that there were valuable documents in the study. Whenever he was at work in there, he'd lock himself in.'

'It sounds as if he was afraid of something,' said Charlotte.

Peter nodded. 'I fancy that he had good cause.'

Chevy Ruddock was the first there. He had to wait an hour before Filbert eventually turned up. The old man was surprised that his partner had decided to hide in the church porch.

'What's wrong with the shed?' he asked.

'I'd rather breathe fresh air.'

'Smoke a pipe the way I do.'

'I've got no taste for it, Bill. I tried it once and I nearly coughed myself to death. My wife told me to leave tobacco alone in the future.'

Filbert smirked. 'Do you always do what your wife tells you?'

'Yes, I do.'

'Then more fool you, Chevy.'

'Agnes always gives me good advice.'

'Then I'll give you even better counsel,' said Filbert. 'Don't ever let a wife feel that she can make you do everything she tells you. She'll only get above herself. You'll wake up one morning and realise that you married a shrew.'

'My wife is no shrew,' said Ruddock, scandalised.

'Give her too much power and she'll turn into one.'

'Agnes is a kind, gentle, loving wife.'

'They all start off like that.'

Feeling his temper rising, Ruddock moved the conversation swiftly to the matter in hand. He explained that the chance of having any visitors during the night was slim, but that he'd wake Filbert up from time to time so that both of them were alert.

'I need my sleep,' complained Filbert.

'So do I, Bill, but we're on duty. We must be awake.'

'You just said that nobody would come tonight.'

'I said the chances are slim, that's all.'

'Then we can snore away for hours on end.' He slapped Ruddock on the back. 'You sleep in the porch and I'll sleep in the shed. That means both of us have a good night.'

'Mr Yeomans will want a report in the morning.'

'Then you'll have to use your imagination.'

'I'd rather tell the truth.'

'That's the last thing you do, Chevy. We must both tell the same tale. We heard noises in the night and, when we went to see what was happening, we met two men climbing over the churchyard wall. Before they escaped, we beat them black and blue. There,' said Filbert. 'Doesn't that sound better than admitting we were asleep all night?'

'I won't tell a downright lie.'

'Then leave the talking to me.'

'I'm known for my honesty.'

'Ask yourself a question: would you rather be praised as a hero for scaring off bodysnatchers or torn to shreds by Micah Yeomans for enjoying a good night's rest? I know which one I'd choose.'

Having dined out again, Paul and Hannah strolled back to the hotel. Both were much more alert this time, but their vigilance proved unnecessary. Nobody came anywhere near them. Paul took her into the building.

'There you are,' he said. 'I told you not to worry.'

'As ever, you were right.'

Before they reached the stairs, however, the manager came over to them with a letter. It had been delivered by hand earlier in the evening and was addressed to Hannah. Seeing the fear in her eyes, Paul thanked the manager, took the letter from him, then led her upstairs. Once in their room, she looked at the missive with apprehension.

'Is it from him?' she asked.

'I hardly think so, my love. This is a woman's hand.'

'Open it.'

'But it's addressed to you.'

'I'd prefer it if you opened it for me.'

Paul obeyed and glanced at the name at the end of the letter.

'It's from someone called Henrietta.'

'Which one? I know three or four.' She took it from him and smiled with relief. 'It's from Henrietta Doyle.'

'Isn't she the actress who was taken ill?'

'That's right. She was cast as Celia, but had to withdraw at the last moment.' Hannah rolled her eyes. 'We both know who replaced her.'

'What does your friend have to say?'

As she read the letter, she gave him a commentary.

'Her husband was coming to Bath today on business so she asked him to deliver this message to me. Having performed here a number of times, Henrietta guessed that we'd be staying at the hotel closest to the theatre. *As You Like It* is one of her favourite plays and she's going to make every effort to watch one of our performances. She sends her love and best wishes.'

'It was kind of her to write.'

'I was so afraid the letter came from that sinister highwayman.'

'Instead of which,' said Paul, 'it's from an old friend and it's put you in good humour again.' He saw her smile freeze. 'What's the trouble, Hannah? Has she said something to upset you?'

'It's what she *hasn't* said that's worrying me, Paul.'

'Explain, if you will.'

'Henrietta Doyle is an actress who, like me, comes fully alive onstage because she simply adores theatre. She writes excitedly about *As You Like It*, but doesn't say a word about having been in the original cast. Nor is there any mention of the indisposition that made her drop out at the last moment.' She passed the letter to Paul. 'We've been deceived.'

A warm day in London had developed into a cooler night. Ruddock didn't mind the breeze that had now started blowing. It helped to keep him awake and to dispel some of the stink lingering in his clothes. Even though it was the dead of night, the city was by no means silent. All sorts of noises came and went, whether it was the clattering of hooves on the cobbles or the distant bellows of a drunken argument. Ruddock had gone to the shed at one point to wake Filbert up but, when he heard the gentle wheezing of a tired old man, he didn't have the heart to disturb him. The important thing was that one of them stayed awake.

It was hours later when he heard a different sound altogether. It was the chink of iron on stone. Ruddock strained his ears. Convinced that he might have heard a spade grating against the wall of the churchyard, he moved on hands and knees to the front of the porch. When he heard muffled voices, he knew that someone was there. Staying low, he crept across to the shed, let himself in and, for once, didn't mind the reek that assaulted his senses. Putting a hand over Filbert's mouth, he shook him awake. The old man reacted as if he'd been attacked, but he soon realised that it was Ruddock looming over him.

'They're here, after all,' he whispered.

Filbert was still only half-awake. 'Who is, Chevy?'

'It's them.'

No more words were needed. They'd already agreed that, if any bodysnatchers did turn up, they'd let them get on with their work. As well as tiring them out, it would distract them. The time to strike was when they were down in the grave, trying to manhandle the coffin. Everything was therefore dictated by Ruddock's keen hearing. Two spades cut into the earth and scattered it uncaringly aside. Occasional curses came from the men. Ruddock even heard one of them spitting. Knowing that the spades could be used as weapons, he and Filbert had brought thick staves and the old man had also tucked an ancient pistol into his belt.

Ruddock waited until the sound of heavy panting gave way to the creak of a coffin lid as someone tried to prise it off. It was the signal to attack. Following the route they'd chosen the previous night, they dodged their way between headstones until they came to the open grave. Ruddock didn't stand on ceremony. He struck one of the men across the back of the head, knocking him senseless. As the other tried to clamber out, Filbert jabbed him hard in the chest with his stave, then waved the pistol in his face.

'Drop that spade or I'll shoot your eyes out!' he yelled.

The man obeyed instantly. By way of thanks, Filbert felled him with the butt of the weapon. It was all over.

* * *

When she awoke that morning, Charlotte no longer felt that she had to get out of bed at once in case their guests needed her. Clemency was far more interested in basking in her husband's love than in making any demands on the household. If either of them required anything, the servants would see to their needs, leaving Charlotte to enjoy some additional time in bed with Peter. She nestled in her husband's arms.

'I hadn't realised that he'd be so important,' said Peter. 'Clemency never told us that her husband did work for the government.'

'All that she could think about was her father.'

'The two men can't be far apart in age.'

'We've only been in his company for an evening, yet I feel as if I've known Jan van Emden for a long time.'

'Yes, he had that effect on me as well.'

'What are you going to do today?'

'The search will continue.'

'Do you still think that Joseph Rafter holds the key?'

'It's more than possible, Charlotte, but there's someone I've been forgetting. Rafter, it seems, did his job well and only fell out with Mr Parry when threatened with a reduction in wages. Abigail Saunders told us that. Rafter was a reliable servant. Even though he'd left Mr Parry's employ, he was chosen to return to the house to supervise the disposal of its contents.'

'That's true.'

'The man who should have done that was Edmund Haines.'

'Why?'

'To begin with, he was still a member of staff. When Rafter left, Haines would have taken charge. The task of helping to clear the house should surely have fallen to him.'

'Then why didn't it?'

'I suppose that Mr Parry no longer trusted him for some reason.' Peter sat up in bed. 'I'm worried that I've been looking at the wrong servant. Joseph Rafter may have no part in Mr Parry's disappearance at all. It might have been someone else entirely.'

'Edmund Haines?'

'It's possible, though we mustn't jump to conclusions. Remember what Abigail Saunders told me. All the servants were kind to her. That includes both Rafter and Haines. Ideally, I'd like to find them both.'

'Have you any idea where they might be?'

Peter brooded for a moment. 'Oddly enough,' he said at length, 'I think I can guess where one of them will be.'

'And where's that?'

'He's with Mr Parry.'

Night had failed to cool Hannah's temper. It was as fiery as ever next morning. When she'd first understood the implications of the letter from her friend, she'd wanted to storm straight off to Vernon Teale's house to tell him that his claim had been exposed as false and that she wanted Elinor Ingram dismissed from the company at once. Paul had managed to dissuade her against such a course of action, arguing that any decision should not be taken until she was in a calmer frame of mind. Though she did her best to suppress her rage, he could see that she was still bent on revenge.

'Why not leave this to me?' he asked.

'This is my fight, Paul.'

'But it isn't, my love, that's the problem. It's not simply a tussle between you and the manager. It affects the whole company. If you cause disruption, it will leave a nasty taste in everyone's mouth.'

She was resolute. 'That woman is not going to play Celia.'

279

'I agree. Mr Teale and I will send her on her way today.'

'She should never have been engaged in the first place,' said Hannah. 'Teale told me that Henrietta Doyle was to play the part, yet it's quite clear from her letter that Henrietta was never offered it.'

'She'll be offered it now,' he said.

'What do you mean?'

'You'll insist on it.'

She bristled with anger. 'I most certainly will.'

'You sent me to do battle with Teale once before,' he said.

'Yes, and you failed to make him agree to my demands.'

'I have a stronger weapon to wield this time – that letter.'

'It was sent to me,' she said, 'and is therefore mine to wield against him. Henrietta has unwittingly explained how Elinor Ingram managed to secure a role in the play.'

'Evidently, she's the manager's mistress.'

'And there was that two-faced liar, inviting us to dine with his wife and passing himself off as a doting husband.'

'That's none of our business,' he said. 'From what I've seen, most theatre managers have mistresses as a matter of course. In a profession with so many desirable ladies, it's inevitable.'

'Since when has Elinor Ingram been desirable?'

'I won't answer that question.'

'Are you saying that you find her attractive?' she demanded.

'My opinion of her is immaterial. What I see is that one actress gets an important role because she sleeps with the manager and that the name of a rival actress – far superior in talent, you tell me – has been used to justify a deception.'

'When I speak to Mr Teale, I won't put it so politely.'

'I can't let you do it, Hannah.'

'It's my right.'

'You'll only inflict damage on yourself and on the company,' he argued. 'The simple fact is that you signed a contract and can be held to it. That doesn't mean Teale will go unpunished. Our first objective is to deprive him of his mistress and send her packing. That will hurt him and infuriate her.' He grinned. 'I'd love to be there when he tells her to leave the company.'

Hannah laughed aloud. 'Elinor will turn into a wildcat.'

'While I'm at it, I'll exact other concessions from him.'

'You'll ask for a financial inducement for me to stay?'

'I won't need to ask, Hannah. He'll offer it at once. There are lots of things I can demand, the first of which is that Henrietta Doyle is invited to replace Miss Ingram. My second demand is the name of the actress who told you that she'd been desperately ill. The woman was clearly part of the conspiracy to win you over. She must go as well.'

'You're right,' she said, after thinking it over. 'It's far better if *you* deal with the manager.'

'I'll have the upper hand this time. Besides,' he went on, 'I'll value the opportunity to touch on another matter altogether.'

'What's that, Paul?'

'I'll ask him about Cosgrove.'

They had never approached Bow Street with such jubilation. Having good news to report, they felt certain that the chief magistrate would overlook their past failings and acknowledge their extraordinary success. They entered Kirkwood's office without any of their usual disquiet.

'We have something to report, sir,' announced Yeomans, grandly.

'Then get on with it, man,' said the chief magistrate.

'As a result of measures that we took, two bodysnatchers were apprehended last night and are now in custody.'

Kirkwood was impressed. 'Did you arrest them yourselves?'

'No,' said Hale, 'they were caught by Ruddock and Filbert.'

'So it's Ruddock we have to applaud yet again, is it?' said the other. 'I must congratulate him in person.'

'He was acting under my orders, sir,' asserted Yeomans.

'But you weren't there when the villains were confronted, were you? Ruddock and his partner were. They deserve the kudos.'

'You haven't heard the rest of it yet, sir,' said Hale. 'When we learnt what had happened, we questioned the two prisoners. Micah got confessions out of both of them.'

'Yes,' added Yeomans, 'they both admitted to being party to raids on other churchyards and one of them – with a little persuasion – told me the name of the professor of anatomy to whom they sold the bodies.'

'That's the best news yet,' said Kirkwood. 'He incited a series of foul crimes. I'm the first to recognise the importance of medical science, but its progress should not rest on the violation of Christian burials.'

'When the word spreads of what happened last night, bodysnatchers everywhere will start to tremble. One of their paymasters has just been taken and been forced to retire from his grisly trade. His arrest will act as a warning to others who flout the law.'

'You both deserve plaudits, Yeomans.'

'Thank you, sir.'

'And so do Ruddock and Filbert.'

'Chevy Ruddock led the way,' said Hale, 'and setting the trap was really his idea.' Aware that he'd just admitted the truth, he

282

was too frightened to look at Yeomans. 'What he couldn't do, of course, was to get a confession out of the prisoners. Nobody can do that as well as Micah Yeomans. Once he has a criminal in his grasp, he can make them sing like a bird.'

'Then why didn't he make Harry Scattergood tweet?' asked Kirkwood, sarcastically. 'Yeomans didn't even have to take the trouble of catching that infernal thief. The Skillen brothers did that for him. Why didn't you interrogate Scattergood the moment you heard of his arrest?' he asked, looking at him. 'You could probably have got him to confess to hundreds of crimes.'

'And I will, sir,' promised Yeomans.

'If you ever find him . . .'

Scattergood had learnt his lesson. Instead of going straight to the brothel where Welsh Mary lived, he took a room in a tavern and spent the night nursing his wounds. In the morning, he'd felt well enough to send for her. He was now lying naked on the bed while she applied a soothing balm to his bruises and sang a lilting ballad in her native language.

'What was it like in St Albans?' she asked.

He jerked convulsively as if her fingers were iron spikes.

Peter and Charlotte went off to the gallery together that morning. Ackford was instructing a client, but Huckvale was free. He was amazed that Jan van Emden had turned up without warning and hoped for the opportunity to meet him. What Huckvale really wanted to hear about, however, was Peter's second visit to Geoffrey Taylor. He listened intently to his friend's report. When it was over, he snapped his fingers.

'Mr Taylor's son hinted that there was something in the wind,' he said. 'Mr Parry had been close to a discovery of some kind.'

'We now know what it was, Jem.'

'Why did he abandon it?'

'I don't know, but he did so with great reluctance.'

'Yes,' said Charlotte, 'Clemency told me that, while her father worked for other people, he was always developing ideas on his own as well. He was wealthy enough to buy the time needed for research.'

'But this latest invention of his put enormous strain on his finances. Parry had to find money from elsewhere,' said Peter. 'When he couldn't do that, he probably became more and more desperate. Geoffrey Taylor blamed Clemency for what happened to her father, but she couldn't be held responsible for his obsession. In my view, he was so determined to continue with his experiments that he eventually turned to gambling as the only solution.'

'I feel so sorry for him,' said Huckvale.

'We all do, Jem,' said Charlotte. 'It would have been so helpful to us if his daughter had been able to tell us much more about his work. Unfortunately, he was very secretive and Clemency showed no interest.'

'That's not her fault. What woman *is* interested in engineering?'

'Given what we've learnt about Mr Parry, *I* certainly am.'

Peter smiled fondly. 'That's because you're unique.'

When the discussion ended, Huckvale had news of his own.

'Harry Scattergood is back.'

'How do you know?' asked Peter.

'One of our informers sent a message. He saw Harry getting out of a coach and limping off into the shadows.'

'But he never uses coaches. Harry always rides on a stolen horse so that he has a means of escape. He'd feel trapped in a coach.'

'I'm only passing on what I was told.'

'It's useful intelligence. When we've time, we'll act on it.'

'You've already arrested Scattergood once,' said Charlotte. 'Does that mean you collected the reward for his capture?'

'Alas, we didn't, my love. The reward was contingent upon his arrest and *conviction*, and he managed to escape.'

'Do you have to catch him again, then?'

'I fear that we do.'

Before he could go on, a knock on the door silenced him. Huckvale went to see who the visitor was. When he came back, he had Abigail Saunders with him. She was carrying two large leather bags.

'I'm sorry to disturb you, Mr Skillen,' she said, nervously, 'but you told me to come here if I had any news for you.'

Knowing that the manager would get to the rehearsal room well before anyone else, Paul was waiting to intercept him. Teale told him that he didn't have time to speak to him, but Paul insisted.

'If you don't speak to me now,' he warned, 'you'll have to talk to Miss Granville in front of the whole company. You wouldn't enjoy that, Mr Teale, because she will be waving a letter she had from Henrietta Doyle at you.'

'What sort of letter?'

'It's a truthful one.'

Paul gave him such a meaningful look that Teale gasped and the colour drained from his face. He hustled Paul quickly into his office. After collecting himself, he first tried appeasement.

'I'm eternally grateful to you, Mr Skillen,' he said, rubbing his hands together. 'Having you at her side has not only reassured

Miss Granville that she is safe, but you've also spoken up eloquently on her behalf.'

'I was shielding you from a more sustained assault. Unless you agree to her demands this time, I'll have to unleash Miss Granville herself on you.'

'I'm sure this matter can be sorted out easily. We are, after all, good friends, are we not? The four of us had such a delightful time the other night. My wife remarked on it only this morning.'

'What sort of remarks would she have made had she known of your relationship with Miss Ingram?'

'I have no relationship with her.'

'The lady may be more honest if I confront her in person and tell her that we know how she came to secure a role in the play.'

'No, no,' begged Teale, 'don't do that, I pray. We must keep Miss Ingram out of this altogether.'

'But she is responsible for this dilemma. Miss Granville accepted your invitation to come to the theatre only after she'd seen the cast that you'd engaged. Henrietta Doyle's name was on the list, but the letter she sent to Miss Granville makes it clear that she was never even considered for the role of Celia.' Paul took a step closer and fixed him with a stare. 'It had already been promised to Miss Ingram, hadn't it?'

'You don't understand, Mr Skillen.'

'Then please enlighten me.'

Teale reeled off a whole battery of excuses, but they fell on deaf ears. Paul simply stood there impassively. When he realised that he could not wriggle out of it, the manager acceded to all of Paul's demands, saying that he would write to Henrietta Doyle that very day. While he insisted that there was nothing improper in his dealings with Elinor Ingram, he pleaded with

Paul to make no mention of the actress to Mrs Teale. He insisted that, by way of a heartfelt apology, there would be a generous increase in Hannah's salary. Everything was settled to Paul's satisfaction. He was even able to gather all the information he'd asked for about Cosgrove's work at the theatre. It turned out to be more extensive than Paul had imagined. Pausing at the door, he had a last question.

'Do you have a message for Miss Granville?'

'Yes,' said Teale, lower lip quivering. 'Tell her that today's rehearsal has been cancelled. I have to speak to Miss Ingram.'

Paul gave his broadest smile. 'You'll have much to discuss.'

Yeomans and Hale were back in their customary seats at the Peacock Inn, but they'd consumed far more than was normal for that time of day. Hale was drinking to celebrate their success, but Yeomans' ale was helping to drown his disappointment.

'We never get full credit for what we do,' he protested. 'We go there to tell him about two important arrests and he sends us off with a sneer about Harry Scattergood.'

'All that Harry deserves is a sneer.'

'I got valuable information out of those bodysnatchers.'

'True, but that was only possible because Ruddock and Filbert had caught the pair of them in the first place.'

'Mr Kirkwood should have shaken our hands.'

'Yes, Micah.'

'Instead of which, he tells us what a clever man Ruddock is.'

'We knew that already.'

'Don't keep on about him,' snarled Yeomans. 'And why did you have to say that setting a trap was really Ruddock's idea?'

The door opened and a bleary-eyed Ruddock tottered in. It took him a moment to locate them. Once he'd done so, he staggered over to their table and stood in front of it, swaying slightly.

'You look exhausted, Chevy,' said Hale.

'I am, sir, but I wanted to know if you'd been to Bow Street.'

'Yes, we have.'

'Was Mr Kirkwood pleased with us?'

'Yes,' replied Yeomans, 'he was especially pleased by the way I'd shaken the truth out of those men. You stopped one crime in its tracks, but I got them to confess to several others. I even scared them into giving me the name of the man who hired them.' He thrust his chin forward. 'Could you have done that?'

'No, I couldn't, Mr Yeomans.'

'What about Bill Filbert?'

'Neither of us have your skills, sir.'

'Remember that.'

'One good thing,' observed Hale, sniffing, 'you don't stink half as much as you did yesterday.' Ruddock threatened to fall, but Hale steadied him with a hand. 'You need your sleep, Chevy.'

'Thank you, sir.'

'When you wake up again,' said Yeomans, 'I have another assignment for you.'

'It's not in another churchyard, is it, sir?'

'No, it's a different sort of task altogether. Harry Scattergood is back in London.'

'What am I supposed to do about it, sir?'

Yeomans had a sip of ale and gargled with it before swallowing. 'Find him,' he said.

Abigail Saunders was eager to know how Clemency was faring. When she heard that Jan van Emden had sailed to London, she felt that it was a touching romantic gesture on his part.

'Any man in that situation would wish to support his wife,' said Charlotte. 'He was detained by business commitments. Otherwise, he'd have boarded the same vessel as his wife and we might never have heard about her problem.'

'Yes,' said Huckvale, 'it was only because they were lost that I stopped to help them. From what I've been told about Mr van Emden, he's the sort of person who never gets lost anywhere. His work takes him to a number of countries and he probably feels at home in all of them.'

'He's a true cosmopolitan,' said Peter, before turning to Abigail. 'You said that you had news for me.'

'Well, first of all,' she said, excitedly, 'let me tell you about my new position. I'm to be in service to a Mr Endsleigh of Regent Street. I'm so pleased to be back in the city again. Wapping frightens me.'

'It is a trifle unruly,' he agreed.

'We're very pleased for you,' said Charlotte. 'How did the offer of this post come about?'

'That's what I need to tell Mr Skillen. He kept asking me about Joseph – that's Joseph Rafter.'

Peter leant forward. 'You know where I can find him?'

'Yes, we'll be working alongside each other again. Joseph is employed by Mr Endsleigh as well. He was good enough to put in a word for me. I'm on my way there now.' She indicated her luggage. 'That's why I've brought all my belongings.'

'I'll come with you.'

'That's very kind of you, Mr Skillen, but there's no need. I can find my way to Regent Street easily. It's not far.'

'I just wish to speak to Rafter. His name has come up so often that I'm curious to meet him myself.'

'Does he know that Mrs van Emden is back in England again?' asked Charlotte.

'Yes,' answered Abigail.

'How did he react?'

'Well, it was strange, really. When she lived with us, he always liked Miss Parry, as we knew her. Today,' she said, 'he was different. He seemed quite upset that she was back here again.'

CHAPTER TWENTY-ONE

Since there was to be no rehearsal, a whole day stretched before them and Hannah was set on enjoying every minute of it. She had been in one of the most beautiful cities in England for days yet seen nothing of it. Fear had robbed her of the delights of Bath. All that she'd done was to scurry to and fro like a frightened mouse. Emboldened by the triumph over the manager and by the promised expulsion of Elinor Ingram and another actress, Hannah shook off all her anxieties. Fine weather beckoned them outside, so they began with a leisurely stroll through the streets. They saw masses of people promenading in the morning sunshine.

'Why are there so many soldiers here?' she asked.

'The war is over, my love. They've returned to their barracks. That's why you see so many splendid redcoats.'

'You'd look wonderful in uniform, Paul.'

'As it happens, I looked quite superb.'

'You never told me that you'd served in the army.'

'It was only for a very short time, Hannah,' he said. 'Have you so soon forgotten the time that I posed as the hero of Waterloo?'

'Of course!' she exclaimed. 'You were the Duke of Wellington to the life. I was able to advise you about using greasepaint and moulding a false nose.'

It had been shortly after they'd been drawn together. Peter and Paul foiled a plot to assassinate the Duke at an event in Hyde Park to celebrate the victory at Waterloo. While the real Duke was safely out of the way, his double – Paul Skillen – duped the would-be killers.

'You are a born actor, Paul.'

'I prefer to live in the real world.'

As they walked on, she remembered something.

'Did you tell Mr Teale of your suspicions about Cosgrove?'

'No, Hannah, and I don't intend to. At the moment,' he went on, 'he's far too preoccupied to think about anyone but Miss Ingram. In fact, he's probably trying to mollify her at this very instant.'

'Elinor will be giving the most animated performance of her life,' she said, laughing, 'and Teale is the deserved victim of it.' She became serious. 'How will he behave towards me tomorrow?'

'He'll treat you as if you were made of delicate porcelain.'

'Is he a vengeful man?'

'He's a very chastened one. I don't think he'll ever again try to smuggle his mistress into the cast of a play under false pretences.

If anyone will have a grudge against you,' said Paul, 'it will be Miss Ingram.'

'Elinor has always had a grudge against me.'

'She'll have an even bigger one now.'

Elinor Ingram was incandescent with fury. Having been promised a role she'd always coveted in a play that would be seen by the high society of Bath, she was instead being told that she was no longer a member of the company. When she recalled the favours she'd had to offer in order to be rewarded with the part of Celia, she started shaking with fury.

'You *used* me, Vernon,' she said, accusingly.

'I loved you, my darling.'

'Is this what your love amounts to – summary eviction?'

'We'll give out that you were taken ill,' he suggested.

'You tried that device for Henrietta Doyle and it failed.'

'How was I to know that she was a friend of Miss Granville's? But for a cruel coincidence, my stratagem would have worked.'

They were in the drawing room of the neat little cottage that he'd rented for her, providing her with a cook as well as a servant. It was a cosy nook and they'd spent hours of pleasure in it. Knowing that she had a temper, he'd expected blazing criticism but nothing on the scale he now faced. As he watched her pacing the room like a caged animal, he was dithering with fear. Eventually, she stopped and turned on him with a wild-eyed savagery.

'I have it!' she said, snapping her fingers. 'I have the solution.'

'What is it?' he gibbered.

'Instead of dispensing with me in this disgraceful way, you simply have to get rid of *her*.'

'That's unthinkable!'

'I find it a quite delicious thought.'

'I have a contract with Hannah Granville.'

'You had one with me until minutes ago. Then you tore it up as if it was utterly meaningless.'

'Miss Granville will be a memorable Rosalind.'

'I could play the role better, infinitely better. Well,' she added, 'it's true, isn't it?' He nodded meekly. 'What does she have that I don't?'

'She has a *name*.'

'I have a name as well. It's Elinor Ingram and it should be given the respect due to it. Give me the chance to play Rosalind and I will eclipse Hannah Granville in every way.' She folded her arms. 'That's my demand, Vernon.'

'It can never be met, alas.'

'Why not?'

'Miss Granville's reputation will bring people flocking to this theatre night after night. Yours, my darling, has yet to reach those heights. It most certainly will one day. Of that, there's no doubt. I will assist your career in every way that I can. At the moment, however,' he said, arms outstretched in a gesture of despair, 'I have to bow to the wishes of my leading lady. Miss Granville will be taking the role of Rosalind.'

'And I'll be supplanted as Celia.'

'It's unavoidable, I fear.'

'All those promises you made were utterly meaningless.'

'I'll make it up to you somehow.'

'Why should I believe a word you say?'

He put his arms around her. 'Elinor, my darling . . .'

'Get out of here,' she said, pushing him away.

'You seem to forget that I am paying for this cottage.'

'GET OUT!'

Ducking the decanter that was hurled at him, Teale decided that it was the moment to beat a retreat.

Having endured the rigours of life in a Wapping tavern, Abigail Saunders was delighted to move to a more sedate environment. When she and Peter called at the house in Regent Street, the servants' door was opened by a man who was clearly the brother of Nicholas Rafter. Sleek and well-spoken, he lacked the shipwright's physique and brusque manner, but the similarities were too numerous to ignore. Hearing that Peter wished to speak to him, Rafter first took Abigail off to meet the rest of the domestic staff, then returned alone. He invited Peter into his pantry and offered him a seat. Rafter was polite and respectful.

'Did you enjoy working for Mr Parry?' asked Peter.

'Yes, I did.'

'Why was that?'

'He was a decent, fair-minded man.'

'Why did you leave?'

'It was impossible for me to stay, sir. When Mr Parry had financial problems, he sought to reduce the wages of the staff. Had it only affected me, I might have accepted the change of circumstance, but others are involved. I have aged parents who rely on the money I can send them.'

'With respect,' said Peter, 'it can only have been a limited amount. Your brother, Nicholas, must earn a much larger wage as a shipwright. Surely, he was in a better position to support your parents?'

Rafter was surprised. 'How did you know that I had a brother?'

'When I was trying to find you, I first made contact with him.'

'What did he say about me?'

'To be candid, he was not very flattering. In blunt terms, he gave me to understand that you and he are estranged from one another.'

'Nick and I haven't spoken for years.'

'Why is that?'

'There are a number of reasons, sir,' said Rafter. 'One of them concerns the way that he treats our parents. It's disgraceful, Mr Skillen. That's all I'm prepared to say.'

'Then I won't pursue the matter,' said Peter. 'Your private life is your own affair. All that I'm interested in is your relationship with Mr Parry and his daughter. You knew them both for a number of years.'

'It was a very happy house until Mrs Parry died.'

'How did her husband respond to that?'

'He became even more of a hermit, sir. He'd lock himself in his study and work long hours on his latest project.'

'What about Miss Parry?'

Rafter paused. 'Miss Parry was profoundly upset by her mother's death,' he said, measuring his words. 'She was still relatively young, you must remember, and took time to . . . adapt to the new situation.'

'Did you like Miss Parry?'

'I had the greatest respect for her.'

'That's not what I asked, Mr Rafter. Since you take such care of your parents, you are obviously a man who believes in duty to your family. There came a point,' said Peter, 'when Miss Parry put her own wishes before her sense of duty. For a young woman to defy her father in the way that she did was highly unusual.'

'It was not my place to comment on the situation, sir.'

'But you must have had an opinion.'

'It's one that carried no weight.'

'May I know what it is?'

'I don't see why you are asking such questions, sir. Time has moved on. What happened between Miss Parry and her father is water under the bridge now.'

'That's an appropriate image for a man who once designed a bridge,' said Peter, amused. 'As to the point you make, I have to disagree with you. What happened in the past illumines the present. My task, in essence, is to reunite a father and daughter. Do you object to that?'

'No, I don't, sir.'

'I sense that you have reservations.'

'I've come to believe that Mr Parry is no longer alive.'

'Oh, there's great doubt on that score.'

Rafter was taken aback. 'Are you quite sure, sir?'

'Someone has gone to the trouble of trying to convince Mr Parry's daughter that her father is dead. I've established to my own satisfaction that he is not.'

'Then where is he?'

'I'm hoping that you'll help me find him.'

The trip to Bath had completely shattered Jenny Pye's expectations. After an uneventful journey, she'd assumed, she would spend most of the time in Hannah's company, watching the rehearsals, helping her to memorise her role, attending all of Rosalind's costume fittings and offering support whenever it was needed. Instead, she'd been held at gunpoint by three highwaymen, then – after Paul's arrival – been able to spend less time alone with Hannah. A practical woman, she was quick to see an advantage. She had relatives living in a village less than ten miles away from the city and had asked for a day off to visit them.

Her cousin and his wife lived on a small farm with their family. They'd always marvelled at Jenny for working in what they believed was a glamorous profession that involved visits to various cities, Paris included, and which gave her the opportunity to rub shoulders with famous people. Jenny didn't have the heart to disillusion them by describing how lowly a position she held and how unexciting her work sometimes was. She did, however, have a captive audience when talking about the robbery.

It was refreshing to exchange her urban existence for country smells and the noise of animals. The simplicity of farm life had a great appeal to her. When she felt it was time to return to Bath, her cousin insisted on driving Jenny there in a dog cart. He climbed into the vehicle with an old fowling gun over his shoulder. She assured him that there was no danger of an attack by highwaymen, but he insisted that they had to be ready for every eventuality. Ten miles seemed to flash past and she was astounded when she caught her first glimpse of Bath on the horizon.

'Remind me what this play of yours is called,' said her cousin.

'It's called *As You Like It*, and it's a comedy by William Shakespeare.'

'I've heard talk of him afore.'

'Would you like to see a performance?' she asked. 'I'm certain that Miss Granville will be able to get tickets for you at no charge.'

He shook his head. 'Plays are not for the likes of us, Jenny.'

'You'd enjoy it.'

'We don't belong.'

It was not a complaint, just a bald statement of fact. Content in his isolated village, her cousin was out of place in a city, especially one as grand and imposing as Bath. As soon as they entered it, he was on edge, glancing furtively at the tall buildings, his dog cart dwarfed by the stylish carriages and magnificent coaches that rolled past. From her point of view, Jenny found that her mode of transport was ideal because it gave her a perfect view of everything around her. When she saw Paul and Hannah walking proudly along a pavement together, she wanted to cry out to catch their attention, but something stopped her.

She had just seen the man who was following them.

Joseph Rafter had changed. Willing to cooperate at first, he was now more circumspect. His answers came less readily.

'I'm afraid that I can't give you more time, Mr Skillen,' he said. 'I've duties to perform and Abby needs her instructions.'

'I won't be long,' said Peter. 'I'll come to the question that brought me here in the first place.'

'Very well.'

'Did you intercept the letters sent here by Mrs van Emden?'

Rafter goggled. 'I can't believe you asked me that, sir.'

'Why shouldn't I?'

'It's an insult.'

'Could I have an answer, please?'

'No, I did not intercept any correspondence addressed to Mr Parry. It would never occur to me to do such a thing.'

'What of the letters that he wrote to his daughter?'

'There weren't any,' said Rafter. 'Mr Parry broke off all contact with her. Why should he wish to write to someone who defied him?'

'I'm only telling you what Mr Darwood confided in us. I'm sure that you remember him.'

'I remember the gentleman well. He came often at one time, then, for some reason, his visits were few and far between.'

'Why do you think that was?'

'After his daughter married,' said Rafter, seriously, 'Mr Parry had no social life to speak of. Hardly anyone was ever invited to the house.'

'If he and Mr Darwood were such old friends, Mr Parry would have trusted him implicitly.'

'I'm sure that he did, sir.'

'So he might have told him something that he appears to have kept from you – namely, that he wrote to Mrs van Emden in the hopes of finding a means of reconciliation.'

Rafter frowned. 'This comes as news to me, sir.'

'I find that rather odd.'

'Why?'

'Mr Parry employed you to run his house. You were closest to him and would have known everything he did.'

'Not necessarily – he was a very private man.'

'If you were in charge there,' said Peter, 'you'd surely have been responsible for sending any correspondence from Mr Parry.'

'That was true, sir.'

'You'd also have seen any letters that came to the house.'

'In the normal course of events, I would.'

'So why didn't you see the mail sent by Mrs van Emden?'

'It's a mystery, Mr Skillen.'

Rafter met his gaze. His face was blank, his eyes glinting, his voice deliberately flat. Peter couldn't decide if the man was being honest or displaying dumb insolence. He tried a slightly different tack.

'When he lost his house,' resumed Peter, 'Mr Parry asked you and Abigail to be there when the servants of the new owner arrived.'

'That's correct, sir.'

'Why did he choose you when he no longer employed you?'

'He asked me as a favour, Mr Skillen. I was glad to help.'

'Yet, by that stage, it was Edmund Haines who had taken over the running of the house. Why didn't he ask Haines?'

'Mr Parry didn't tell me, sir.'

'You must have wondered.'

'It wasn't something that worried me.'

'My information is that he found Haines especially trustworthy. Were you aware of that?'

'Edmund repaid that trust.'

'Then why was he overlooked when the house was changing hands?'

'We don't know that he was, sir,' said Rafter, evenly. 'It may be that he was asked to take on the task but refused for some reason. There's another possibility, and it's not as strange as it may sound: Mr Parry simply forgot to ask him. He was drinking a lot and his memory failed him all the time.'

'He didn't forget you, though.'

'No, I was touched by that – especially as we didn't part on the best of terms. It was good to work briefly with Abby again.'

Still unable to decide how honest the man was, Peter pressed on.

'What made you think that Mr Parry was dead?'

'The last time I saw him, he looked desperately ill.'

'Did you speak to him?'

'No, sir,' answered Rafter. 'Before I could do so, he disappeared into the crowd. In one sense, I was relieved. I'd prefer to remember him as he was before . . . things changed for the worst.' He stood up. 'I must go now, Mr Skillen. We're not really allowed to have visitors, you see.' He opened the door. 'I'll show you out.'

'Let me ask you one more thing,' said Peter, rising slowly to his feet. 'What happened to Edmund Haines?'

'He did what I did and sought work elsewhere.'

'And did he find it?'

'So I'm told.'

'I'd very much like to find him.'

'All I can tell you is that he now lives somewhere in High Barnet,' said Rafter, 'but I don't have the address.'

Peter smiled. His visit had yielded a vital piece of information.

'I think I know what it might be,' he said.

In the wake of Harry Scattergood's escape from one of the cells at Bow Street Magistrates' Court, the reward money for his capture had been increased even more. His rumoured disappearance from London meant that he was out of reach of the Runners, but that didn't stop them trying to gather information about his whereabouts. Dozens of informers – some of them, thieves themselves – were on the lookout for Scattergood's return. The city was his private gold mine. He wouldn't desert it for long.

'He's definitely back,' said Yeomans. 'I feel it in my water.'

'There have been sightings of Harry. Sooner or later, someone will tell us where he is.'

'We'll take charge of the arrest ourselves, Alfred. I'm not letting the Skillen brothers get their greedy hands on him this time.'

'Paul is still in Bath,' said Hale.

'Long may he stay there!'

'And Peter must be busy somewhere. He's not working at the gallery, I know that. Gully Ackford has had to hire someone to help him out. The Skillen brothers both have business elsewhere.'

They were ambling along the Strand, keeping their eyes peeled and enjoying the occasional glances of appreciation they received.

Yeomans and Hale were well-known figures, lauded by law-abiding citizens as much as they were reviled by the criminal fraternity. As they passed a side street, they saw a man stepping back smartly into a doorway.

'That was Reuben Walters,' said Hale.

'They must have let him out of Newgate.'

'He swore to kill us, Micah.'

'That little rat couldn't kill anyone,' said Yeomans, laughing. 'A good fart would blow him over. One thing about Harry Scattergood – he had good reason to hate us as much as Reuben, yet he's never made the slightest threat against us.'

'He might if we actually manage to arrest him.'

'I don't think so. It's all a game to Harry. He's been the winner so far. Next time, I swear, we'll give him a very nasty surprise. We'll win the game once and for all.'

She was a miracle-worker. Scattergood didn't know if it was the magic of her kisses, the curative power of her caresses or the sorcery of her songs, and he didn't care. The simple fact was that Welsh Mary had brought him back to life again, simultaneously subduing his pain and stimulating his desire. They were in a different room in a different tavern now. Keeping on the move was his long-established ritual. Instead of taking time off to visit Welsh Mary whenever he could, he'd brought her with him. It had been a resounding success. She was not only there to do his bidding day and night, he had the gratification of knowing that he was not sharing her with other clients. There had been many other women in his life, but none made him feel that he'd found Elysium. Scattergood wanted more of her.

* * *

Hannah was glad to see Jenny return to the hotel and invited her into their room. Paul was already there.

'How did your visit go?' he asked.

'Oh, I had a lovely time,' replied Jenny. 'I haven't seen them for ages and they were so pleased to see me. My cousin drove me back here.'

'That was good of him.'

'I saw the two of you walking along the main street.'

'Yes, rehearsals were cancelled for today.'

'Did you realise that someone was following you?'

'No, we didn't,' said Hannah. 'It wasn't Elinor Ingram, was it?'

'No, it wasn't her.'

'Then who was it?'

'It was that man who travelled with us on the coach,' said Jenny. 'Mr Cosgrove. Is he being paid to guard you?'

'He's being paid by someone,' said Paul, bitterly, 'but it's not us. While you were away, I discovered that he was working with those highwaymen.' Jenny was shocked. 'Yes, I know it's hard to believe, but there's no doubt about it. I haven't challenged him, as yet, because he's the one person who will lead me to those three villains.'

'Including Cosgrove, there'll be four of them against one of you,' protested Hannah. 'Even you can't fight against those odds, Paul. You need help. Send for Peter.'

'What can he do? Peter has problems of his own and they'll keep him more than busy. No, my love, this is something I'll have to handle by myself. I can't expect any assistance from my brother.'

As Peter rode out of the city, Jem Huckvale was alongside him. Both men were armed. The first stage of the journey was passed largely in silence as Peter speculated on the significance of what he'd been told by Joseph Rafter. While it was unwise to rule out the possibility of a curious coincidence, he felt that it was highly unlikely. Memories of his earlier visit to High Barnet came surging into his mind. Having forgotten all about Sebastian Alderson, he was now trying to recall every word that the man had uttered to him. After a while, he became conscious that he had a companion.

'I'm sorry, Jem,' he said. 'I was miles away.'

'So was I.'

Peter smiled. Whenever he caught Huckvale with an expression of silent joy on his face, he could read the younger man's mind. He was thinking fondly of Meg Rooke.

'I knew there was something odd about Mr Alderson,' said Peter. 'When he paid for that funeral, he ordered the cheapest coffin possible.'

'We don't know that.'

'Yes, we do. We both saw that coffin. It looked like something that had been made very quickly and with little care. It was the sort of thing you'd see at a pauper's funeral.'

'The man inside had *been* a pauper,' said Huckvale.

'Granted, but Mr Alderson, who paid for the funeral, is very rich. While I didn't expect him to spend a vast amount on a complete stranger, I thought he'd pay for something better than that.'

'Perhaps he did.'

'I don't understand.'

'Perhaps he paid for one coffin and was given something that was nowhere near as good. I doubt if the gentleman looked closely at the coffin. It's something I never do when I go to a funeral.'

'I catch your drift now,' said Peter. 'You're suggesting that

Mr Alderson was tricked by the undertaker who took a larger fee yet made a coffin worth only a fraction of the amount. It's possible, I suppose. He was not the most prepossessing individual, was he? On the other hand, he showed such pride in that poor, afflicted daughter of his. No,' he decided, 'I don't think he'd try to deceive Alderson – or the vicar, for that matter. Whoever he really was, the deceased was buried in the mean coffin ordered for him.'

'Why does it worry you so much?'

'It tells us something about Mr Alderson's character.'

'You said he was kind and considerate.'

'He was, Jem, and I still admire what he did. He's a Good Samaritan, if ever there was one. There's just something about him that troubles me.'

'And you want my opinion of him, is that it?'

'No, it isn't.'

'Then why were you so keen for me to come with you?'

'I may have a very important job for you to do.'

Once her dresser had settled back in, Hannah decided that she would like to visit the spa and taste the celebrated water. Since Jenny would act as her chaperone, Paul was no longer needed. He seized the opportunity to take a second look at the home of Roderick Cosgrove. On his earlier visit, he hadn't been invited into the house because Cosgrove claimed to have company. From the way that the man had confided the information, Paul had assumed that the visitor was a woman. In the wake of the discovery that Cosgrove was, in fact, an accessory to the highwaymen, he now questioned that assumption. Paul began to wonder if Cosgrove's visitor might instead have been one of the men who'd robbed the coach.

Now aware that they'd been followed by the man that morning, Paul was more circumspect, looking over his shoulder at regular intervals and, when turning a corner, waiting a few minutes to see if anyone was dogging his footsteps. There was no sign of Cosgrove or anyone else. He could move freely about the city. When he got to Cosgrove's house, he found a vantage point from which he could watch unseen. Paul had come prepared. Hidden beneath his coat were two pistols.

What he was hoping for was a glimpse of the man who'd led the highwaymen. Though he'd been wearing a mask at the time, there'd been distinctive features about the man. The description given him by Hannah had been similar to those from Jenny and Mrs Vellacott. Ironically, the joint portrait they'd painted of the man made him sound rather like Paul himself. He was chasing his mirror image. It was telling that Cosgrove had given a less detailed description of the leader, claiming that he was distracted by the pain from his injury. At the time, Paul had believed him. That was no longer the case. Cosgrove was the highwaymen's spy. He shared their guilt and deserved to be punished accordingly.

If Sebastian Alderson was astonished to see Peter Skillen again, he kept his surprise hidden behind a bland smile of welcome.

'What brings you back here?' he asked as he took his visitor into the library. 'It's a long ride from London.'

'You don't need to tell me that, sir.'

'Do you bring news of the arrest of the grave robbers?'

'Unhappily,' said Peter, 'I don't, but I hope to find them in due course. Once I take on a task, I see it through to the end.'

After a lengthy time in the saddle, Peter was glad to be offered a seat. Taking the chair by the desk, Alderson studied him.

'How is Mrs van Emden?' he asked.

'Much to her delight, her husband has arrived from the Netherlands. That's why I didn't subject her to the same journey again.'

'That's very considerate of you, Mr Skillen.'

'Being considerate is a trait I share with you, sir. When you took an interest in that dying man, you showed extraordinary concern for a fellow human being in distress.'

'I hate to see suffering of any kind.'

'Most people turn away from it.'

'Then I am the odd one out and proud to be so.'

There was a long silence. While Peter wondered how best to proceed, Alderson was trying to work out the reason for his return. Each was waiting for the other to make the first move. In the end, Peter tired of being evaluated by the other's searching gaze.

'Why was the deceased buried in such a mean coffin?' he asked.

'What an absurd question,' replied Alderson, with a laugh of disbelief. 'Are you seriously claiming that you came all the way from London simply to ask me that?'

'Other questions may arise out of your answer, sir.'

'I'm tempted to tell you to mind your own business, Mr Skillen.'

'I can't do that. Somebody tried to persuade us that the man in that grave was George Parry. We are convinced that he was not. As a result, the coffin has taken on a special interest for me.'

'I don't see why it should.'

'Its quality is at variance with the generosity of the purchaser.'

Alderson became peevish. 'What did you expect?' he said. 'A velvet-lined coffin of the finest oak with brass handles?'

'I expected something that reflected your character, sir.'

'I did my best to save that man's life.'

'You deserve full credit for that, Mr Alderson.'

'Then I'd be grateful if you'd stop criticising me.'

'No criticism is intended, sir. I just wish to understand why you ordered the cheapest coffin available.'

'I don't have to answer to you for the way that I choose to spend my money,' said Alderson, pompously. 'I found the fellow in the most dire condition, sought medical assistance and did what I could to make his last few hours on earth as comfortable and dignified as possible. Why should I spend a large amount of money on his funeral when a simple coffin was just as serviceable as the most elaborate casket?'

'If we followed that reasoning,' said Peter, tartly, 'every one of us would be buried in a crude wooden box. Are you happy at the prospect of your funeral being conducted solely on the principle of serviceability?'

'I refuse to discuss this any further.'

'Then we can move on to the next question.'

'There'll *be* no next question, Mr Skillen.' He rose to his feet. 'Good day to you, sir.'

'Tell me about Edmund Haines.'

'I know nobody of that name.'

'Are you sure, sir?'

'I'm absolutely certain.'

It was a categorical denial, but Peter had seen the way that the man's mouth had twitched involuntarily at the mention of Haines. He got up from his seat and confronted Alderson.

'Now you see why I was compelled to return, sir,' he said, calmly. 'Edmund Haines was one of Mr Parry's servants. You happened to have chanced upon a dying man identified as George Parry. When I was told that Haines lived in High Barnet, you'll realise why your name came into my mind immediately.' He sharpened his voice. 'I think that Haines is a member of your domestic staff.'

'That's not true.'

'He might, of course, be using another name – just like that man in the cheap coffin.'

Controlling his anger, Alderson drew himself up to his full height.

'I give you my word as a gentleman,' he declared, as if taking an oath, 'that Edmund Haines is not a member of my domestic staff. You are at liberty to speak to everyone under this roof. Each one of them has been with me for years. Since I didn't need an additional servant, why on earth should I employ one?'

Peter was unruffled. 'I seem to have made a slight mistake.'

'It's time for you to leave,' said Alderson, ringing a small bell. 'I hope that our paths never cross again, Mr Skillen.'

'I'm sorry to have bothered you, sir.'

The door was opened by a servant. Peter bade his host farewell, but all that Alderson did by way of a reply was to glare at him. The servant escorted Peter along the passageway and into the hall before opening the front door. Another servant was waiting outside, holding the reins of Peter's horse. After thanking the man, he mounted the animal and rode off at a steady canter.

Teeth clenched and jaw muscles undulating, Alderson watched through the window until Peter disappeared out of sight. He then moved to the desk to write a swift message. Summoning a servant once more, he handed him the letter and gave him his orders. The man headed for the stables at once. Minutes later, he left the house and kicked his horse into a gallop. Back at the window, Alderson saw him go. What he didn't see, however, was the rider who came out of a side street and followed the servant who'd just been dispatched. Emerging from his hiding place at last, Jem Huckvale was thrilled to be involved in the chase.

Charlotte Skillen had heard the story of their courtship before, but Jan van Emden's version provided several new details. Attracted by her beauty, he was also struck by what he saw as Clemency's vulnerability. It had aroused a protective urge in him. While she had given the impression that the whole of their relationship had been conducted in secret, he admitted that he'd approached her father to ask for his permission to call on her. It was brusquely denied with the excuse that she was already spoken for.

'I just didn't believe it,' said van Emden. 'When a woman's heart has already been given to a man, you can see it in her eyes. I saw it in yours, the moment I met you, Charlotte. But it was, thankfully, absent from Clemency's eyes. She didn't belong to anyone else. What I saw was a gorgeous young woman pleading to be rescued.'

'And you responded,' said his wife, squeezing his hand.

'Why was Mr Parry so antagonistic towards you?' asked Charlotte. 'Was it because you were a foreigner, or did he think the age gap between you and Clemency made a marriage unthinkable?'

'Both were elements in his rejection of me,' he said, 'but the main problem was that I dared to argue with him on the subject of engineering. We are a small, flat country that is essentially a trading nation. Enormous efforts have been made over the years to reclaim land from the sea, a feat of engineering that I believe is unparalleled. Mr Parry disagreed.'

'Father could be very argumentative,' said Clemency.

'Reasoned argument is one thing, my darling, but he had no time for that. Because I dared to disagree with him, he was shaking with fury. He said that Ironbridge was a greater piece of engineering because it was the first single-span cast iron bridge in the world. The Netherlands had produced nothing to match it.'

'That's a matter of opinion,' said Charlotte.

'Mr Parry claimed that Britain was the greatest industrial nation on the planet and that countries like mine followed in its wake. There's some truth in that, of course, but I stubbornly maintained that our skill at land reclamation is worthy of the highest praise. It annoyed Mr Parry.'

'You should have agreed with him,' said Clemency.

'I'm proud of my nation's achievements. I wasn't going to dismiss them in the way that your father did. Doing my best to remain polite, I refused to bow to his exaggerated claims. From that point on,' he said, sadly, 'I knew that any contact between Clemency and me would have to be secret. I was caught up in a debate I could never win.'

'You won my love,' said his wife. 'It would have been so much easier had Father accepted you as a son-in-law, but that was beyond him.'

'Only at the start,' Charlotte pointed out. 'He did mellow in time and made efforts to get in touch with you.'

'I wish I'd been aware of that, Charlotte.'

Her husband was philosophical. 'I doubt that he'll ever approve of me,' he said. 'I'm still too old for his daughter and I'm still a champion of Dutch engineering.'

'I think he'd be prepared to make allowances now,' said Charlotte.

'We must all hope that he's still alive.'

'Oh, he is. I've never known Peter more certain about something.'

'If he does find Mr Parry, he'll be doing us an enormous favour.'

'He's doing what he was hired to do. This is far more than a task to my husband. It's a mission.'

* * *

Peter had to wait for the best part of an hour. He and Huckvale had agreed to meet at a village not far from High Barnet that boasted a small but comfortable tavern. It was a good place to rest and to analyse the conversation he'd had with Alderson. The man had clearly been needled by the reference to the coffin in which the bogus George Parry had been buried. Instead of being praised for the kindness shown towards the stricken man, Alderson had been censored. In retrospect, Peter found that one of the man's first questions took on more significance. He'd asked if the grave robbers had been caught and there was the slightest tremor in his voice. That set Peter thinking. Huckvale eventually arrived and entered the tavern. He rushed over to his friend's table.

'Well?' asked Peter, looking up. 'Have you found him?'

'I might have done.'

Having watched the house for a long time, Paul Skillen came to the conclusion that Cosgrove was not at home. Nobody had come out of, or gone into, the abode. It was time for Paul to rejoin Hannah. Before he could quit his carefully chosen position opposite, however, he saw someone approach on a bay mare. The rider was tall, lean, elegant and close to his own age. All his instincts told Paul that he was at last looking at the leader of the highwaymen, the person who'd stolen Hannah's pendant, then caused her untold grief by stalking her. The man was finally within reach. When he saw him dismount outside Cosgrove's house and tether his horse, Paul felt a surge a joy. It was only momentary. His hat was suddenly torn off from behind and his head was struck hard by the butt of a pistol.

CHAPTER TWENTY-TWO

While enjoying his time with Welsh Mary to the full, Harry Scattergood was keenly aware that he had to dispose of the booty from St Albans. His visit to the town might have ended in failure, but it was offset by earlier successes. Jewellery, silver ornaments and a host of other small items were kept in bags under whichever bed he and his lover were sharing at any one time. They needed to be converted into money. Now that he'd recovered sufficiently from his wounds, he felt able to dispose of his loot. Welsh Mary made no protest. She knew full well that the expensive rings, brooches, necklaces and so on would be incongruous in the brothel that was her home and would arouse the envy of the other women. It was enough for her to have been allowed to wear some of them as she pranced naked around the room.

In his early years as a thief, he'd have taken everything to a dolly shop, home of a disreputable pawnbroker who'd always buy his wares, albeit at insultingly low prices. As he progressed, Scattergood dealt with other fences, discerning men who'd only receive stolen goods if they were of good quality. He was able to get better deals that way. In recent years, he'd relied on an old friend who would buy almost anything he was offered and ask no questions about its origin. There was a pattern to their business dealings. Scattergood would arrive at the house, display his latest plunder, be outraged at the prices offered for it, threaten to go elsewhere in future, gain concessions, reach a compromise and shake hands on the deal.

That was exactly what happened yet again. In less than ten minutes, he was leaving the premises discreetly by the back door with a large amount of money in his purse. Unbeknown to him, however, there was something different about the transaction this time.

Peter and Huckvale were in the saddle almost immediately, going back over the route that the younger man had just taken. To hold a conversation while cantering, they had to shout to each other.

'How far is it, Jem?' asked Peter.

'We should be there in less than half an hour.'

'And you say that it's a farm?'

'It was at one time,' said Huckvale, 'but I didn't see any animals there. The rider I followed went straight to this large barn. When he dismounted, he ran towards it.'

'My guess is he was carrying a warning letter.'

'You must have scared Mr Alderson.'

'He couldn't wait to get rid of me. When I realised that Haines was not part of the domestic staff, I fancied that he might be employed somewhere else by Alderson. That's why I'd asked you to hide in that side street.'

'Someone came out of the stables not long after you'd left. He was riding hell for leather. I had a job to keep up with him.'

'It sounds to me as if it was worth the effort, Jem.'

'I hope so.'

Because he'd been careful to keep out of sight, Huckvale had brought back only limited information, but it was enough to excite Peter and reinforce his suspicions.

'It's a pity you didn't get to see inside that barn,' he said.

'I might not have seen anything but I heard the noise loud and clear.'

'What sort of noise?'

'It's difficult to describe,' said Huckvale. 'It was a sort of clanking sound I've never heard before. I still can't decide what it was.'

'Could it have been some sort of agricultural machine?'

'I don't think so.'

'Why do you say that, Jem?'

'It's just a feeling I have. There's no hay or straw stored in that barn. I'm sure of that. It's being used for another purpose altogether.'

The visit to the baths had been an education. Neither of them could believe that Roman civilisation had been so advanced, creating majestic buildings that defied the passage of time and contained features that astounded them. Hannah and Jenny were less complimentary about the spa water itself, supposedly healthy but having a foul taste that seemed to linger. At no point had they felt in danger or that they were under observation. Since they were in places where plenty of people milled about, there was a sense of safety they could take for granted.

Hannah was glad to have Jenny back with her. As well as offering unquestioning support to her, the dresser understood the need for discretion with regard to Hannah's relationship with Paul, knowing instinctively when to make herself scarce. Alone together, they enjoyed each other's company.

'Whenever I see Roman ruins,' said Jenny, 'I think about the plays they must have seen in those days. Huge crowds went to see work by their playwrights. They're hardly ever heard of today.'

'It's a question of fashion,' said Hannah. 'There's no taste for plays of that period any more.'

'Shakespeare has survived – why haven't they?'

'He's better, Jenny, and he's English.'

They'd arranged to meet Paul at the hotel and expected to find him waiting for them. When there was no sign of him, Hannah collected the key, then led the way up to their room. As soon as she unlocked the door, she saw the letter awaiting her on the bedside table. Confident that it had been written by Paul, she snatched it up and opened it. Jenny saw her stiffen in horror.

'What's happened?' she asked.

'It's Paul,' gasped Hannah. 'He's been kidnapped.'

The dresser gulped. 'We must get help at once.'

'No, we can't. There's a warning in the letter against involving anyone else. If we do that, Paul will be killed. He means it, Jenny.'

'Who does?'

'The man who's been stalking me ever since we got to Bath. He sent this letter. I had others from him. He was the leader of those highwaymen.'

'And he'd really *kill* Paul?'

'I don't doubt it for a second.'

'But there must be some way to rescue him.'

'There is, Jenny. This is a ransom demand.'

'Then it will have to be paid at once.'

'He's not asking for money,' said Hannah, with a shudder. 'He wants a night alone with *me*.'

The Runners were so pleased with the information brought by Chevy Ruddock that one of them bought him a pie and a pint of ale to wash it down. He felt that he was appreciated at last. The three of them were in their usual corner in the Peacock Inn.

'How did you do it, lad?' asked Yeomans.

'I found out which fence Harry Scattergood used,' said Ruddock. 'He might have been out of London for a short while but that didn't mean he'd stop thieving. He can't help himself.'

'You're right there,' agreed Hale.

'When I heard he was back, I knew he'd have some booty to get rid of, so I talked to some of our informers and finally got a name out of them.'

'Who was it, Chevy?'

'Israel Goodman.'

'We know the rogue.'

'He's as crooked as a corkscrew,' added Yeomans, 'and we've tried to arrest him a number of times. Unfortunately, we could never catch him with stolen goods in his possession. We've searched and searched that filthy house where he lives, then had to give up.'

'You'd have caught him red-handed if you'd been there when Harry went in. I was watching through the window of the tavern opposite the house.'

'Then why didn't you arrest the pair of them?'

'It wasn't as easy as that, sir. Goodman has two ruffians standing outside his door. I couldn't tackle them on my own, Besides, I was after Harry Scattergood and not his fence. So I sneaked around to the back of the house,' Ruddock went on, 'because I knew that Harry would leave that way. Then I followed him.'

'Where did he go?'

'He's staying at The Mitre in Eastwell Street.'

'Then he must have money,' said Hale, 'The Mitre's expensive.'

'Harry's there with a female friend.'

Yeomans guffawed. 'She's his trull, his whore, his doxy,' he said. 'Women like that sell their friendship by the hour.' He got to his feet. 'You did well to come for us. Nobody could arrest Harry by himself. We'll take all reinforcements.'

'But I've only just had my first bite, sir,' said Ruddock, through a mouthful of pie.

'Eat the rest on the way there.'

'What about my ale?'

'We'll take care of that,' said Yeomans, grabbing the tankard and emptying half of its contents down his throat before handing it to Hale. 'Finish that off, Alfred. We're in a hurry.'

When they got within a hundred yards of the place, they slowed their horses to a trot. Peter saw that Huckvale's description had been accurate. Though there was a farmhouse, a yard, a cluster of outbuildings and a sizeable barn, there was no sense that they were looking at a working farm. The only animals visible were a few hens pecking at the ground in search of food. As they got closer, Peter heard the loud clanking noise that Huckvale had mentioned and he also spotted something that had eluded his friend. In the field behind the barn, the sun was glinting on something half-hidden in the grass. From that distance, it was difficult to make out exactly what it was.

As they rode towards the yard, they were aware of being watched from a window in the farmhouse, but nobody came out to challenge them. After tethering their horses, they walked to the barn and opened the door to peep inside. What they saw made both of them gape in amazement. They were looking at a huge engineering workshop, reminiscent of the one that Geoffrey Taylor owned. The doors at the far end were wide open, letting in the light and revealing that what they'd seen glinting in the sun was an iron railway that ran the length of the barn before going out into the field beyond and describing a complete circle.

Chugging along the line was a large, ugly, noisy contraption, comprising a boiler, six wheels, a tall funnel, a small funnel and a bewildering arrangement of pistons. As it left the barn and went out into the field, it was driven by a stocky man in rough, oil-stained clothing and a greasy cap. Belching smoke, the steam engine gathered speed and made a complete circuit of the railway before coming back into the barn and slowing to a halt. Watching the machine's progress with great interest was an older man in shabby attire. Both he and the driver were far too engrossed in what they were doing to notice the arrival of the visitors.

Peter had to raise his voice to be heard about the noise.

'Mr Parry?' he shouted.

The older man turned, peered at them, then waved to the driver. When various levers had been pulled, the engine hissed. The visitors moved forward.

'Are you George Parry?' asked Peter.

'Yes,' said the older man, uncertainly.

'You must make allowances for him,' warned the driver, getting down from the engine and eyeing them warily. 'He gets confused.'

'Do you like it?' asked Parry, indicating the machine. 'We built it together. It's mine.'

'Who are you and what do you want?' demanded the driver.

'We're friends of Mr Parry's daughter and we've come to take him back to her.'

'He's going nowhere. He lives here now.'

Parry was confused. 'I don't have a daughter any more.'

'You heard him,' said the driver, squaring up to them.

'Is this all he does?' asked Peter.

'It's important work. Steam locomotives like this will change our lives one day. They'll pull carriages that take people all over the country.'

Huckvale was dubious. 'I don't believe that.'

'But if it did happen,' said Peter, alive to the possibilities, 'it could indeed cause a revolution in transport. The inventor of this steam engine would stand to make a fortune.' He looked at Parry. 'Do you hold the patent?'

'No,' said a stern voice behind them, 'Mr Alderson does.'

Peter turned to see the gun pointing at him.

The women were in turmoil. Horrified to discover that Paul had been kidnapped, they were reeling from the ransom demand for his release. It had made Hannah's flesh creep.

'Whatever am I supposed to do, Jenny?' she cried.

'You must never put yourself in his power,' said the other. 'There's no telling what that man might do to you.'

'Paul's safety is the most important thing.'

'We have no idea where he is.'

'That's not true,' said Hannah. 'He was going to take a second look at Mr Cosgrove's house. That's where he must have been seized.'

'I think you should tell the manager.'

'No, I can't do that.'

'We need help and he's the best person to give it.'

'You didn't read the letter, Jenny. It forbade me to turn to Mr Teale or to anyone else. If I do, I'll be signing Paul's death warrant.'

'What a dreadful thought!'

'There *has* to be a way to rescue him,' decided Hannah, face distorted by sheer terror. 'We must try to keep calm. We can't make sensible decisions when we're in this state.' Eyes closed, she breathed in deeply, then exhaled slowly, repeating the process several times. When she felt she'd achieved a measure of control, she opened her eyes again. 'There's a question we must ask ourselves, Jenny.'

'Is there?'

'What would Paul do in this situation?'

'He could never *be* in an identical position.'

'This is a crisis,' said Hannah, 'and he's dealt with many of those in the course of his work. I know exactly how he'd react.'

'Do you?'

'He'd send for Peter.'

'But his brother is still in London,' argued Jenny, 'and it would take ages to reach him.'

'Not if I sent a message by courier. It might arrive in the early hours of tomorrow but I know that Peter would respond at once. He'd ride all night to come to his brother's aid.'

'Could you hold off this monster until then?'

'I'll have to somehow,' said Hannah. 'I can't possibly succumb to his demand. It's unthinkable.' She thought of Paul's predicament. 'And yet . . .'

When he regained consciousness, Paul Skillen found that he couldn't move, see or speak. Bound and gagged, he had a blindfold over his eyes. Desperately wanting to put a hand to the throbbing pain at the back of his skull, he was tied to the stout wooden chair in which he was slumped. He tried hard to concentrate so that he could work out where he was. The place was cold and dank. He could hear a steady drip nearby. When he struggled slightly and made the chair move a few inches, there was a slight echo. Paul decided that he was in a cellar. His guess was soon confirmed. He heard a door being unbolted above him, then feet came down stone steps. The next moment, someone undid his blindfold and snatched it off. He blinked several times before his eyes became used to the lantern that was held close to his face. His visitor was a tall, lean, well-dressed man with a cultured voice. He wore the mask he'd used when robbing the stagecoach.

'Good day to you, Mr Skillen,' he said. 'I'm sorry to offer you such mean accommodation, but you've become rather a nuisance to me. There is, however, hope that your life may yet be spared. All that Miss Granville has to do is to spend a night in my arms.'

Consumed by rage, Paul did everything he could to escape from his bonds, straining every muscle and rocking to and fro. But it was a futile exercise. He was held tight by his bonds. The man laughed.

'I had a feeling that Miss Granville would choose a spirited lover for her bed,' he said. 'She'll have another one tonight. And when it's over, I'll reward her with this.'

Taking an opal pendant from his pocket, he let it dangle tauntingly in front of the prisoner's face. Paul shuddered. It was the gift he'd once given to Hannah.

'I leave you with an intriguing thought. Does Miss Granville love you enough to save your life?'

Laughing all the way, he went back up the steps and took the lantern out through the door. Paul was plunged into darkness yet again.

They took no chances. Aware of Scattergood's reputation for avoiding arrest, the Runners had several men surrounding the tavern. Since it was Chevy Ruddock who'd actually followed the thief to The Mitre, they let him enter the building with them so that he could be directly involved in the capture. Micah Yeomans didn't stand on ceremony. Issuing threats to the landlord if he failed to obey, he demanded the master key to the bedrooms, then led Hale and Ruddock upstairs. Most of the rooms were empty so the doors were already unlocked. Two that they let themselves into had only a single occupant. The last one was more promising because they could hear the creaking of a bed and the unmistakable sounds of passion. Yeomans turned the key in the lock, flung the door open and rushed in to see two bodies threshing around under the sheets.

Ruddock turned away in embarrassment, but the others ran to the bed, grabbed the sheets and tore them back with a flourish. Primed to overpower Scattergood, they were instead looking at a wrinkly old man on top of a full-bodied, pale-skinned woman of middle years. The old man looked over his shoulder in dismay.

'We're doing nothing wrong,' he said, plaintively. 'We were married this morning.'

* * *

Though he'd never seen the man before, Peter identified him at once.

'You must be Edmund Haines.'

'That's right.'

'You were one of Mr Parry's servants.'

'I still am.'

'You look more like his keeper to me.'

'I'm responsible for saving his life,' said Haines, angrily. 'If it hadn't been for me, he'd have starved to death.'

'What's wrong with him?' asked Peter.

'He went through a very bad time. It affected his mind. All that he remembers is how to work on one of his inventions.' He nodded at the steam engine. 'This is the latest one.'

'Yes, but it's not *his*, is it? Alderson stole it from him.'

Haines levelled the gun at him. 'I was warned that you were too clever for your own good. How did you find us?'

'I followed Mr Alderson's messenger,' said Huckvale.

'That was a big mistake.'

'Why?'

'We can't allow you to leave here.'

Haines was a wiry man of middle years with a narrow face and dark eyes. The driver, meanwhile, picked up a weapon of his own, a large iron pipe that lay on the ground.

'Does that mean you're inviting us to stay?' asked Peter.

'Those are my orders,' said Haines. 'Yours won't be the first bodies to be buried here. You'll be joining the late George Parry.'

'Are you talking about me?' said Parry, confused.

'Keep out of this.'

'I don't understand what's going on.'

'I think that I do,' said Peter, as he realised what must have happened. 'A fake George Parry had to die so that the real one could slave away here for someone else's benefit. That other poor wretch was not stolen from his grave by bodysnatchers. He was dug up by *you*, wasn't he?'

Haines smirked. 'We brought him back here for a second burial,' he said. 'Nobody will ever be able to find him.'

'What was his real name?'

'We've no idea. Mr Alderson needed someone on his last legs. I found him half-dead under a hedge. That much was true.'

'Do you hear that Mr Parry?' asked Peter. 'Did you know that they lowered your coffin into a churchyard in Islington?'

Parry was bemused. 'None of this makes sense to me.'

'You just do as you're told,' said Haines, harshly. 'I'm not your servant any longer. You take orders from me.'

The distraction was exactly what they'd been hoping for. While Haines was turned towards the old man, Peter leapt forward and grabbed the barrel of the pistol, turning it upwards and causing Haines to pull the trigger. The shot went harmlessly up into the air. Peter then tripped him up and twisted the weapon out of his hand before diving on top of Haines and pummelling him with both fists. Before the driver could move forward to help, he was intercepted by Huckvale, who dived head first at him, burrowing into his stomach and taking all the wind out of him.

Haines, meanwhile, was fighting back and getting in a relay of punches, but Peter was younger and in far better condition. He was also infuriated by what they'd done to Parry, stealing his invention and virtually turning him into a slave. At the gallery, Peter gave lessons in boxing, but he was skilled at wrestling as well. He knew how to grapple and put an opponent in an excruciating hold. Once he'd quelled all resistance, he battered the man into submission.

Huckvale, however, was up against a much stronger opponent. He'd ducked under the flailing pipe to struggle with the driver and even managed to make him drop his weapon to the ground. He, too, was fit and strong, but he could not hold off the bigger man for long. When the driver had shaken his arms free, he got his hands around his opponent's neck and squeezed hard. All of Huckvale's energy began to drain away. The pain was intense and his eyes began to mist over. Though he continued to fight, there was no power at all in his fists. He was on the point of passing out completely when there was a loud grunt and the driver's fingers lost their grip instantly. Before Huckvale knew what was happening, the driver had sunk to the floor with blood pouring from a head wound.

George Parry stood over him with a hammer in his hand.

'I couldn't let him kill you,' he said, simply. 'That was wrong.'

Peter was back on his feet. 'Are you all right, Jem?'

'I am now,' said Huckvale, massaging his throat.

'I'll take that, if you don't mind, Mr Parry,' said Peter, relieving him of the hammer. 'Thank you for helping us.' He looked down at the two bodies. 'Let's get the pair of them trussed up, Jem.'

'Is it right, what you said earlier?' asked Parry, hopefully. 'They told me that Clemency hated me.'

'It's not true. She loves you and misses you and has come all the way from Amsterdam to find you.'

Parry's face lit up. 'Is that true?'

'Yes, it is,' said Peter, gently. 'Everything will be explained in due course. We'll look after you now.'

Having dispatched a courier, Hannah returned to her room at the hotel. Jenny was waiting to hear what had happened.

'He's in the saddle already,' said Hannah, 'and promises to get the letter into Peter's hands as soon as is humanly possible.'

'I still think there's too long a delay.'

'It simply means that I have to put off that ogre for a while. I've thought of one way of doing it.'

'What's that?'

'I'll refuse even to consider his demand until I have proof that Paul is still alive and unharmed.'

'That's very wise of you.'

'I'd like you with me at the time, Jenny.'

'Yes, of course,' said the other. 'I can't say that I'm looking forward to seeing that hateful man again, but I'll give whatever support you ask.' She lowered her voice. 'Have you considered that . . . well, that Paul might already be dead?'

'I'd feel it here, if he was,' replied Hannah, putting a hand to her heart. 'My only fear is that he might be hurt in some way. That's why I'll insist that he's unharmed.'

'And then what?'

'I'll do what I said and consider his demand.'

'You could never agree to anything as disgusting as that.'

'I didn't say I was going to agree to it, Jenny. All I'm committing myself to is thinking it over – or, at least, of pretending to do so. I'm banking on the fact that it will buy me a night to make my decision.'

'And then what?'

'I'll just pray that Peter can come to our rescue.'

'What if he doesn't get your message in time?'

'He may already know that his brother is in trouble,' said Hannah. 'They are identical twins with a strange insight into each other's minds and behaviour. When Peter was caught up in a

329

crisis last year, Paul knew by instinct that he needed help and he provided it. I'm just hoping that the same thing may happen now with the roles in reverse. Before my courier even reaches him, Peter might be on his way to Bath.'

The arrival of her husband had turned Clemency van Emden from a nervous and fearful young woman into a person with charm, poise and self-confidence. The more Charlotte got to know them, the more the age gap between husband and wife began to disappear. They were supremely happy in each other's company. As the three of them chatted in the drawing room, serious discussion was relieved by bursts of laughter. Charlotte came to feel completely at ease. For their part, they found her a caring hostess and a friend in whom they could place absolute trust.

'Clemency has been telling me about the shooting gallery,' said van Emden. 'It sounds like a remarkable place.'

'Charlotte actually works there,' said his wife. 'She puts me to shame. I didn't know that a woman could do such things.'

'I'm not sure that it's entirely suitable work for a woman,' said her husband, 'especially one as refined as Charlotte.'

'My life has none of the excitement that she enjoys. Charlotte's been involved in all kinds of adventures.'

'Peter and Paul have the major share of adventure,' said Charlotte, 'so they court the greater amount of danger.'

'Don't you fret over Peter's safety?'

'I've managed to grow out of that over time.'

'Your husband is a very courageous man,' said van Emden, 'and so is your brother-in-law. They seem to have chosen a life that keeps them in almost permanent jeopardy.'

'Strangely enough,' said Charlotte, 'they prefer it that way.'

When she heard the sound of hooves outside, she looked through the window and saw that Peter was riding towards the house and towing a horse behind him. Excusing herself, she went to open the front door herself. Peter dismounted and was given a welcoming hug. After summoning a servant, he handed over the animals and stepped into the hall with his wife.

'What happened?' she asked.

'We found him at last.'

'Where is he?'

'I hired a gig so that Jem could bring him back in relative comfort. I'm not sure that Mr Parry could have ridden here. He's not in the best of health,' said Peter, 'and his mind wanders a little. Before they meet him, you ought to prepare Clemency and her husband.'

'Why can't you do that, Peter?'

'I have to leave immediately.'

She was startled. 'Where on earth are you going?'

'I'll take a fresh horse and ride off to Bath. Paul needs me.'

'How do you know?'

'It's the way I always know, Charlotte. He's my brother and I sense that he's in trouble. As for what happened to us,' he went on, 'Jem will explain when he gets here. Suffice it to say that Haines had betrayed his old master whose genius as an inventor was being cruelly exploited by Alderson. Haines and his assistant are now in custody. Thanks to an understanding local magistrate, Alderson is also behind bars.'

'Is that all you can tell me?'

'You'll hear the rest from Jem. Meanwhile, advise Clemency to be very gentle with her father and not to expect too much from him.'

'Is Mr Parry ill?'

'You'll see for yourself.'

'What about—'

'I must go, my love,' he said, interrupting her and giving her a farewell kiss. 'My brother is calling for me.'

Now that his eyes had grown used to the gloom, Paul was able to make out more of the contents of his prison. From the size of the cellar, he reasoned that it was below a large house. Various things had been stored there, but the items that attracted his attention were the wine racks. All that he could see were fuzzy outlines of necks of bottles sticking out from them. He wished that he'd been able to explore the cellar to the full, but that was impossible. Paul could hardly flex his muscles, let alone move around. Sounds from above alerted him. The door was unbolted, then his captor came down the steps with the lantern again. In his other hand, he was carrying a letter. He waved it under Paul's nose.

'Your dear lady has replied to my demand,' said the highwayman. 'She refuses to consider it until she has evidence that you are alive and unharmed. See for yourself, Mr Skillen. I'm sure that you recognise her hand. The stationery has the faintest hint of her perfume.'

To his disappointment, Paul saw that the letter was genuine. Before he could read it, it was whisked away from him.

'We will have to arrange a sighting of you,' said the man, 'just to satisfy her. Then it will be *my* turn for satisfaction. Miss Granville cares for you enough to offer the most precious thing in her possession to effect your release.' He stared into Paul's blazing eyes. 'Yes, I may have the predatory instincts of an animal but they are softened by a gentlemanly sense of restraint. Miss Granville was at my mercy once before, but why take something by force when I can have it willingly handed to me? Who knows?' he went on, grinning broadly. 'I might even let you watch.'

By way of a punishment, they made Chevy Ruddock buy a round of drinks, then the three of them sat at their table in the Peacock Inn.

'It was *your* fault,' said Yeomans, jabbing a finger at him.

'I swear that I watched him going into The Mitre,' said Ruddock. 'I followed him to the door.'

'You should have kept watch on the place and sent for us.'

'Don't be too hard on him, Micah,' said Hale. 'When all is said and done, Chevy is the only one of us who actually saw Harry Scattergood in the flesh and he certainly did stay at The Mitre. When we described Harry to him, the landlord confirmed that. For obvious reasons, he didn't give his real name.'

'No,' said Ruddock, chortling. 'Fancy calling himself Micah Yeomans!'

Hales laughed. 'Harry always did like a jest.'

'You can both stop sniggering,' ordered Yeomans, as he raised a menacing fist. 'I saw nothing funny in what he did.'

'In a way,' said Ruddock, 'it was a sort of compliment to you.'

'Yes,' added Hale. 'You're such an important figure in his life.'

'Shut up!' growled Yeomans.

'Be glad, Micah. The fact is that we almost caught him.'

'It's always a case of "almost" with Harry Scattergood.'

'We may have failed at The Mitre, but we did have a big success at that church. With the help of Chevy and Bill Filbert, we caught two bodysnatchers and the surgeon who was paying them. That was a triumph.'

'It certainly was,' said Yeomans, ruefully. 'But Kirkwood only ever remembers the things we do wrong.'

'That's not true, sir,' said Ruddock. 'There's something I haven't mentioned before.'

'What is it?'

'Mr Kirkwood wrote to thank me for what Bill and I did that night. My wife was so proud that I'd got praise from the chief magistrate. Agnes said that I deserved a promotion.'

Yeomans glowered. 'You get a letter and we get *nothing*?'

'Didn't he send *you* a commendation as well, sir?'

'No, he didn't.'

'He never does,' said Hale.

'That's not fair,' said Ruddock.

'It happens all the time,' complained Yeomans. 'Nothing we do can please Kirkwood. He's far more likely to send his congratulations to the Skillen brothers than to me.'

'Well, they are more successful than us, sir. The truth is that, if we don't catch Harry Scattergood soon, they'll do it for us. Truth will out. Peter and Paul Skillen are simply better than us.'

Eyes like molten lava, Yeomans rose to his feet. 'What did you say?'

'Whatever it was, I was badly mistaken,' said Ruddock, hastily backing away. 'I won't disturb you any further. Goodbye.'

Clemency was so exhilarated by the news about her father that she was unable to remain seated. She stood at the window with her husband on one side of her and Charlotte on the other. It seemed an age before a trap finally came along the street.

'That's him!' cried Clemency, excitement turning instantly to anxiety. 'Oh dear!' she exclaimed. 'He looks so old.'

'When I've shown Mr Parry in,' said Charlotte, 'I'll get the full details from Jem.'

'Thank you.'

'Do you want to be alone with your father?' asked van Emden.

'No, Jan,' she said. 'You're my husband and his son-in-law. You have a right to be here.'

'Then I'll stay.'

Seeing the gig pull up outside the house, Charlotte went to open the front door and watched Huckvale helping his passenger out of the vehicle. She went forward to greet Parry, then took him by the arm to lead him into the house.

'Clemency and her husband are in there,' she said, pausing at the door. 'They've been waiting a long time for this moment.'

His tears began to trickle. 'I thought I'd lost her.'

'She's come back to you.'

Opening the door, Charlotte stayed long enough to see him enter the room and let out a cry of joy as Clemency ran to embrace him. It was an affecting scene. Conscious that she was intruding on a private moment, Charlotte gently closed the door.

In the letter containing the ransom demand, Hannah had been told to hand her reply to the hotel manager. She'd obeyed the order. Who collected it, she didn't know but it obviously reached its intended recipient because she had a reply. It was delivered to her room by the manager.

'Who brought this?' she asked.

'It was a youth,' he replied. 'He said that a man paid him to hand it over, but has no idea of his name.'

'I see.'

'Will there be anything else, Miss Granville?'

'Not at the moment.'

Thanking the manager, she shut the door behind him and opened the letter. Jenny Pye watched her face as she read it. Hannah blanched.

'He wants to meet me within the hour.'

'Where do you have to go?'

'A cab will pick me up outside the hotel.'

'What if it's a trick?' asked Jenny. 'He's just trying to lure you out of the safety of the hotel.'

'He gives me a firm promise that that's not the case. Read what he says.' She handed over the letter. 'I'm inclined to believe him.'

'Well, I'm not. I don't trust him.'

'He spared me when he robbed the coach, Jenny. Remember that.'

'You won't be so lucky next time.' After she'd read the letter, she handed it back. 'I'll go with you.'

'I fear for Paul.'

'So do I,' said Jenny. 'I don't believe they'll release him at all.'

'I'm looking at it from his point of view,' Hannah told her. 'Paul will be mortified that I'll see him at someone else's mercy.'

'He'll be even more upset at the price you're asked to pay.'

'Hopefully, I won't have to pay it. If I can cause a delay, Peter will get here eventually.'

'Your courier won't reach him for hours yet.'

'I told you before. He may not be needed.'

Keeping his horse at a gallop, Peter Skillen ignored the discomfort of the long ride and relied on his knowledge of geography. Somewhere before too long, he'd need to change to a fresh mount. He tried to remember where the next coaching inn would be. Speed was of the essence. His brother was in jeopardy.

* * *

During the short time when there was some illumination in the cellar, Paul had made a quick note of his surroundings. He'd been particularly interested in the position of the wine racks. Though they were several feet away to his left, he knew that he had to reach them if he wanted any chance of escape. Paul began to rock to and fro in the chair, building up a steady rhythm until two of the legs began to leave the floor each time. He kept going until he was on the point of toppling over altogether. It took a final lurch to his left to achieve his aim. As he crashed to the floor, he banged his head and bruised his shoulder, but he was more than willing to endure the pain.

He now had some movement. It was slow and laborious. By twisting and turning, he inched along the floor towards the wine rack. His efforts soon made sweat break out on his face and stream down his body. From time to time, he collected a mouthful of dust from the floor, spitting it out with disgust. Paul was less worried about his agonising progress than in the filth soiling his clothes. By dint of his snail-pace movement, he finally reached the wine rack and paused for a respite. When he felt strong enough, he swung his head around so that he came into contact with the neck of a wine bottle. After a few minutes of experimentation, he managed to hook the edge of his gag around the glass neck. By working at different angles, he eventually contrived to pull the gag away from his mouth. The relief was overwhelming. He could breathe properly at last.

Rewarding himself with a rest, Paul came to the most difficult bit. He got his mouth around the neck of the bottle and pulled it towards him in tiny instalments, each time having to back away a little. Every muscle was throbbing now. Every movement brought a stab of pain. It was the thought of what might happen to Hannah that drove him on. He cursed himself for letting himself get into such a humiliating situation and knew that he could only find redemption by escape. There was some way to go, however, and it involved real danger.

Working in the dark made everything more difficult. With the bottle in his mouth, he went into reverse and edged himself away until he came to what he believed would be a bare stone wall. His aim was to smash the bottle. It might leave him with a bad injury in his mouth or even damage to his eyes. At the very least, he feared, there'd be facial lacerations. They had to be suffered. Broken glass was vital if he was to cut through his bonds. There was a lot of painstaking manoeuvring before he got the bottle parallel to the wall. Holding it as tightly as he could in his mouth, he tried a practice swing. The bottle thudded against the wall, jarring his mouth. He tried again, putting more effort into it this time. Sweat was pouring out of him now and his mouth was on fire but he had to keep going. The image of Hannah being molested by the highwayman gave him extra power and courage. He closed his eyes, swung his head as far to one side as he could, then brought it back hard in the opposite direction. Striking the brick wall, the bottle burst apart and glass went everywhere.

Paul lay on the floor in a pool of liquid, not knowing if it was wine or his own blood.

Evening shadows were starting to blend into darkness as Peter mounted the fresh horse. The ostler holding the reins for him pointed out that a coach would be leaving soon and that it might be sensible to travel with it for safety. Spurning the advice, Peter kicked the horse into action and galloped off.

* * *

338

When the cab arrived at the hotel to pick her up, Hannah was in for a surprise. She found a woman with a veiled face waiting for her. From the sound of her voice, Hannah could tell that she was young and well educated. Refusing to answer any questions, the woman conducted Hannah and Jenny out to the waiting vehicle. After they'd climbed in, the newcomers were each handed a blindfold.

'Please put them on,' instructed the woman. 'We don't want you to see where we're going, do we?'

Having used the broken glass to cut himself out of his bonds, Paul rubbed his sore wrists and ankles. He then began to assess the damage, feeling gingerly for any wounds. There were minor cuts on his face, but it was his hands that had taken the real punishment. Both had gashes from which blood was still oozing. Tearing the gag in half, he wound a piece of the material around each hand to stem the flow. When he tried to get to his feet, he realised how bruised and unsteady he was. Aching all over, he took time to loosen his limbs and regain his balance.

While he was at last free from the gnawing ropes, he was still locked in a dark cellar with a bolted door between him and liberty. If they simply left him there, he'd have no means of getting out. Then he remembered what the highwayman had told him: Hannah would be allowed to see him. The prospect horrified Paul. He hated the idea that Hannah would view him in that condition, dirty, dishevelled and with blood on his hands, face and clothing. He would feel shamed.

After the initial joy of the reconciliation, Jan van Emden decided that it might be better to leave his wife alone with her father. They had a lot of unhappiness and misunderstanding to repair. Two people who'd been deliberately kept apart were now back together again, all their earlier differences forgotten and forgiven. Closing the door gently behind him, van Emden joined Charlotte and Huckvale in another room.

'It's a miracle,' he said. 'I never dreamt that this would ever happen. Mr Parry has been brought back from the dead.'

'That's the literal truth,' said Charlotte. 'There was a time when we were all convinced that he really was in his grave. Jem has been telling me how they tried to convince us of that.'

Huckvale took his cue. 'Haines was behind it all,' he explained. 'He was responsible for preventing any letters from passing between father and daughter. And it was Haines who sent that message to Mrs van Emden about her father's supposed death. Mr Parry was right not to trust him. He was sly and cunning. He knew that his master had been working all hours on an important new project and he managed to sneak into the study to look at the designs. Even though he didn't know much about engineering, he could see that Mr Parry had invented something very special.'

'But he didn't have the money to develop his ideas,' said Charlotte, 'so he tried everything he could to raise it, forced eventually to gamble all that he had on it.'

'Once he'd lost the house,' resumed Huckvale, 'he was in despair. He turned to drink to block out the shame of it and eventually ended up on the streets.'

'What did Haines do in the meantime?' asked van Emden.

'He went in search of someone who'd be evil enough to steal Mr Parry's invention and make a fortune from it. In the end, he found Mr Alderson.'

340

'The first thing they had to do,' said Charlotte, 'was to rescue Mr Parry from the streets and convince him that they'd come to save him.'

'Instead of that, they kept him locked up on a farm and made him work on his invention. If it had been a success, he wouldn't have got a penny for it. Alderson would have pocketed all the money.'

'What about Mr Parry?'

'Once Mr Parry had done what they wanted,' said Huckvale, 'Peter thinks that Alderson would have had him killed.'

'The ruthless devil!' exclaimed van Emden.

'Fortunately,' said Charlotte, 'he's been rescued and is back with someone who loves him. I'm sure that Clemency will nurse him back to full health.'

'We both will, Charlotte.' He shook Huckvale's hand. 'Thank you so much for what you did. You and Peter have been heroic.' Jan van Emden looked around. 'By the way, where *is* Peter?'

Riding towards the crest of a hill, he could see a fingerpost silhouetted against the sky. He reined in his horse so that he could peer at the numbers carved into it. Peter was relieved to see that he was over halfway to his destination. It gave him the encouragement he needed to carry on at the same furious pace.

It was only when they were inside the house that they were allowed to remove their blindfolds. Hannah and Jenny blinked for a few moments, then looked around. They were in the hall of what seemed to be a gracious residence. Still veiled, the woman beckoned them along a passageway, then indicated a doorway. Making an effort to still their nerves, the two of them went into the drawing room to face the man they'd met once before. He was leaning nonchalantly against the marble fireplace and wearing a mask that he touched with a finger.

'It's a necessary precaution,' he said. 'I'm sure you understand why. But have no fears, Miss Granville. When we're alone together, I will, of course, remove it in the darkness of the bedroom.'

'Where is Paul?' she demanded.

'Don't be so hasty. Why not sit down and relax?'

'I want to see him *now*.'

He smiled indulgently. 'I'm amenable to all your requests.'

When he turned towards a corner of the room, they realised that there was someone else there and that he, too, was wearing a mask. Hannah and Jenny recognised him as one of the other highwaymen. Both were jolted at the sight of the pistol in his belt. In response to a gesture, the man left the room.

'Mr Skillen will join us in a couple of minutes,' said their host. 'Now, may I offer you a glass of champagne?'

Paul was poised and ready. Much of the pain had eased and he could now move freely. When he heard the bolt being drawn back above, he quickly hid himself in an alcove. Someone came down the steps with a lantern, then stopped in amazement at the bottom of the flight. He stared at the upturned chair, the broken bottle and the discarded ropes. Before he could even begin to work out what had happened, he was struck from behind by Paul, who smashed a bottle of wine against his skull and sent him pitching forward on to the floor. Snatching the pistol from the man's belt, Paul used the butt to knock him out completely. He then picked up the ropes to tie him securely and put the gag in place.

'There you are,' he said. 'Let's see if *you* can escape, shall we?'

Pistol in one hand and lantern in the other, he crept up the steps.

Seated beside Jenny on a sofa, Hannah seemed very composed when she was, in fact, trembling inside. She had resolved to show no weakness. The highwayman was tall, debonair and possessed of a kind of natural authority that was hard to resist. Hannah tried to assert herself.

'If Paul is injured in any way,' she warned, 'the ransom is out of the question.'

'You're not in a position to haggle with me, Miss Granville. I hold the advantage here and I mean to use it.' Hannah and Jenny quailed. 'And it's no good expecting help to come. The servants have been given the evening off. Apart from my accomplice whom you just met, the only person in the house is my sister. She came to fetch you, but she won't be taking you back tonight.'

Hannah was angry. 'Would you dare to hold me against my will?'

'I'll do whatever I wish,' he said, with a smile.

'I looked for some consideration from you.'

He strolled across to her with a taunting laugh and put a hand to the side of her face. She tossed her head to get clear of his touch. Taking her by the arm, he pulled her to her feet without the slightest effort, then held her by the chin, intending to kiss her.

'Leave go of her!' shouted Paul.

They turned to see him in the doorway, holding the pistol. Alarmed at the state he was in, Hannah let out a scream. The highwayman stepped away from her and regarded Paul with a measure of admiration.

'It seems that I underestimated you,' he said.

'That was bad judgement on your part,' said Paul, motioning with the pistol. 'Move right away from Miss Granville or I'll shoot.'

The highwayman raised both hands in a gesture of surrender, then made a sudden dart towards Hannah, getting behind her so that she became his shield. Arm around her neck, he applied enough pressure to make her protest.

'Put that down or I'll break her pretty neck,' he said. When Paul levelled the pistol at him, he laughed contemptuously. 'You wouldn't dare to fire it in case you hit Miss Granville.'

Paul took a step to his left, aimed at the man's ear and pulled the trigger. He hit the target perfectly. With a howl of pain, the man released Hannah and put a hand to the side of his head to feel the blood-covered remains of his ear.

'I should have told you,' said Paul. 'I work at a shooting gallery.'

The highwayman was enraged. One hand to his ear, he ran to the fireplace and picked up the poker with the other hand. He came charging at Paul and swung his weapon vengefully. After stepping nimbly out of the way, Paul leapt forward to attack the man, punching him so hard to the face and the body that he made him drop the poker. All that the other man could muster was token resistance. With blood still streaming down the side of his face, he was soon lying unconscious on the floor. Hannah ran across to Paul.

'What have they done to you?' she asked, worriedly.

'I did most of it myself,' he told her, 'and it's not nearly as bad as it looks. Let's round up the sister I heard him mention. That will be three of them to hand over. I daresay there'll be a large reward coming.'

'I've already got my reward,' she said, hugging him.

'There'll be another one for you. He told me that he was going to give you that pendant I bought you. I'll be able to do that myself now.'

Walking across to the highwayman, he tore off his mask. 'You won't need this any more, my friend. Your days of robbing coaches are over.'

When the gallery closed at the end of the day, Gully Ackford went straight to the house to hear what had happened. He was delighted that George Parry had been found and returned to his daughter, albeit in poor health. Huckvale explained how they'd rescued him from the farm. He, Ackford and Charlotte were together in the dining room.

'What was the machine like?' asked Charlotte.

'It was the most peculiar thing,' said Huckvale, 'but it can travel at over ten miles an hour.'

'That's impossible,' claimed Ackford.

'Don't be so sure, Gully. We saw it puffing away. On the drive back here, Mr Parry told me he was inspired by the steam engines he'd studied at mines in Cornwall and in Wales.'

'What about his other inventions?'

'He'd been forced to sell most of the patents. The only one he kept was for his steam locomotive. He'd pinned all his hopes on that. At least he now owns the patent again.'

'I never thought that you'd ever find him.'

'They persevered,' said Charlotte. 'That was their secret.'

'Peter was suspicious about that makeshift coffin,' said Huckvale. 'That's how it all started.'

'Where is Peter?' asked Ackford. 'Is he with Mr Parry?'

'No, Gully,' said Charlotte. 'He's on his way to Bath. Paul is in difficulty.'

'What sort of difficulty?'

'He doesn't know.'

'It must be serious if Peter is haring off to help him.'

'I just hope that he gets there safely,' said Charlotte. 'I don't like the thought of him riding alone through the night.'

Having returned to the hotel, Paul had taken his clothes off so that Hannah could bathe his wounds. For the most part, they were superficial and, once the blood was washed away, the scratches were largely invisible. The gash in one hand was more serious and they'd sent for a doctor to come and attend to it. Left alone, they adjourned to bed and celebrated their reunion. They fell asleep in each other's arms. Paul had always been a light sleeper. Hearing a rustling sound early next morning, he was instantly awake and got out of bed to investigate. A letter had been pushed under his door. He picked it up and was startled by the familiar handwriting. It belonged to his brother. After reading the letter, he dressed quickly and slipped out of the room quietly so as not to disturb Hannah.

Paul got downstairs to find Peter fast asleep in a chair. The night porter, a grizzled old man, told him that his brother had arrived much earlier in a state of urgency.

'At first, I thought it was you, Mr Skillen,' said the porter, looking from one to the other. 'I can't tell the two of you apart. When I told the other Mr Skillen that you were perfectly safe, he breathed a sigh of relief. He didn't want to disturb you, so he wrote a letter and I slipped it under your door.'

'Thank you,' said Paul. 'You did the right thing.' He looked down at his brother. 'He's ridden all the way from London to help me. I feel cruel, having to wake him up.'

He touched Peter's shoulder gently and it was enough to bring him awake. Screwing up his eyes until he got used to the light, he then noticed the bandaging around his brother's hand.

'What happened?' he asked.

'I had a spot of bother.'

'It felt like much more than that. It's the reason I came.'

'You're more than welcome,' said Paul, embracing him, 'and your journey is not in vain. There's unfinished business. Three villains are already in custody, but there are two more to be apprehended.'

Peter yawned. 'If I can stay awake, I'll be glad to help.'

'Do you have any weapons?'

'I have two pistols and a sword.'

'That's all we'll need,' said Paul, putting an arm around his shoulders to lead him out. 'Let's find our horses. I'll explain everything on the way.'

Roderick Cosgrove had been well rewarded. When he became aware that Paul was watching his house, he arranged for one of the highwaymen to creep up behind him. They'd delivered Paul to their leader and had each been given money for their efforts. The two of them had spent the evening drinking, before going on to a brothel where even more alcohol had flowed. In the early hours of the morning, they'd staggered drunkenly back to Cosgrove's house and fallen asleep in chairs.

They were awakened by a thunderous knocking on the front door. Since the lone female servant was too frightened to respond to the summons, Cosgrove dragged himself to his feet and lumbered along the passageway. Opening the door and prepared to send the caller on his way with some ripe language, he was astonished to see Paul standing there.

'How did *you* get here?' he asked, quaking. 'You should still be tied up in that cellar.'

'So it *was* you who helped to put me there,' said Paul. 'I thought as much. You're a confederate of those highwaymen.'

'That's not true.'

'I've come to arrest you, Cosgrove.'

'You've no reason to do so, Mr Skillen.'

'I have every reason.'

Cosgrove reacted like lightning. He first tried to slam the door, but Paul managed to get his foot in the way. Swinging around, Cosgrove ran down the passageway, went into the room where he'd been sleeping and locked it behind him. His accomplice was still only half-awake.

'What's happening, Roddy?' he asked.

'Get up!' yelled Cosgrove, yanking him to his feet. 'We have to get out of here fast.' There was pounding on the door. 'Come on!'

The two of them ran to the rear of the house and out through the back door only to discover that Peter was waiting for them with two pistols cocked. They came to a sudden halt.

'How the devil did *you* get here?' asked Cosgrove. 'It's magic.'

'Not really,' said Peter. 'My brother will explain.'

They heard a loud noise as the locked door was shattered. Paul came sauntering out into the tiny garden. The two prisoners were utterly bewildered.

'Which one of you is *Paul* Skillen?' asked Cosgrove, spluttering.

'You'll find out at the trial,' said Peter.

A week later, everything had returned to something akin to normal. The smoke of recent events had finally cleared. Rehearsals were going so well that Hannah felt safe enough to send Paul back to London, after extracting a promise that he'd return for the first night of *As You Like It*. On his journey back home, Paul was carrying newspaper accounts of his exploits in arresting three notorious highwaymen and their accomplices. Having collected handsome rewards for the capture of the gang, he and Peter had now returned to their work at the gallery. They were there with Huckvale when Jan van Emden called on them.

'My first duty is to pay you for your services,' he said, handing over the money. 'It's twice the amount agreed with Clemency because you gave us so much help.'

'We're very happy that we were able to find her father,' said Huckvale. 'How is he now?'

'He's so much better after the ministrations of Charlotte and Clemency. Between them, they've worked wonders.'

'And you've persuaded him to go to Amsterdam with you,' said Peter. 'That was a real achievement.'

'It's only until he's fully recovered,' said the Dutchman. 'My father-in-law's ambition is to return to England to resume his work. We've been in touch with Geoffrey Taylor and he's agreed to join forces with Mr Parry to develop his latest invention.'

'Does he have the money to invest in the project?'

'Yes, he does,' said van Emden. 'I'm helping to finance his work.'

'Then you could stand to make a lot of money,' said Paul. 'Peter and Jem have seen this steam engine of his. They say it has potential.'

'It has great potential,' agreed Huckvale.

'Mr Parry just needs time and money to make some refinements,' said Peter. 'He must be gratified by your interest in the project.'

'It's more a case of duty than interest,' admitted van Emden.

'It's something I feel that I have to do. Privately, I have considerable doubts. Let us be honest, shall we? Mr Parry is talking about a steam locomotive that will carry hundreds of passengers large distances at speed.' He shook his head with incredulity. 'It will never happen.'

EDWARD MARSTON has written well over a hundred books, including some non-fiction. He is best known for his hugely successful Railway Detective series and he also writes the Bow Street Rivals series featuring twin detectives set during the Regency, as well as the Home Front Detective series.

edwardmarston.com